A GAME OF MINDS

Also by Priscilla Masters

The Martha Gunn mysteries

RIVER DEEP
SLIP KNOT
FROZEN CHARLOTTE *
SMOKE ALARM *
THE DEVIL'S CHAIR *
RECALLED TO DEATH *
BRIDGE OF SIGHS *

The Joanna Piercy mysteries

WINDING UP THE SERPENT
CATCH THE FALLEN SPARROW
A WREATH FOR MY SISTER
AND NONE SHALL SLEEP
SCARING CROWS
EMBROIDERING SHROUDS
ENDANGERING INNOCENTS
WINGS OVER THE WATCHER
GRAVE STONES
A VELVET SCREAM *
THE FINAL CURTAIN *
GUILTY WATERS *
CROOKED STREET *
BLOOD ON THE ROCKS *

The Claire Roget mysteries

DANGEROUS MINDS *
THE DECEIVER *

* *available from Severn House*

A GAME OF MINDS

Priscilla Masters

severn
House

This first world edition published 2020
in Great Britain and the USA by
SEVERN HOUSE PUBLISHERS LTD of
Eardley House, 4 Uxbridge Street, London W8 7SY.
Trade paperback edition first published
in Great Britain and the USA 2021 by
SEVERN HOUSE PUBLISHERS LTD.

British Library Cataloguing in Publication Data
A CIP catalogue record for this title is available from the British Library.

ISBN-13: 978-0-7278-9082-5 (cased)
ISBN-13: 978-1-78029-723-1 (trade paper)
ISBN-13: 978-1-4483-0444-8 (e-book)

This is a work of fiction. Names, characters, places and incidents
are either the product of the author's imagination or are used fictitiously.
Except where actual historical events and characters are being described
for the storyline of this novel, all situations in this publication are
 fictitious and any resemblance to actual persons, living or dead,
business establishments, events or locales is purely coincidental.

All Severn House titles are printed on acid-free paper.

Severn House Publishers support the Forest Stewardship Council™ [FSC™],
the leading international forest certification organisation.
All our titles that are printed on FSC certified paper carry the FSC logo.

Typeset by Palimpsest Book Production Ltd.,
Falkirk, Stirlingshire, Scotland.
Printed and bound in Great Britain by
TJ International, Padstow, Cornwall.

ONE

C laire didn't know what she was doing here. She hadn't known Grant's sister, had never even spoken to her. Maisie was, after all, the reason that they had split up, using her illness to manipulate her brother back to her side. But Claire had promised Grant she would be here and she wasn't one to break a promise. So here she was, wearing the only black dress she possessed, sitting at the back, alone.

Looking around at the packed crematorium, Claire realized Maisie had had lots of friends. She had been sick for all of her life but plenty of people must have loved and admired her. Grant was, of course, right at the front, feet from the coffin, at his mother's side. Pale, but resolute, in a dark suit and black tie, unruly black hair temporarily tamed, eyes focused ahead. She had watched him follow the coffin as it had been wheeled in on its bier, holding his mother's hand tightly, comfort seeping almost palpably from one to the other. He looked unfamiliar and she realized, almost with a smile, that she had never seen him in a suit before. He was normally a casual dresser which suited his dark features and hint of a beard. Her pirate, she thought, with another smile. As though he'd sensed her presence as he passed, his eyes had flicked along the row to find her. He'd given her a small, jerky nod of recognition, the merest hint of a smile. And he'd mouthed a 'thank you' as he'd drawn level. His mother did not look her way but kept her gaze on her daughter's coffin, her hand tightly gripping her son's.

There was a waft of air as the people sat down and the service started.

There were numerous readings, mostly passages from pop songs, joined by Kipling's 'If' and Robbie Williams' 'Angels'. There were tears, some silently mopped by handkerchiefs, others noisy with sniffs, and as Claire noted the small size of the coffin, she too felt sad. Maisie had not chosen to be born with cystic fibrosis. God knows she had gone through some pain and suffering. Just twenty-three years old, she'd been dealt a shit hand. Luckily she'd had a brother who had stayed by her side, to the cost of his own relationship with Claire. She watched the back of his head, bending towards his mother, at one point putting his arm around her and drawing her head towards his shoulder; all of which led Claire to make her own conclusion. Now it was his mother who needed him.

Grant's eulogy was touching and unbearably sad. He spoke about his sister's terror of the illness, of her apprehension and sadness that the future her friends looked forward to – relationships, marriage, children – would be denied to her. His mouth twisted with grief. He allowed one hand to brush his own tears away.

His voice shook as he spoke. 'I admired Maisie for her bravery, felt honoured to be her brother and glad that I could be there for her when she needed me.' His eyes flickered in Claire's direction. Was he seeking absolution for his abandonment? She focused on his words. 'The illness that she was born with was a curse, but we never gave up hope of a cure or genetic engineering.' His smile was twisted. 'Some new antibiotic, stem cells, a miracle. We devoured each new piece of research voraciously. As a family we found it hard to deal with, but at least we were there for each other.' He looked up again, this time towards the heavens. 'But it didn't come in time.' It was his admonishment to Him above. 'I shall never forget my sister's courage or the love and gratitude she expressed whenever I spent time with her . . . We both knew that one day her luck would run out.' He wiped a tear from his cheek and scraped his throat noisily before continuing.

'Maisie could generally find something funny to say even in the bleakest of times. She had a dry wit as well as a positive outlook. She'd often say that we wouldn't have been so close had she not been ill.' He looked up, pain making his face strained and unhappy, his skin tone deathly pale.

'The odd thing is I can't imagine what life would have been like had Maisie *not* been ill.' He stood still, blinking away tears which reached everyone in the room. 'We would have lived our lives differently. She would have had boyfriends, gone to university. We would have had our separate lives, gone our own way. But as it was, we were bound together.' He looked uncertain, as though he wasn't sure what to do or say next. Then he moved away, the curtain threaded around and the coffin was gone.

For a moment the people simply stood, as though they couldn't believe what they had just seen. And then they started to file out to Ed Sheeran's *Perfect*. A quick check of the front row confirmed something which Claire had vaguely registered. Of Maisie's and Grant's father there was no sign. His abandonment of them was complete.

Grant met her eyes again as they filed past. He managed a smile and she responded with a nod, her emotions too mixed up to analyse.

Like guests at a wedding there was a line-up outside. Grant's mother treated her to a frosty look before giving her a grudging nod and holding out her hand. Claire held it for a moment, muttering her condolences. Grant grasped her hand. 'Thank you for being here, Claire.' He kissed her lightly on the cheek. It was a polite, social kiss. She moved on.

Outside a slight breeze stirred the air, wafting the scent of flowers and newly mown grass towards them. Floral tributes were laid across immaculate lawns peppered with memorial stones. An oasis on the edge of the city, the view beyond rows of houses interspersed with green walkways, the sound of traffic distant and otherworldly. But the sun beamed down, insensitive as ever, to the funeral of such a young woman.

Claire stood on the edge of the clusters of people, some in black, others in bright colours they possibly imagined Maisie Steadman would have appreciated. She scanned the faces. Apart from Grant and his mother she knew no one. Grant and his mother were still dealing with the line-up. There would be no opportunity to speak to him privately so, intending to slip away unseen, she moved a distance off, switched her phone on and picked up a message.

'Hi, Claire.' She didn't recognize the voice. Not until he introduced himself.

'It's DS Zed Willard here. I don't know if you remember me, but I could really do with your advice, maybe help. Is it possible we could meet up? Soon if possible. Anyway, give me a ring back on this number and I'll . . . erm, explain.'

She stared at her phone. What the heck could *he* want? He sounded agitated. She moved further away, stood under a tree and redialled. DS Willard picked up at once. 'Claire.'

'Hi.' Her greeting sounded listless. Her 'What can I do for you?' was unenthusiastic.

'I have a problem,' he said, speaking quickly. 'And I think you might be able to help.'

'Really?'

'Yes.'

'Well, give me some idea what this problem is?' She hoped he hadn't picked up on the flatness in her tone.

'It's better if I meet up with you. It's a bit complicated. Hard to explain over the phone. Where are you now?'

'At a funeral.'

'Sorry. No one close to you, I hope?' Mere politeness. He was anxious to spill out his own problem, not absorb hers.

'No.'

'Can you get to the station?'

'Hanley?'

'Yeah.'

'OK.' She was curious now. What could be so urgent and complicated? 'It'll take me nearly an hour.'

'Thank you.' His voice was sounding more relaxed now he'd handed over 'the problem'.

'I owe you one.'

She ended the call, put her phone back in her bag and glanced across to the clusters of people still standing around Grant and his mother. Grant had his arm around his mother's shoulders and her head rested against him. Her shoulders were heaving.

Then he looked across, spotted her, said something to his mother and walked towards her.

Her heart went out to him. Closer, he looked wrecked. There were lines around his eyes as though he hadn't slept for a month.

And now she felt awkward, with nothing to say, so hid behind a banality.

'That went as well as . . .' Her voice died away as she met his eyes. They were lifeless. 'God, Grant,' she said. 'I'm so sorry.' And without working anything out or really thinking about what she was doing, she put her arms around him and kissed the stubbly cheek.

He dropped his head and spoke against her shoulder. 'I've always looked after her,' he said, broken. 'I've always been there for her. Beck and call, you might say.' Then, in an outburst, he said, 'I feel like shit. I think I should get roaring drunk. You're coming to the wake?'

'I can't.' She knew she was letting him down. 'I can't.'

His eyes misted over. 'Work?'

She nodded.

He grabbed her arm. 'When am I going to see you? Properly? For a real talk?'

She avoided looking too deeply into the dark eyes. They had a habit of robbing her of free will. 'I don't know. Things are complicated.'

He reacted angrily. 'How do you mean complicated? What's complicated about us?'

She glanced past him towards his mother, standing, watching them. And this time hid behind an irrelevant truth. 'I have a lodger these days.'

His head jerked up. 'You mean you've moved someone else in?'

'No. It's not like that. He's a colleague . . .'

'He?' He'd picked up on it straightaway.

'An Aussie over here on an exchange.'

He could not have looked more shocked had she slapped his face. His features crumpled. He looked like a disappointed little boy.

'It's not like that,' she said quickly. 'He's married. He's just over here on a short-term contract. And . . .' She tried to lighten his mood. 'You know what rental properties in Hanley are like.'

But Grant looked puzzled. He put his head on one side and regarded her, his expression unconvinced, his dark eyes suspicious.

'OK,' he said finally, and walked away leaving Claire wondering. Why hadn't she made a date with him? Just dinner wouldn't have hurt. Why couldn't she have said he looked nice in a suit? Why hadn't she at least kissed him more warmly? Given him something more? She watched him as he was swallowed up by people, and then she left.

TWO

Claire had met Zed Willard over a previous case and while they hadn't exactly hit it off, they had found a détente and a mutual respect. Though what on earth possessed him to ask for her help now she couldn't begin to imagine. Curiosity propelled her forward.

It was a shit journey to the Hanley police station battling through traffic hindered by road closures caused by water mains leaks and apologized for by Severn Trent. The Hanley station was the hub of Stoke-on-Trent's law enforcement – modern, huge and ugly – but Claire couldn't find a parking space. After a few minutes driving round and round she parked on the road straddling double yellow lines and decided if DS Willard wanted her here he could bloody well pay the parking fine.

She approached the front desk and spoke to a bored-looking officer who could barely lift his eyelids.

In response to her request he gave her a lopsided grin and picked up the phone. 'You want to take a seat?'

'No,' she said, 'I'm fine. I'd rather stand.'

But he hadn't finished his hospitality spiel. 'Cup of tea?'

'Thanks,' she said, suddenly thirsty. She'd had nothing since breakfast, which had been hours and hours ago.

'Milk and sugar?'

'Milk. No sugar.'

He was back in a suspiciously short time and handed her a cup of weak, milky tea. But it tasted good, made with fresh milk rather than the synthetic stuff. And, in a nod to the city's nickname, the Potteries, it was in a china cup.

Two sips in DS Zed Willard was standing in front of her. She hadn't seen him since the summer. He was still stocky but had lost a bit of weight, fat turned into muscle – maybe a few evenings at the gym? But his hair was still unruly, thick and dark, his blue eyes very bright in contrast and his grin was as warm as if he was greeting an old friend rather than a passing work colleague. She stood up, balancing her cup of tea. Their eyes were level as his grin broadened. 'Good to see you, Claire. Thanks for coming. I really appreciate it. Sorry to drag you away from your funeral.'

'That's OK. You did me a favour. And I was ready to go anyway.' She couldn't help adding, 'I couldn't find a parking space outside so am square on some double yellows. I just hope I don't get a parking ticket, Zed.'

He looked a bit concerned. 'Are you on the . . .'

'Yes, on the road in. Otherwise, I'd have had to park in the multi-storey.'

'Just have to hope you don't get booked by a PC on his first day trying to impress us all.' Contrasting with his tone an hour or so ago, he now sounded light. Relieved.

'If I do, Zed, I'll blame it all on you.'

It wasn't ruffling his good humour. 'OK, Claire. You do that.'

'So what's this all about?'

He looked around him. 'We need to talk in private. Walls have . . .' He tapped his ear. He led the way along the corridor, chatting as he went. 'So whose funeral was it?'

'My ex's sister.'

'Ex? What – the pirate-looking guy?'

'Yeah.'

'Ex's sister?' His eyes landed on hers.

'Yeah.'

He stopped walking. 'A bit young then?'

'She had cystic fibrosis. She was just twenty-three. His kid sister.'

'Oh.' He was silent for a moment before sneaking a sideways glance. 'Ex?'

'Yeah. We broke up over a year ago.'

'But you still went to his sister's funeral.' It was almost an accusation until he followed up with, 'That's nice. She was a good friend of yours?'

Claire shook her head and was thankful that DS Willard had just pushed open the door to one of the interview suites. It saved her spitting out the cliché: *It's complicated.*

She waited while he closed the door behind them and indicated a seat. He was a man who liked to take his time, his movements, like his sentences, ponderous and deliberate. She imagined his work would be the same, measured and thorough. Not given to impulses or hunches but the result of facts rather than fantasy. He didn't speak straight away, but sat with a frown on his face, both hands resting, palms down, on the table as though at any moment he would spring up.

She risked a joke. 'Surely *you're* not in need of a psychiatrist's help?'

He managed a watery smile, but it was accompanied by a troubled frown.

Then he looked up. Oh, God, she thought. I hope he hasn't dragged me here because he's going through a traumatic divorce and wants a shoulder to cry on. Two men in tears in one day was the last thing she needed. She didn't prompt him.

And at last he started talking. 'Do you recognize the name Jonah Kobi?'

It took her mere seconds to connect the name to the story. 'Unfortunately I do. He killed some young girls. Schoolgirls, weren't they?'

'Yes. Four.'

She was puzzled now. 'But he was convicted of the murders, wasn't he? He's gone down for life, surely?'

Willard nodded. 'Yes.'

She waited for him to explain, wondering where she fitted in. Most serial killers were not interesting in her opinion. They were untreatable psychopaths who derived satisfaction from holding the power of life and death over an individual. Most were cruel and many held strange beliefs, that they had a God-given right to murder. Unfortunately, in her role as a forensic psychiatrist, she had met a few too many of these unsavouries. Mostly men but one woman too. They were, in general, devoid of any normal human emotion. As though a vital switch had failed to connect, they lacked pity or empathy and did what they did because they could. Because people were there, because . . .

Because nothing. Of all the serial killers she had met, not one of them had had any real reason for killing. And yet there was often a cruel pattern in their logic. They killed women they thought were prostitutes, women with red hair, men who walked the streets searching for loose homosexual love, the homeless, the old. All targets. And interestingly, from a research point of view, each one stuck to a similar MO, forming a terrible pattern and leaving their stamp on victims and crime scenes. Some collected bizarre trophies of their crimes: eyes, other body parts, items of clothing, as others might collect thimbles or pictures or works of art. Their methods too were uniform: knives, screwdrivers, axes, rarely guns (not satisfying enough) or they strangled with bare hands. What few of them had was a documented, treatable psychiatric disease. They simply had a personality disorder. They were sociopathic, psychopathic, narcissistic, paranoid, amoral, antisocial. There was no shortage of words to describe them. The sub-classifications were almost endless. But one thing united them. Their reason: because they felt like it. Freedom from the burden of a conscience let them loose on an unsuspecting victim. The 'perp' was unlikely ever to change. They might pretend to; some even tried to but the tendency was always there and at any moment, like the chronic infection that had blighted Maisie's lungs, it could burst through. They belonged in prison. Thankfully the condition, in its most severe form, was rare. They might be a danger to society but they weren't interesting. From what she remembered about the case, Jonah Kobi had fitted the profile perfectly. A narcissistic personality disorder. There were far more interesting and curable psychiatric diagnoses to occupy her work time. The disorder meliorated only with time. Old psychopaths are less of a threat and the older they grow the less of a threat they become. She felt her own interest start to wane.

'So where do I come in?'

He fidgeted, frowned. His eyes dropped. Then his words came out in a rush. 'There was a query about a fifth girl.'

She scraped her memory. 'As far as I remember, Kobi was convicted of four murders. Not five.'

'The CPS decided not to charge him with the fifth. They felt they wouldn't get it to stick and they had enough on him to put him away for life. There was no forensic evidence to link them and, unlike the other four, we never found her body. But the time-line was right and the profile. Marvel Trustrom was the right age and the area fitted – within a radius of ten miles of the Potteries. Kobi was killing between 2012 and 2015. Marvel disappeared in 2013. Her death slots in neatly between the killing of Jodie Truss and Teresa Palmer. She was fourteen years old, a schoolgirl, like

the others. There is a slight difference in that she was abducted
on a Saturday so wasn't in school uniform.'

'The others all were?'

'Yeah. But everything else fits, Claire. She'd gone by bus to
the Potteries Shopping Centre and we believe she was abducted
from there.'

She felt the first prickling of interest. 'But you haven't found
the body?'

'No. But come on, Claire. How many schoolgirl killers are
going to be out there, in that time frame and from the same area?'

'The other girls were abducted on school afternoons?'

'Ye-es.'

She sensed his hesitation and prompted him. 'Go on.'

'The other four girls' bodies were found within hours in various
locations with little attempt to conceal them. Petra Gordano and
Jodie were abducted on their way home from school, last seen at
the bus stop. Their bodies were found less than a day later – one
of them dumped at the back of the bus depot and the other in
Hanley Park. Teresa's body was dumped in a recycling wheelie
bin outside some printer's offices and Shelley Cantor's body was
weighted down and found in Westport Lake. That was how we
finally found Kobi. The Staffordshire Wildlife Trust had put up
some cameras looking for unusual water birds or something.
Anyway, one of them picked up his car number plate.'

'It's interesting,' she mused, 'that his mode of disposal was so
careless, but you say that Marvel's body has *never* been found and
I take it he's given you no clue as to where it might be?'

DS Willard shook his head. 'Even Shelley Cantor's body was
bound to be found soon. Westport Lake is used by families and
fishermen.'

'They were all killed the same way?'

Willard nodded. 'Strangled with their school ties.'

He was looking eagerly at her, like a puppy hoping to be taken
for a walk. 'Do you see anything of interest there?' he asked.

She tried to wriggle away. 'Really, Zed. It's nothing to do with
me. Don't you have a cold case review – or something?'

'That isn't the answer.' He was looking intently at her. 'I'm
sure,' he said, 'that the truth lies within Kobi. He's playing with
us, keeping back this last card.'

'Is it that important?'

His response was a grave nod. 'Her dad's dying. He has cancer and has weeks to live. He wants to be buried or cremated with his daughter. He's desperate for us to find her body.'

Now she realized why Zed Willard had appealed to her so urgently. Inwardly she heaved a big sigh. 'Since Kobi's been in prison has he said *anything* about Marvel?'

'He's denied it consistently. Said it's nothing to do with him.'

'He admitted the others?'

'Yeah. In the end. At first it was a typical "no comment" interview. But when we presented him with the facts, he and his solicitor tried plea bargaining.'

'His defence?'

Zed Willard ruffled his hair. It was an unconscious but endearingly boyish gesture. 'The usual, troubled upbringing, career damaged by a spurious and malicious allegation.'

'Was there one?'

'So it seemed. He was a teacher at a private girls' school in Macclesfield. In 2008 a schoolgirl called Miranda Pullen made an allegation of sexual impropriety. After an investigation the allegation was deemed to be false. But in the light of subsequent events . . . It makes you wonder, doesn't it?'

'Wasn't Kobi seen by a psychiatrist when he was charged?'

'Yeah. A guy called Wilson.'

'Terence Wilson?'

'Yeah. That's the one.'

'Based over in Stafford, at St George's?'

'Yeah.'

'So why haven't you gone back to him for help?'

'He's dead,' Willard said bluntly. Then added, 'Which is why I'm calling on you.'

'Was Marvel's disappearance mentioned at the trial?'

'No.'

'And in the intervening years you've found no sign of her?'

'Nope.' He sighed. 'I wish.'

'If you haven't found the body,' she pondered, 'you're convinced she *was* murdered? She wasn't simply a runaway?'

He shook his head. Then nodded and turned his bright eyes on hers. 'I just want him to confess, Claire, tell us where he hid her body and fulfil the wish of a dying man.'

'I take it Kobi got life?'

Willard nodded. 'With a recommendation he serve a minimum of forty years.'

She nodded. 'So no get-out-of-jail-free card if he cooperates. We can't use that as a lever.'

'No.'

'And you want me to interview him at—'

'Stafford jail.' Sensing victory, or at least acquiescence, he grinned. 'Not exactly far.'

'You think *I* can squeeze a confession out of him when you failed?'

'To be honest you're our only hope, Claire. We thought you might be able to pick up on stuff. Ask the right questions. I can't think of another approach that might work. We've interviewed him . . .' He ran his hands through his hair again. 'Numerous times.'

'And how does he respond to that?'

'He just stonewalls us.'

'If he is guilty of Marvel's murder what possible motive could he have for not confessing? It wouldn't make any difference to his sentence.'

'I know.' He gave an achingly naive and hopeful grin at her. 'You're the psychiatrist, Claire. Could it be one-upmanship? He still has something over us? Is he mocking us because we don't know everything? Is it even possible he thought he might use it to reduce his sentence at some point in the future?'

'I don't know.'

'I just don't know what else to do, Claire. I feel so sorry for Marvel's dad. If he dies before we find her I'll feel we've failed him.'

He spoke again. 'Kobi's teasing us, Claire. Stringing us along. And there's this poor guy dying day by day who just wants to know where his daughter is.'

She nodded but he hadn't finished trying yet.

'You have a knack of finding out the truth.'

She smiled at the blatant flattery.

'You're a psychiatrist. You'll know the right approach, the best questions to ask, the way to trip him up.'

'And you've failed to get the truth out of him.'

Willard drew in a deep sigh. 'You think we haven't tried?'

She smiled.

'On the book Marvel is down as a missing person but there isn't anyone in the station who doesn't believe she's dead and that Kobi killed her.'

Zed Willard leaned back in his chair, and as she watched him she sensed something more personal. A few lines had deepened around his mouth and eyes. She spoke gently. 'It isn't just the fact that Marvel's father is dying, is it, Zed?'

'I was sort of involved in the case. I was the one who had to tell Petra Gordano's mother that we'd found her daughter's body. Claire, she was only thirteen. An only child.' He bowed his head. 'Kobi's first victim. I'll never forget the look on her mother's face. She was' – he searched for a word – 'destroyed.' He paused. 'It isn't something you can be trained to cope with. It stays with you.' He balled his right hand into a fist and she realized his feelings extended in hatred towards the man he believed responsible. 'As long as we haven't solved every single one of his victims' murders he's won.' He put his elbows on the table and, angry now, met her eyes. 'That stinks. If *you* can worm your way into the cesspit of his mind, maybe you'll persuade him to give Marvel's body up. You're my only hope.'

His appeal was like a fishhook and just as difficult to extricate herself from though she tried. 'I think you have rather exaggerated ideas of my capabilities.'

'You can do it, Claire.'

She stayed silent. Actually the art or science of forensic psychiatry didn't have a great track record and neither did she. People's true nature could be kept hidden even from professionals. She'd misjudged a previous patient who had died, defended a friend who had turned out to be guilty. Mistakes were made. Psychiatrists are not some infallible oracle. They are simply an informed opinion. And sometimes they are wrong.

She began to explain. 'It's nice of you to have such faith in me, Zed, but . . .'

'Please,' he said. 'If you met Tom you'd want to help him.'

'OK,' she said reluctantly, 'I'll do what I can. But I don't hold out much hope. If Kobi did murder her he's held out so far. And there isn't any carrot I can hold out to him as reward for his telling us. He will serve life and he'll know it. There's no point appealing to his conscience. He doesn't have one. So even if he does have the answers we want I have no leverage. And he might not be connected. You might be wrong.'

He gave a wry smile and shook his head. 'Course he murdered her. There are hardly going to be two serial killers operating at the same time in the same time frame, the same profile and the same MO in and around one fairly law-abiding Staffordshire city that has a relatively clean track record.'

'If you haven't found the body,' she pointed out, 'you don't know whether the MO's the same. And there are the obvious differences.'

'OK,' he said impatiently. 'I grant you that but please try.'

'Besides,' she said thoughtfully, 'it wouldn't be *two* serial killers. It would be one serial killer and the other a single, isolated event. Or else a schoolgirl runaway.'

Willard was chewing his lip and she caved in. 'I'll need to see photographs of all the girls,' she said, adding, 'including Marvel.'

'OK.' He smiled.

'There weren't any more incidents around that time were there?'

He shook his head and his face told it all. Angry and defensive. Bordering on hostile. 'I can be convinced of the long arm of coincidence, but he did it.' His face was suddenly vicious. 'He bloody well did it. Denying it is just his way of winning. But life is a long time, Claire. He knows he won't be out this side of seventy. If ever. And all that time he'll be in the stinking flea pit we call prison. He'll have to put up with violence against him, shitting into a cracked toilet, sharing a cell with another psycho. Prison isn't what is portrayed in the press. It's living in a shithole with a whole load more psychos who'll beat you up if you so much as look at them wrong, half of them out of their flea-brains with drugs their so-called family smuggle in for them, and that's not counting the drone drops.'

She smothered a smile. DS Willard, it seemed, had no illusions about the present-day prison system.

'OK,' she said again, 'I'll speak to the family and I'll speak to him, see if I can get any more out of him than you already have.'

'Thank you.' His anger had turned to humility.

'But I'll need all the police and Dr Wilson's psychiatric notes including his past family, medical and psychiatric history as well as every single detail of Marvel. Her character, pictures, the circumstance of her disappearance as well as the details of the other four girls. I'll need access to friends as well as family.'

'Hey.' He looked cheered now. 'I owe you one.'

'Then you can pay my parking fine.'

He chortled at that and looked almost happy, almost carefree. She knew why. He'd passed the baton on in a difficult race. So she added a note of encouragement. 'Zed,' she said, 'if there's one thing I do know about serial killers, like other repeat offenders, they like attention. Prison robs them of that. They move from being a celebrity to a nobody surrounded by other nobodies. No one cares any more whatever they do or say. Their status has gone. They have left their world, entered into a dark place and lost control. Maybe his thirst for attention will persuade him to tell me something he's kept from you. We'll see.'

'Thanks,' he said again, his smile bordering on warm, inviting.

She shook his hand, giving out the clear message, *let's keep this formal.*

She had enough complications in her life.

THREE

I t was two thirty by the time she arrived at Greatbach Secure Psychiatric Unit. Tall grey walls reached through an archway; the modern part of the hospital which housed the Day Centre and Outpatient clinics was out of sight, round the back. Even for Claire who worked there, walking underneath the arch felt forbidding. She'd never quite got used to it.

She was still in time to help Salena Urbi, her registrar, with the outpatient clinic. Salena was a beautiful and clever Egyptian whose insight into psychiatric diagnoses and intelligence was only matched by her work ethic. They greeted each other with a grin. 'Simon has been seeing your patients,' she said, flashing white teeth. 'He's getting on really well.' She accompanied her words with a wink and a giggle.

Simon Bracknell was her Australian lodger, also her registrar. Finding out he was staying in seedy lodgings and realizing she had four empty bedrooms, she'd offered him the top floor of her house and he'd jumped at it. Since Grant, the ex-boyfriend she still hadn't quite managed to discard, had moved out she'd come to the conclusion that Number 46 Waterloo Road, Burslem, was far too big for a single person. She could have moved but since her decorator Paul Mudd had done up the place from top to bottom the house felt too much like home – albeit rather a large one. Having Simon on the top floor had worked out really well. So far. With pale skin, thick glasses and freckles he might not be the archetypal tanned, surfing Australian, but in his carefree casual nature he fitted the bill. It had been a few weeks after he'd moved in that he'd confessed he was married – to Marianne who was currently still in Adelaide. Presumably Simon rang or Facetimed periodically but he rarely mentioned her, and in the time he'd been living in Waterloo Road his wife had not visited. Not yet, at least.

He came out of the interview room as she passed and he and Salena filled her in on the patients they'd seen so far. They split the rest of the clinic between them and by five thirty only had notes to write and the usual discussions.

'How did your funeral go?' Simon asked.

'Grim and sad.' Anxious to change the subject, she continued quickly, 'When I switched my phone back on I had a message.'

They looked vaguely interested.

'Do you remember DS Zed Willard, Salena?'

'The detective who was involved with the Dexter Harding case?'

'The very one.'

'Not really. I think I might have met him once but I don't recall.'

'He's asked me to look into a case of a serial killer.'

She frowned. 'To consider parole?'

'No. To try and find a missing victim.'

'One of his?'

'Apparently so.' Now she was frowning too. 'That's what they believe anyway.'

Salena picked up on her doubt. 'You don't sound very convinced.'

'You know me. I withhold judgement until I'm quite sure.'

'You're going to see him at the prison?'

Claire nodded.

'Rather you than me,' was Simon's contribution. 'You'll be dealing with a nasty, sticky little insect. And so,' he tacked on casually, 'how *is* the boyfriend?'

By the jangling of her earrings, Claire knew Salena's head had whipped round.

'Grieving.' She then ran out of words. She never could quite encapsulate Grant Steadman in words. He was a presence rather than simply a person. At one time she would have sworn they would marry and have a family but, without a word, for six months, he had simply disappeared. Only later, much later, had he told her why – to be at the side of his dying sister, Maisie.

Simon and Salena exchanged meaningful looks and Claire smiled.

Sometimes psychiatrists were just too darned perceptive.

She rang the ward to ask if there were any problems and Astrid Carter, one of the senior psychiatric nurses, assured her all was calm.

That meant she could head home. But as she drove through the traffic Claire felt guilty about Grant. 'Which is bloody silly,' she said out loud, grasping the steering wheel. 'He was the one who abandoned me without so much as a word.' She still dialled his number on the car phone. Perhaps recognizing the number, he picked up right away,

'Hi.' His voice sounded thick. At a guess he'd kept his promise to get roaring drunk.

'Grant.'

It was hard to say whether he was pleased to hear from her or not.

'Are you pissed?'

'Not yet. Not quite. Not enough. What did you ring about anyway?' He was slurring his words.

'I just wondered if you wanted to come over tomorrow evening?'

'To Waterloo Road?' Instant sobering up.

'Yes.'

'Oh.' He sounded taken aback. 'You sure?'

'Yes.' God, she'd forgotten just how awkward things were between them.

'I'd love to come. Is seven too early?'

'No. I don't think so.' She paused. 'How's your mum?'

'Not as bad as I thought she'd be. She's coping. Some of her friends have been popping over to see how she is. People can be quite kind. She's wondering whether to go back to Cornwall or stay here.'

'It's early days yet.'

Another of those rich chuckles. 'Not like you to resort to clichés, Claire.'

He knew her so well, inside out, outside in, upside down.

And that was the point. In our lives there is often one person. Just one person who understands us better than any other. Better than mother, father, brother, sister. They are your second skin, your natural partner, the one piece of humanity whose shape complements yours.

For her that one person, that second skin, that natural partner, was Grant Steadman with his husky voice, so appealing, so laden with insight, always ready to test her because he knew that lightened her mood, distracted her from dark thoughts.

Silence dropped between them. Maybe he too was thinking the same thoughts. Finally Grant spoke. 'See you tomorrow, then.'

FOUR

Simon's hired Nissan Micra was already in the drive and as she opened the front door he called out, 'Cup of tea?'

'That'd be lovely.'

He was in the kitchen, preparing some pasta and sauce that smelt good. Garlicky and meaty. A tin of tomatoes was on the side. He saw her sniffing and peering towards the pots. 'Plenty for two,' he offered.

'Nice. And I just happen to have a bottle of Italian wine which will go very well with it.'

'Ready in ten minutes.' As they sat round the table, both sipping the tea, Claire wondered how she could possibly ask her lodger to make himself scarce the following evening because her 'boyfriend' was coming round.

'You want to talk about the funeral?'

'Not really. What can I say? They're all pretty awful. Maisie was just twenty-three. She'd gone through so much. She'd had a heart and lung transplant but her body rejected it. Then it was just a matter of time.'

He nodded. 'Poor girl.' He paused before asking his next question, a little glint in his eye. 'And the ex?'

She put her hands to her face. 'Doesn't quite feel like an ex,' she confessed. 'I've asked him over tomorrow.'

He jumped in. 'I'd better make myself scarce then.'

She eyed him and smiled. 'Thanks.'

They sat companionably, drinking tea. After a few sips Claire put her mug on the table.

'I've never asked you,' she said. 'Your wife? Does she mind your being over here for so long – being without you?'

She'd noticed that men with ginger hair often have a very pronounced blush and Simon Bracknell was no exception. 'Oh, heck,' he said awkwardly. 'I was going to ask you about that.'

She raised her eyebrows.

'I mean . . .' His blush deepened, making the freckles on his nose less pronounced, less of a contrast. 'I . . .'

'Spit it out,' she said gently. 'Or rather let me guess. You'd like her to come over?'

'How would you feel about it, Claire?'

'It's fine.' But even she could hear the hesitance in her voice. Having Simon on the top floor was a bit different from having a married couple up there. For a start she would be outnumbered, and they would probably want to use the shared kitchen more frequently. Honesty compelled her to add, 'For a time, at least.'

He nodded and looked past her. 'To be honest we've been through some sticky waters. We need some time together.'

This was getting worse. Now she sensed a warring couple. 'And you thought the best way to deal with that was to scarper over here?'

'She lost a baby a year ago.' He looked even more ashamed. 'Since then . . .'

She guessed. 'No sex?'

'Fucking psychiatrists,' he said, looking even more embarrassed. 'Is there no place you won't explore?'

She shook her head. 'You should know. So how is she now?'

'Different. I thought it best if I absented myself for a while.'

She nodded. 'And has that helped?'

He grinned. 'Given the ten thousand miles or so between us at least sex isn't much of an issue.'

She couldn't help herself. She giggled like a schoolgirl.

'But she's agreed to come over. I thought if she could come to your place for a day or two just to get over the jet lag we could do some travelling maybe. A bit of sightseeing. Scotland, Wales, Ireland and of course there's plenty of England too.'

She felt compelled to ask, 'How long would she come over for?'

'A month, I thought, but we won't be spending too much time with you.'

'OK,' she agreed, 'but we'll play it all by ear. You too. OK?'

'Great.' He almost rubbed his hands together and she grinned at him.

'You're fond of her, aren't you?'

He nodded. 'Sort of childhood sweethearts.'

'Touching. And Simon, I'm sorry about the baby.'

'Hell. She was just three months gone. It didn't seem real to me. I was just getting used to the idea. But Marianne was heart-broken. I hadn't realized how much it meant to her but truthfully I can't really say I was too.' He eyed her. 'And now you're going to hate me for being a hard-hearted arse.'

'No,' she said. 'It's just a male thing, isn't it? Now is that pasta ready? I'm starving.'

As they ate Simon switched subjects. 'So tell me about your serial killer?'

She forked in some spaghetti. 'He murdered four schoolgirls between 2012 and 2015. In 2013 another girl, Marvel Trustrom, went missing but her body's never been found. There are anomalies in the case and no obvious link. Though he confessed to the four schoolgirls he's always denied having anything to do with Marvel. The CPS convicted him of the murder of the four girls but had no evidence to charge him with Marvel's disappearance so left that one out. Bad for the girl's family. The police, however, have always bracketed Marvel's disappearance with the others. Her father is dying and is appealing for help to find his daughter's body so they can be buried together. It's a terrible story,' she reflected.

Simon leaned back in his chair. 'Well, the police are naturally anxious to solve major crime and keep their figures looking healthy, so sometimes they shoehorn major crimes into a known perp. I can see it from their point of view. It's tempting. Trouble is . . .' He pushed his glasses up his nose and smiled at her. 'I don't need to spell it out to you.'

She shook her head.

He did anyway. 'No body, no evidence and presumably no witnesses. And now on top of all that they have a time limit.'

'Yeah.'

He forked some of the spaghetti into his mouth. 'I wonder what he's like.'

'Kobi? Who knows. Probably perfectly ordinary – at least on the surface.'

'Mmm. So how are you going to approach this?'

'I thought I'd arm myself with some facts first, speak to the girl's dad and the rest of her family, explore the other victims' circumstances and then interview him.'

'Sounds good.' He took a deep swig of the wine. 'Have you got anything from his past social and medical history?'

'Waiting for that to come through from the police and his previous psychiatric assessment. I've already applied for a visiting order. He doesn't have to see me though I suspect he'll at least grant me an interview.'

'Lucky you,' he said, and raised his glass.

FIVE

Friday 13 September, 6 p.m.

In spite of the unlucky warning of the date it felt good shopping for something special to cook. Simon had emerged as she had arrived home and announced he was visiting friends in Manchester and wouldn't be back until Sunday evening so she had a whole hour and an empty house to prepare – food and herself. And yet something held her back. She recognized something in Grant that she'd previously turned her back on. When faced with a conflicting situation he was a runner. 'So, Claire,' she lectured herself as she peeled some fresh prawns, 'remember that. When things get tough . . .'

The seafood risotto she'd planned meant peeling a lot of shellfish and all had to be fresh. Finally all was done by six thirty so she opened the wine and lit the log burner. It wasn't really that cold but the log burner made the atmosphere intimate and cosy. She sat watching the flames before going upstairs to shower and change into a midnight-blue dress, short-sleeved and relatively plain. She didn't want to overdo it, make it appear that she'd dressed up for a special dinner date. This was simply a 'mate' coming round for supper. At least that was what she told herself. The drawback to this was she'd forgotten how sexy Grant was, how he turned her guts to water and her free will to soft plasticine. But when she heard the doorbell ring all the old, familiar feelings flooded back.

Grant, wearing jeans and a dark red shirt, had a bottle of wine in one hand and a bunch of night-scented stock in the other. She smelt the peppery, fresh scent the moment she opened the door, almost before she breathed in the sharp tang of his aftershave. Simon didn't wear 'man scent' as he called it, so the scent of aftershave had been missing from the house. Grant was grinning at her as he handed over the flowers. He knew how they always lifted her spirits, particularly stock with its country garden look and fresh, clean scent. He bent and kissed her cheek with a grin that was more like the Grant she'd known and so loved, and she reached out her hand to cradle his neck and hold him there. She drank in the scratchy feel of his chin. Grant was no precise shaver. His lips felt warm and soft, the scent of soap and spice and shaving cream almost heady. Then he broke the moment, drawing back, sniffing and peering round her. 'What's cooking?'

'Wait and see.'

He followed her into the kitchen, his eyes taking it all in, the freshly painted walls and ceilings, the newly polished wood tiles. 'Looking good,' he said.

'Yeah. I got a local guy to do it from top to bottom.' She giggled. 'His name's Paul Mudd.'

'Fitting for a decorator.' He ran his fingers over the sash window frames. 'He's done a good job, Claire.'

She knew how he felt. Disconcerted. He'd been replaced. But she felt different too except in another way. He'd only just walked back in here and she felt as comfortable as though she'd slipped on a pair of slippers. She had to keep reminding herself that this pair of slippers, however well worn, was quite capable of walking away. She stood and looked at him and he took in the appraisal without blinking. It was as though their eyes were communicating without words, awkwardness, hesitation or duplicity, just honesty. His eyes weren't questioning but now looked back at her with a hint of mischief.

'So do I pass the test?'

She simply handed him a glass of wine.

He looked around him. 'Where's your lodger?'

'Away for the weekend.'

Grant raised his eyebrows and she felt bound to add, 'I didn't chuck him out for the duration, you know. He volunteered. He's got friends in Manchester that he wanted to visit.'

Grant looked both amused and sceptical.

He had the look of a pirate. Dark curly hair, thick eyebrows, dark eyes, a thin, almost menacing face – when he wasn't smiling. He was only a little taller than she. His build was muscular but his hands were the delicate hands of an artist – not a pirate's hands at all. He had long, slim fingers, well-shaped nails. More suited to carrying a paintbrush than a cutlass. His hands were his true beauty. They were the clue to his artistic tendencies. And his personality too was more artistic than piratical. But there was nothing feminine about him. He had a certain steeliness, an underlying selfishness, the habit of running away and, buried deep beneath that, vulnerability and neediness. But he was soft-hearted too and this mix had been why he had rushed to his dying sister's side but backed away from explaining the situation to her. As she stirred the risotto she homed in on another characteristic. Once he had made up his mind about something or someone, he did not change, but was as constant in his opinions as the four points on a compass.

They sat down, Claire still tossing ideas around, while on the surface Grant was telling her about his mother's plans.

'She's missing the sea.'

'She has lots of friends in Cornwall.'

'She's looking at houses this weekend.'

There was a subtext, each of them asking questions about the future. A chasm to be crossed that grew wider every day. She had bought him out of the house they had planned to refurbish together and refused to let him back into her life because Claire was familiar with abandonment. Soon after her birth, her French father had abandoned both her and her mother. Her mother had blamed her for his leaving, calling her the 'French Frog' and making her the focus of her bitterness. Right up until she had met Mr Perfect David Spencer and they had produced the perfect son, Adam. After which her mother had virtually ignored Claire.

Watching Grant pour the wine, she reflected. Was it possible that with the death of his sister he had changed? He was still talking about his mother. 'At a guess,' he said, 'she'll move down there some time later this year.'

'I hope she'll be happy.' The words came out automatically.

'Yeah.'

They knocked glasses across the table and Claire continued her appraisal. The jeans and bright shirt suited him better than the mourning clothes. He chewed his lip and she sensed he was about to tell her something. She realized then she'd always believed he would come back. But, with this new insight, she also believed he would not stay for ever. She was a psychiatrist and she could read the signs. Her job taught her to have insight into people's motives and character. That was why DS Zed Willard had asked her to speak to Jonah Kobi, because part of her job was to interpret subtle body language like the foot that was tapping underneath the table as though it wanted to run and the fact that Grant was unaware of it as he continued his update.

'They only came up here because they have a really good cystic fibrosis unit in Stoke. It was what Maisie wanted. And of course, I was here to study at Keele. But Mum's got a part-time job down there which she can walk back into. The house up here is only rented and she's got enough to buy somewhere, just a flat probably, in Cornwall.'

Claire took a spoonful of risotto, tasting the salt on her tongue as though it was the brine of the sea. 'And you? Are you intending to go back down there?'

He licked his lips and met her eyes, a furrow between his thick eyebrows.

'Are you?' she repeated.

He laid his hands flat on the table, palms down. Then he shook his head. 'No. Whatever happens I'm not heading back down to Cornwall. It doesn't feel like home to me.'

Home, that word which sat between them. This had been his home. But she couldn't ask him.

'Claire,' he said, his voice quiet and tentative. 'I'd really like to move back in.' He was avoiding looking at her. 'Here.' He followed that quickly with, 'But of course that's up to you.'

The right words were difficult to find.

She drew in breath, pressed her lips together, about to say, *I really need to think about this.*

He lifted his eyes and there was that steely determination in them. She'd forgotten how long and thick his eyelashes were or how your soul could melt when you let yourself be drawn into his dark eyes and roguish features. She couldn't help but smile.

He grinned and reached for her hand across the table. 'What I'd really like, Claire,' he said, 'is for us to be married. Having lost Maisie, I'd really like a family. I know first of all we'd have to be genetically tested. I couldn't bear to bring a child into the world to suffer as Maisie did or to have to say goodbye to her or him.'

Claire sought refuge in the research she'd done when she'd realized just why Grant had abandoned her without even a word.

'An individual must inherit two non-functioning CF genes — one from each parent — to have CF. If both parents are carriers there is a 1 in 4 (25 per cent) chance that both will pass on the non-functioning gene, which would result in a pregnancy affected with cystic fibrosis.'

When she'd learned about Maisie, she had paid to be screened for the CF gene. She was clear. Any children they had would be clear. But for now she was thoughtful and didn't say anything. He took a sip of the wine and lifted his gaze to her, his face changing. He looked jaunty and mischievous.

'I've started up an interiors business.' His eyes flashed towards hers for approval. 'I've always liked the market of creating an individual look, something other than the minimalist stuff that's so popular, all that stark white, a bit of grey and the same old ornaments. Big telly, plain walls. No patterns, no interest, no individuality. Awful modern art which no one can really understand but pretend they do.'

'You think there's a market for this in Stoke?'

'I do.' His face was still merry. 'The Potteries was filled with ceramics artists, painters, designers and these days there is still that pool of talent.' He gave her a sly look. 'And haven't you got a friend who's a talented potter?'

'Gina.' She was surprised he'd remembered her. He'd only met her a couple of times and she hadn't realized he'd been absorbing her conversation quite so deeply.

'Yes. Gina, the one who mixes Japanese folklore with fantastic animals.'

She nodded and his face lit up with enthusiasm. 'I know the Potteries are here because of clay and coal. But talented artists were drawn here because of the opportunity and the encouragement people like Wedgewood and Spode gave them.'

She watched him, drawn into this other side of him, this creative other world he lived in – so different from hers which peered inside diseased personalities and aberrant minds.

'I like creating and encouraging talent. I think I can do it.'

She simply nodded, poured them both another glass of wine and was thoughtful.

He pressed on. 'I didn't do anything with the money you paid me for the house. It can go back and help pay off the mortgage if you like. I want to realize my dreams, Claire. And you're part of that. I need to be here with you. I need a home and family.' His smile was appealing. 'I also need a workshop.'

She felt her own feelings draw her back.

He hadn't finished. 'If my little dream comes true I think it'll be good for you too. We were happy.'

She resisted the temptation to point out the tense. 'Grant,' she began. 'I'm really not sure about your moving back here. Let's wait, see how things go.'

It checked him. 'OK,' he said, his face changing and his gaze dropping to the floor. 'I know I played it all wrong about Maisie but I am here now, Claire, and I will never leave you again.' His eyes fixed on her face. 'I know you, Claire. You aren't a person to rush into things. You'll want to spend some time thinking about this.' He looked at her ruefully. 'I'd better stop at this one glass of wine. Don't want to lose my licence.'

She filled his glass up.

SIX

Monday 16 September, 9 a.m.

Salena gave her a sly look. 'How was your weekend?'

The truth was the weekend had flown by. Grant, by her side, felt as though he had never left and the same was true for her. They had laughed and talked, made love, cooked together and on the Sunday had walked along the Trent and Mersey canal, taking a detour to a city pub. He had left late on Sunday night, pressing his finger to her lips when she had tried to speak.

'Next time it will be for ever,' he said in his husky voice. 'But be sure, Claire.'

Why couldn't she believe him? How deep are the scars of an early rejection? No word for six months . . .

'So . . .' Claire simply blew out her cheeks and answered her registrar's comment. 'Lovely,' she said. 'Grant came over and we spent some time together.'

Salena's eyes sparkled with mischief. 'Oh yes?'

Claire nodded. 'I'm taking my time, not committing myself. But, Salena . . .'

Salena gave her a wicked smile.

'I don't want to rush into anything.'

And Salena's perfect eyebrows managed to form a direct question. *Oh really?*

'And *your* weekend?' She knew perfectly well that Salena had been on call and would have been on the end of a phone and/or based in the hospital. 'Have you concerns about any patients?'

Salena groaned. 'Ilsa,' she said.

Ilsa was a beautiful Danish woman married to a wealthy, local businessman, John Robinson. She had been suffering panic attacks and developed a habit of self-harming. She'd finally been referred by her private GP who hadn't known what else to do with her. Salena and Claire had tried anti-depressants, a short course of ECT and some cognitive behavioural therapy as well as group therapy. And gradually the real Ilsa had peeped out, a funny, intelligent woman who really should have been teaching Scandinavian Studies at Keele University. That was her talent and the original reason why she had ended up in Stoke-on-Trent. Between them, Ilsa and John had two stepchildren and a child of their own, Augustus, eight, who appeared to be cared for almost solely by a nanny. Ilsa had told her that her access to her own son was controlled by her husband which had led Claire to label him as 'controlling'.

She had interviewed John Robinson at some length and had found him difficult to work out. A wealthy businessman who seemed cold and detached. His interpretation of his wife's illness was one of complete confusion. At times he appeared bullying towards both Salena and Simon, not uncommon among relatives who were frightened or mystified by a mental diagnosis. *'Can't you make them better?'* was the confused plea.

'So what's the problem, Salena? She's nearly ready for discharge, isn't she? She's been here for more than two months.'

Salena nodded and sat down in the chair opposite. 'And that's the trouble,' she said. 'She *is* ready for discharge. But her husband has no idea how to deal with her. If we send her home she'll start on the old self-harming route again.'

'We have her on the right medication and she can attend therapy sessions here. She's happy to go home?'

Salena was frowning now. 'We-ell, she's saying she should be at home with her son.'

'So what's the problem?'

Salena's frown deepened. 'She's now saying that John is having an affair with her best friend, Maggie.'

'That's a new one.'

'She appears absolutely convinced.'

'It could be true.' Claire smiled. 'We might not find him the most attractive of men but he's wealthy. And beauty, as they say . . .'

'I know. But some of the scenes she was describing, if they're not true, then she is psychotic. She's describing them as vividly as if she was a fly on the wall.'

'That is troubling. I'll talk to her later. Any other concerns?'

'If she's psychotic how reliable will she be caring for her son?'

'I see what you mean.'

There had been one incident when Ilsa had taken the boy shopping and had gone home without him, forgetting he'd been left in the store's crèche. John Robinson had instantly hired a nanny, a Swiss girl. Two days later Ilsa had been shipped off to a private clinic in Birmingham.

Claire was silent for a while, then she shook her head. 'There's no option, Salena. She has to go home. She's been here long enough. The bed bureaux is putting pressure on me. We can keep an eye on her as an outpatient, see her weekly, check her mental state and monitor her medication, but you know as well as I that she will go home. I can't keep her here indefinitely.'

Salena stood up, tall and willowy with a vague scent of patchouli that clung to the air around her. 'I know that as well as you but we both know that that could cause Ilsa Robinson to relapse.'

'One of the frustrations of our work.'

Simon arrived then, still yawning. 'God, that was a hot weekend,' he said. 'Sometimes I have trouble keeping up with my Aussie friends.' He grinned at Claire. 'Sorry I'm late.' He smothered yet another yawn. 'Hope I didn't disturb you when I got in Sunday night – or was it early Monday morning?'

'I don't know. I didn't hear you at all.'

'Good.' He rubbed his hands together as though celebrating something exciting. 'So when do you get to see your serial killer?'

Salena's perfectly shaped eyebrows lifted and her head swivelled round sharply.

'I don't want to visit him until I've got a bit more background, hopefully from the family. I'll wait for the notes and all the police files as well as the dead girls' photographs to come through. Then I'll have to wait for clearance – and his permission to visit. As I don't have anything to use as an inducement and it's pretty pointless appealing to his better nature, he might not agree to see me. I'll be honest.' She eyed them both. 'I'm not optimistic about this outcome. I'll delve into his past medical and psychiatric history.

See if there's anything there that'll work but he's stonewalled the police and I don't really think I'll fare any better.'

Salena's expression changed to one of sympathy while Simon continued to look intrigued. 'Sounds time consuming.'

'Don't worry; I won't be neglecting my work here.'

'I didn't mean—'

He tried to retrieve the remark and Claire justified her stance. 'If I have a job to do I must do it properly.'

They spent the rest of the morning speaking to patients on a prolonged ward round before Claire picked up some sandwiches from the canteen and returned to her office where, next to a large pile of outpatient notes, was a parcel marked with her name in thick black felt-tip pen, alongside the words *Jonah Kobi* and in brackets *from DS Zed Willard*. For a moment she didn't open it. Inside this brown paper parcel lay the stories of the deaths of four girls. She took a bite of her sandwich and still didn't break open the seal. Pandora's box, she thought, but without any hope left inside. Instead it was the story of a killer and the devastation he left behind.

She took another bite of the sandwich while she wondered what Kobi looked like. What was his story?

She broke the seal and opened the first page, a neatly typed up and concise past medical history and assessment by Terence Wilson, the psychiatrist who had interviewed him. So there it was.

A police mugshot was pinned to the front. She took a while to study it. Thin face, dark hair, staring boldly into the camera with more than a hint of arrogance. No surprise there. He was an unremarkable-looking man, someone you would not have looked twice at if you passed him on the street.

Age: thirty-eight. So now he would be forty-one.

She read on. History teacher. She spent some time digesting this fact. A history teacher who must have hated his pupils. As he had taught the First World War, Henry VIII and his six wives, the Russian revolution or the battle of Waterloo, he had planned to kill girls like the ones who faced him.

Terence Wilson had begun his report with a neat and unemotional precis.

Convicted of the murders of four schoolgirls between the
years of 2012 and 2015. Each one strangled and the bodies
carelessly disposed of. Asked to interview with a view to a
psychiatric diagnosis.

Claire almost smiled. Well, good luck with that one, she thought.
     There was no mention of Marvel Trustrom. Dr Wilson had stuck
to the known facts and the crimes Kobi was accused of. He had
begun with an overview of his character:

Jonah Kobi is of average height and weight with a confident,
intelligent manner and good eye contact. He comes over as
pleasant and engaging. His appearance is smart. He is slim
and fit looking without appearing over muscular. He has
worked as a history teacher, initially at a private girls'
school. In 2008 one of the pupils, a thirteen-year-old girl,
made an allegation of inappropriate behaviour. There was
no evidence to support this allegation and eventually Mr
Kobi was deemed blameless. But he left the school two
years later and took up supply teaching in numerous schools
in Staffordshire and Cheshire, which is where the four crimes
were committed.

Claire read on.

He is the younger by two years of two brothers. His father
is a manual worker, his mother a housewife. He describes
his parents as conventional, 'a bit boring'.
     His childhood appears to have been unremarkable. He
graduated in history at Birmingham University in 1999.
He was briefly married in 2003 but he and his wife split up
after two years and have had little contact since then. It
appears to have been an unsatisfactory relationship.
     I have interviewed Mrs Marie Kobi, Mr Kobi's ex-wife,
who insists their sex life was normal and that they
were simply incompatible. Interestingly, she claims not to
have been surprised when he was found guilty of the murders
of four young girls, but when questioned didn't enlarge or
offer any tangible explanation for this. It is worth mentioning

that his sister-in-law (his ex-wife's younger sister), Chloe,
remains fiercely loyal to him.

Claire smiled. With their manipulative charm psychopaths are very
good at inspiring devotion.

Mr Kobi's past medical history is unremarkable consisting
of the usual childhood illnesses. He insists he is medically
fit both physically and mentally.

She was beginning to taste Jonah Kobi, anticipating their encounter
with some relish.
    She bent her head and read on.

His older brother works in Dubai as an engineer.
He has no children.

There was plenty more which she scanned before she arrived at
Terence Wilson's summing up.

There is a certain arrogance in Mr Kobi's manner, a superiority
and condescension, but towards me he was polite, restrained
and articulate. It was only when I dug deeper and asked him
if he had known any of the girls personally that he shrugged
and said they were all of a kind.
    What sort of a kind?
    Privileged, arrogant, thinks their attractiveness makes them
superior. They can tell lies with *impunity*.

Claire underlined that last word. So the allegation made by the
girl at the Macclesfield school had acted as a trigger factor. He
had stayed at the school for a year after her allegation had been
dismissed, no doubt encountering the girl and her friends on a
daily basis and so the wound and damage to his ego had festered.
This then would be where her interview would begin. With Miranda
Pullen who had lit the spark.
    As for Kobi, she had no illusions that he would tell her the
truth. She would have to dig deep and read between the lines.
Sometimes she thought of psychiatry as a guessing game, hit or

miss. There was no definitive blood test to prove a positive or negative. At other times she realized psychopathy was nearer to a scientific equation: underlying personality disorder plus narcissism plus circumstance plus trigger factor equals the explosion, i.e. the crime. Put the right components together and the consequence was almost inevitable. She stared at the walls of her office and wondered. What worms would she unearth in Kobi's story? He might play her like a kitten with a mouse. And maybe to give his game extra flavour he would play her along until Marvel's father was dead. He might refuse to see her, as was his right. She almost picked up the phone to explain to DS Zed Willard that she was too busy with her own work and that the likely outcome was that Kobi wouldn't tell her anything new. Her hand actually reached for the phone but she stopped, held back by an image of Marvel's father, dying, in despair, wanting to know his daughter's fate, possibly feeling he had let her down. If there was any chance of alleviating this terrible grief then surely she had a duty to do what she could?

She spent another hour combing through the notes, but she didn't pick up on anything that referred to Marvel's death or any other murders or disappearances other than the four he was finally convicted of.

She closed the file with a vague feeling of depression. Enough for now. She could examine the murdered girls' profiles and details of their deaths later.

Salena and Simon Bracknell knocked on her door and filled the small office with their noisy chatter. They'd brought her a coffee and discussed their roles for the coming afternoon. Rejuvenated with two cups of strong coffee they said they could manage the wards and there was no clinic this afternoon, which left Claire free to begin her contact with Marvel Trustrom's family.

'By the way,' Simon said as they were leaving, 'I should know soon when Marianne's due to get here.' His words were accompanied by an anxious grin which set Claire wondering.

Was he concerned his wife would change her mind about the visit or was it more to do with being reunited with her? Whatever, she worried that even her home life was about to become a bumpy ride.

SEVEN

I n the six years since Marvel had vanished from sight, life for the Trustrom family had moved on.

DS Willard had written a note to that effect and clipped it to the front of the file bringing Claire up to date. Two years after their daughter had disappeared, Tom and Dixie Trustrom had separated. Dixie now lived with their younger daughter, Clarice, in Acocks Green, Birmingham. Tom still lived in the family home in Gillow Heath, near Biddulph, Stoke-on-Trent, with his partner, Yvonne. Marvel's older brother, Shane, was now married with a baby and Sorrel, the sister closest in age to Marvel, worked as a beautician in Cellarhead, where the Leek to Stone and Hanley to Cheadle roads crossed.

Claire contacted Marvel's mother first thinking, mistakenly, she would be the more sympathetic choice. Dixie Trustrom was now working in Birmingham as a helper at a school for disadvantaged children and she was patently reluctant to have any contact with Claire, even when Claire explained in detail her involvement in the case. 'I know Tom is sick,' his wife said, in a tight, hard voice, 'but we've been apart for four years now. We were no help to each other when it happened. There's nothing I can do for him now. I can't help you.' Her voice had risen in a desperate panic. 'Understand this, Dr Roget – we're not good for each other. We just caused each other hurt. Every time we looked at one another we simply saw our murdered daughter.'

'So you believe your daughter is dead?'

Dixie's voice was incredulous. 'Of course I do. I don't mean to be rude, Doctor, but look at the facts.'

Claire kept her cool. 'And you believe that Kobi killed your daughter?'

'Yes.'

'So why do you believe that, in spite of confessing to the other crimes, he's consistently denied it and kept her body hidden?'

'He wants to draw out the torture. To twist the knife,' Dixie said bitterly. 'Other parents of his victims have buried *their* girls, found some sort of closure. Something we couldn't have. And now Tom is dying. We lost our girl six years ago. And look at the anguish it's still causing him. That poor man . . .' Claire heard her voice break. Unbidden the thought entered her mind. *Could you not have held his hand? Consoled him in some way? Did you have to cut him loose?*

'I'd like to speak to you about the day Marvel went missing.'

'Look,' Dixie Trustrom said, 'I'm sure your motives are perfectly honourable but I don't want to meet up with you. I work with disadvantaged children now, children that I can actually do something for. It helps me as well as them. As a family we've all moved on. Shane is married. Sorrel has a good job and Clarice is hoping to go to university next year. She lives with me and we . . . we just don't talk about it. We've all moved on – except Tom – and I suspect that's because he's dying. It's making him focus on death. The rest of us want life.' That note of desperation was back, more intense than before.

'You know he wants to be buried with her?'

'Ye es, though I think it's morbid. Wherever her body is Marvel ceased to exist once she'd walked out of that door.' As though to make up for her refusal to meet up, she added, '*He'll* see you, Dr Roget. Marvel was his special . . . little . . . girl.'

Was Claire imagining it or was there a hint of irony in her voice?

'He'll be only too anxious to talk about her.' This time Claire could have sworn Dixie Trustrom *was* mocking something or someone.

Dixie finished with a more sincere sounding: 'Sorry,' and the line was cut, but Claire couldn't rid herself of the instinct that something here was very wrong.

If it wasn't the hard-heartedness of the mother, what was it?

Dixie was proved right. Marvel's father was only too anxious to meet up with Claire but not until Wednesday. He explained he had a hospital appointment on the Tuesday.

The intervening day was filled with a series of pointless meetings about funding for some ring-fenced acute outpatient beds in the local hospital. And as always, whenever there was separate funding between physical and mental health, it led to prolonged 'discussions' which turned into impassioned arguments, and in the end nothing was settled. Claire walked out of the meeting with a sense of frustration. Two hours wasted. Nothing achieved.

Salena was away until the end of the week at a conference on bipolar disease and the current trends in treatment since Lithium had fallen out of favour. Simon Bracknell was working flat out but still had time to quiz her further about the weekend with Grant.

'So how did it go?'

'It went well.'

He winked. 'Not giving much away, are you, Claire?'

'No. I'm taking it one step at a time.' She tried to divert the subject. 'So when does Marianne arrive?'

'I'll let you know exactly when I'm picking her up.' A mischievous smile lit his face. 'So did he stop over?'

She felt herself flush. 'Mind your own business,' she said, and he guffawed.

And Grant? Wisely he was leaving her alone to make up her own mind. And she had. If he wouldn't commit – not really – then neither would she. Maybe this easy come, easy go, suited them both.

Wednesday 18 September, midday

Looking at Tom Trustrom, Claire agreed with the assessment that he probably had only weeks to live. She'd agreed to meet him at his house, an inter-war semi in Gillow Heath, a small, rural conurbation near Biddulph. It was the same house they'd all lived in when Marvel had been taken, part of a row of eight which lay opposite open fields and a pathway. It was a quiet neighbourhood, the front garden neat and ordered, paintwork perfect, one car, a red Nissan Micra parked in the drive. As he'd opened the door Claire had noted the unmistakable fingerprint of cancer, the Belsen-like thinness, the hollows beneath the eyes, the bony wrists, the jaundice and the acceptance of his brief future portrayed in the droop of his shoulders and that extreme, painful tiredness as though the brief walk to the door had exhausted him. The clothes that must once have fitted him hung as though there was no body inside. However, he looked at her with a smile which held a hint of light and optimism, as though he believed she could offer some sort of absolution. The Holy Grail he was seeking, the body of his daughter. As she shook his hand she wished she shared both his optimism and his conviction, but was aware that she had yet to confront Jonah Kobi and she had the feeling that the encounter would damp any optimism she might feel of a resolution.

Yvonne proved to be a quietly attractive woman in her late fifties with salt and pepper hair. She stood behind her partner as he lowered himself into the sofa and threw a blanket over his skinny legs. In spite of her efforts she looked as tired as her partner and prematurely grief struck. The room they'd ushered her into was neat, cream and beige, with the underlying scent of death hardly masked by a lavender-scented candle burning on the centre of a pale oak coffee table. It was Yvonne who opened the conversation while Tom made himself comfortable, arranging and rearranging cushions behind his back.

'Tom and I met at one of the victim support meetings,' she said. 'My husband died as the result of a hit-and-run and they never found the driver. We sort of bonded over that. Dixie hadn't wanted to go.' She couldn't resist a swift catty dig. 'I think she was in denial so Tom had come all alone. He looked so' – she fished around in her memory for the right words – 'so lost, so lonely. I knew just how he felt. I was widowed and felt the same unfairness of it all. The same anger. Both of us, you see, had lost someone precious and we didn't even have a person to blame.' She gave a little ghost of a smile and glanced across at him with a touching, soft affection. 'I still dream that one day there will be a car crash and they'll get some DNA or something and someone will finally own up to having killed my husband.' Another quick glance across the room. 'And Tom hopes for the same. But time's running out.' Her face sagged. 'He wants to see that man confess. He wants his daughter's bones cremated with his own so he'll be whole again.'

She was a softly spoken woman, who wore little make-up except for mascara which emphasized her limpid brown eyes and long lashes. Her voice was soft, her feet bare, toenails varnished pale pink. She spent a moment searching Claire's face before falling silent, waiting for either Tom or Claire to take over.

Tom Trustrom studied her through tired eyes before he spoke.

'So you're Dr Roget,' he said, 'the psychiatrist trying to extract a confession from that . . .' He gulped. 'That monster.'

She nodded. 'I take it Detective Sergeant Willard has been in touch with you and explained my role?'

'That's right. He's pinning my last hope on you.'

It gave her an opening to prepare him. 'Tom,' she said, 'it's quite likely that Kobi won't tell me anything he hasn't already confessed to.'

Tom nodded. 'I realize that. Have you seen him yet?'

Claire shook her head and didn't confess she hadn't received the visiting order yet. 'I thought I'd talk to you first and examine his files.' She dropped into jargon. 'Familiarize myself with the background.'

'I haven't much time left, you know?' His voice was soft, his eyes suddenly bright almost as though he visualized heaven. It took her aback.

She nodded her agreement. Pointless to try and pretend otherwise. 'Tom, Mr Trustrom, I'll be honest with you. I don't hold out much hope of getting anything out of Jonah Kobi. He's kept silent for nearly four years. He has nothing to gain by telling us the circumstances of your daughter's death. Or where her body lies.' She felt bound to tack on, 'If he is responsible for her disappearance. You understand that? I don't have magical powers. In the end it will be up to him what he tells me.'

Tom Trustrom nodded, his head drooping but whether from disappointment, acceptance or tiredness Claire couldn't guess.

Yvonne stood up. 'Let me make some tea.'

The universal panacea. 'Thank you.'

When Yvonne had left the room, Claire settled back in her chair. 'Tell me about your daughter, Tom. What was she like? Tell me about the day you last saw her.'

He didn't respond straight away but spent a moment gathering his words together. 'I went looking for her, you know. Took the car round the streets just hoping I'd see her. She was a lovely girl. Nice natured. A bit trusting. Naive. You know. Kind . . . but a bit needy.'

Claire tucked the word away. *Needy. How so?*

Tom gave a short chuckle. 'One minute she could look the innocent schoolgirl. The next she was wearing clothes that seemed too old for her, slapping on the make-up, looking like . . .' He ran out of words.

Claire nodded, encouraging him to continue with a bland agreement. 'I suppose lots of girls are like that at that age. Sleeping with a teddy bear at home but when they're out so sophisticated.' She watched him carefully. Was she imagining this? Was there something furtive in his manner? Some evasion?

'Tell me more about the day she went missing.'

'It were a Saturday in November. The weather was horrible and rainy. Blustery. We all felt a bit . . . cooped up in the house. Four kids' – he looked around him – 'and this place isn't big. Sorrel and Marvel had been at it like a pair of cats. Quarrelling.'

'What were they quarrelling about?' Claire asked the question quietly. It could have little bearing on the case.

'Oh, those bloody charm bracelets.' The frustration was flooding back. 'We'd bought Sorrel and Clarice a charm because they'd done well in their ballet exams. And Marvel made such a bloody fuss. She always wanted what the other ones had. She was a bit prone to that. Jealousy. We thought Marvel should be getting on with her homework and stuff, but she made such a fuss about the charm and said whatever we said she was going up Hanley to get one. You know, why should her sisters have something she didn't. Drove us mad, it did.' He'd forgotten for a moment. 'So off she goes. Caught the bus up Hanley in the most unsuitable clothes considering the weather. I said to her, "You'll get soaked".' He chuckled, still in the moment. 'She just gave me one of them looks.' He chuckled again before he remembered. 'I thought she'd get the charm, perhaps meet some friends, maybe grab a burger. At least it would get one of them out of the house. I did suggest she take one of her sisters with her. Huh. That went down like a lead balloon.'

'Do you think she was meeting someone that day?'

Now he looked annoyed and defensive. 'I would have said if she was. I would have told the police, wouldn't I? They interviewed her two best friends, but Karen and Lara said they'd gone to the pictures.' He stopped again, puzzled now. 'Except . . .' Claire resisted the temptation to prompt him, '. . . they hadn't asked our Marvel if she wanted to go with them.'

There was a tinge of sadness here while Claire wondered whether Karen and Lara were such good friends.

'If she had . . . maybe . . .' And his voice trailed away.

'Marvel had a mobile phone?'

'Pay as you go.' Another rueful smile. 'She'd run out of credit, else again . . . maybe . . .'

They were both silent. The world, history, events, full of maybes.

Yvonne broke the silence, re-entering with a tray of rattling teacups and a look of concern at Tom and accusation towards Claire. Tom held his hand up to ward off any intervention.

'What was she wearing that day?'

'I can't remember.' He looked away.

Yvonne opened her mouth as though to speak and clamped it tight shut. 'Milk? Sugar?' It was not what she had meant to say.

Questions were lining up in Claire's mind. She needed to delve back into Kobi's file, take a look at the girls he had killed and compare them with Marvel's profile. Serial killers are suckers for habit. And tend to stick to the same victim type. Blonde-haired, red-haired, dark-haired – whatever. So the first question was why a Saturday? Why would Kobi have gone for a girl not wearing his preferred outfit? Could it be because the police were closing in with officers around schools and vigilant parents sitting in cars waiting to take their daughters safely home? Was that why he had struck on a Saturday? She might discuss it with her colleague, Edward Reakin, who was the clinical psychologist attached to Greatbach. He'd thrown a light on many a case before but, as she sipped the tea and watched Tom Trustrom, even here, with the girl's father, something felt like a misfit. Without answers to the little questions she would not find the truth to the larger one.

Or were they all wrong and this was not Kobi's work but another killer? Kobi had provided them with a convenient explanation.

As the three of them made small talk and drank their tea, at the back of Claire's mind doubts were compounding. Tom and Yvonne seemed to have a hidden language. Each would start a sentence, eyes on the other, and then stop abruptly. Perhaps there is always some conspiracy between partners. Which begged the question: was there one between her and Grant? Or was it missing? Was *that* what was missing? He had had a conspiracy to care for his sister but had not shared that with her. He kept secrets.

Instinctively she put her finger on something when she asked one particular question. 'Have you had any contact with Kobi?'

Yvonne and Tom looked at each other guiltily. Exposed. And then Tom nodded. 'I wrote to him,' he said. 'Appealed to him to tell us the truth. Two or three times but the letters were opened and returned. He never got back to me.'

No, she thought. The appeals would have amused him. Answer the questions that were so distressing the girl's father? No.

'So he didn't even *deny* responsibility?'

Tom shook his head and put his finger right on the pulse. 'It was as though he wanted us to suffer. To hang on. Always to wonder. Never have answers.'

She nodded. 'I believe you're alone in the family wanting this . . .' She hesitated to use the word. 'Closure? Dixie'– she'd chosen not to use the epithet of ex-wife – 'and your son and other two daughters aren't pushing to find out what happened to Marvel?'

'They're not bothered,' he said without rancour. 'They just want to get on with their lives. Put it behind them. They don't want always to be known as the brother and sisters and mother of a murdered girl. They want to forget about her. Pretend she never existed.'

Claire made a hand gesture meant to indicate sympathy and understanding, waiting for the inevitable bitterness to creep in.

'But *they're* not dying,' he finished.

'No.'

She put her cup firmly back on the saucer and stood up.

'When do you think you'll get to see him?'

'I have to wait for the prison's permission as well as his,' she explained and then paused. 'Tom,' she said, 'don't get your hopes up. Even if he does agree to see me it doesn't mean to say that he'll give me any valid information. You understand that? If my assessment of his character is correct he's just as likely to feed me misinformation.'

'You're my best hope. My only hope that you'll find my girl.' His voice now was thin, reedy, desperate.

'I'll do my best,' she said, addressing them both while trying to ignore the raw appeal in Marvel's father's eyes.

Outside she switched her phone back on to a bright message from Grant. *Any chance I can buy you a curry tonight?*

She tapped out her response.

EIGHT

She'd told Grant she'd walk up to the local curry house. It was a pleasant walk through streets lined with various shops, some still open, others with steel shutters guarding them, many sporting For Sale notices or, even more optimistically, To Let. These days Burslem wasn't a high crime area. Traffic was light and the evening pleasantly warm. The walk up to the India Cottage was a familiar one, the incline only a mild pull on her legs as she quickened her pace. While she walked, she thought. Rita had let her know that the visiting order had come through. Tomorrow, at three o'clock, she would be meeting Jonah Kobi and could begin to form her own opinion of him. In many ways she was excited by the challenge, even if at the same time she was realistic enough to acknowledge that the chances of Kobi confessing to her were slim, particularly at their first encounter. If anything, he would spin it out.

But for tonight, now, she was glad of the distraction. And whatever else she might say about Grant Steadman, he was certainly that.

He arrived a few minutes after her. Stood in the doorway, peering around, grinning and biting his lip before striding across the room, bending and kissing her on the lips, his own still cool from the evening air. Then he sat down opposite and couldn't wait to deliver his news. 'I've got a commission,' he said. 'My first.'

'That's great. Go on. Tell me more.'

'A guy who owns a massive historic house in Cheshire. Wants a complete refurb. Says it's too old fashioned and he has big plans for a fresh start.'

'Really? Congratulations. Well done.' They clinked glasses. 'Let's hope it's the first of many. How did he hear about you?'

Grant looked cocky. 'Word of mouth, I guess.'

Something compelled her to add, 'Just make sure he isn't stringing you along, Grant. Make sure he pays up.'

Grant looked a little hurt. 'Gosh, Claire, don't be such a pessimist. You don't have to make me out to be a complete idiot, you know. Have some faith in me.'

She reached across the table to touch his hand. 'Just warning you, that's all. I'd hate to see you taken advantage of.'

Grant simply nodded, still frowning. He hadn't forgiven her yet. 'It's the beginning of a future,' he protested sulkily.

She smiled. And after the briefest of moments his face softened too into that well remembered grin.

'Yeah.' He squared his shoulders, leaning back in his chair. 'It'll take a lot of time, a lot of work, a lot of sourcing of materials. And I guess he won't like *all* my ideas.'

'Have you been round the house?'

'A couple of times now. I've met him but it was only today that he confirmed I've got the job. I've been through costings with him and he's agreed, advancing me enough money to get started.'

'Wow. So what sort of look will you be going for?'

He spent the next few minutes describing a look that combined avant-garde with traditional, age with innovation, sculptures and pottery, fabrics and here and there some iconic antiques, pictures mixing Impressionism with tradition. 'And,' he added, still fizzing with the moment, 'I'm really paying attention to the lighting.'

'You're going to be busy.' She felt a tinge of chagrin. It all sounded so creative compared to her usual week of ward rounds, clinics and, from now on, prison visits.

He nodded. 'Might have to outsource some of the work but I'll oversee it all.' He put his wine glass down. 'And you? What's new in the mental health world?'

She told him a little about her current task and Grant listened carefully, making few comments. 'You mean you'll have to visit him in prison?'

She nodded. 'I'm going tomorrow. Prison is hardly foreign ground to me.'

He looked concerned. 'Is it safe?'

She almost laughed. Prison officers, CCTV everywhere, panic buttons, locked doors. 'Yeah.'

'How many times will you have to go?'

'As long as it takes to either find the girl's body or be satisfied that Kobi's just stringing me along and didn't do it in the first place.'

'Do you think he did?'

She reached across the table to touch his hand again, smiling now. 'You should know me better than that.'

He was curious now. 'Will you know as soon as you meet him? Some sort of instinct?'

She laughed. 'I'm not a clairvoyant, you know. I won't ever be sure if he's telling me the truth. Sociopaths . . . psychopaths . . . are adept at deception.'

'I couldn't do your job,' he said, and she raised her glass to him. 'And I couldn't do yours.'

They ordered hardly glancing at the familiar menu. Quite smoothly he introduced another subject. 'So how's your brother, Adam?'

'Adam is getting married.'

'Lovely,' was Grant's response. 'When?'

'Next March.'

'Nice.' And then with a cheeky look in her direction, he threw down a challenge. 'You want to enter the lions' den on your own, Claire, or might you need a man on your arm? Some moral support?' He looked around at the other diners before returning his focus on her with an affectation of sheer innocence. 'Nothing worse than attending a wedding on your own.'

All she could do was smile, shake her head and change the subject, asking when his mother would be moving back down to Cornwall. Grant answered her questions but both knew there was a subtext. Would he be at his mother's beck and call as he had been at his sister's? Popping down to Cornwall when his mother, this time, needed a picture hanging? Would a desperate plea from her result in yet another disappearance with no explanation? Looking at his face, still animated from his news, she read underlying doubts and guessed that her face reflected the same. Grant had always been able to read her mind but wisely he said nothing; neither did she and they veered back to the other subject which was occupying her mind. The waiters placed their food on the table and Grant asked why DS Zed Willard was taking such a personal interest in this.

'He had to break the news to the first victim's parents and then hear about the other girls' murders, knowing it was the same person. It's stayed with him so he really wants to convict Kobi of this fifth crime. Mop up an unsolved murder case and maybe part of him wants to grant a dying man his last wish. Having failed to prevent the subsequent murders he may even feel a bit responsible.'

'Sounds like this Willard chap has a bit of a conscience?' Grant was thoughtful.

'Yes, he does.'

'Hmm.' Grant speared a piece of lamb balti. 'The girl's dad really is dying then?'

She nodded and kept her voice low. 'Not much doubt about that. I would say he's got a couple of weeks. Not much more. Not by the look of him. The trouble is Willard seems to think I have magic powers, which I don't. He thinks by asking the right questions and interpreting the responses that I'll be able to squeeze the truth out of Kobi. And it isn't just for Marvel's father. It's for him too. An unsolved murder is an embarrassment to the police. It was convenient to park it in Kobi's garage. But it isn't necessarily the truth. Willard wants this tied up. He thinks I can do it.'

'You sound doubtful.'

'Because I am, Grant. Looking at Kobi's profile, he's a devious sod. Intelligent and he's kept schtum for years.' She stopped. 'Why? Why would Kobi confess to all the crimes but deny this one, hide the body too? He won't get any time off his sentence. If Kobi murdered Marvel Trustrom he stepped out of his usual MO and then stepped right back into it for the last two murders. Killers don't usually alter their MO. They sometimes escalate – a sexual predator might become a rapist who might then become a killer. An assault might become a murder, but then they don't slide back to their original ways.'

'Were the girls raped?'

'It doesn't look like it.'

'Oh.' He looked relieved.

'And another thing. I've read pages of court transcripts. He was fond of "boasting" about his crimes. Part of the satisfaction he felt was watching the parents of the murdered girls squirming. Few of them stayed for the whole trial. His words and attitude were as harrowing as was the cynical, careless dumping of the bodies.'

Grant was silent and as she watched his face cloud over Claire reflected. For all his piratical looks, Grant was tender-hearted. While she had learnt to accept the vagaries and variations of mental diagnoses he had no experience of it. His dark eyes were troubled and sad.

'I don't know how you do it, Claire. I think you're amazing.'

Perhaps it was at that point that she realized how easily they'd fallen back into their old relationship. It was like a *pas de deux*. He had been waiting in the wings to lift her, to support her, for her to soar like Baby in *Dirty Dancing* held aloft by Patrick Swayze.

They finished their meal, arguing amicably about the bill. Grant wanted to pay up but Claire insisted on fifty-fifty.

And somehow Grant sensed that this night she wanted to be alone. He gave her a lift back and they parted with a chaste kiss on the driveway. Simon's car was there but no lights were on. The entire scenario felt strange. She turned and waved him off but he'd already reversed out and was heading down the road. Would it always be like this? she wondered. A strange relationship, somehow out of kilter? A train that had missed its rails. Something lost that could not be retrieved?

She put her key in the door and turned it.

NINE

Thursday 19 September, 8.50 a.m.

The day began full of surprises. And for the first time she wondered why Kobi was serving his sentence at HMP Stafford. Stafford was a Category C prison, mostly housing sex offenders. Was Kobi being classed as a sex offender? Before she visited him she wanted the full story so rang DS Zed Willard to ask him.

'Ah,' he said, 'I forgot to tell you.'

'Forgot?'

'Two years ago Kobi got married so they moved him closer to his wife.'

'Married? Wife?'

On the other end of the line, Zed groaned. 'There are some headcases around.'

'Obviously.'

She picked up the picture of Kobi again. He wasn't an unattractive man facially. But who, in their right mind, would marry a lifer and killer of four schoolgirls, who tossed their bodies out of the car as though they were no more than a discarded sweet paper? However, it was a subject she had often mused about. One day, she vowed, she would write a paper on the reasons why a woman might marry a "lifer".

'Tell me more.'

'A woman called Jessica had been writing to him almost from the moment he was convicted. The friendship sort of . . .' He hesitated. 'Progressed.'

'Right.'

'And two years ago they got married. He got permission to be moved nearer to her so she could visit.'

'You might have told me he was married.'

'Yeah,' he said. 'Sorry about that.'

'I will need to speak to her.'

'OK. I'll send through her contact details.'

'*After* I've interviewed Kobi,' she emphasized. 'I'm seeing him later today. I need to prepare my interview.'

'Sorry about that,' he said again. 'I bet you have enough to do.'

She bit back the obvious retort. 'Listen, Zed.' She used his name awkwardly. 'I'm very unlikely to unearth anything in the first interview but in the event that I do I will keep you up to date.'

He managed a small chuckle. 'Thanks.'

She looked at the papers on her desk and the number of unopened emails as well as the pile of letters Rita, her secretary, had left for her to sign. Besides reviewing some parole appeals she had ward work to carry out. It wasn't fair to expect the registrar to manage the entire workload.

She rang the ward and was reassured there was nothing they couldn't manage and spent the next two hours working through papers and responding to emails. She was totally immersed and quite unconscious of the passage of time. By midday she was ready to start planning her approach to Kobi. She massaged her shoulders which were tensed up and opened the file at the point she had marked.

She needed to learn everything she could about Kobi before she met him. Each tiny splinter of fact was a potential weapon which could pierce his armour. She was sure that Kobi, just as she was preparing to interview him, would be preparing ways to deflect her interest while at the same time keeping her visiting until he was bored. He would mislead her, inwardly laughing as he did so. But there are rules to psychiatry, well-trodden paths to follow and Claire intended to follow them to the letter.

Step 1: Listen
Step 2: Tag
Step 3: Question
Step 4: Confront
Step 5: Solve
Step 6: Approve

She was pretty sure she'd get as far as step three, but after that . . .?

She would be in freefall.

What intrigued and continued to intrigue her was if he had killed Marvel why had he broken up his pattern only to return subsequently to his usual MO? Only one logical possibility presented itself. Was it possible that this crime had a different motive from the other four? Had Marvel's death been an impulse rather than a structured plan? Had he acted without planning, without stalking, without thinking? Acted out of character?

She was doubtful. Because the strange thing is that if you dig deep enough into a damaged mind you usually unearth some bizarre logic in the perpetrator's actions. We might not follow their reasoning but there is a trigger, some crazy reason why they acted as they did that one anomalous time. Once you followed them down this particular rabbit hole you had a key in your hand which could possibly unlock their psyche.

Walk along the railway tracks and you will reach your destination.

So as, yet again, she opened Kobi's file, she was searching for specifics. Little pointers, clues. She spent some time studying the photograph on the front. He stared into the camera, jaw tight, brown hair neatly, almost militarily, cut. A thin mouth and an expression that mocked the photographer and anyone else who cared to look. He looked perfectly composed, ordinary enough, someone you would not notice if you passed them in the street. Not really any clue as to his character.

Which was probably why the girls had suspected nothing. They had climbed voluntarily into his car even as the papers were running the headline 'Schoolgirl Killer'.

She turned the page and read again Zed Willard's brief descriptions of the court cases for the four girls Kobi had been convicted of killing: Petra Gordano, Jodie Truss, Teresa Palmer and Shelley Cantor. When Zed had first drawn her in to the case, her initial thought had been that these murders would have a primarily sexual background, but in none of the cases was there any mention of sexual activity. Their clothes had been undisturbed – except for the school tie.

She spread the pictures of the four girls across her desk, leaving Marvel's photograph face down. She wanted to focus on certainties before posing questions. The police had issued two photographs of each girl, one in the school uniform she had been abducted in and the second, very different picture, had been lifted from their social media profiles. In each case it was hard to believe that the two pictures were of the same girls.

Petra Gordano, the first victim, had been killed in 2012. She was thirteen years old, the youngest of Kobi's victims. This was the girl whose death DS Zed Willard had broken to her parents, something which had obviously stayed with him ever since.

The first school photo showed a cleanly scrubbed little girl with dark hair and dark eyes staring earnestly into the camera, her hair plaited neatly behind her back. She looked a sweet child. Innocent.

Claire picked up the post-mortem report next. Facial injuries, broken nose, fractured zygomatic arch consistent with a punch and a slap before she was strangled. Her body had been found at the back of the bus depot, which had no working CCTV, the day after she disappeared. There had been little attempt to hide it. It hadn't been wrapped or covered but discarded as carelessly as a cigarette butt and covered with rubbish. The place of disposal as well as the fact that she had lain there overnight must have torn her parents apart, a final insult to their daughter.

Petra had still been dressed in her school uniform, knickers and underwear not disturbed. Her school bag had never been found.

Method of abduction? Petra went to school in Newcastle-under-Lyme and caught the school bus home on most days back to

Knypersley where she lived. But on Tuesdays she had hockey practice and had to catch the ordinary bus so she was always later home, which was why the alarm hadn't been raised for a few hours . . . and which led Claire to wonder. Had Kobi stalked her? Watched her, learnt her habits? If he had selected her, why her? Claire picked up the photograph again. Apart from the fact that she looked half Italian with a sallow complexion and dark hair, there appeared nothing particularly remarkable about her.

For an answer she turned to the second photograph. Pouting into the camera, an over-the-shoulder shot, make-up heavy with winged eyeliner, hair tousled, and she appeared to be wearing nothing except a pair of enormous hooped earrings. You could just see the mound of her breasts, the photograph reaching almost down to her nipples.

How had she been taken? CCTV from the Newcastle bus station showed her waiting for the bus, but she had not boarded. Presumably then the point of abduction had been at the station but out of sight of the cameras. The weather had been blustery and cold and Petra would have had a long walk at the other end. Her house was half a mile from the bus stop up a steep hill. Maybe it had been easy to persuade her into a nice warm car which would drive her all the way home. But instead she had been strangled with her school tie. Claire spent a while digesting the facts.

She had dealt with a few sociopaths and psychopaths. Too many. Nothing, she felt, should surprise or shock her, so this disdainful disposal was hardly surprising. But it did show that Kobi hadn't considered the consequences of his actions. Petra had not been raped and nothing was missing apart from the school bag. If Kobi had kept it, it had not been found when police had searched his house.

Even without reading the detail and turning over the remaining photographs, she could almost predict the other three abductions, murders and method of disposing of the bodies. Careless. The serial psychopathic killer walks a tightrope. He wants recognition, for people to applaud or shrink in horror from his crimes. But he must balance that with the imperative need for anonymity. Once he's been found the fun stops. The higher the profile of the crimes the harder the police and all their resources would spend searching for him so the greater the risk. But the greater the risk the more potent the adrenaline rush. And so he constantly veers between public awareness which he interprets as respect rather than revulsion and the need to remain anonymous.

He wants people to find the bodies, feel fear over the killings and puzzle over his identity. And, like many killers, he wasn't going to stop except by being caught. These people are mad *and* bad and the one thing no psychiatrist ever forgets is that they are a very real danger to society. Luckily they are very rare.

She turned back to the notes.

Only two months after Petra Gordano's body had been found, when the police were searching for him, Kobi had killed again.

Jodie Truss had been a little older than Petra. Fifteen. She attended school in another part of the Potteries, near Fenton. Her body had been found late the same night in Hanley Park, propped up against the wooden sign looking, so a member of the general public said later, 'as though she'd had one too many'.

After Jodie had come the two-year gap during which the police believed Marvel had been killed. Claire bypassed her for the moment and focused on the crimes Kobi had been convicted of.

On a warm October day in 2014 Teresa Palmer, fourteen years old, a pupil and resident of Stone, a town almost ten miles south of Stoke-on-Trent, was walking from school to her home on the Walton estate, a distance of just over a mile. Claire knew Stone well. At one point, liking the atmosphere of the pretty market town which boasted a lovely high street as well as canal-side pubs and a weekly street market, she had considered buying a house there. But in the end she'd opted for Burslem and the Victorian home she and Grant had done up.

Teresa had left school with a few friends and they had wandered down the high street but parted company at the bottom, two of the girls heading up the Lichfield Road. Teresa had continued on her own. And that was the last sighting of her – alive. The next time she had been seen it was a corpse dumped in a wheelie bin, found not by the police but by a horrified employee of the printer's. She had been dropping a black plastic bin liner into the bin when she had seen long brown hair.

In appearance Teresa was similar to the other two girls. Innocent schoolgirl to siren in three easy moves. The police had spent an extensive search of the area in and around Stone, combing the

CCTV cameras along the high street as well as using ANPR to search for a likely car. But Kobi had outwitted them; they had found nothing.

And so they had waited.

And then had come the breakthrough. But again this had cost a young girl, fourteen years old, her life.

Shelley Cantor was the last of Kobi's victims. She was the one whose body had been weighted down and dropped in Westport Lake. Claire narrowed her eyes, alert to this. There had been some inept attempt at concealing the body with rocks placed in her school bag. There was another difference: Shelley Cantor was from Congleton, this time another market town but almost ten miles north of Stoke-on-Trent and in Cheshire. Another charming place standing on the River Dane with stories and legends of its own. Shelley had proved Kobi's nemesis. The RSPB camera had captured images of him dragging a heavy and lumpy package to the water's edge. And his car number plate was easily read. Then it was a matter of time. Half an hour actually, before Kobi was being bundled into the back of a police car and the rest was, as they say, history.

Too late for Shelley, Teresa, Jodie and Petra.

The photograph of Shelley told the same story as the other girls. Schoolgirl by day, siren by social media.

Claire left Marvel's profile until later. It was almost two o'clock. If she knew one fact about prisons it was that they lived by the clock. It would soon be time to meet Kobi.

TEN

Thursday 19 September, 3 p.m.

E ntering a prison gives you an instant sense of gloom, of freedom vanishing behind you, of natural light being extinguished. Every door opened is another one locked behind you, distancing you from the outside world. Claire was a visitor but it still gave her a feeling of dread. She hated the places. Hated the metallic clanking, the sounds of anger and frustration that spilled into the main areas. Noise everywhere and CCTV eyes watching all the time. She might be a visiting psychiatrist but even so there was no ducking the rules, no mistaking the authority of the prison officers, the 'screws' who watched her every move, searched her bag and put everything in a locker except a notebook, recording machine and a pen.

Notices everywhere. *No mobile phones. Nothing sharp* . . . the list went on and on. So many things forbidden. Entering a prison is always the same. Security, locks and bolts, identity checks, communication between gate and nerve centre, accompanied by strange noises that are difficult to source or attribute to humans: groans and shrieks, shouts and screams. Untangling the noise from the echoes is impossible. And the inmates walking around either looking like bruisers or figures stepping out of a Lowry picture, stooped and old before their years. Even the younger ones. There is a strange uniformity about prisoners as there is about prison. A feeling of leaving the real world behind as indeed you are.

A woman officer led her to the interview room, commenting, 'I don't envy you, Doctor. He's a right cool customer, that one. You won't ruffle *his* feathers.' She spoke in a strong Potteries accent and was slim built but looked tough, wiry and strong and, at a guess, could give as good as she got. Her dark hair was scraped into a thin ponytail which swung as she walked. She held the door open. 'I'll go get him,' she said. 'Good luck.'

Presumably she had some idea what the purpose of this visit was. She hadn't asked. Claire sat down, opened her notebook, prepared to switch her recording device on and waited.

Moments later she heard footsteps.

He was standing in the doorway appraising her as she was him. She saw herself through his eyes. Nothing remarkable. Medium height, light-brown hair, straight and to the shoulders with a swept across fringe. Slim, bordering on thin, in cream trousers and a black shirt, pale face, just a hint of make-up – nothing heavy, a touch of mascara, a smear of foundation, pale lipstick. She knew what he was thinking. *Plain. Not my type. No threat. No problem here.* She could read it in his face, which visibly relaxed as he studied her and gave a mock flourishing Regency bow.

It was a relief to know how far she was from his preferred type.

The officer broke into their thoughts, urging him forwards. 'Go on then, Kobi. Get in there. Give the doctor what she wants.'

He strolled towards her, sitting down opposite, the table between them. His movements were controlled and neat, but his gait was slightly stiff as though he spent too much time in his cell, which didn't surprise her. He would be a natural target, although in a Category C prison, surrounded by sex offenders, he was, arguably, safer here than in many other gaols. He held out his hand. Dry skin and a firm grip. 'Dr Roget, I presume.'

He rolled the 'r', emphasizing its French sound. 'Nice to meet you.' She had to dig deep to find the sarcasm in his voice. Superficially it sounded perfectly polite.

As she had anticipated, Kobi was good looking but in a negative way. His features were small and neat, a thin, rosebud mouth, hazel eyes, a small, snub nose, a pale, smooth complexion. It wasn't so much that he was good looking as that his looks were unremarkable, forgettable, with nothing out of order or dominant. It was a face which would be hard to recall, difficult to describe. Like her he was of medium height, medium build, with light-brown hair cut very short.

And a steady, unflinching gaze. He hadn't looked at her directly until he was sitting down when their eyes were level. She took a while to study his face. He was thinner than his mugshots but his eyes were clear and watchful, still appraising her. He showed no sign of nervousness but met her eyes without any facial expression, not even a flicker of his eyelashes. Which was, considering his past, disconcerting. If she sensed any emotion it was, possibly, fleeting amusement. Possibly even a hint of disappointment.

He set his mouth in an accommodating smile and waited for her to open the conversation.

'Thank you for agreeing to see me, Mr Kobi.' Like him she kept her tone neutral and polite.

His mouth twisted. 'My pleasure.'

She continued smoothly. 'I know you already know who I am but just for formality's sake I'm Dr Claire Roget, a forensic psychiatrist.'

He gave a brief jerky nod this time. And then responded, 'Roget.' Again, he rolled her name around, pronouncing the 'r' like a native. 'It's French, isn't it?'

She narrowed her eyes. Did he realize he had gone straight to her Achilles heel? Identified the French Frog?

She kept her mind focused and her aims clear. Rule one: set the parameters.

'Would you prefer me to call you Jonah or Mr Kobi?'

'I couldn't give a fuck what you call me.' His voice was lazy now, disinterested and in spite of the curse, held no anger.

'Do you know why I'm here?'

He nodded then spoke in a smooth voice, his accent patrician, possibly affectedly so, considering his background. 'Of course.'

'You understand that the police believe you are responsible for the murder of a fifth victim?'

A faint smile crossed his face. He leaned back and folded his arms in an attitude of utter disdain. 'I understand this much, Dr Roget. Correct me if I'm wrong, but the girl whose body was *never* found'– he tossed his head – 'I can't remember her name . . .'

She knew perfectly well Marvel Trustrom's name was on the tip of his tongue.

'Her dad is sick and he wants me to tell him where I've hidden his daughter's body assuming, of course, that I killed her in the first place.'

She waited and let the silence extend.

'*You* think I know where she's buried and you *think I* might be persuaded to share that *little secret*' – he wiggled his fingers at the childish words – 'with you.'

He kept his eyes trained on her face as he spoke, searching for her response before continuing. 'I suppose, being a *psychiatrist*' – again that mockery – 'that you've formed your own opinion as to why, having come clean over four girls' deaths, I've decided to keep this one to myself.'

'I try not to form opinions, Mr Kobi, until I have all the relevant facts.'

'Very wise, Claire.' His words were a sick pat on the back.

Again, she waited, sensing the enjoyment Kobi was deriving from the encounter.

He smirked. 'And you think I might tell all? Spill the beans?'

'You might.' Her tone remained affectedly disinterested.

'Why? Why would I do that?' He leaned in so she could smell coal tar soap and coconut shampoo. He had prepared for this meeting. 'As a psychiatrist you must be really interested in motive?'

'Sometimes.'

'Do you think because this girl's father is dying that you might evoke pity in me?'

She shook her head, keeping her eyes trained on his. The one thing she would avoid at all costs was to use pity as a reason for a late confession. If he had expressed sympathy for a dying man she would not have believed him. Kobi's eyes were cold.

She directed her full attention towards him. 'How did you know that Marvel's father is ill?'

There was a lifting of the corners of his mouth. It was nothing like a smile. 'The investigating officer, DS Willard, came in and told me himself. Nice of him.'

'Right.' She was angry now. Willard should have told her he'd mentioned this to Kobi. He'd had plenty of opportunity to share that particular piece of important information. It had given Kobi a head start, time to prepare. To suppress her crossness and regain her equilibrium she glanced down at her notes. 'I want you to understand, Mr Kobi, I'm not here to unpick the court's original verdict. You've been found guilty of four murders, all of them young girls. Anything you tell me will not influence an appeal, a reduction in sentence or the decision of the parole board. Neither will it cut any ice with the CPS.'

Kobi smirked. 'Not a lot in it for me then?'

'Frankly, no.'

'So why should I help?'

This was the quandary she'd prepared for. Focusing on Marvel's father's plight would be a pointless argument. You can't appeal to an emotion a person can't feel. But Kobi would sniff out a lie and sense any insincerity on her part. She might gain ground by using the fact that he had a new wife. She tucked that card up her sleeve. Curiosity and boredom are useful tools and Kobi had plenty of both here as well as time to reflect.

Watching Kobi, she wasn't getting the impression that he was hugely anxious to flaunt his crimes. He was icily calm as he faced her. Quite in control as she gave her next prompt.

'Do you want to say anything about Marvel Trustrom?'

He clicked his fingers in mock recognition. 'Of course. That's her name.'

She gave a slow nod and he continued with his play act.

'Trustrom. It's an unusual name, isn't it?'

'I don't know.' She was getting irritated with this polite version of cat and mouse.

'I've noticed that Marvel's murder appears quite different from the others. Why do you think that is?'

His eyes flicked up to hers. 'Possibly because I didn't kill her?'

So that was the game he was playing. He was going to string this one out for as long as he could – without giving anything away – while she probed. 'Tell me what you know about her disappearance.'

He wasn't fooled. 'Only what I've read in the papers, Claire.' The skip to her Christian name felt like an ice cold barb as he continued smoothly. 'I think she was from some little place just outside Biddulph, wasn't she?' His tone was that of idle curiosity.

Claire mimicked his tone. 'I believe so.' Then she moved on to probe. 'How did all this start, Mr Kobi?'

He smirked. 'You've really got time for all this? Going right back to the beginning?'

'Your parents?'

This time he laughed out loud. 'Rejected me? No. They were too stupid to do anything quite as interesting as that.'

'Your brother?'

'Jack?' Again, he shook his head.

'So when did it all begin?'

This time he folded his arms behind his head while he watched her. 'You already know, don't you?'

'Refresh me.'

'I suppose,' he said, speaking as casually as if she had asked him whether he wanted red wine or white, 'that the tendency must always have been there.'

She waited and caught the first scent of anger.

'To want to have power over someone who had belittled me.'

'So that was the beginning?'

Slowly he nodded. 'Yes. When that little bitch . . .'

She supplied the name. 'Miranda Pullen.'

'When she made that totally spurious allegation. I didn't even fancy her. She was just someone with such a big head she was convinced she was irresistible. And she wasn't. Far from it. Disgusting little—'

She stopped the rant. 'But Miranda wasn't your first victim, was she?'

'I toyed with the idea.' Interesting that his response to that jibe was defensive.

She was perfectly aware that Kobi was enjoying this little trip down memory lane. Showing off. DS Willard owed her a stiff drink subjecting her to this. But she ploughed on. 'I take it the four girls whose murders you were convicted of were all killed for the same reason?'

'Silly little girls. Arrogant creatures posing in that ridiculous way on social media.' He almost spat the words out. But she couldn't resist a little skip of joy. She'd provoked him, burrowed into his skin like a tick. That little spit of emotion had slipped out instinctively. He hadn't been able to suppress it.

Like a dropped stitch in knitting, she picked up on the word. 'Silly?' She knew she would proceed along this path, maybe putting in the odd slick of mud for him to slip on but never letting Jonah Kobi forget why she was really here. 'In what way were they silly, Jonah? Because they were frightened?'

He batted away her query. 'Girls of that age,' he said disdainfully, 'are all pathetic, thinking every male on the planet fancies them.'

She took up his comment. 'Whether they were like that or not they didn't have the chance to develop into women, find careers, a partner, maybe have children.'

His expression became even more disdainful. And then, unexpectedly, he leaned forward, his face almost touching hers, his expression fiery and earnest. 'And what sort of women would they have made, do you think, Dr Roget? Gossips, nosey, spiteful, little bitches manufacturing lies about men.'

'Is that your opinion of women?'

'Nearly all.' His gaze on her was steady and appraising.

She changed tack. 'Who have been the women in your life?'

His face screwed into a sneer. 'Have you really got time for all that?' He wafted his hand around. 'You really want to play the hereditary game?'

'This isn't a game.'

'Isn't it?'

She responded calmly. 'The women in your life?'

'We-ell . . .' He was stringing this along, pretending to think. 'My mother was ordinary. Very ordinary. She was boring.' He leaned back in his chair, folded his arms behind his head. 'She wasn't good at anything. Her conversation was dull. She wasn't even a good cook.'

'Is she still alive?'

Kobi gave a deliberate yawn. 'I have absolutely no bloody idea. In fact, I couldn't give a fuck about any woman, in my life or otherwise.'

That, she suspected, was an untruth, spoken to put her off the scent. He had a wife.

'Your sister-in-law,' she said. 'Your ex-wife's little sister, Chloe?'

No response. 'You seem to have her trust and affection.' She paused before plunging back in. 'And then, of course, there is your wife of . . .' She pretended to consult her notebook. 'Two years?'

She saw the flash in his eyes and hoarded the fact, squirrelling it away like a secret treasure.

'What about your father?'

'What about my father?' He was looking guarded now, apparently surprised at the question.

Finally. 'He married my mother, didn't he, stupid bastard?'

'Do you hear from him?'

His response was a sneering, 'No.'

'Was there anyone you were close to as a child?'

He closed his eyes. 'I really can't remember. What's that got to do with the purpose of your visit anyway? What'll that tell you?'

Claire affected a nonchalant tone. 'Well, you never know where something will lead, do you?'

Kobi sat back, watched her and started drumming his fingers on the desk. Softly at first, but she knew he would gradually increase the noise and tempo. Just to annoy her.

She smiled at him and picked up her bag. This provoked Kobi into blurting out, 'I didn't kill her, you know. It wasn't me. That's why it's different.'

She took a moment to study his face then nodded. 'OK,' she said. 'Well, we'll leave it at that for today, shall we?'

As she gestured to the warder and watched Kobi being led away, she knew this would be a battle. He reached the door and turned around, gave her a challenging stare, a slightly disapproving shake of his head, and then he was gone.

ELEVEN

Friday 20 September, 8.20 a.m.

As she drove into Greatbach the next morning her mind was still sifting through the interview. While displaying little concern at most of her questions she had definitely found some weak points. The anger which he felt towards the girl who had made the original complaint against him had spread to encompass many of her contemporaries. And while there had not been a flicker of emotion when she had mentioned his ex-wife or her sister he had definitely shied away from reference to his current wife. As interesting as the question why had she married him was the follow on: why on earth had he married her? Had she appealed to his narcissism? Apart from these two chinks he was just as she had anticipated.

But if he wasn't guilty and Marvel was dead, someone else must have killed her. And Zed Willard was right. The chance of there being a second killer of a schoolgirl in this area and in that particular time frame was remote. Maybe she needed to look at this from another perspective. Rather than focus her attention on Kobi perhaps it would be a good idea to turn the spotlight on the victim. She had been a teenager. Fourteen. Was it possible she had absconded? Had the quarrelsome family Tom had inadvertently described persuaded her to leave? Could she still be alive? Could this be why her body had never been found? Or was it because Kobi wanted to keep them all guessing? Until they found a body they couldn't be certain of the girl's fate.

The questions would continue to frustrate her. As she turned into the car park her thoughts turned back to another subject that vexed her: Grant, always hovering on the edge of her mind. She'd already sensed his mother's rivalry and dislike of her – at a chance encounter at a restaurant and then at his sister's funeral – which was understandable. And his mother would win, replacing his sister in that she would become increasingly needy, demanding his presence and attention, perhaps laying down conditions, because buried deep in Grant's character was a sense of guilt and inadequacy, as though Maisie's illness been his fault rather than a result of his mother and father's genetic code. Maisie had been cursed while he had not. He would always be burdened with the feeling that he had not done enough for his family. And this guilt was so much part of him, buried so deep in his character that she could never release him from that curse which had been implanted when his father had walked out on his wife, son and very sick daughter, mirroring the exit of her own father. Perhaps this was why they had such a strong bond. A shared experience. She parked the car, climbed out into a bright, damp day, locked up and crossed the courtyard. What to do next? How does one fight a personality who feels such a heavy burden of guilt? She blew her cheeks out in frustration and entered the code to open the door. Some problems had no easy answers. Just like her patients and colleagues, who were waiting.

Ilsa Robinson being just one of them. She thought carefully about this outwardly beautiful, troubled woman and wondered why she did not feel more sympathy for her plight. Ilsa was now claiming that her incapacitating anxiety and depression were a result of having a controlling, manipulative husband. Claire had met him on more than one occasion and had caught no hint of that. But it is hard for an outsider to make a judgement on a marriage and John Robinson could be smart enough to conceal any hint of pathological behaviour. Ilsa was also now claiming that her husband was having an affair with her best friend, Maggie, and wanted rid of her. She also claimed that he was trying to alienate her from her eight-year-old son.

Claire walked slowly along the corridor, trying to put her thoughts in order and work out where the truth lay. John Robinson, notwithstanding his wealth, had struck her as stolid, unimaginative and anything but a lothario.

For now, she shelved that particular problem and returned to the one that was taking up permanent residence at the back of her mind. Kobi.

In her office, hoping to see light through the fug, she closed
the door firmly – most staff could interpret this wish to be alone
– sat at her desk and flipped over the two photographs of Marvel
Trustrom before placing them alongside the eight pictures of the
other four girls. As with the others there were two photographs,
one of Marvel in her school uniform and the other taken from
Marvel's social media, her supposedly glamorous image. And
immediately she could see what was wrong. Whereas the other
girls all had dual personalities, innocent schoolgirl and siren, the
school picture showed a plain, pudding face staring out at her and
the social media picture was not much different. No make-up could
disguise Marvel's plainness. Unlike the other girls, Marvel had no
talent with make-up. And rather than look confident, her expression was pleading. Even in two photographs the difference between
Marvel and the other four girls was marked. She fumbled in the
file and brought out two more pictures which Zed Willard had
held together with a paper clip, a note pinned to them.

> The family gave us these pictures taken a month or so before
> Marvel vanished. We didn't release them to the press.

Claire smiled. In these pictures someone had cut and blow-dried
Marvel's one claim to beauty. Thick, red-gold hair to her shoulders.
It was not quite enough to make her beautiful, but it was, at least,
something.

She placed all the pictures side by side. And the longer she
stared at them the more her flesh began to crawl with a hundred
centipede feet, the instinct that this was not Kobi's work. The
feeling spread from the tingling in her toes to an awareness of
every single hair on her scalp.

Wrong.

Kobi had given her some sort of distorted explanation for his
crimes. He felt mocked by these sexually precocious, attractive,
budding young women. Staring down at the plump face that
appeared from the photograph, Claire knew Marvel would not
have provoked this feeling, the very reason behind Kobi's murders.
And the more she stared at the five different faces, the more Marvel
stood out as different.

The police would have wanted Kobi to be guilty of this crime and he would have enjoyed stringing them along either with vague hints or at least avoiding denial. But what was the real story?

Questions bubbled up in her mind, one after the other.

Was that the real reason why her father was so anxious to learn his daughter's fate, because he too sensed that the truth had not been unearthed? She thought back to her meeting with Tom. Was there an element of guilt there? She studied the photographs again, trying to divine some clue. There was an appeal in the girl who stared out. Was it an appeal to be liked? To be loved? By her family? Tom had described feeling cooped up in the house. The girls had been quarrelling. So how had the rest of Marvel's family, her mother, sisters, brother felt about that last day? So far she'd had no access to them and Dixie Trustrom did not appear to share her ex-husband's ambition to discover her daughter's fate. The questions kept coming. Why not? And what about the rest of her family? Did they not want to learn her fate? Again: if not why not? Was it really because they were all trying to 'put it behind them' and 'move on with their lives'? Or was there another reason? Were they afraid to speak to her because they worried that when she lifted stones she might find something unpleasant underneath? Did they have something to hide? Claire felt her mouth twist. Everyone has something they want to hide. As with Kobi, Claire had no right of access to Marvel's parents, brother or sisters. She couldn't force them to cooperate. But she knew this case would gnaw at her, because now she'd got involved she wanted to know the truth just as much as Tom Trustrom or DS Zed Willard.

Unfortunately her instinct was that this case might well prove unsatisfying. Even if the answer did lie with Kobi, he was perfectly capable of holding out and she had no other leads. Like a bluebottle in the bedroom thoughts buzzed around, distracting her, until, in desperation, she picked up the phone and rang DS Willard.

But he didn't pick up and she didn't bother leaving a message. She wasn't sure what message she'd have left anyway.

Psychiatric units are busy places, unquiet, bustling with both staff and patients, and Greatbach was no exception. The staff, in general, battle on with obstacles, some thrown at them by the government who aren't slow at snatching an opportunity. One of the latest directives the psychiatric services had received was to reduce the number of suicides. Claire had read the manifesto, all 140 pages of it, and her response had been how? Did the government not believe they were doing all they possibly could to prevent this tragedy? All the same a meeting was scheduled for later this morning and she was expected to attend. As she pushed open the door to the conference room she could feel resentment bubbling up.

Every year people of all ages decide they would prefer to die than to live and that is an unshakeable fact. What can a government manifesto do to alter this? Particularly when mental health services were the paupers of the NHS. Some interventions could help, but for others the depression was too deeply embedded. Many of these tragic cases had never consulted a doctor but had concealed their morbid wish from even their nearest and dearest. How many times had Claire heard the refrain from bereaved families: I didn't realize . . . Some 'suicides' were unhappy accidents. Unintentional, the traditional 'cry for help'.

The meeting dragged on with a few objectives set but Claire felt weighted down with pessimism that any one of them would prevent even one determined suicide bid.

Meetings. The day was filled with them.

Five p.m. was the time they had set for the multi-disciplinary case conference on Ilsa Robinson to review her approaching discharge. As she surveyed the people around the table, Claire wondered if any of them shared her doubts about this case. Salena met her eyes and grinned, her dark eyes sparkling as she touched her hijab and pulled it across her mouth. Simon didn't look too happy and yet his wife should be with him soon. Next to him was Edward Reakin, their clinical psychologist. Edward was a tall, prematurely stooped man in his mid-forties with a balding pate. He had had his own demon to deal with when his wife had blatantly flaunted an affair. Edward had never got over it and had confided in Claire that he would never trust a woman again – except her. After the Grant Steadman business she had not even tried to dissuade him. He smiled at her across the table, that sad, slightly hesitant smile as though he did not expect it to be returned. He did not realize how much he was valued. As a psychologist he often shed new light on their cases. Whereas a psychiatrist focuses on the sick mind, Edward's priority was behavioural. He watched and listened. Salena and Simon were already sitting down as Claire poured herself a beaker of water and settled into her seat.

'Right,' she said. 'Shall we look into Ilsa's problems? Edward?'

He sat back in his chair, relaxed and thoughtful. 'I don't see that any of our cognitive behavioural therapy has helped.' He hesitated, looking round the room, and she caught that frisson of doubt. 'It seems as though' – he looked around apologetically – 'she is resistant to our therapies so there's not a lot of point in keeping her here. We have to stick to the criteria, Claire. She's passed the acute stage of her episode. Her medication's kicked in. At the moment she doesn't appear be a danger to herself or to the wider public.'

It was interesting, his use of that word, resistant.

'It's her husband who isn't helping,' Simon said quietly. 'Every time he visits she deteriorates but at some point we are going to have to let her go. I mean, where else can she go but home?'

Claire felt herself tense up.

Salena shrugged. 'I can't see Mr Robinson putting in any real effort to make things better. He tries but he seems almost . . . afraid of her. I've interviewed him on four occasions. His suggestion is that she returns to the clinic in Birmingham for a month or so before going home.'

Inwardly Claire sighed. Ilsa's case was proving unsatisfactory, the end result sliding away from them like an eel in a river. 'I'll speak to him,' she said. 'I'll ask Rita to make an appointment.'

Edward spoke up next. 'She's worse than she was. When I went in earlier she was squatting down in the corner. It *looked* as though she was terrified.' Again, Claire wondered why the emphasis was on that word and why his grey eyes looked troubled.

'Is she psychotic?' Claire looked around the table at her colleagues for an answer but they all shook their heads before she answered for them. 'I've had no evidence she is.' She followed that up with: 'Have you found her delusional, Edward? Paranoid?'

'Possibly all those,' Edward said quietly. 'But possibly not. She's not fitting into any of our neat little boxes – unless she's very manipulative and pulling the wool over all our eyes.'

She couldn't help smiling with the rest of them. 'Well, that was unhelpful.'

Salena offered an explanation – of sorts. 'Maybe that's the problem. Maybe she doesn't really want to go home. Maybe she's frightened to go home.'

They all digested her suggestion, their faces dubious.

'Last time I spoke to her,' Edward said, 'she begged me *not* to send her home. She said she was frightened what might happen.'

Both Simon and Salena nodded. 'We got the impression that she wants to go home but for some reason she's apprehensive.'

'Apprehensive?' Claire echoed. 'Why?'

Edward Reakin frowned. 'Her husband? Some inner demon?'

She smiled. 'Are we descending into spook talk? Or do we think that John Robinson is an abusive husband?'

'I've asked her that,' Salena said. 'She says he's controlling.'

'To what extent?'

Salena shook her head. 'That was the point at which she chose not to answer.'

They were all thoughtful. They were perfectly aware that psychiatric illness could appear supernatural, that anxiety and depression could translate into psychosis, which in turn could make it seem as though a person was inhabited by a demon. We are most afraid of something we can neither see nor understand. And mental illness is, most of the time, invisible.

Afterwards they might analyse their light comments, sift through all that had been said, but at that time their way forward appeared unclear.

They discussed a few more patients but none was as concerning or as puzzling as Ilsa, who remained in Claire's mind. When the meeting had broken up Edward stayed behind. 'So how are you getting on with your tame murdering psychopath?'

She gave a long sigh. 'It's going to be a long haul, if I get anything out of him at all. He's not going to play ball. He'll mess me around until he's bored with the game.'

'You mean he's denying the fifth murder?'

'Yes,' she admitted, 'he is. To get anything out of him is going to take time.'

Edward nodded. 'Time the girl's father might not have.'

'I could really do with speaking to the other members of Marvel's family to study the family dynamics.'

'Why?'

'I don't know,' she said, almost laughing. 'I just feel if I get to understand this girl I might be able to use it for or against Jonah Kobi.'

She looked at his kind face and hardly needed to ask the question. 'Can I trust you?'

His response was a smile.

'Everything about this case feels wrong.' Again, she hesitated. 'A bit like Ilsa. I feel I'm being deliberately led along a track.'

He raised his eyebrows. 'You picked up on that too?'

'Yeah, but I don't know exactly what it is that I've picked up on. Is it possible that, like Kobi, she is playing us?'

'To what end?'

'I don't know. Kobi might be clear cut. He's locked up, safely put away. With Ilsa I don't know what's going on but it feels unsafe.'

He smiled and his worn, tired face lifted. She could see that once, before baldness and that cruel exposure, he must have been an attractive man.

She put a hand on his arm. 'If you do have any ideas, Edward, I'd really appreciate it if you'd share them with me.'

He nodded. 'If you want you could let me have Kobi's notes and I'll take a look at the police files.'

'Thanks. I might do that. In the meantime, I'd better go up and spend some time with Ilsa.'

TWELVE

Ilsa was lying in bed, the sheets pulled right over her face. She didn't move as Claire closed the door behind her and gently pulled the sheet back. Ilsa's eyes remained tightly closed but Claire knew she was awake. 'Sit up, Ilsa,' she said. 'I need to talk to you.' Ilsa moved, slow and elegant as a cat, until she was sitting bolt upright, her eyes focused on Claire with a perplexed expression.

Ilsa was a beautiful woman in her mid-thirties, with white-blonde hair and high cheekbones. She had once had a sporty physique, according to her husband. She had been a minor tennis star but now she was looking gaunt and her expression was apprehensive almost to the point of terror. She dropped her legs to the floor. 'I know I should go home to be with my boy but inside . . . In here . . .' She banged her chest. 'I know I shouldn't go back there.' Her eyes were round and frightened.

'Why not?'

Ilsa didn't answer but moved her gaze to stare out of the window. 'He is a bad man,' she said finally. 'And when I am near a bad man something could happen.'

Claire paused. It sounded like a threat. 'What?'

Ilsa's eyes, forget-me-not blue, looked incapable of deceit.

'I don't know, Dr Roget. It's as though a dark cloud comes over me.'

Claire felt her scepticism grow. 'Do you see the cloud in here?'

'No. That's why I feel safe and want to stay.'

'And that dark cloud, what does it hide?'

Ilsa's response was to shake her head. 'I don't know.'

'If you don't go home, Ilsa, where do you suggest you do go?'

'Can't I stay here, Dr Roget?'

Claire shook her head. 'No.' And she repeated the points she had made at the meeting. 'You've passed the acute stage of your episode. The medication's kicked in. You're not a danger to yourself or the general public. We have no justification in detaining you.' She couldn't stop herself from adding, 'And there will be other patients who need admitting.'

Ilsa's eyes grew hard then, a cold, icy blue. She shook her head and held up her hand as though to ward off this judgement. She tossed her hair and her voice was angry. 'Is that your only concern, that you need to put someone else in my bed? What if I am in danger *from* . . . my . . . husband?' She almost shouted the last few words.

'Are you telling me you're the victim of domestic abuse?'

'Not physical abuse,' she said quickly. 'Although one day he might resort to that. No. Mental abuse. Dominance, control. Mental cruelty.' Her voice was getting higher. 'He wants to control me. My mind. Make me do things I don't want to do. And then he will divorce me. And then he will marry his mistress, the woman who was once my best friend. Tsstt.' She made a spitting sound.

Claire watched her. John Robinson was not your typical wealthy businessman. His financial success had more to do with brains, good decisions and luck rather than ruthlessness. In her opinion he was not unsafe. But . . . who knows what goes on behind closed doors? A cliché, like many clichés, grounded in truth.

'It's been suggested that you spend some time in the clinic in Birmingham to prepare you for your return home.'

Ilsa's eyes remained tightly closed as she shook her head. Then she opened them, eyes wide. 'My son.' It was all she said before she squeezed her eyes tight shut again. 'I need to be with him. I need to protect him.'

'From what?'

Ilsa opened those forget-me-not eyes wide. 'From his father. I need to be there to keep them apart.'

And that, Claire reflected, was just what John Robinson did not want to happen. But Ilsa's apprehension was infectious, and it was infusing her with a sense of something dark approaching. She was frowning now as she looked out of the window, at patients wandering aimlessly, staff walking purposefully, clusters of gossiping nurses and the tea trolleys, collected, being returned to the kitchens. It was ironic that this family, so outwardly prosperous, was, in reality, damaged, dangerous and disturbed. Families, she thought. Hers, Grant's, the Robinson's and Marvel's family. All unhappy in different ways. Close the doors on them and the misery intensifies.

6 p.m.

It had been a long day but it wasn't over yet.

Back in her office she tried Zed Willard one last time and this time he picked up. 'Hi, Claire. How did your first visit go?'

Surely, she thought, he wasn't expecting a miracle? A quick confession followed by the GPS location of the missing girl's body?

'Much as expected. Zed. He denies killing Marvel.'

'And you believe him?'

'I don't know yet.'

'When?'

'I'm not a miracle worker. If I had more detail I might be able to catch him out. As it is I don't have a lot of ammunition in my approaches.' Even though he wouldn't be able to see it she couldn't resist a smile. 'For the time being I'm keeping an open mind.'

'You've got our notes?'

'Yes. They've arrived safely.' She hesitated. 'I hope it's OK but I intend sharing them with Edward Reakin, our clinical psychologist.'

'Anything that'll help, Claire.'

'The trouble is, apart from those extra photographs, all I know, at the moment, is in the public domain. I know what she was wearing when she was last seen. I know what she looked like. If I'm going to catch him out I need something that only you and the killer would know. What I don't have are the family dynamics. I haven't met any of her friends. There are very few interviews with people who knew Marvel. The whole thing looks – well – sketchy and a bit impersonal. No one's opinion is off the record. It's all polite and too careful. I have no flavour of her except to guess that she was a bit of a misfit. Tom hinted at her being jealous of her sisters. What was she really like, this girl? Was she likely to abscond? I need to get a flavour of her. I want to know what her catchphrases were, her perfume, her habits. Her friends. Was she always bonded to her mobile phone? What happened to the mobile phone? There's so much missing from this investigation, Zed.'

Had she known him better she might have inserted the word, sloppy.

'We never found the phone,' he said grumpily. 'According to the service provider it was switched off almost to the second when she left home.'

'Which probably means *she* was the one who switched it off. Isn't that odd?'

'Maybe saving the battery. Our thinking was that she was coerced into meeting someone. We thought at the time Kobi.'

'And now?'

'We thought he could have persuaded her to switch her phone off. The other girls' phones were switched off pretty soon after they were abducted. It fitted in,' he finished defensively.

'Do you think it was a chance meeting? Through social networking?'

DS Willard hesitated and she pressed on sensing the thin end of a very fat wedge.

'That wasn't the way he operated, was it, Zed? They were chance encounters. Not assignations made through social networking. You did, at least, check her phone records and any computer she had access to?'

'Of course.' DS Willard cleared his throat noisily.

'The others were picked up randomly, weren't they? Pure chance.'

When he was still quiet, she pushed him. 'Look, Zed, I need something more intimate. I'd like to speak to her brother and her sisters. Her mother if possible. Can you persuade them to talk to me?'

His response was a noisy *huff*.

'Have you at least got their contact details?' She hesitated. 'I've spoken to Marvel's mother but she wasn't prepared to help. I think she's buried the past, decided that whatever happened to her daughter, she's over it. To be honest I'm not sure she wants to be involved at all even though . . .' She stopped, uncertain where she was going with the words. She wasn't a mother herself (and if she continued with her on/off relationship with Grant was unlikely to ever be one). But this total lack of interest where a daughter's body lay, along with the true story of her disappearance, felt abnormal. She was perfectly aware that response to a violent tragedy affects people in different ways. She had met the entire gamut of responses in her time. Some people bottled it up, pretended it had never really happened, while for others it sparked a crusade. Suicide among siblings as well as parents of a murdered child was more common than in the general population and marriages frequently split apart as had the Trustrom's. The repercussions could be unpredictable and far reaching.

She waited before adding, 'This is going to be a long haul. Longer than Tom's got. Kobi is not going to crack any time soon whatever questions I throw at him.'

On the other end of the line there was silence.

'I'm happy to see him again, Zed, but I need something more. A tempter. I need something that makes me appear more knowledgeable than I am.'

She tried to clarify. 'Something that makes *him* want to impress *me*.'

'You think that'll work?'

'Yes, I do. Like many killers what he actually wants, however dangerous it might prove, is recognition along with accolade.'

'OK. I'll gather some stuff together and bring it over.'

Replacing the handset, she felt better. At least she was beginning to work to a plan. She had only one thing left to do before she could head home for the weekend.

She crossed the corridor to her secretary's room and left a note asking Rita to make another appointment with John Robinson. She needed to discuss his wife's discharge and possibly list some warning signs he should be wary of – a return of the self-harming, inappropriate behaviour, signs of delusion, paranoia, psychosis. He would need to watch her carefully.

But . . . the little voice said, voicing her brief moment of doubt. She knew Ilsa's case inside out. There was no record that John Robinson had ever assaulted his wife. Mental abuse might be harder to prove. She could interview him again and form her own judgement. All the same, as she shut down her computer, she had a second's doubt. What if she was wrong and she was sending Ilsa back to harm?

THIRTEEN

A moment of weakness was waiting to ambush her. Driving home her car phone 'somehow' found Grant's number and pressed Call. He didn't pick up right away, but she didn't want to leave a message. She ended the call, feeling a bit deflated. It had been a long day and she would have liked a chat – maybe over a drink? Not to be.

Minutes later, he called back. 'Claire? Did you just ring?'

'Yeah.'

'Oh, that's nice. Was it about anything special?'

His voice, husky and intimate, sounded as if he'd just got out of bed.

Years ago, she had realized that the sexiness of a man is implanted deep in the memory and waits, ready to resurface. That is why a delicate touch, a whispered phrase, a sudden look can be so erotic. It brings memories flooding back of shared nights, of long periods spent in bed, of touching, of love making, the feel of his mouth hard, sometimes soft, against hers. She sighed and shoved it all aside. But when *she* spoke she could hear a distinct waver in her voice.

'No, not really. I just wondered if you fancied a drink.'

'What, now?'

'Yeah.' She got the feeling his mind was not one hundred per cent on this conversation and added, more sharply than she'd meant, 'What are you doing?'

'Now?'

'Yeah.'

'Looking at swatches of material and paint shades.'

'Grant,' she said again and fell straight into cliché, 'we need to talk.'

'Now?'

'Face to face,' she said. 'Not over the phone.'

'Come here then.'

'Where is here?'

He chuckled. 'Ah, you don't know, do you?'

She waited.

'A rented house,' he said, 'in the Westlands.' And he gave her the address.

'I'm still in my work clothes.'

'I've seen you in those before. And I'm wearing paint-spattered jeans. Just come round, Claire. If you feel the need to talk just come over.'

She was there in twenty minutes, standing in front of a small, detached bungalow with the unloved air of a rented property. She pulled on to the drive and the front door opened. He'd been telling the truth about his clothes. The jeans were ripped and paint-spattered, his shirt similarly decorated. It looked as though he'd been using his clothes as a paint shade card. But he looked achingly anxious and gave her a slightly querying smile. 'I hope this business bloody well works,' he said ruefully, as he kissed her on the cheek and led her into a sitting room, the back wall of which held French windows and overlooked a neat lawn but little else except a fence at the back. He saw her looking. '*Chez* Steadman, temporarily,' he said. Then added with a shrug the cliché, 'It does for now.'

At the back of the room was a glass-topped dining table strewn with wallpaper books and swatches of material, a few *Interiors* magazines and dirty coffee mugs, a large scribbling pad with squared paper and a bunch of pencils. He followed her glance and smiled and some of his enthusiasm rubbed off on her. She bent over the table and studied his designs.

'And can your client afford all this?'

'Oh, yeah.' He disappeared into the kitchen, returning with a bottle of wine and holding two wine glasses by the stems. He shoved some of the papers to the side and poured them both a glass. Then, eyes focused on her, he waited for her to speak.

'I had the test for cystic fibrosis,' she said. His eyes flickered up and he waited, still without speaking. He was not going to make this any easier for her. 'I'm negative.'

He gave the ghost of a smile, dark eyes flickering. 'Me too,' he said, frowning.

'So why didn't you have that test before?'

'Because,' he said wearily, 'I didn't want to know. So I didn't have the test until after Maisie had died. It would have seemed somehow disloyal.'

'You're a strange guy,' she said.

His response was a shrug. He took a sip of the wine, put his glass back on the table and waited while she put forward her second objection to resuming their relationship.

'Your mother,' she said, and he nodded, as though he had anticipated this. 'She's going to need you too.'

'I'm her only family, Claire.' Already he was on the defensive and she saw this would be the tricky road ahead. 'I'm all she's got left.'

She continued doggedly. 'So when she's low or depressed or needs a picture fixing on the wall, she'll just pick up the phone and you'll go?' She could already see that if they got back together again this would be their most frequent topic for argument. A source of chronic friction.

Grant tossed the ball back in her court. 'And what would you *expect* me to do?'

A clever move on his part. And she had no answer.

'Mum has friends in Cornwall,' Grant said, frowning. 'She's going back there. But actually I was looking a bit farther forward.'

Now it was she who was frowning. 'What do you mean?'

'Well . . .' He took a deep breath and seemed to gain confidence. 'Put it like this. You and *your* mother are not exactly close.'

She could feel her temper rise.

And that was her fault? And what did that have to do with it? Was he expecting her to become a surrogate daughter to his mother who disliked her on sight? Recalling the brief glimpse she'd had at the funeral of his mother's rigid back and carefully coiffured hair Claire couldn't see it. So she looked at her ex-partner for explanation which he gave in a way. 'Your job is important to you.'

She nodded.

'And . . .' He wafted a hand over the papers and plans. 'I'm determined to make a go of this, Claire.'

She couldn't stop herself. 'So?' It sounded brittle and hostile.

'My mum could help with childcare,' he said lamely.

'From Cornwall?'

'I don't think she'd stay there if she had a role up here.'

Her mouth dropped open. This wasn't just looking way into the future but was making a whole kettle load of assumptions.

Grant was grinning now. He knew what he'd done, taken the wind right out of her sails because he'd anticipated this very conversation, solved the problems, or so he thought, and now he waited while she digested this. It wasn't so much that he had raced way ahead of her; she hadn't even considered her life following this particular path.

She might be teetering in his direction, but she wasn't quite ready to fall back into his arms just yet or into this proposed life plan. Perhaps sensing this Grant changed the conversation and started leafing through his sketch book.

She was contemplative for a moment. She hadn't realized that this would be such a serious, large-scale venture. Grant had always been the lazy, easy-going sort. She was looking at a different side of him, a driven businessman. Imaginative, clever and talented.

She picked up her bag, feeling she didn't quite know this new man. Maybe he sensed her distancing from him. His voice was resigned. 'You going already?'

'Mmm.'

He didn't try to stop her but as she slipped her coat on he put his hand on her arm. 'At least think about what I've said, Claire. We both need to spend some time thinking about what we really want from life – and a relationship. You have your job and I need something too.' She nodded and he walked her to the door.

He brushed her cheek with his hand. 'It's a difficult job you do.' She glanced back at the table. 'Yours too,' she said, 'though mine isn't exactly creative.'

And that was that. He touched her lips with his own, but she drew back to look at him. His eyes were serious. 'Think about what I've said.'

And somehow she was back in her car, driving away.

FOURTEEN

Monday 23 September, 8.15 a.m.

The visiting order had been on her desk as she'd arrived at work that morning.

So he was asking to see her. What, she wondered, would be his stance this time around?

The thought occupied her mind right through her morning's work.

3 p.m.

The warder gave her a nod of recognition this time round. She had the feeling she would be seeing quite a bit of her and her colleagues before she was through.

Kobi was already sitting down when she entered. He stood up, an unexpected gesture of politeness. But there was a gleam in his eye as though even the gesture was a mockery. His expression was guarded, his eyes watchful. And his lips were pressed tight together as though he wanted no words to escape accidentally. But there was an energy around him. He couldn't hide his excitement at the

encounter. And her compliance to his bidding. Kobi was capable
of composing his body language, but he couldn't hide the energy
radiating out from him.

She gave him a curt nod and opened her file, removed a
photograph and placed it face down on the table between them.
Kobi made no attempt to turn it over though he ran his eyes over
the back of the picture and the labels the police had stuck there
along with a date.

'Do you know what this is?'

The look he directed back at her had completely recovered its
equilibrium. He was now cocksure. 'Let me see,' he said, finger
theatrically placed on chin, a device she would learn to anticipate
and loathe.

'Is it a photograph?' His tone was as light and teasing as though
he was playing twenty questions.

She didn't respond but waited for him to continue.

And he did. 'Looking at the date it wouldn't be a saucy picture
of little Petra Gordano, would it?' His eyes challenged her.

Claire pasted a bland smile on to her face. 'Clap, clap,' she
said, her tone ironic and her eyes cold as she turned it over. Her
overriding thought was that she hoped Petra's mother hadn't ever
seen this.

The photograph was from the police files. Behind bus stations
are generally seedy areas, places where drunks and drug abusers
congregate with the homeless. A place where rubbish is dumped.
The car must have pulled up for less than half a minute. Her body
had been flung to the side, face down, hair rippling down her back,
school skirt rucked up, the school tie clearly visible, knotted tight
enough round the back of her neck to give an obvious cause of
death. Claire had seen the post-mortem pictures too – congested
face, tongue protruding, eyeballs bulging. From this picture alone
no one could have said whether Petra Gordano had been a pretty
girl, but one suspected she might have been. Around her was
discarded detritus: fast food polystyrene trays, newspapers, the
odd plastic bottle or two.

According to the accompanying police report her body had been
thrown from the car, the contusions all inflicted post-mortem. She
had not been raped and there were no other injuries.

Kobi's eyes were cold and disdainful as he glanced down before looking up at Claire. 'As I said,' he said in his icy voice, 'a silly . . . little . . . girl.'

Claire folded her arms and leaned in across the table, knowing they were being watched by the electric eye that bulged in the ceiling. But, as psychiatrist to patient, the sound had been turned off to preserve confidentiality. 'Tell me,' she said idly, 'how you picked Petra up. How you decided she was the one . . .'

Kobi's eyes flickered and he thought for a moment before responding.

'I didn't decide specifically on her. She wasn't special. It could have been any one of them.'

'Them?'

'They were standing in the bus station, waiting for a bus to take them home. They were all laughing and flicking stuff on their mobile phones, hands over their mouths, giggling.' For effect he opened his mouth, gave a few falsetto squeaks then smothered the sound with his hand, but not before Claire had seen his mouth simpering, like a teenager, wobbling his head and staring down into his palm as though it held a mobile phone.

She was used to psychopaths, sociopaths, patients with personality disorders, narcissists and patients who tried their hardest to evoke fear, but something in Kobi's acting skills chilled her. He had studied this group of girls enough to be able to convincingly morph into them. 'How did you get her to go with you?'

'Her friends all got on another bus,' he said, speaking quietly and openly now in his normal voice. 'She'd missed hers. I pulled up and said I was going to Biddulph if she wanted a lift. I said I was a friend of her parents.' Again that smirk. 'No one ever remembers their parents' friends. She looked me up and down, decided she could trust me, and got in. Big mistake.' He leaned back in his chair and flipped his hands out, palms up in the classic pose of disclosure. 'Simple as that, Dr Roget.'

So however many times a mother advises their daughter not to accept lifts from strangers, it really is as simple as that?

'And then you pulled over and . . .?'

'Look at it this way, Claire . . . I was planning on her being the first of many. You understand?' He sneered. 'I always knew I would reduce the number of these parasitic young women.'

'You killed her and tossed her body out but you kept her school bag.'

That inspired an unexpected flame of fury. 'You think I killed her for a few pencils, some crappy books?'

She tried to hide the fact that this was news to her. 'You looked inside?'

And for the first time since she'd met him, she could see Kobi had lost his lines. His mouth opened, fish-like. He shut it again and frowned.

Without commenting, Claire made some notes and softly closed the buff folder. She waited a moment before opening the second folder. But instead of reading from it she searched that cold face and appealed to Kobi's vanity.

'There was increased police presence,' she said. 'And Jodie's murder was only two months after Petra. It must have been hard to pick up that second girl.'

Kobi saw right through it. 'Not very subtle, Claire,' he said disdainfully. 'You'll have to try better than that.'

Oh, don't you worry, she thought. I will.

'I just changed area a bit,' he said airily. 'Went to the other side of Stoke. The police,' he said, 'have little imagination and are under resourced. All I had to do was move a little. It wasn't hard. The police were hanging around Newcastle bus station. As if I'd go there again,' he derided. 'In fact, I drove right past them as I headed out to Fenton and hung around the school – or *academy*.' He gave a mocking little chuckle at the word. 'It was another rainy day in Stoke, another little girl who didn't want to get wet.' He leaned in so close she could see his yellow teeth. 'Time to have another crack at the whip.'

She schooled herself. *Focus on what you need to achieve from this. Think about Marvel. Think about the fact that her body is lying somewhere. Think about her dying father.*

'Her school bag looked heavy. She was walking like a snail along the pavement, feet splashing in puddles.' Kobi's eyes were half closed as he revisited the scene. 'She wasn't wearing a mac. I almost' – he wagged a finger – 'felt sorry for her.'

Kobi was enjoying relating his tale. Serial killers need an audience; their victims are no good. They're all dead.

'I wound the window down and said she looked cold and sympathized with her. God, she was so bloody grateful to get in the warmth of the car. "June," I said, "and it's bloody freezing."

Rainwater dripped on to the seat and then to the floor. It took ages for my car to dry out.' He gave her a bold stare. 'She was grateful.'

'And how did you feel when you dumped her body at the park?'

'Ye-es,' he mused. 'A bit unimaginative of me, wasn't it? Rainy day. Local park. But . . . it gave me an identity. The Rainy Day Killer.' He giggled. 'Or The Schoolgirl Killer.' He giggled again. Of all the sounds that chilled Claire this was the one she found worst. That sharp, hysterical giggle.

Inwardly she shuddered, trying not to link the pictures she had seen of Jodie Truss, well-developed for a fifteen-year-old, body dumped just as carelessly, propped up at the gates of the park. It had taken less than an hour to find Jodie's body and the police had already linked this second murder of a schoolgirl to the same killer. Maybe Kobi was right. Maybe that simple change of area had enabled him to kill again.

She didn't want to thread through the circumstances around the murder of all four girls but would change direction. It might disconcert Kobi, knock him off balance. 'You were working as a teacher when Miranda Pullen made that allegation.'

In spite of his self-control, Kobi blinked and missed his lines.

'That must have had quite an impact on your career.'

His mouth fell open. He was unprepared for this. She also picked up on his reluctance to talk about her. Because . . .? She'd beaten him, won that round. It took him a while to gather a response, find his lines and make a feeble attempt at regaining control.

'Don't you want to know about my childhood fetishes, Claire? Whether I kicked my father out of bed, slept with my mother, anally raped my brother?'

'I know your family background from the police reports,' she said, ice in her voice. 'I hardly need to go through all that Freudian stuff with you.'

Kobi blinked and although it was the tiniest of triumphs she returned to her analysis.

'After Jodie you had the nickname The Umbrella Killer.'

He snorted at that. 'They couldn't decide what to call me,' he crowed. 'The Rainy Day Killer, The Schoolgirl Killer or The Umbrella Killer. In the end, wisely, they settled on The Schoolgirl Killer.'

He sat back, self-satisfied, arms folded.

'And, of course, the day Marvel disappeared was another rainy day, wasn't it?'

He nodded, guarded now, uncertain where this was leading. 'And so the police had put extra officers out on the beat on days when it was raining. But not at weekends.'

He ignored her comment, continuing with his own version. 'And then Teresa,' he said. 'What a lovely hot day. An Indian Summer. Don't you just love those, Claire?' He was in his element now. 'Off her guard. Poor thing, boiling hot, struggling to walk the distance home. But of course our killer only strikes on rainy days so when that nice man comes along and offers her a lift and a nice cold Coke she's only too glad to accept. Poor thing.'

'They got you in the end.' She hadn't been able to resist it.

'Ah' – he tapped the side of his nose again – 'but not until after I'd dumped poor little Shelley in the lake. And by then, Claire, quite frankly, I was getting bored with the game anyway.'

He folded his arms and pressed his lips together. Interview over.

She stood up, pressed the buzzer and left, knowing he was silently reaching after her.

Don't you want to know about Marvel?

He might not have said them aloud, but the tendrils of his words followed her down the corridor as, accompanied by one of the prison officers, she walked back out into the open fresh air.

FIFTEEN

Back at Greatbach, sitting in her office, chewing an apple and a piece of cheese, she poured again over the notes of all four girls Kobi had been convicted of killing, searching for something new, something that connected them to Marvel. But there were still missing facts that she couldn't ignore. Apart from Shelley Cantor's body, two of the other three girls' bodies had been dumped by the side of the road. Carelessly tossed out of the car as though he wanted them found as soon as possible. Even Teresa Palmer's body in the wheelie bin had been a half-hearted attempt at concealment.

And Kobi must have known that, even in November, Westport Lake was a busy centre for fishermen, families and birdwatchers. Which led her along a different track. Had Kobi known the RSPB had set up concealed cameras around that area? Or, with his warped sense of fun, had he been edging nearer, seeing how close he could inch towards discovery without actually being caught? Identification from lens to car number plate was elementary policing. Particularly when they were searching for a man who had killed before, generally using the same MO. If Kobi was responsible for Marvel's disappearance too, why would he have hidden Marvel's body only to revert to type with Teresa Palmer in the following year?

She wrote the questions down as she flicked through more of DS Willard's notes, feeling some sympathy for the police. They must have had one hell of a job when they had failed to find Marvel, then another girl had been killed and only a month later Shelley had been reported missing. Searching for a body is bad enough without the press and the public baying for blood. The police had not been certain whether Marvel had been abducted from near her home, or from Hanley, where she had been heading. The details of her final shopping trip were unclear. The jeweller's had a record of a silver charm – a pair of ballet shoes – having been bought on that Saturday, but the purchase had been made in cash and the store's cameras badly placed. It had not been possible to identify Marvel as the shopper.

The area surrounding Biddulph was semi-rural with large areas of scrubland and there were numerous obsolete shafts from the nearby Chatterley Whitfield mine which had closed in 1977. The week before she had vanished, Marvel had been spotted heading for a disused railway track which led from Biddulph south towards the Potteries and north towards Congleton. It was muddy for most of the way, tangled with brambles and almost impassable, blocked in parts by branches and fallen logs and even in November on the day Marvel had been spotted she had been similarly dressed as the day she had vanished: short skirt, flimsy shoes, denim jacket. She would have slipped and slid her way along the track as for days before there had been heavy rain. But that day she had been identified by two independent witnesses, one a woman looking out of her window and the other a jogger who too had been heading that way. Wisely he'd decided against slithering around in the mud and had stuck to the road instead. This sighting had diverted and delayed the police investigation as they had wasted time battling their way along the entire track, in both directions, finding no sign of the missing girl. But it had raised the question: had she been meeting someone up there?

To add to the difficulties, almost as deliberate as an obstacle race, near Biddulph there was a recycling plant which, in 2013, had been a council tip. It had been a filthy, smelly old place, a rich source of methane and carbon dioxide. Today it was sanitized and well monitored. But seven years ago, when Marvel had gone missing, a body could have been hidden on the site and so the police had wasted more time, practically tearing it to bits, wearing protective face masks against the smell.

Reading through the documentation, the point that struck Claire was the story *behind* Marvel's shopping trip. She'd wanted the charm because her sisters had one each. But it was more than that. What she had really wanted was the image of a graceful dancer. Claire sifted through her file and found a posed family photograph. Her two sisters, then eleven and twelve, had been standing at the front, feet in the ballet first position, turnout 180 degrees, hands beautifully placed. Both were elegant little dancers. Marvel, standing behind them, had pulled her hair across her face in the classic pose of not wanting to be there, not wanting to be seen. Her stance was awkward, her head hanging down, shoulders dropped – another classic pose. But of shame this one. Claire put her hand over her mouth and remembered what it had felt like to be an outsider. Somewhere there would be similar pictures to this of her mother, stepfather, half-brother and herself, wishing she was anywhere but there. Marvel would never look like her sisters. Acquiring the tiny piece of silver was simply a way she could fantasize.

She turned her attention to Marvel's brother, Shane, then a confident eighteen-year-old, staring into the camera with a chal-lenging confidence. There was something cocky, self-assured about him. A tall, slim, good-looking boy with a straight, fearless gaze.

Mother and father stood stiffly apart, as though even then they were not a happy, united couple. Tom was almost unrecognizable when compared to the sick shell of a man she had met. He was tall, quite handsome in a flashy sort of way. Marvel's mother looked calm, facing the camera with a slight smile.

Claire reverted to the police records and the missing girl. She unearthed the last point that had lain across the police's guilt. As it had been a Saturday, they'd relaxed their presence, catching up with office work instead of patrolling the streets, watching schools, bus stations, shopping centres. Making the dangerous assumption that the schoolgirl killer was, like most of the population, sheltering indoors from the rain?

Claire read on.

In such wet weather in a short skirt, denim jacket and flimsy shoes, Marvel would have been soaked quickly and probably grateful for the warmth and shelter of a proffered car ride. Like Shelley.

Was there a geographical clue in the fact that Kobi's first victim and Marvel had lived within a couple of miles of each other though they went to different schools? Marvel lived in Biddulph and went to the local comprehensive, while Petra was from nearby Knypersley but attended an independent school in Newcastle-under-Lyme, ten miles away. Claire searched further. They had attended different primary schools too as Petra's parents had only moved into the area when she was eleven. Their ages were close but in every other respect they couldn't have been more different. Petra was an only child, living in a detached house in a more affluent area. Marvel's home must have been cramped, a sold-off, ex-council house with three bedrooms for four children. The three sisters had shared a room while Shane would have had his own private space. Claire put the photographs of the two girls side by side and tried to divine anything else. Petra had an intelligent, animated face while Marvel looked different. Stolid, resigned. Claire peered at the picture and read deep unhappiness, a lack of self-esteem which did not appear to affect any of the other family members. She frowned. Why her? What was different about Marvel?

Staring at the photos wasn't going to give her the answer so she turned back to Kobi's past. The subject on which he had mocked her. To a psychiatrist the police notes on him were irritatingly sketchy, chunks missing, questions she would have asked never touched on, points she would have focused on glossed over. Too little about his early home life, close relations, potentially damaging life experiences. The story of his ex-wife, for instance. There was no detail on Marie Kobi, only her name and the relevant dates were documented. They had married in 2003, separated in 2005 and divorced in 2008. And that was it. No interviews, no further detail. But then the police perspective and her own would hardly be the same. They wanted a conviction, whereas her training was to constantly ask why. Once they had unearthed the fact that Kobi had been a schoolteacher accused of inappropriate sexual behaviour against a pupil they had enough of a motive. But for her it was just the beginning of a story. What had been the substance of the allegation? Luckily Terence Wilson had documented it in his neat, precise writing. It was alleged that Kobi had slipped his hand inside the girl's blouse after keeping her back for using her mobile phone during lessons. No witnesses. The police had never interviewed the girl but, Googling her name, Claire could see plenty to interest her. Even though Kobi had been found blameless, Miranda Pullen, who had been thirteen at the time of the alleged assault, had profited out of the story when his crimes had hit the headlines. Ignoring the findings of the school investigation, she had claimed to be the one who had recognized his 'killer instinct'. Miranda had sold her story – or rather *a* story – to one of the tabloids. And what a story she'd concocted.

Lurid, way beyond her original allegation of a single incident, there was a highly imaginative tale of his trying 'for ages' to get her on her own, staring at her in class, making comments that could be construed as sexual invitations. In spite of the seriousness of the circumstances and the result of these fairy tales, Claire couldn't help smiling. There was nothing here that could be proved or disproved and, in her opinion, most of this was the result of a fertile imagination and a greedy palm. It told her more about Miranda Pullen than Jonah Kobi. Kobi just wasn't that stupid.

The articles conveniently ignored the fact that Kobi had been suspended for almost a year on full pay and ultimately found not guilty. It had been a long time for his anger to stew before he had been finally discharged with 'no case to answer'. Not surprisingly he'd left the school the following year. From then he had not had a permanent job but had gone into supply teaching. Two years later he had committed his first murder.

Prior to Miranda's possibly false allegation there was nothing. No documentation of previous cruelty either to women or animals. No violent assaults. No brush with the law. And apart from being caught speeding over thirty, he had passed what was then known as the CRB, the Criminal Records Bureau investigation, mandatory for anyone working with children or vulnerable adults. Nothing had been flagged up. So had this one complaint festered enough for a previously blameless Jonah Kobi to erupt into a killer? Revenge turning into indiscriminate murder?

Weaker trigger factors had been known, but not in Claire's experience. Kobi must always have been a gun cocked ready to fire. All Miranda Pullen had done was to release the safety catch.

And yet, two women believed in Kobi. His ex-wife's sister and the woman who had married him, his current wife.

She rang DS Willard and told him she was still happy to progress with her interviews but she needed access to these two women.

'I can get you their details, Claire, but I can't guarantee either of them will speak to you.'

'It's interesting,' she said, 'that his first marriage only lasted two years, yet his ex-wife's sister still believes in him?'

'Yeah, well, it's often the way, isn't it?' he said dismissively. 'It's often the family who feel tainted whereas an "outsider" can afford to be magnanimous.'

DS Willard's attempt at psychology made her smile.

'And even more surprising that someone has been prepared to marry him.'

Willard's response was another cynical huff.

But she had no chance to pursue his thoughts. There was a knock on her door. Rita stuck her head round, mouthing, 'Mr Robinson's here.'

She returned to the real world and her current patient load.

'I've got to go, Zed,' Claire managed. 'Just give me Chloe Barker's contact details as well as those for the current Mrs Kobi.'

'I'll see what I can do but I can't promise anything. And Claire – thanks.'

She could hardly respond with *my pleasure*.

SIXTEEN

John Robinson had the effect of unsettling her, and she could never quite work out why. He was physically unprepossessing, plump with a balding head and pasty features. He moved in an ungainly waddle, with thick thighs and feet splaying apart. His eyes were small and pale, lids hooded and his mouth was tight and mean, reminding her of pictures she had seen of Henry VIII. She had questioned Ilsa about why she had married him. Ilsa had shrugged. 'He pursued me,' she'd said. 'Flowers, dates, smart restaurants. He told me he loved me.'

Robinson was careless about his lack of physical appeal. Today he was wearing a rumpled grey suit with an open-necked white shirt and brown brogues. He smelt vaguely of rosemary and mint. As he sat down he gave a loud, impatient sigh.

She pasted a smile on her face and shook his hand. 'Mr Robinson.'

'Dr Roget.' Both were aware they were going over well-trodden ground.

'We intend to send your wife home.'

He stiffened and shifted forward. 'I can't have her home,' he said.

She was taken aback. 'Why not?'

'I just don't want her home,' he said bluntly. 'Not right now. If you say she's cured—'

She had to interrupt him then. 'Your wife will always be vulnerable,' she said. 'The way you treat her, with compassion and understanding, may well avoid any future episodes.'

His only response was to raise his eyebrows.

'Her panic attacks and delusions have a root cause in a lack of confidence which is part of her personality.'

He frowned. 'You're sure?'

Claire pressed on. 'We all have our weak spots.' And now she had to tackle the most difficult aspect. 'It will help Ilsa hugely if you're supportive, encouraging, helpful. This will restore her confidence in herself and slowly but surely she will improve. We hope to send her home on medication which we'll gradually reduce until she can, hopefully, come off it altogether.'

John Robinson looked troubled. 'I'm not sure she's ready to come home.'

'She will continue to improve over time.'

'How much time?'

She smiled and shook her head. 'Hard if not impossible to say.'

'What about her returning to the clinic for a month or two and a phased return home?'

'I can arrange it if that's what you'd prefer.'

'I'm not sure what I prefer,' he said.

That was when Claire realized John Robinson was struggling. She waited while he collected himself. 'She can be . . . unpredictable.'

'We'll follow your wife up with clinic appointments, some more CBT and further counselling.' She tried to impart an optimism she wasn't feeling. 'I have confidence that with home support she'll do well.'

'Home support?' He looked puzzled. 'Do well? What exactly does that mean? They're empty phrases, Doctor. You don't know how bad she was.'

'I was here when she was admitted.'

That was when Robinson snapped. 'I'm out at work all day. She would be alone and . . .' He frowned. 'Who knows what she might get up to?'

'Maybe a friend could stay with her while you're at work.'

Robinson's frown deepened. 'Maggie's her only real friend and she can be very unpredictable with her. And what about Augustus?'

A muffled alarm rang in the back of Claire's head. She had a duty of care towards her patient. She had other patients who needed that precious mental health inpatient bed, but at the same time she sensed a dark miasma which surrounded Ilsa Robinson's case. Too insubstantial to put her finger on.

'And if I decide to move her back to the private clinic in Birmingham?'

'If they have a bed and Ilsa agrees, I'll arrange it.'

But once he'd left, she couldn't shake off the feeling that one of them would be the loser.

SEVENTEEN

S he spent the evening at the gym, trying to work off some of her unease. Kobi was temporarily displaced as the focus of her concern. Ilsa Robinson and her husband lay at the back of her mind and however much she sweated over the pedals of the exercise bike it did little to distract her.

Finally, after fifteen minutes on the Nordic Track Treadmill, she succeeded in moving her focus back to Kobi. She had applied to visit him again next week but really wanted to speak to Chloe Barker and Kobi's current wife first. Possibly they would help her break the deadlock. She drove home and, feeling the need to confide in someone, climbed the stairs to the top floor, finding Simon in his room, watching a TV programme on his iPad. He switched off when he saw her face. 'What's up?'

She unburdened her concerns and he listened without comment. He might know nothing about Kobi and couldn't help her reach the truth, but he did know Ilsa and could give his honest opinion. Her worry was that she should keep her in for longer than just another week. But she had other patients on the list, two with serious depression. If she could not admit them to a secure unit, they might attempt suicide. Her duty of care was to the wider population. Not to just one troubled lady.

'I don't think she's that bad, Claire.' Then he added, 'Is she?'

'She's puzzling me. And I'm bothered about why her husband doesn't want her home.'

He yawned. 'Ultimately she's his responsibility – not ours. If we find her fit for discharge and have advised him to take care with her then that's his business. Maybe a private clinic isn't such a bad idea?'

'A private clinic with no resident psychiatrist?'

His eyes wandered back towards the screen of his iPad and she got the hint.

'OK, well, thanks. I'll have another think about her in the morning. For now I'm having a long, hot bath and bed.'

And hope that gives me a few hours' peace of mind, she thought, as she descended the stairs again. Maybe having her registrar on the top floor wasn't such a great idea after all.

Tuesday 24 September, 9.45 a.m.

Chloe Barker sounded crisp over the phone and surprisingly businesslike, but while she sounded reluctant to speak about her sister's ex-husband, she was not overtly hostile to a meeting and agreed to attend Greatbach later that afternoon.

'I'll come over at four,' she said. 'I only work in Congleton. May as well get it over with.'

Not very flattering, Claire thought, but let it ride and gave her instructions on how to find her office.

Why was Kobi's ex-sister-in-law still prepared to defend him? Had she not been shocked at his actions? Had she been hoodwinked by his charm? Was she gullible? Vulnerable? Sentimental? Naive? She hadn't sounded it over the phone. Neither had she come across as the sort of woman who would derive enjoyment from vicarious notoriety. Was she a Christian who extended forgiveness? Or was it simply intrigue? There is always some of that surrounding a killer. People are curious. Even relatives who thought they'd known them well.

Claire reminded herself that Chloe Barker had known the man before he had turned killer.

Maybe that was the answer.

It was five o'clock before she arrived, a petite woman in her early thirties, with wary eyes, but a businesslike manner and confident air which was eroded slightly by a crooked smile that made her appear slightly cynical. After an awkward start and introduction, Claire moved round to the subject of Kobi.

'Tell me about the time when you first met him.'

Chloe Barker crossed her legs and looked thoughtful. 'When Marie brought him home I was a schoolgirl, round about fourteen,' she said without a flicker of irony. 'He was sweet to me.' She gave one of her lopsided smiles. 'He'd help me with my homework and treat me like an adult.' She looked Claire straight in the eye. 'My parents were very patronizing. I was hardly allowed to go out even with my friends, but once or twice Jonah let me tag along with him and my sister. I suppose I sort of hero-worshipped him. He was the first guy to make a fuss of me. You don't forget that.'

'Was he ever . . . inappropriate towards you?'

'No. He was just sweet. Really nice. He seemed to understand me. Knew just what to say. Yes, he kissed me, but not in a sexual way.' She bit her lip and her eyes flickered across Claire's face who could read the subtext and had to address it. 'Did you . . . want him to pay *more* attention to you?'

Chloe Barker blushed. 'Truth? Yes, I did.'

'Do you still have any contact with him?'

'No. I did write to him when he was on remand and he wrote back. Told me I should forget about him and get on with my life.' She gave a small, embarrassed noise. 'Easier said than done. I never have forgotten him. He was . . . an influence on my life.'

'And when he and your sister split up?'

'It was like a thunderbolt. I never really understood why. Marie never confided in me. Just said they were incompatible and when I asked Jonah he got quite nasty and said I should keep to my side of the court. I think he was trying to push me away.'

'Have you wondered why?'

'I've come to the conclusion that he liked young girls and didn't want me too near.'

Liked young girls? Hardly.

'OK.' Claire reached out and touched the woman's hand. Her distress was palpable.

'So when his crimes came out?'

Chloe didn't answer straight away but sat rigidly. 'I, umm . . .' She sniffed, rifled through her bag, found a tissue and blew her nose. 'This is the awful thing, Dr Roget. I wasn't surprised.' She blew her nose again. 'I think I'd always . . .' She was running out of words. She made a brave attempt at a smile. 'I felt he was . . . dangerous. I don't mean a killer,' she added hastily. 'I mean, don't you sometimes think a man who appears dangerous can seem attractive?'

Claire nodded. And now it was time to work her way around to the still missing girl.

'Did you see much of your brother-in-law after he and your sister broke up?'

Chloe shook her head. 'I had his mobile number and email

address. I'd send him stuff – I was reading English in Manchester and would ask him for help and advice, which he freely gave.'

'Did you meet up at all?'

Chloe shook her head and looked slightly shamefaced. 'I did suggest it but he said it wasn't a good idea.'

'You understand why I've been asked to intervene?'

Chloe nodded. 'The missing girl.'

'Do you know anything about Marvel Trustrom?'

Chloe shook her head. 'He's never mentioned her – or any of the other girls. It's as though he thinks I don't know.'

There was something infinitely sad in her face, like a child who has just found out there is no Father Christmas.

'Have you visited him in prison?'

Chloe shook her head. 'He won't allow it.'

'Is there anything else you can add?'

'No.'

And Claire felt bound to apologize. 'I'm sorry to have upset you.'

Chloe Barker tried to shrug it off. 'It's OK. Really. It's OK. One day I'll look back on it and it won't seem so . . . awful. It's just that it's all being raked up again.'

'I know. I'm sorry,' Claire said again. 'But Marvel's family deserve the truth.'

'Whatever it is?'

'Yeah. Whatever it is.'

'What do you think, Doctor?'

'Whether he killed her? Probably.'

'And the reason he's keeping it back?'

'Who knows. You're still fond of him, aren't you?'

Chloe's face softened. 'Yes, I am.' She felt she should explain. 'It's as though there were two people, Jonah, my friend whom I always liked and Kobi the killer. I realize he did kill those girls, but he never would have harmed me. Everyone else, including my sister, can vilify him. Why should I? He never did anything bad to me.'

If he had, Claire thought, *you'd hardly be here today, would you?*

Chloe gave another of her strange, twisted smiles. 'Jonah may be a killer but he's not a liar, you know. If he says he didn't do it then he didn't.'

Claire found it hard not to smile at this gradation of faults. But the irony of her stance appeared lost to Kobi's sister-in-law.

And that was the trouble. Once caught and charged Kobi had pleaded guilty. But he had continued to deny any knowledge of Marvel's disappearance. Claire thanked her and Chloe left.

Now Claire had seen Kobi through someone's eyes who'd been fond of him, she had a different perspective. The kaleidoscope had twisted.

EIGHTEEN

Wednesday 25 September, 11 a.m.

She visited Ilsa on the ward and sat down with her, still troubled by the decision she was about to finalize. As an inpatient they could monitor their patients hour by hour, change medication within minutes, note serious incidents. Above all watch and sometimes prevent assaults, meltdowns and suicide attempts. Do their best to carry out that government directive. As an outpatient they would be cutting her free. She recalled Edward Reakin's words. Possibly psychotic, possibly not. As Claire entered the room she sensed that Ilsa was withdrawing into herself. She was sitting in the corner, in an armchair, frowning, her mouth working as she muttered. She didn't look up when Claire entered but continued with a slight rocking movement and the continual working of her mouth. If anything, she seemed even more distant and detached.

'You'll soon be going home.'

Ilsa didn't respond.

'John is, I believe, getting the house ready for when you return from the clinic.'

No response.

'You'll see your son.'

Still no response.

'I think he's planning for Maggie—'

Ilsa's head shot up. 'No,' she said. 'Not in my house.'

Claire kept her voice calm. 'I understood she was your friend.' She pursued the subject. 'Maggie is a good friend, isn't she?'

This provoked a soft huff. But there were questions it was her duty to ask.

'You know where you are and why you're here?'

'Yes.'

'And now?'

Ilsa's expression was pure cunning. Instinctively Claire leaned forward and touched her hand. 'You need to tell me,' she said, 'what you want to do. You're not powerless, you know.'

Ilsa made no response.

'You need to tell me if you really are happy to go home.'

Ilsa leaned forward. 'Nothing you can do will make any difference. John won't win, you know.'

'Won't win what?'

'This round.'

'He doesn't need to win, Ilsa. There is no competition.'

Ilsa licked around her mouth. 'There's always a competition. Life is a competition.'

'In some ways, yes. But *he* isn't my patient, Ilsa. You are.'

'Maybe he wants me out of the picture so he can carry on with Maggie.'

'That isn't the impression I get. He seems very fond of you. He just wants you to get better.'

'He's good at deceiving people.'

'Why would he do that?'

For the first time since Ilsa had been admitted Claire saw a mischievous smile as she responded. 'Who knows?'

Claire made her decision. 'I'm going to ask Edward Reakin, the psychologist, to spend some time with you so we can work out a care plan for your discharge. And it will be one that puts you first. Understand?'

Ilsa nodded.

As Claire left the room, she felt worried. Something here felt dangerous. Ilsa was far more manipulative than she had realized. What was she really capable of? She must call on Edward, she thought, as she wrote up the notes and left the ward. As she passed Ilsa's door, she peeped in. Ilsa was sitting on her bed looking pleased with herself.

Grant rang at lunchtime wondering if they could meet up, but she had to say no. 'I'm sorry but this Kobi thing is taking up a lot of my time. I'm really behind at work.'

'Oh.'

She felt unaccountably irritated at his disappointment. 'Come on, Grant, this is how it is.' She felt like adding the same tired, worn, old phrases, that this wasn't just a job. Like the police it was more a way of life. But that would have been pointless and unnecessary and she'd said it all a thousand times before. Instead she suggested, with a heavy weariness, that they meet tomorrow. 'And I'll give Adam a ring, see if he and Adele are free.' His response was a dissatisfied grunt. Both he and she knew perfectly well what she was doing, using her half-brother as a foil. While he was there they would not be able to discuss their 'future'. In fact, she didn't want to discuss their future at all but wanted to leave it out of focus. She was deliberately putting it off. And Grant's 'Great' was ironic.

NINETEEN

Thursday 26 September, 12.30 p.m.

The day wasn't turning out quite how she'd anticipated. HMP Stafford had rung her at nine o'clock saying that Jonah Kobi was asking to see her – urgently.

Again? It was a repetition of Monday. And what had she gained from that interview? Nothing. It was all part of his game, but she made a two-hour gap in her day to see him anyway.

'Well, well, well,' Kobi greeted her as she entered the room, making that polite gesture of raising himself from the chair and holding out his hand. 'If it isn't my dear friend, Dr Roget.' He turned and spoke to the prison officer. 'Come to interview me over a murder she's not quite sure whether I did or did not commit. She's wondering now what, if anything, I have to tell her.' His smile broadened as he continued addressing the prison officer. 'What do you think?'

The officer was not playing any game. He remained expressionless as a soldier on parade and, with a swift check at Claire, he left them alone.

Kobi lowered himself back into the chair. A smile played around his mouth as though he was really enjoying these interviews, but it didn't quite ring true. Claire kept her eyes on him. His confidence was hollow, his mouth wavering and uncertain. He was, she decided, uncomfortable.

'Nice to see you again, Claire.'

She didn't respond. Instead, she said, 'What's so urgent you wanted to see me today?'

'Maybe I remembered something. Now what was it?' He put his finger on his chin.

She waited, glancing pointedly at her watch.

'Miranda,' he said. 'Have you spoken to her?'

'Not yet.'

'Why not?'

'I'm not convinced she'll be of help.' She turned the topic. 'Unlike your wife.'

His mouth tightened. 'Why do you want to talk to her?'

'Sometimes,' she said casually, 'background information can be useful. Give you another perspective.'

He'd lost his swagger.

'Why did you marry her, Jonah? You're unlikely ever to live together or have a normal married life. So why marry? What's the point? Is it because you won't ever be expected to have sex?'

His face darkened but he managed a tight smile. 'Well. You're the psychiatrist. Why do *you* think I married?'

She leaned back in the chair and delayed responding, as though only now was she giving the question consideration. 'To have someone on the outside,' she said slowly. 'A voice. A representative. Possibly a means of making a plea for release. Someone you could manipulate, Jonah? I'll find out,' she said, 'because I intend to speak to her.'

He didn't like that. He leaned forward. He smelt clean. Soapy, his breath scented with toothpaste. 'I would have thought more interesting, is why did *she* marry *me*?' He treated her to one of his wide 'open' smiles.

She trotted out the notes she'd read. 'There are well-documented reasons why women take an interest in a lifer.'

'Such as?'

She played along. 'Wishing to reform a "bad character". Sharing in notoriety, a sort of negative fame. Sometimes they have' – she paused delicately, observing his responses – "tendencies" themselves. There is a recognition of the same type.'

Kobi stiffened.

She continued smoothly, pretending she had seen nothing. 'They can have a genuine interest in a killer's personality. There arc the oncs motivatcd by curiosity having read something or heard something that catches their interest. There are the fantasists. And then there are the reformers. So which is it, Kobi?'

He responded quickly. 'That's for you to work out.'

'And then,' she picked up, 'the relationship moves on, in stilted form, often a disappointment – to both. I will be interviewing Jessica to decide for myself which category she falls into.'

He didn't like that. 'Who told you her name?' He snapped out the words.

'Oh, come on, Kobi. It's hardly difficult to find out but actually DS Willard told me about her.'

'About her?'

'Only the bare bones, her name. Very little else.'

Something flared in his eyes. She'd touched a sensitive spot. Claire couldn't resist pressing her advantage. 'Yes,' she spoke to herself. 'I think that would be a good idea.'

'And if I forbid it?'

She looked down at her hands, still relaxed, lying on her lap. 'I don't think you can do that, Kobi.'

He tried another tack. '*She* doesn't have to see you. She can't know anything. She wasn't on the scene until later. It would be . . . pointless. A waste of your time.'

'You might have confided in her.'

He shuffled in his seat and she realized why he had so wanted to see her. Not to give her information but to extract it.

'I'll stop her.'

She raised her eyebrows.

'I'll tell her not to meet you.'

'So you have control over her?' She kept her voice low and slow.

And for the first time Kobi wasn't quite sure how to respond.

She smiled, drew in breath and proceeded. 'I'm not exactly short of women to interview about you.'

'Like?'

'I've already spoken to Chloe.'

He looked surprised. 'But she's just a kid.'

'Not anymore.'

'You can leave her out,' he said. 'She doesn't know anything. She was just an innocent.'

'That was my conclusion. But then there's Miranda.'

'Miranda?' he jeered. 'You'll learn nothing from her. She's a trumped-up little liar.'

'Yes,' she agreed. 'But why you? That's what interests me. Why didn't she make an allegation against one of the other teachers? I wonder if she sensed something wasn't quite right about Mr Kobi, history teacher.'

If she'd touched a sensitive spot before this was raw. He sucked in a deep breath and she caught a glimpse of the fury against this schoolgirl. She weaved her fingers. If she could only use this blind anger. 'Miranda, of course, is the smart one. She not only got you suspended while the enquiry went on, but she made a packet of money from selling her story to the tabloids when you were found guilty of the girls' murders.'

Kobi drew in a couple of deep, scooping breaths and struggled to regain control. His eyes burned.

She'd got under his skin.

She still felt dirty after she left the prison. It wasn't the building itself, which was actually clean and smelt more of pine disinfectant than anything else. It was Kobi's character. It was rubbing off on her. If he was playing a game then so must she.

But the question she had asked Kobi stayed in her mind. Why *had* Miranda picked on Kobi?

For now, she shelved the question. She'd made a promise to Grant. She rang Adam, her stepbrother, on the way home, to see if he and Adele were free. It was time she saw him and his fiancée again. Besides, she was wondering how they would absorb the tricky family situation into their wedding plans. At least she'd have Grant at her side to smooth over any family awkwardness.

Adam didn't answer the phone and she left a jaunty message. 'Hi, Ad, big sister here. It's Thursday. Don't suppose you fancy trying out a Greek meal tonight with me and Grant? Ring if you do and bring Adele.' She paused before adding, 'Love you' and making a kissing noise as she turned out of HMP Stafford's car park.

TWENTY

T he visit to Kobi had reignited interest in the woman who had made that damaging allegation. She pulled over and found Miranda Pullen's contact details in her notebook. Miranda now lived in Stratford-upon-Avon, Shakespeare's town, though when Claire had visited it last year there had appeared little left of Mr Shakespeare.

The voice that responded on the phone was crisp, clean and as decisive as sliced lemon. But when Claire introduced herself and gave the reason for her call Miranda was instantly guarded and she quickly mounted her high horse. 'I don't quite see how I can help,' she said. 'My contact with Mr Kobi goes back to well before he began his killing spree.' *Which hadn't stopped her selling a lurid account of her one-time teacher to the tabloids and making a packet of money out of it.* Claire had scanned the stories and found no sympathy for his victims, only a sharp self-protectionism and justification for her original allegations. Psychopaths come in all shapes, degrees and sizes. And no one now cared whether the stories she'd told were true or false.

There were veiled allusions to him making 'suggestions', watching her 'in a particular way', attempts to isolate her from her friends. Nothing actionable. If there was any truth behind the story it was buried in a dung heap of lies. Whatever – the papers had lapped it up and would have paid well for 'insight' into a notorious serial killer.

'It's true that your allegations pre-date his crimes,' Claire agreed, 'but fairly obviously there is a possibility that it was those allegations . . .' She paused, aware she was about to cross a line. Instead she substituted her original words with a safer version: 'Might have woken some dark instincts in him.'

As she'd anticipated, Miranda quickly sprang to the defensive. 'You can't know that.'

'I've read the articles, Miranda, as well as the police files and the post-mortem reports of the dead girls.' She didn't repeat her request for an interview.

The response this time was a heavy silence.

Eventually Miranda capitulated. 'All right,' she said. 'All right. If you think it might help. But I'll only meet at *my* time and at a place of *my* choosing. I don't believe I can help you find that girl for a minute but . . .' Something changed in her voice. It lifted a few notes and acquired brittleness. 'I don't like all this being raked up again. It was a long time ago. I don't want my family being exposed to notoriety.'

Then you shouldn't have gone so public with your little stories.

'I'm getting married next year. I don't want to start married life with this cloud hovering over me. I just want it over. Dead and buried.'

Unfortunate words.

They finally arranged to meet on the following Wednesday, at a hotel a little off Junction 14 of the M6. Miranda said she was 'on the road' that day and this would be the most convenient hook-up point.

Claire put the phone down, acknowledging a surprising detail: Kobi might be a serial killer, as slippery as a wet snake, but of the two she preferred him to Miranda Pullen. If she had to make a choice at all.

5.30 p.m.

Edward Reakin was waiting outside her office to speak to her about Ilsa. He closed the door carefully behind him.

He sat down and looked at her awkwardly. 'Sorry to bother you,' he said. 'I know you're busy.'

'It's OK, Edward.'

'I've just spent some time with Ilsa,' he said. 'I'm not sure what we're going to achieve here.'

'Elaborate.'

'She believes her husband is having an affair with her friend but' – he looked troubled – 'I'm not sure this is a genuine delusion.'

'Why not?'

'It's the way she says it, almost casually.'

'You think she's playing with us? To what ends?'

'That's what I can't work out. It's almost as though she has a secret agenda.'

'What?'

Edward simply shook his head. 'Whatever it is, she's hiding it from us. Maybe what she needs is to go home. Return to reality. Pick her life back up but her husband won't have her home. Says he needs time.'

'For what?'

'That is another puzzle. To protect their son, perhaps? Because he still feels she needs specialist help? Or is there another motive? Ah . . .' He held up his hands 'Claire,' he said, 'something is very wrong.'

'I feel that too, but we can't justify keeping her in because we *feel* that something is wrong.'

'Her husband has suggested she go back to the private clinic in Birmingham.'

'That might not be a bad option, Claire.'

'Your instincts have been right before. I'll talk to Ilsa and book the clinic, discuss the possibility of having a psychiatrist visit her there. We're only on the end of the phone. Her medication has been sorted. She's not acutely anxious or depressed. I don't judge her to be a suicide risk.'

'Decision made then?' He smiled and looked relieved and then added, 'I don't know what her game is.'

'Game? Is that what it is, a game?'

'I just get the feeling she's hiding something vital from us.'

'Then that settles it.' On behalf of all the patients who desperately needed a psychiatric inpatient bed, she felt angry. 'Greatbach isn't the place for a game.'

Edward was almost out of the door when she added softly, half hoping he wouldn't hear, 'I only hope I'm not wrong here.'

6 p.m.

Adam still hadn't rung back.

Next to claim her attention was DS Zed Willard on the phone. 'I just wondered where you are with your interviews?'

'Not sure I'm getting anywhere, Zed,' she said. 'I have arranged to see Miranda Pullen next week – if she doesn't cancel.'

'Why her?' He sounded surprised. 'She probably made the whole thing up as a dare.'

'That's what I'm hoping to find out.'

'He was found not guilty of sexual misconduct,' he reminded her.

'Which doesn't necessarily mean he's innocent. It only means he wasn't found guilty. And when she made her allegation, the rules for sexual propriety between pupil and teacher were less stringent. I don't know if she'll throw any light on Marvel's fate, Zed, but I do think she will give insight into Kobi's character. Why she picked on him. There will be something there, some small and subtle clue. Teenage girls can be very perceptive of the opposite sex. They pick up on things other age groups miss out on. Let's face it. Kobi is never going to confess unless we have more leverage.'

'His wife?'

'I'll get to her. She might well fulfil that role but the first inkling of real emotion I've seen was when I mentioned Miranda Pullen, which is why I'm anxious to meet up with her. He was clearly still furious with her. Nothing else stirred him like that. Not a mention of his sister-in-law who professes to be a real friend or even his wife had such an effect on him.'

On the other end DS Willard blew out his lips in frustration and hid behind his usual mantra. 'Well, you're the psychiatrist.'

And her response was just as hackneyed. 'I wish I had a pound for every time I heard that particular phrase.'

She felt she should climb down. 'How is Tom?'

'I haven't heard anything this week, Claire.'

'But he's . . .?' It seemed brutal to use the words *still alive* so she omitted them, leaving the sentence dangling in the air for DS Willard to catch her meaning.

'As far as I know.'

And that was the end of the conversation.

She put the phone down, omitting to add that one of the papers she was considering writing for the psychiatrists' journal was to look into the reasons why women married lifers when there were no conjugal rights in the UK, and as far as the current home secretary was concerned this privilege was unlikely to be granted any time soon. Her mind wandered. There was the converse of men marrying women killers, though it was much rarer. There were only two cases in the whole of England, Northern Ireland, Scotland and Wales. Possibly because fewer women committed murder. Or possibly because men were less likely to fit into the categories she had so far dreamed up: sentiment, notoriety, curiosity or conversion.

Still no word from Adam and, as always, where her half-brother was concerned, she felt guilty and anxious.

TWENTY-ONE

Thursday 26 September, 6.15 p.m.

She was anxious to get home, wash, change and make it to the restaurant before eight. At last Adam had texted her, leaving a message that he and Adele would meet her there. Grant had texted he would pick her up at seven thirty and she'd smiled, knowing his idea of time was as elastic as a rubber band and had little to do with clocks or the appointed time. The one time he would *not* turn up at would be seven thirty. Maybe six or twenty past, possibly as late as eight. He was . . . unpredictable. Though, she reminded herself, the last two times they had met he had more or less stuck to the appointed time.

And just to prove the point he turned up early, at six forty-five, while she was still in the bath soaking away the day. She heard Simon let him in, a few exchanged words and then, unmistakably, Grant running up the stairs and knocking on the door. 'Claire.'

'Hey,' she said. 'You're early.'

'Hmm,' was his response. No apology or explanation. In his mind, unpinned from the clock, neither was necessary.

It felt natural to pull the plug, wrap a towel around her and meet him in the bedroom. He was sprawled across the bed, in jeans and open-necked, check shirt, hands underneath his head. He watched her, saying nothing – it was all expressed in his wide grin, the rogue smile taking it all in as she dressed in a Joseph Ribkoff, calf-length dress, black with a panel of brilliant verdant green and a split that reached halfway up her thigh. 'Bloody hell,' he said. 'Smart wear for a taverna.' His grin spread even broader. 'If things were different, I'd say give me a twirl.'

He would do this, drop in and out of her life casually. While he was there all seemed natural. And when he wasn't that seemed OK too. She too had moved on.

So she obliged him with his twirl and dropped down beside him on the bed. 'I just felt like dressing up,' she confessed. 'I always seem to be in work clothes and I'm sure they carry the scent of Greatbach or the prison or of something or someone equally unpleasant.'

'Whereas I,' he said smugly, 'carry the scent of paint and wallpaper paste.'

She propped herself up on her elbow. 'So how's it going?'

She didn't really need to ask. She'd caught his look. She knew when Grant Steadman was pleased with himself.

And she was right. He put his arm around her and pulled her to his chest. His shirt was open. She felt the scratch of his hair, coarse compared to the softness of the hair on his head. 'Pretty good,' he said. 'We'll be finished in a month or so.'

'So quickly?'

'Well, there's no structural work only paint and the finishing touches. And even better a few of his mates who've been round to take a sneaky peak, like my work, and want to commission me. Looks like' – he stopped and kissed her cheek – 'I'm on my way.'

And isn't it odd and unfair. After years spent fretting that her boyfriend did not have a 'proper' job she felt a tinge of envy. Her own career of delving into damaged minds seemed mundane and vexatious; his creative and artistic.

'And the lady of the house?'

This brought a troubled frown. 'Is away. He wants it done before she gets back.' He half closed his eyes, long lashes hiding his misgiving.

'I only hope she likes it. It sounds a risky strategy to me.'

He gave her a naughty look now. 'Considering how exacting some women can be,' he said mischievously, 'I would have thought so.' He leant in and found her lips with his own.

She'd forgotten how good he tasted.

She nestled into him and thought how easy it would be to let him back into her life – for ever. She'd meant to say, *Let's not get serious tonight, Grant, let's leave "us" out of it. Adam and Adele will be full of wedding plans. Let's just enjoy the evening. Please?* But he was making it hard.

He kissed her gently on the cheek as she slipped on her shoes. 'You really want to walk up – in those heels?'

'I was hoping I'd be chauffeur driven.' And now the memories were flooding back. Grant's driving, slow and prone to distractions, chatting by her side. With an effort she sat up, crossed to her mirror, fixed her make-up and brushed her hair.

Although she now loved Adam and his fiancée, Adele, and enjoyed these periodic meetings as well as the way he called her Sis, she was dreading the day of their wedding. Dreading meeting her mother again and stepfather, being forced to witness the way they doted on him and could hardly bear to look at her. She wanted to scream at her mother sometimes. *It isn't my fault that Monsieur Roget abandoned us. Maybe it's yours. Certainly, I shouldn't have to pay all my life for his walk-out.* And when she allowed herself to reflect on her father, whom she could not even remember, she knew there was an echo of the way Grant had vanished from her life, even if it had only been for six months. Maybe that was why she was hypersensitive to the subject of abandonment?

But misgivings and fears aside, the evening and the dinner were splendid. Every time she met up with her half-brother she was struck by what a balanced, incredibly nice man he was. He and Adele chatted easily, but did not bore about the wedding details. They showed interest but not undue curiosity about her current case load, even asking Grant about his interiors business. Grant kept them amused with his stories of the paunchy businessman and his attempt to impress the so far missing wife. 'She must be really special. He's sparing no expense, changing everything from kitchen units to Danish taps, from swatches of material to the latest in gadgets. Next he wants to build an indoor gym and swimming pool.'

'Wow.' Adele laughed with the others. 'What on earth is she going to think when she gets back – her entire house gutted?'

'Not sure,' Grant said, slightly uneasy.

There was a sudden halt in their conversation. Adam and Adele exchanged glances and Claire knew they had had conversations about her and Grant's relationship.

Grant kept his eyes on her, the long, curling lashes flirting as he ate his food, and accompanied by his signature wicked grin. She sensed his mood. Teasing. The talk eventually returned to details of the wedding and finally she addressed the dreaded subject. 'I suppose our mother will be there.' Even the words 'our mother' seemed a lie. Adam and Adele exchanged swift glances which, inexplicably, seemed to include Grant but exclude her. It was Adam who spoke, ruffling his copper-coloured hair and giving an apologetic scraping of his throat. 'Of course,' he said.

Adele stretched her hand across the table. 'Claire,' she said in her soft voice. 'I know life hasn't really been . . .' She started again. 'I know Adam's . . .' Another false start. 'I know your mother hasn't always been fair to you. I know you've had a difficult time but let's hope this is the beginning of a détente. Peace between you.' She gave a swift, worried glance at her fiancé. 'We've done our best, Claire.'

Claire simply nodded, trying to swallow the bile that had risen and suppress the resentment she felt that Adam and Adele should need to intercede on her behalf – with her own mother. Suddenly it was anger and hatred that bubbled up.

And when, an hour and a half later, Grant drove her home and hesitated on the doorstep, waiting to be invited in, she shook her head. 'I'm not in a great place. Sorry.'

She shut the door on him.

TWENTY-TWO

S he'd spent a sleepless night, tossing and turning, taking in turns who to resent most: Adam and Adele for the happiness denied her; her mother, for obvious reasons; or Mr Perfect David Spencer for being just that – the perfect stepfather. In the end she'd given up on sleep and come in to work early.

Because the great advantage of work is the distraction it provides.

Her curiosity was now directed towards Jessica Kobi for two reasons. The first was a genuine reason. Had Kobi confided in his wife any details which might help her learn Marvel's fate? The second reason was to provide details for her research into why women married lifers.

There was no record of Jessica Kobi having gone public with her unusual marriage choice so it would seem that money was not her motive. Claire had pictured her as a high-maintenance, brassy blonde, a woman with a loud voice addicted to fame or rather notoriety. But the voice that responded to her call and introduction was soft and sounded intelligent, which made Claire even more curious.

'Yes, Jonah spoke of you,' she said in response to Claire's introduction. 'He said you would probably call.'

'You understand why I've been asked to involve myself in your husband's case?'

'I do.' She didn't enlarge. Obviously a woman who did not feel the need to fill silences.

Claire waited for a clue. But on the other end of the line was silence. It was being left to her to provide the cues.

'Would you be happy to come in and talk to me?'

'I'd have to run it past Jonah first.'

'OK.' Claire gave her her contact details and let Jessica take the lead.

'When were you hoping to speak to him again?'

'I have an appointment with him next week,' Claire said. 'Tuesday afternoon.'

If he doesn't cancel, she added mentally.

'I hope you get what you want.' *Was there a hint of mockery in her tone?*

Claire put the phone down thoughtfully.

I hope you get what you want.

What *did* she want?

The truth. Only that. One could take this statement as a polite expression or a genuine wish, though she doubted it. Much more likely was that the pair of them were sniggering behind their hands at this psychiatrist running around in circles in search of a schoolgirl who had been missing for six years without any clue as to her fate. It was an uncomfortable vision.

Doubts trickled like cold water through her mind. Oh, she thought in frustration, why had DS Willard involved her in this?

She had two clinical case reviews that afternoon which took most of the next couple of hours. Everyone wanted their say: community psychiatric nurses, ward nurses, psychiatrists (in the plural as both she and Salena were there but not Simon) and Edward Reakin. One of the cases under review was that of a paranoid schizophrenic who had had multiple brushes with the police. Usually little more than shouting and twice he had locked himself in public toilets, cut his wrists and refused to come out. Daniel Price was not a danger to society but he was a danger to himself. The decision was made to adjust his medication and move him to sheltered accommodation where he would be supervised twenty-four seven.

The second case up for review was that of Ilsa Robinson and the decision when to transfer her. She caught Edward's eyes and he gave a troubled shake of his head. Claire felt a ripple of unease which passed around the table like a Mexican wave. Discharging a patient carried some risk. Patients could relapse and the progression of some diagnoses could be unpredictable. It was always a matter of patching up holes. Claire left the meeting with a heavy heart and a sense of guilt that she was letting this patient down. But she had a list of eight more vulnerable patients who would benefit from an inpatient bed.

Edward caught her just as she was leaving. 'I took a look at your guy's notes.'

'Oh yes?'

'He's devious and clever. He doesn't fit into the usual criteria, no evidence of alcohol abuse or overt aggression. Everything he does is organized. Interesting that there's no other criminality. Nothing he does is accidental or random. It's all planned and his narcissism is practically off the scale.'

She listened, agreeing with his chilling assessment.

He put his hand on her arm. 'Be careful, Claire. He will try to manipulate your opinion.'

'Thank you, Ed. And thanks for your help with Ilsa.'

She spoke to John Robinson and explained their decision. His response, over the phone, was hard to gauge: relief or concern?

He tested her. 'You're sure of this?'

'As sure as I can be of anything.'

She arranged for Ilsa to be discharged to the clinic on the following Friday.

Simon met her in the corridor, a broad grin on his face. 'She arrives tomorrow morning,' he said. 'I wonder . . . could I . . .?'

She didn't need to ask who was coming on Saturday morning. It was obvious and Simon looked happy. The wife, Marianne.

His hopefulness was as eager as a puppy's when promised a long walk. But underneath his excitement she also sensed his anxiety.

And it left her with a dilemma. She didn't particularly want to be there for the hopefully joyful reunion. On impulse she picked up her phone, connected with Grant and made a suggestion. The weather forecast promised fine weather, great for a coastal walk. Add to that fine food and wine. Grant listened to her suggestion before asking only one thing. 'Where?'

'Wales,' she said. 'Where else?'

TWENTY-THREE

Monday 30 September, 9 a.m.

The weekend in Wales had proved to be wonderful. Claire had found a beautiful hotel on the coast, near Aberystwyth, with a pool, five-star restaurant and plenty of bracing walks

along the coast overlooking the Atlantic rollers. She'd packed a
case early Saturday morning, picked Grant up from his house and
headed straight off, for once glad to be abandoning home. She
wasn't looking forward to having a second guest and already
suspected there were unresolved tensions between the couple that
could only make things even more difficult. Let them have the
place to themselves for the weekend and, hopefully, start to sort
themselves out. Simon was on holiday for the next week and
Salena would cover the weekend. She'd felt her spirits rise as
Grant opened the door and she saw him, happy, grinning, dressed
in walking trousers and heavy boots. He threw his bag on to the
back seat, climbed in and kissed her hard on the mouth making
her wonder how many of those bracing walks they would actually
manage.

Sometimes weekend romantic breaks work out. At other times
they almost seem to fuel rows and disagreements. But she felt she
and Grant had reached a status quo. There were silences between
them, but they also had some long chats and it was good to be
away from the Potteries and work.

They ate in the restaurant on the Saturday night, enjoying the
quiet hotel, hearing the waves wash over the beach. They toasted
their evening and Grant watched her. 'This,' he said, 'was a very
good idea.'

They did manage to swim in the hotel pool and braved the rain
which was confounding the weather forecast, sheeting down,
almost obscuring the cliff path ahead which was muddy and slippery on the Sunday giving them an excuse for extreme laziness.

But all good things come to an end. Sunday evening saw them
heading back to their separate addresses. As Claire dropped Grant
off outside his house his mask slipped. 'I wish I was coming
home,' he said.

Claire almost said, *Then why don't you?* The words were in her
mouth, ready to spill out. She looked at him and felt the pull that
made it hard to separate. But something tugged her back. 'Grant,'
she said. He was watching her very closely, maybe realizing the
doubts that lay in her heart. Then he kissed her. A hard, defining
Goodbye Kiss. Uncompromising. He opened his door, closed it
behind him, picked up his holdall from the back seat and was gone
without a backwards glance or saying anything more.

She drove home still in a daze, feeling she might regret *not* saying those words when they had seemed so obvious, so fitting, so right. They would have dropped quite naturally and sequentially into the chumminess they had achieved over the weekend, but something had held her back and now the moment was gone. And like many significant moments perhaps it would not return.

The house had been quiet as she'd let herself in. Simon's car had been in the drive so, presumably, he and his wife were upstairs. She'd stood at the bottom, straining to hear any sound. But it had been silent. At a guess Marianne would be jet-lagged and Simon would be upstairs. She felt excluded. Wishing Grant was beside her, she showered and slipped into bed. When you have grown used to your partner lying beside you, a double or king-sized bed can seem as big as a continent.

Although Jessica Kobi had promised to contact her with a suitable time and place to be interviewed, so far Claire had heard nothing from her. Maybe Jonah was forbidding his wife from speaking to her. But all else seemed peaceful and Claire was enjoying the lull. The wards were being managed. Salena was due a couple of days off. Simon was on his week's leave. All seemed peaceful.

Tuesday 1 October, 11 a.m.

She almost regretted having to leave Greatbach to head back to Stafford prison.

Driving through heavy rain, she wondered whether today she would learn anything further from Kobi. Or would it be another wasted journey?

He was already in the visitors' room, apparently studying his fingernails as she peered through the glass optic. But she knew he knew she was there. He glanced up as the prison officer opened the door and she stood in the doorway. He half stood up, his polite move, and smiled at her as she sat down.

'I understand you've spoken with my wife.' His tone was pleasant. They could have been at any social gathering.

Her response was deliberately bland. 'I did. I hope to meet up with her at some point.' She omitted to mention her academic interest. He leaned back, folded his arms and lowered his gaze, waiting for her to open the interview. 'Tell me, Jonah, why do you think the MO of the person who abducted Marvel is different to the crimes against the other girls?' She'd chosen to distance him from the perpetrator. It was a deliberate ploy. Rather than accusatory this consultative technique gave the suspected perpetrator status, a chance to air some fantasy of his own, the opportunity of involving him, as an outsider, in the investigation, speaking about the crime objectively, casting the killer in the third person and relieving him of the burden of suspicion. It could also give a killer an opportunity to applaud his own crime. And there was always the chance that some detail would leak out.

Claire recalled a lecture she had attended, given by Heidi Faro, her predecessor, when advising about interviewing patients diagnosed with a narcissistic personality disorder. 'Let them talk,' she'd said. 'That is eventually what gives them away, this need to speak and be listened to. They want to be admired, revered. Give them the rope and let them do all the hanging themselves.'

Heidi had been right. But Kobi was too clever to swallow this bait even if it denied him accolade. He leaned forward so close she could see the pores on the side of his nose, watch his eyelashes flicker, feel his breath on her face. And watch him smile. 'Well, Claire,' he said, 'it could always be a copycat killer.' His voice was soft. 'Someone who didn't *quite* get it right.'

She kept her expression deliberately neutral. 'I suppose it could be.'

There was a brief silence before he proffered another explanation. 'It could always be that the girl herself was different.'

Ah!

'In what way?'

He appeared to be deliberating over how to answer this. 'There are the obvious differences,' he said.

'You mean her appearance.'

'That and the crime itself. Think of it this way, Dr Roget.' The way he rolled his 'r's' set her teeth on edge. It seemed a deliberate taunt though how he could have known about her unhappy home life and father's abandonment she had no idea. Perhaps he'd just read her emotions and hit lucky. He kept his voice so quiet she had to strain to hear him. 'Maybe I'm just guessing – just as you are. Maybe I don't have the faintest idea why this girl was selected for different treatment than the ones *I* chose.' He couldn't prevent the triumphant smile from spreading across his face.

She sat forward, elbows on the table. 'You're still denying her murder then?'

Kobi followed that up with a sly, sideways look. 'I'm simply doing what you're doing. Discussing different scenarios.'

'Maybe.' Time to change subjects.

'I'm meeting Miranda Pullen tomorrow.'

Apart from a flash in his eyes she could not be sure he'd heard her.

She closed the subject down. 'Tell me about your wife.'

He shrugged. 'As in . . .?'

'How did you get together in the first place?'

'You enjoy reading romances?'

Her turn to shrug.

'She wrote to me. One of many.'

'She wrote to you saying what? That she believed you were innocent?'

'I can't remember.'

'Surely you can? You must have continued with the correspondence.'

'I must have done, mustn't I?'

'So how did the relationship progress?'

He looked bored. 'It just did.'

'So you married her – because you were bored?'

'Sort of.'

She prompted him. 'You must get quite a few letters.'

He replied, 'You wouldn't believe how many . . .' Then he shook his head. 'Not really.'

This was the first time she'd felt connected. This was the first statement he'd said that rang true. There was even a ring of humility in his tone as he continued, 'Once you're sentenced and out of the headlines people soon forget about you and move on to someone else.'

'What did Jessica say that made you feel particularly connected?'

He gave her question some thought and answered with a certain amount of veracity. 'Sympathizing, saying she understood about teenage girls, that she'd been a little bugger in her time, and it was a wonder no one had strangled her. She sounded intelligent.'

He tapped his index finger on the desk. 'Her English and grammar were good.'

'And when you actually met her, how did you feel?'

'Huh. That's an interesting one.' He put his finger on his chin, pretending to think deeply. 'I thought she was attractive, interesting. Intelligent. Perceptive.' He snapped his fingers. 'Put it like this. We clicked.' He gave a bland smile.

He was feeding her lines and they both knew it.

'How do you *feel* about her, Jonah?'

He narrowed his eyes. 'I fancied her.' He gave a spurt of laughter. 'So transparent, Claire,' he scolded. 'You're trying to find out the depth of my sociopathic personality.' Then the anger bubbled up again. 'Do you not think I've been through enough psychiatrists to almost write the fucking textbooks myself?' He banged the table causing one of the prison officers to peer through the window.

Claire wafted him away with her hand and moved on. 'Why do you think *she* married *you*?'

He looked disinterested. She felt the detachment from him, his attention slide away. 'Who knows? Who cares? I don't. It seemed a good idea at the time. That's about all I can say.'

She tried again. 'You love her?'

Another burst of laughter. 'Love? What a wonderful sense of humour you have. Love under these circumstances? Shall I get philosophical, Claire, and ask in a thespian tone, *lerv*? What is *lerv*?'

She felt annoyed now. She was wasting time here. And she was learning nothing.

'Have you ever discussed your crimes with her?'

His response and body language were casual, hands still on the desk, but his eyes were wary. 'What do *you* think? Why don't you ask her?'

'I shall, when I meet her.'

He chewed his lip, thought for a moment, then admitted, 'We did speak about Petra and Jodie.'

He was reeling out a tiny length of rope. 'And the others?'

'Too repetitive,' he said.

Claire dug her fingernails into the palms of her hand as she thought how Shelley Cantor and Teresa Palmer's parents would respond to this dismissal of their daughters' murders. *Too repetitive.*

She made a feeble try. 'And after Petra and Jodie next in the sequence would be Marvel.'

'Would be. Yes.' His mouth curved. 'Except . . .' he said, wagging his index finger at her, in that irritating gesture.

'Except,' she picked up, 'that you have not confessed to Marvel's murder.'

Kobi deliberately tipped the interview into farce, putting a finger on his chin again. 'Oh no,' he mocked, speaking in pantomime falsetto. 'That's right. I haven't, have I?'

Claire kept her voice low and controlled. 'This isn't a joke, Kobi. This isn't fun. This is serious. I have a job to do, plenty of patients needing my attention. We have a dying man here. A missing daughter. A family who . . .' She had been about to say *cannot move on* but that was untrue and Kobi quickly picked it apart.

'Then I suggest you return to your patients and to that family who' – he wiggled his fingers – '"cannot move on" Except they have, haven't they?'

She eyed him steadily wondering how much he knew, how much was bravado and how much a clever device to twist the knife into her, Tom Trustrom, DS Willard, or anyone else who was affected by this girl's disappearance. Because that was what it was. A disappearance. No one could say she had been murdered. Girls did disappear in various circumstances and many of them never turned up again. They weren't all murdered. They weren't all dead. Some still walked the streets. Incognito.

'OK,' she said. 'Let's go back to November 2013.'

Kobi's response was to wet his lips and wait, his eyes trained on Claire.

'Let me remind you, Jonah. It was pouring with rain. A Saturday. You were in Hanley?'

His eyebrows lifted. 'Was I?'

'Maybe marauding? Cruising? Looking for . . .' She deliberately chose a word that would appeal. 'Entertainment?'

She expected anger or a denial but Kobi simply laughed. Genuine humour this time. 'You won't catch me out that way.'

'Let me remind you. You would have been supply teaching then.'

'Correct.' He could have been a games master on a TV quiz show.

She switched subjects. 'You dumped Shelley's body in Westport Lake,' she said, 'watched by a birdwatcher's camera. Was that a mistake?'

He jutted his chin forward. 'Guess.'

'I think you'd had enough of the game. I think you wanted to be caught.'

There was a flame of anger now. He looked around him. 'And spend my life in a dump like here?'

'That was always going to be the end result.'

Claire remembered back to the time, the panic that had spread around teenage schoolgirls in the whole of Staffordshire and Cheshire, the extra police drafted in to watch girls going home from school. A fear that the crimes would spread, maybe to Derbyshire or Shropshire or even country wide. The extracurricular activities that had been curtailed. And try telling any fourteen-year-old that they can't go shopping after school, that they must always stay in pairs, be accompanied. Girls who are latchkey young women and rebellious, girls who are gifted with the conviction that they will live for ever and never grow old. Girls who believe that carrying a mobile phone acts as protection.

She managed to inject some admiration into her voice. 'One thing's always puzzled me. With all the publicity. All the warnings. How on earth did you persuade Shelley Cantor to get in the car with you? The schoolgirl murders had been well publicised. Surely she was on her guard?'

Something flickered in his eyes. She'd caught him on the hop. She'd already looked at Shelley's abduction notes. Either the girl had been dragged into the car or the weather had persuaded her into a warm interior rather than struggling through snow. The clothes she'd been wearing had been school blazer, shirt, skirt, ankle socks and shoes. Hardly prepared for the polar conditions that had swept down the country. There was another possibility: that he'd had an accomplice. Just as Myra Hindley had persuaded children into Ian Brady's car, a female accomplice would allay any fears. But if there had been one she had not come forward or been identified. Kobi's car had held traces of Teresa Palmer and Shelley Cantor. No one else.

She frowned and gave Kobi the opportunity to recover his equilibrium. 'Look, Claire.' He spoke in a soft, reasonable voice. Probably the very same voice he had used to lure young girls into his car, in spite of their having been warned by recent events not to travel with people they did not know. 'You're looking in the wrong place.' He locked eyes with her, willing her to believe him. 'I didn't kill Marvel Trustrom.'

'So if you can't help me find her body to satisfy a dying man, why did you allow me to interview you?'

'Maybe boredom,' he said. 'Or maybe something else.' He shuffled forward in his chair, earnest now. 'Maybe being a killer myself, knowing girls of that age so well, I can understand events a bit better than you. Maybe I can help you.'

In spite of herself Claire was listening – hard.

'You need to look a bit closer to home. Look *inside* her family.'

As she looked into those clear eyes she wondered. Was this the truth? Was Kobi actually trying to help her? Or was it all part of the game?

She decided to play it anyway, throw the dice. 'OK, Kobi,' she said, 'enlarge on that.'

Her belief was still that he was looking for attention. He didn't know anything. He couldn't have insight into the mechanisms of Marvel's family. But, as a killer, his perspective might just be useful.

'OK,' he said steadily. 'You're wondering how I know about the family?'

'Yes.'

'I get the papers here,' he said, 'and we have the internet with certain sites forbidden. I've followed the case. You have the father who claims he's dying.'

She'd wanted to correct his statement but something in Kobi's eyes stopped her. He leaned forward. She could see the size of his pupils, the flare of his nostrils, the slackening of his mouth. 'He says he's dying but I guess you haven't seen his medical notes, have you?'

She shook her head, began to say, *I don't need to*, but stopped before the words were out.

Kobi continued. 'Check Marvel's dad's medical history. It's possible' – he opened his eyes wide – 'that he is *not* about to die.

It's just that his conscience is, at last, catching up with him.' He reached across the table. 'At least look into it.'

She kept her head still, neither nodding an affirmative nor shaking out a negative.

'So my suggestion is that you look first at Tom before investigating Marvel's mother, brother and two sisters.' He grinned. 'Since Marvel's disappearance the family's split apart, haven't they? Like an old, rotten, dead tree.'

Claire didn't respond. Her instinct was still that this was Kobi playing his game, wasting time, diverting her attention. He would love to see her scurry around, asking irrelevant questions, making herself look silly, feeling now, even from behind the prison walls, that he was in control. She shook her head, smiled and stood up. She was not going to allow Kobi to pull her strings.

But he hadn't finished with her yet. 'Think about it, Claire,' he said urgently, reaching out to touch her hand and something in his voice caught her attention. 'What have I got to gain by making it all up? I'm in here for life. I know that. I've got a wife outside. We'll never live together. I'll never fuck her. We'll never have a family of our own. I am paying for my crimes with my life. I won't get parole. So what do I get out of it?'

She headed for the door before turning around. 'I shan't come again, Jonah – not unless you really can help me with Marvel's case. And I don't mean trying to shift the focus on to the Trustrom family. It's a waste of my time. I have a hospital full of patients and endless queues of outpatients too. If you have something concrete to tell me let the prison warder know and I'll call. Otherwise it's goodbye, Mr Kobi. Thank you for agreeing to see me in the first place but I can't say you've really helped.'

The expression on his face stuck with her as she took the three steps towards the door. He should have looked crestfallen, but he didn't. He looked . . . triumphant.

She knocked on the door and the prison warder let her out.

TWENTY-FOUR

After such a day home should be peaceful. But even here there was no respite from conflict.

She heard the voices as soon as she opened the door that evening. 'Oh yeah, pull the other one. It's got bloody bells on it, mate.'

As Claire let herself in and stood in the hall, she sensed the woman's hostility like a dark cloud rolling down the stairs. The woman, presumably Simon's wife, was descending, Simon galloping down behind her. Both stopped and stared. This was her house, but in this instant it didn't feel like it.

Simon stepped in front of his wife. 'Claire,' he said, his face flushed and uncomfortable. 'This is Marianne.'

Claire held out her hand to the small, dark-haired woman with tight lips. 'Pleased to meet you,' she said, expecting at the very least a return of civilities.

But Marianne Bracknell ignored the outstretched hand and studied her. 'So you're Claire, are you?' She looked at her husband and then back at Claire. 'Sorry to break up your little twosome.' Her voice was positively venomous. 'Did he tell you he was married?'

'Yes. Of course. From the first.' Though that wasn't one hundred per cent true it was near enough.

And, by her response, Claire suspected Marianne sensed this. 'Oh, really?'

Claire winced at her scepticism. She tried once more to be pleasant to the petite woman bristling with anger. 'You've had a nice weekend, Marianne?' She didn't dare look at Simon who was even more flushed and embarrassed than usual at his wife's hostile outburst.

He managed to conjure up an answer for both of them. 'Yeah,' he said. 'Thanks. Lovely.'

The three of them stood awkwardly in the hall until Claire made the first move towards the stairs. 'I've been to the prison,' she said. 'I need a shower.'

Sitting in her bedroom, still slightly damp, she now regretted her decision to share her home with her colleague. His wife was nothing like she'd imagined.

She heard pots and pans clanking in the kitchen but couldn't face sharing the space with them. Twenty minutes later there was a soft knock on her door and Simon popped his head round. 'I'm really sorry,' he said. 'Since she lost the baby she hasn't been herself at all.'

'Well, I don't suppose your moving to the UK helped.'

'It was the wrong move. I know that now. I should have stayed there, with her, but when I saw there was an opening here . . . It's so important for my career. I need the experience.'

She held her hands up. 'Well, it's your decision,' she said. 'Your wife, your problem, but Simon, I'm not sure I want this sort of situation in *my* house.'

'No. No. I quite understand. I'm sorry. I'll . . .'

She anticipated his offer. 'There's no need for you to leave right away. Just sort it. Please?'

He nodded then grinned. 'We've left you some tea in the oven. Marianne's a great cook.'

She smiled and the mood between them evaporated.

But her house no longer felt like her home. The impulse to ask Simon to move into the top floor had backfired. Now it was she who was the outsider.

She spent the evening in her bedroom, watching a film on her iPad. The next morning she couldn't even remember what the film had been.

Wednesday 2 October, 8 a.m.

Even though there was no sign of either Simon or Marianne the next morning, she bolted her cereal and coffee and only felt at ease when she'd backed her car out of the drive and started to plan her day.

Today she was due to meet Miranda Pullen, the girl who had flipped the trigger. Whatever the rights or wrongs of her allegations Claire felt Miranda must have sensed something about her teacher. What was it?

At least the meeting would give her something to focus on

because so far her contact with Kobi felt unsatisfactory. She had learned nothing about the fate of Marvel Trustrom. Anything she did learn would probably come from another source. Kobi had suggested she look into Marvel's family. Was it possible he was right?

But unwittingly Kobi had given something away. He didn't want her to speak to his wife. And judging from the fact that Jessica had not contacted her, she wasn't too keen on speaking to her either. Claire's curiosity was aroused. She *would* pursue this lead. So when she had completed the ward round she dialled the number she had for Jessica Kobi using the hospital landline which would come up as an unknown number rather than her own mobile. After a few rings it was answered by a very wary voice. Claire outlined her proposal for a meeting, and it was quickly obvious that Kobi had got there first. 'Jonah doesn't want me to meet up with you,' she said apologetically. Then added, 'I'm sorry.'

Claire couldn't quite work out whether the reluctance came from Jonah or from Jessica herself. Whatever   she intended to pursue this course.

She wasn't going to take no for an answer.

'Why do you think your husband doesn't want us to meet?' Claire asked the question even though she already knew the answer. Kobi liked to write his own lines, didn't he? And that included his wife's lines too. He liked control, even from inside the prison. The other end of the line was silent. She pursued her advantage. 'What harm can it do?' she urged. 'Besides, would he need to know?'

'He'll know all right.' Jessica paused before adding, 'There's nothing I can tell you that he won't already have said to you. I didn't even know him at the time of the murders. It was afterwards.'

'I just wanted your take on it, Jessica, that's all.'

Her response was sharp and guarded. 'Take on what?'

'On the search for the missing girl. Has he ever mentioned her to you?'

'No.'

She'd answered too quickly. 'I thought he might have said something to you that might help us find her.'

'Well, he hasn't. I can't help you, Doctor.'

'Please?'

There was a long, tired sigh on the other end of the line as though she had been asked this question too many times before. 'Don't you guys ever give up? It was years ago. My husband has denied all knowledge of the girl. He had nothing to do with her. It didn't even fit the profile of his crimes. I've been married to him for just three years – the girl disappeared four years before that. Leave us alone?'

'He might have inadvertently said something?'

'I don't get it, Dr Roget.' She was riled now. 'How do you think I can possibly help you?'

'Men confide in their wives, Jessica.'

Her response was sharp and quick. 'Not when they're in prison. And not Jonah. Some men might confide in their wives the details of their crimes. Not him. We don't talk about them. We stick to . . . other subjects.'

Like what? Claire thought. *Politics? The weather? Impending holidays?* What else was there to talk about other than the events which had incarcerated him?

It had registered that Jessica hadn't called the crimes horrible or dreadful or even disgusting. Jessica continued, 'Some men might get off on it. Describing their crimes to their wives. Not Jonah. And . . .' Even over the phone Claire sensed her smiling. 'Some wives might even get a kick out of it too. Our relationship isn't like that.'

'So what is it like?'

There was a pause while Jessica Kobi thought up an answer. 'A sort of mutual respect,' she said. 'We find each other interesting.'

'Why did you marry him?'

Jessica's answer was defensive. 'What's it to do with you?'

'You know I've been asked to help – for the sake of Marvel's family, in particular her father. Knowing what attracted you to Jonah might just help us find the answer to what happened to this girl.'

'Hmm.'

Her scepticism hung in the air. Claire could have given up, put the phone down and abandoned this line of enquiry but she didn't. She pursued her quarry. 'I think it would be good if we met up – even if it is just the once.'

'All right.' Her voice was sulky. 'How are you fixed for next Friday? In the afternoon? I'll come to you. I know where you are.'

Back in her office, she browsed through DS Willard's notes again, this time focusing on the two last girls: Teresa Palmer, the fourteen-year-old whose body, still in school uniform, pristine white shirt and green and grey tie, knotted around her neck, had been crumpled into a wheelie bin; and Shelley Cantor, Kobi's last known victim, who had been found at the bottom of Westport Lake, rocks in her school bag keeping her weighted down. But, of course, the RSPB nesting box had been watching and recording as Kobi had dragged the girl's body over the sandy gravel, to the water's edge and then waded out until it was deep enough for her to sink. All recorded. A basic mistake, Claire thought. Surely he would have known this body's disposal was bound to be more public than simply tossing something out of a car? Had he wanted to be caught? Or, more likely this, had he not cared? That would fit in with his character. A complete disregard for the rules of normal society. But at least Shelley's death had led to Kobi's conviction and stopped him murdering any more girls. Jonah Kobi had finally been caught and charged.

And the city and the two counties breathed again. Teenage girls were let off the hook, allowed out for shopping trips or meeting up with friends for coffee. Life began again as though the colour had been leached back into the city.

Kobi's picture had been splashed all over the media and plenty of his ex-pupils had surfaced to write their own blogs and tweets and tell the world that they'd always known he was a weirdo. Except no one had really known, had they?

And among that plethora of girls Miranda Pullen had surfaced again and profited well from the story she told which was probably no more a fabrication than any other of the tall tales.

Where had Marvel's story fitted in to this?

And what would Jessica Kobi have to say about her husband?

It was four o'clock when Miranda Pullen finally rang and in a tight voice said she would be at the hotel in twenty minutes.

Eleven years brings quite a change as a schoolgirl morphs into a young woman though there was still the hint of a truculent teenager hovering just beneath the veneer of sophistication. Miranda Pullen was now in her twenties and had obviously thrived. She walked in on high heels and a smart, grey power suit, neatly striped hair in a bob and immaculate make-up, carrying a large, expensive-looking handbag. Her eyes were watchful, her manner guarded. In the intervening years Miranda Pullen had learnt something of the world. Claire shouldn't have been surprised but she was. This was a brittle woman who kept tight control. She walked elegantly towards her, head held high, wafting expensive perfume and displaying white, even teeth. Everything about her shrieked prosperity, success, confidence. She showed absolutely no vulnerability. Claire watched her carefully. This was a woman who was used to looking after herself.

'At a guess,' she said, sinking into one of the deeply upholstered armchairs, 'you're the psychiatrist who's been,' she wiggled her fingers in speech marks, 'involved with Mr Kobi.'

It was interesting that years later Miranda still called him by his teacher's title. Claire would have smiled but she didn't. Instead, she nodded. 'That's right,' she said, equally briskly. 'I'm Claire Roget, consultant forensic psychiatrist. I've been asked to speak to Mr Kobi to see if we can learn the fate of Marvel Trustrom.'

Miranda snorted. 'Well, good luck with that one.'

'Thank you.'

Claire had lined up her questions one after the other, but the woman's composure slightly nettled her.

Like the police before her, Miranda displayed certainty. 'He did it, you know.'

Claire ignored the comment and pressed on. 'How many of your allegations about Mr Kobi were true?'

Miranda smirked and lifted her perfectly shaped eyebrows. 'Excuse me?'

Claire simply waited.

She soon got a sulky response. 'I might have . . . embellished some of it.'

'Did he actually do *anything*?'

A cunning look crossed her face. 'He kept me back after lessons,' she said, tossing her hair.

'Why?'

'Oh, tried to make out I was using my mobile phone. But I

wasn't.' Her lipsticked mouth became a thin, unattractive scar. 'I
knew it was so he could look down my blouse, watch me cross
my legs.'

This didn't even deserve a response.

'Did he actually touch you?'

'Who's to know? There were just the two of us in the room.'
She gave the self-satisfied smile of a woman who believes she is
irresistibly attractive and flicked her hair away from her face. 'And
he's in prison and likely to stay there. So who' – she leaned her
face towards Claire's – 'is to know?'

'It must have taken quite something to persist in your story
when the tabloids became interested.'

The eyelashes flickered at the word 'story', but Miranda was
losing none of her equilibrium.

'And of course, he was found innocent.'

That provoked a laugh. 'Well, they were wrong, weren't they?
And if they hadn't made such a mistake maybe one or more of
those girls would still be alive.'

'How much money did the tabloids pay you for your story?'

Even that didn't faze Miranda. 'Enough to pay off my student
loan.'

And again, unexpectedly, Claire again found herself on the same
side as Kobi. She disliked the girl intensely. She drew breath.

'And look at me now,' Miranda crowed. 'I have a good job.
A car. I'm getting married next year. Notoriety has served me
well.'

Claire studied her face. Did she not realize she was the one
who had lit the spark? And if she did feel she was in any way
responsible for the four murders would she care? In her own
way Miranda Pullen was as much a psychopath as Kobi.

'What was he like? What made you home in on him?'

'Creepy.'

'In what way?'

Miranda Pullen crossed her legs. 'The way he'd stare at you.'
She frowned. 'You know in books they say a man undresses the
heroine with his eyes?'

Claire jumped in, interested in her use of words. 'Do you class
yourself then as a heroine?'

Miranda became thoughtful. 'Look,' she said, 'you're the

psychiatrist. Male teachers respond in a certain way to teenage girls. They play along with them. Mr Kobi – well, he just didn't engage. He was wooden except when he looked at me. I began to wonder . . .' She drew in close again, enjoying the feeling of confidentiality. 'I began to wonder if I'd be able to tempt him. It became a sort of challenge.' Her expression changed, became almost coy. 'I tried a few tricks but he wasn't biting. I began to wonder whether he was gay – or bi or simply impotent.'

'He'd been married,' Claire reminded her.

'Yes, but it didn't last, did it? And lots of gay men marry just as a smokescreen.'

'And now he's re-married.'

That drew a chortle of laughter. 'Some marriage,' she said disparagingly.

'So you wanted to bait him.'

For the first time since she'd arrived, Miranda coloured. 'What's he like now?' she asked in a small voice.

'I've only met him when he's been in prison for three years. He's probably changed.'

Miranda was silent, working out her response. 'Some people might have found him attractive . . . then.'

And Claire saw through it. *She* had found Kobi attractive. But he had ignored her. And so she had extracted her revenge. That was how it had really been.

And possibly realizing her cover had been blown, Miranda shuffled in her seat. 'Is that all or is there something else you'd like me to go through with you?'

Claire shook her head. 'But you're convinced he is responsible for Marvel's disappearance?'

Miranda's response mirrored Zed Willard's. 'Who else?'

The question rang in her brain all the way home. *Who else?*

She was deep in thought as she turned into her drive. Simon's car had gone so she assumed he and Marianne had gone out somewhere. Hopefully somewhere where they could sort out their differences. She couldn't cope with a warring couple under her roof. But she felt some sympathy for Simon's wife. She'd miscarried her child. And then her husband had taken a contract on the other side of the world. A double loss.

She was so absorbed in reflections she almost didn't notice a girl standing in the shadow of the trees that marked her boundary. Waterloo Road, Burslem, had once had a reputation for being a red-light area. But in the last five years it had been cleaned up. The girls had gone, probably elsewhere. Claire stood still for a moment trying to make out the girl's features. She wasn't speaking, and although the night was cold she was wearing a micro skirt, long black shiny boots and T-shirt. They looked at one another. Claire didn't say anything. To offer, *Can I help you?* would have been fatuous. It was obvious that the girl was hoping for business. She was slim, average height, had thick, dark hair that rippled down her back and looked young – perhaps not even twenty. Claire locked the car and took a step towards her front door. When she looked back, she felt that the girl wanted to speak to her. She half-turned but someone else was walking along the street. With a heavy tread, determined, focused. Masculine. The girl shrank back against the hedge. A miasma of fear seemed to form around her. A hand reached out and the girl slipped away back into the night.

It is strange how a street in a densely populated urban area can suddenly seem empty of people. The girl had vanished somewhere out of the arcs of light cast by the lampposts. It was as though she was never there. As Claire turned away from the street towards her front door, she realized the encounter had brought something home to her. Girls vanished for many different reasons. Many were never found. Some were trafficked, others descended into drugs, prostitution or simply formed a new identity. A few were murdered, their bodies not found for years; some remains were never found. And this might be the end result of the investigation into Marvel Trustrom's fate.

They might never know.

TWENTY-FIVE

She might have resented the tense atmosphere between Simon and his wife, but the house seemed eerily quiet without them and she took a moment to steady herself. 'Stupid,' she told herself.

Walking through into the kitchen she found that Simon had left
a note on the kitchen table simply saying they'd headed off for a
few days' holiday. Good idea. Claire put her bag down and linked
her phone to the charger. She had the place to herself – again.
Bliss. It felt a welcome situation but also strange, foreign and
unreal. A bit lonely and isolated. Even though it was late she was
tempted to pick up the phone, speak to either Adam or Adele or
even Grant, but she desisted. She wanted to think. She needed to
think. She always had concerns about a number of patients and
usually a glass of wine and the peace and quiet of home settled
her mind. But not tonight. Her mind was disordered. The case of
Jonah Kobi and the missing girl was disturbing her.

She slept badly that night, tossing and turning through turmoil,
dreams of the dead girl now alive, now dead. Body tossed somewhere but never found, Kobi wagging his finger at her, as though
he was a schoolteacher telling her off for poor spelling or not
handing in her homework. He had assumed a dominant role in her
mind, and when she woke she was hot and sweaty. She showered,
slipped on her dressing gown and went online to read the news
headlines as she drank some coffee.

When you first wake and read the headlines, they do not initially
sink in.

She read them three times before realizing what was being said.
And then she understood.

Just a small paragraph.

> Police are to reopen the case of missing schoolgirl, Marvel
> Trustrom.

There it was, in black and white. Why hadn't Willard told her they
were going public with this? To flush something or someone out?

> It is understood that in the hope of finding out the truth behind
> the disappearance of schoolgirl Marvel Trustrom, who disap-
> peared in 2013 and whose body has never been found, a
> forensic psychiatrist has been visiting Jonah Kobi, the teacher
> currently serving four life terms for the murder of schoolgirls
> Petra Gordano and Jodie Truss in 2012, Teresa Palmer in
> 2014 and Shelley Cantor in 2015.

There was some detail about Kobi's past and the murders but nothing new.

She sat back in her chair, sipped her coffee slowly and gave herself time to absorb this news and the anger she felt at her involvement being leaked to the press. It didn't actually name her but there were few psychiatrists in Stoke-on-Trent and only one forensic psychiatrist. Her. For anyone in the know it wouldn't take long to point a finger at her name.

So who had provided this particular little story? Anyone could have fed it to them. There were quite a few people now who knew she'd been asked to visit Kobi and plenty more who were aware that she actually had. It could be any one of a number of people: a prisoner, a prison guard, Kobi himself, Mrs Kobi, Marvel's family, Tom Trustrom or his partner as well as someone from the police or even a work colleague from Greatbach. It could even be Miranda Pullen trying to extract a few more pounds from her largely made-up story. It meant nothing. And yet it had drawn her attention to something. Claire sat back and touched her forehead in exasperation. She should have realized this. There it was, staring her in the face and she had somehow walked straight past it. The newspaper article correctly described Kobi as a teacher, briefly mentioning the allegations that had led to him resigning his post in the Macclesfield school and taking up employment as a supply teacher working at various schools in and around the Potteries. Which schools? What she needed was a more detailed work record. Every single school he had worked at in the years between 2010 and 2016 when he had finally been convicted of all four murders.

She looked more carefully at the dates. Petra had been killed in April 2012. Only two months later Jodie Truss had died. Marvel's disappearance had been in November of 2013. Then in October 2014 Teresa Palmer had met her end, and finally Shelley Cantor in the November of 2015.

She rang DS Willard, who denied having fed the story to the press. In fact, he sounded outraged at the leak and was so defensive it handed her an advantage. Which she used.

'I need a detailed list of all the schools Kobi worked at between 2010 and 2016.' When she sensed his hesitation, she added, 'I take it you have them?'

'Of course. But, Claire. It's a long list. Some of those schools he only worked at for a couple of days.'

'I still think I'd better go through them. Did he ever work at the school where Marvel attended?'

'Yeah. A couple of times. But he didn't teach her class. He taught the older girls.'

'OK, well, if you wouldn't mind emailing it over to me.'

'Yeah. Of course.'

Thankfully he didn't ask her how she was getting on.

She scanned the article again. In spite of the sensational headline there was nothing new in it apart from the fact that she was involved. That this was being made so public made her uneasy. She preferred to work in secret, behind closed, preferably locked, doors. Something else made her skin prickle. Would the leaking of her involvement to the press have any consequences?

So what next?

The temptation was to follow Kobi's suggestion, drop down the rabbit hole and look into Marvel's family. But it could have been a device flung in front of her merely to deflect her from the truth.

Maybe Jessica Kobi would be more enlightening, but for now she needed to focus on her work here, in Greatbach.

She had a morning spent with the police and the CPS advising on the parole panel. Always a worry and always a responsibility. Were you letting a wild animal out of its cage to prey on some unwary member of the general public or some old crony they had a score to settle with? On the one hand you had a prisoner who wanted out (or at least most of them did). Others, particularly lifers, having spent a significant number of years behind bars, in the protected environment of a prison, were fearful of stepping to the outside where they had lost connections and there was often no family, no friends and the support given to them by the state was lacking. To the outside world they were always ex-cons whereas inside they were the norm.

Get it wrong and you robbed a prisoner of a chance of life outside. Get it wrong and you let a wild animal out of its cage.

Today they were considering three cases. An armed robber who had held up a building society, a killer and an elderly man who had abused young boys in the late nineties. Claire had interviewed each one at length, making an assessment. The case conferences would go on for most of the day leaving Salena Urbi to cover the wards, which meant she wouldn't see Ilsa until later on, when she would prepare her for formal discharge the following morning.

Sometimes Claire ruminated over the consequences of the decisions made by the parole board but today her conscience was more focused on Salena Urbi's workload, so she headed upstairs to the ward once the conferences were finished. And as anticipated, Salena was struggling.

Ilsa was sitting in the corner, her face immobile except for her lips which were moving in some internal conversation. An argument judging by her fixed scowl and impassioned expression.

Claire began with innocuous questions. 'Are you ready to be transferred to the clinic in Birmingham for a little while before going home?'

Ilsa turned her pale eyes on Claire. 'I want to go home.'

Claire sat down in the armchair. Why was she uneasy about this change of mind? 'Why don't you fall in with your husband's suggestion? And then in a couple of weeks you can go home to John and Augustus.'

Ilsa drew in a sharp breath. 'Claire,' she said, 'I want you to remember something.' Claire waited. 'Remember this. I believe my husband and my "best" friend are plotting to kill me.' She was watching her intently.

Claire stiffened. 'Why would they do that?' Was this fact or a paranoid delusion?

'I know he is having an affair with her.'

'He denies it.'

Ilsa's smile was stiff. 'He would,' she said. 'My husband likes to pretend. One of the things he likes to pretend about is that he is a good man, a devoted husband.' Her expression was snake-like.

Claire played it safe. 'That's certainly my impression.'

Ilsa looked at her pityingly but with a touch of contempt. 'So you are fooled too.'

'I don't think so. But Ilsa, you're a lot better now. You don't need to be here. It's time for you to go.'

'OK. But remember this. It's important Claire.'

As Claire left the room half an hour later, she wondered. Ilsa appeared convinced about this affair between her husband and best friend. So who was the one who was deluded – or lying? John or his wife?

If John was lying, he was a consummate actor. The temptation was to trust his version of events and put Ilsa's version down to her precarious mental state. But . . .

She documented it all the same and knew that she was not in any danger of forgetting Ilsa's words.

Remember this. There had seemed a special significance in the words and the way she had spoken them. Almost a threat? What was she planning? Why had she planted that seed of doubt?

Claire wrote up her notes, spent more time discussing the case with Astrid.

And so the day passed.

At five o'clock, Rita rang. Jessica Kobi was waiting for her downstairs.

TWENTY-SIX

It's hard not to form a picture of someone you are about to meet. Claire was intrigued, her curiosity bubbling up like an underground spring. This was a first for her, interviewing a woman who had married a lifer *after* his sentence. The voice on the phone had sounded decisive and in control when she would have thought that a woman marrying in such circumstances, especially to someone who had committed multiple murders of young girls, would have been just another victim, someone who had problems forming normal relationships. After all – what was in it for her? What on earth could be *her* motive?

A do-gooder – someone who believed they could reform him?

Notoriety? Maybe capitalising on it: writing articles, novels, selling her story, perhaps even extracting further details of his crimes that she could use in some way?

A love of intrigue?

She leaned back in her seat, rolling her pen between finger and thumb, analysing.

Was it possible there was another explanation? Surely, surely the motive for marrying a serial killer could not be love? That beautiful, selfless emotion? How could she fall in love? Why had Kobi married her? It didn't make sense.

But thoughts of love led her along another pathway. She retrieved her mobile phone from the bottom of her bag and, before she could change her mind, texted Grant. *Hey, you. Fancy cooking for me tonight?*

She watched the screen for some response, and when there wasn't one she reluctantly switched it off. She could not have it pinging in the interview.

The first thing that struck her about Kobi's wife was how petite she was. Almost childlike though she was in her early twenties. The second observation was that though the packaging was different – Jessica had arrived in ripped jeans and biker boots – there were similarities between Jessica and Miranda Pullen. Jessica was similarly self-assured, with a disconcerting gaze. Although she was small, she looked strong and entered with an assured stride, dropping into the chair with a silent challenge. Surely, Claire thought, she was just the type that Kobi hated? She had a clear, clean, freckled face which was easy to read, grey eyes with long lashes. She wore no lipstick and very little foundation. Her main adornments were four ear piercings which reached along the pinna and a nose stud. Her hair was stripey brown, shoulder length, thick and straight and her gaze was direct. She held her hand out as Claire greeted her.

'So we meet at last,' she said, her mouth twisted with some of her husband's cynicism.

Claire nodded and indicated a chair opposite.

She began by thanking her for coming and Jessica Kobi responded with a regal bend of her head in acknowledgement. Then she waited for Claire to begin the interview.

'Mrs Kobi,' Claire began, only too aware of the questions she really wanted to ask.

Kobi's wife waited.

'Do you understand why I've become involved in this case?'

Jessica Kobi gave a sharp intake of breath which could have been interpreted as an expression of irritation. Claire chose to ignore it until she spoke.

'Of course I do,' she said. 'The one girl whose body has not been found.' She folded her arms and looked confrontational. 'My husband has assured me he knows nothing about this girl's disappearance. You understand?' In case Claire hadn't got the message, she repeated more forcefully, 'He denies it.'

Claire nodded. 'And you believe this to be the truth?'

Jessica Kobi slowly unfolded her arms and spread her hands out. 'Why would he lie to me?'

'Perhaps because this is the one murder he has not been convicted of and thus could have a renewed sentence?'

Jessica Kobi blew out her cheeks in derision. 'Come on, Doctor,' she said. 'What bloody difference can it make? Jonah's been handed four life sentences. Life times four. He's unlikely to come out. Ever.' She spat the last word out with vitriol.

It gave Claire an opportunity to delve. 'Would you want him to come out?'

Kobi's wife shrugged. 'I don't know,' she said. 'It isn't really part of the deal.'

'The deal?' Claire was struggling to understand her.

Jessica Kobi gave a twisted smile. 'Life means life. That's what they say, isn't it? It's what they want. Throw away the key.'

'If he did come out,' Claire said slowly, 'how would that impact on your marriage?'

That drew another twisted smile. 'It's certainly not what I signed up for.'

Another golden opportunity. 'So what *did* you sign up for?'

Jessica's smile this time was pure cynicism. 'None of your business,' she said. 'That is between me and my husband.'

And Claire nodded. *Fair enough.*

Remembering that an appeal was more likely to bear fruit than confrontation she angled her next question appropriately. 'Are you able to help me at all with the investigation into Marvel Trustrom's disappearance?'

Strangely enough the name had an effect on Kobi's wife. Her mouth opened as though to protest. But then she closed it again. 'I . . .' Then: 'No. I'm not.'

Claire moved on. 'When and how did this romance between you and Jonah start, Jessica?'

Kobi's wife studied her for a moment before smiling. It was

not a nice smile. There was no warmth in it. Only coldness, hostility and mockery. 'You're the psychiatrist,' she said. 'Work it out.'

Though Claire groaned inwardly she kept her voice steady in her reply. 'You read about him in the paper and thought he looked interesting?'

Jessica's look was pure disdain. 'That'll do,' she said.

After a pause Claire pursued the subject. 'Why marry?' she asked. 'Why not simply write to each other as friends?'

Jessica's answer was strangely soulless and unconvincing. 'They need someone on the outside,' she said woodenly. 'Someone they can trust.'

'But what's in it for you?'

The grey eyes slid over her with even more disdain. 'Does there have to be something in it for me?'

Claire tried another tack. 'Wouldn't you prefer to have a partner on the outside?'

Jessica shook her head leaving Claire puzzled.

'What job do you do?'

The innocuous question caused Jessica Kobi to look wary. 'I'm a teacher,' she said. 'I just graduated.' She smiled. 'In history.'

Did that give Claire a clue? 'Did you know Jonah before all this?'

Jessica shook her head.

'Did he ever teach you?'

'I went to school in Shrewsbury,' she said. 'I don't believe Jonah ever taught there. If he did he certainly didn't teach me.'

'Is there a connection between the fact that you both studied history?'

That was the point at which Kobi's wife disengaged. 'I don't see that's anything to do with the focus of your enquiries,' she said and stood up.

Claire appealed. 'Please,' she said, 'all I want is to satisfy a dying man's request for us to locate his daughter's body so they can be buried together.'

Jessica gave a squeal of laughter. 'And you think I can help by tricking my husband into confessing to something he didn't do.'

'You're convinced of that?'

Jessica Kobi bent over the desk. 'Yes, I am,' she said.

Then she was gone, leaving Claire unaccountably uncomfortable.

It can take a while to have a handle on a person's character. But Jessica Kobi's personality defied any classification. Having spent less than a quarter of an hour in her company, Claire was still unsure what sort of person she was or why she had married Kobi. There was a reason, she was sure, but she could not work out what it was. And that spread around in her head like a virus.

She thought she'd had enough shocks for one day, but she was due for one more. Having forgotten to switch her phone back on she had missed Grant's response. His battered Peugeot was in the drive and the scent of cooking greeted her as she let herself in. He stood in the doorway of the kitchen, spatula in hand, striped butcher's apron knotted around his waist. It felt so good to see him that she simply walked up to him, put her arms around his neck and kissed him full on that soft mouth. When his mouth was free, he laughed. 'It's only spag bol,' he said. 'No need for a fuss,' and returned to his pan of pasta. Something meaty bubbled in the pan next to it. Then he turned around. 'You all right, Claire?'

He'd always been quick to pick up on the subtle signs.

'I have had a shit day,' she said. 'And I need more than a hug.'

He looked warily at her. 'Before or after tea?'

When they were finally sitting down and he'd grilled her about her shit day's work, while she'd relished the feeling of having someone to offload to she'd finally exhausted the subject. 'Let's change the record,' she said. 'What about your day. How's the job going?'

He rested his fork on the side of his plate, frowning, his dark eyes troubled.

'I can't work the guy out,' he said without explanation. 'He treats everyone like a lackey. Even me sometimes.' He blew his cheeks out. 'But God, he pays well. He's set up a standing order. No quibbles about the price of anything. For a businessman he's careless about money, doesn't check the receipts. Personally I think he just wants to impress people. Or else he's trying to buy someone's affection.'

'The missing wife?' She wound the spaghetti round her fork.

'Maybe.' Grant shook his head. 'But she still hasn't shown up.'

'Perhaps she's abroad.'

'Yep. But he is an odd guy.'

'You don't have to like him, Grant,' she pointed out reasonably, 'you just have to make the place how he wants it.'

His frown deepened. 'And that's the trouble, Claire. He doesn't really know what he wants. He wants something but I don't think he's quite sure what.'

She wound another coil of spaghetti round her fork. 'Does he need clear ideas? Isn't that why they employ someone like you?'

'Yes. But I need some idea of what they hope to achieve.'

She frowned. 'I wouldn't know where to start.'

He laughed at that. 'And sometimes neither do I.'

She poured out another half glass of wine.

And he continued. 'The house is really nice as it is. It's an old house. It's not possible to turn it into exactly what he wants.'

'Right. You can do it, can't you?'

'Ye-es. Sort of – inside, at least. But he says his wife's difficult to please.' He caught something in her eye. 'Claire?'

'What's the man's name?'

The truth was she'd already guessed it.

TWENTY-SEVEN

Monday 7 October, 7.45 a.m.

The morning drive brought a call on her car phone from DS Zed Willard trying to sound friendly, but actually she could tell he was chivvying her along. 'Uh, just wondering how things were going with Kobi?'

'I haven't arranged to see him again,' she said, compelled to add, 'I'm getting nowhere with him, Zed. It's a waste of time. He's told me absolutely nothing and his wife insists he didn't have anything to do with Marvel's disappearance.'

'And she'd know,' he jeered.

'If anyone does,' she countered.

He still persisted. 'You couldn't appeal to his conscience?'

Had the situation not had at its heart a tragedy Claire might just have squeezed out a laugh. 'Zed,' she said, as gently as when she taught fourth-year medical students. 'Psychopaths and socio-paths don't have the full gamut of emotions. They experience anger but not fear, impatience and irritation but not the capacity for restraint. They certainly can't experience guilt or sympathy or empathy. Unhappiness translates straight to anger. Fear makes them lash out. I can't tap into Kobi's conscience because he doesn't have one.'

'Oh.' It came out as a frustrated sound. 'So what can you appeal to?'

'His vanity, his wanting to play along, to keep me interested enough to continue to visit him, a wish for entertainment.'

'You can do this?'

'I have to let him stew, but Zed, I'm not convinced it'll lead to any solid facts about the disappearance of Marvel. He's quite capable of making things up just to make sure I carry on visiting him.'

'But he did it?' Willard's voice was just that little bit too eager.

'I don't know. If I have anything concrete to tell you I'll be in touch. OK?' She was as anxious to end the conversation as DS Willard was to prolong it. 'I'm doing what I can behind the scenes, I promise. But for now I have nothing to add, nothing to help you.'

'Maybe something'll turn up,' he said grumpily.

'Maybe. And Zed, send me that list of the schools Kobi worked at when he was supply teaching.'

'I'll get around to it,' he said, still not engaging. 'But it goes on for ever. We're talking six years here.'

'It'll be through an agency,' she said. 'They'll have a record.'

Driving into Greatbach, Claire's mind moved back to her patients. Ilsa had been transferred on Friday to the clinic in Birmingham. Maybe she should simply wash her hands of the whole affair. But at least she understood now why John had been adamant he didn't want his wife home. It seemed he was employing Grant to trans-form his home and, hopefully, through that, his marriage? There was a sort of twisted logic in all this. Well, good luck to the man though she doubted a home refurbishment would solve all of Ilsa and John Robinson's problems.

She was hardly distracted as she battled her way through a

clinic of outpatients, all with their own troubling problems. Depression, anxiety, two ex-policemen, witnesses to a particularly gruesome crime, who now suffered from PTSD. At the end she dictated her letters while eating a sandwich and drinking strong coffee. Then she climbed up to the top floor to check on her inpatients.

Three hours later she returned to her office and a note from Rita on her desk saying that Mr Jonah Kobi wanted to see her again. At the bottom she'd added a further note. *He sounds desperate and says please do come!*

Maybe this time, she thought, he might give her something concrete about the case. She looked at her watch. It was four o'clock. Most of her work was finished. She could afford to visit him and then, maybe, take her bike out along the towpath. The afternoon was golden and the temperature as she left Greatbach unseasonably warm. It was her favourite time of year when all the colours on the trees seemed to brighten before they faded and the leaves fell.

Kobi was already sitting down when she entered the visitors' room. And he was looking thoughtful, almost pensive. Probably working out how to justify this summons. His eyes flickered as he thanked her for coming. Was she imagining it, was there a note of humility in his voice? Or was he acting? She sat down and placed her notebook in front of her, leaned back in the chair and regarded him steadily.

'What did you want to see me about? You'd better not be messing me around.' She'd meant to sound firm but not quite so snappy, and he looked surprised, jerked out of his complacency. He didn't answer straight away but licked his lips, wondering whether to speak.

'Kobi?'

Much of his arrogance had melted away. He looked genuinely troubled. 'I don't know how to convince you,' he said. 'But you're looking in the wrong place.'

'Convince me of what?'

He met her eyes then. 'I didn't kill her,' he said. And then with urgency, he continued, 'It has none of the hallmarks of my work. Claire, surely you can see that? Why *should* I take the rap for someone else's crime?'

He was sounding convincing. She needed to test him with an idea she had.

'OK,' she said finally, 'let's talk about the years after you'd left the school at Macclesfield.'

Kobi looked puzzled. He couldn't work out why she was taking this route instead of pressing him. And, unable to see where this was heading, he was also wary, his eyes flicking around the small, empty room.

Nothing to see there, Kobi.

'If, as you say, you are innocent of the abduction of Marvel Trustrom, there was more than a two-year gap between the murder of Jodie Truss, and Teresa Palmer.'

'I told you. I did some travelling.'

'But you returned to work.' She spoke with assurance, as though she knew this for certain. *Damn Willard. Get me that list.*

'I did some supply work.' This was dragged out with reluctance.

'Where?'

'Around the place.'

This was a new sensation – Kobi on the hop.

She'd touched on something he hadn't wanted to share.

'Can you give me a list?'

He shook his head, frowning. 'I can't remember everywhere. Schools around the Potteries – mainly.' He shifted uncomfortably in the chair.

Oh, Mr Kobi, she thought. *I'm treading on your corns, aren't I?*

'OK.' She stood up as though to go. 'I can easily find out.'

'You haven't even asked me why I wanted to see you – what I had to tell you.'

'OK. Go on.'

'You spoke to Jess.'

'Yes.'

The silence between them extended. Kobi licked his lips.

'You're worried she might have told me something?'

He gave a quick jerk of his head.

'I did find her interesting to talk to. And, of course, Miranda too.'

And then he burst out. 'Couldn't stand the posh little madams,' he said. 'Fucking cunts the lot of them.'

She didn't enter the discussion but continued smoothly, 'But when you were found innocent of misconduct you didn't leave the Macclesfield school straight away. You stayed on for another year. Why?'

'That's obvious. If I'd gone straight away the allegation would have followed me. I'd never have got another job however desperate they were for a history teacher.'

'You must have resented the "posh little madams" even more.'

'What do you think?'

'Finally leaving in 2010.'

His eyes flickered. He was wondering where all this was leading.

'So you were supply teaching at the time when Marvel went missing.'

'You're not listening.' He banged the table. 'I said I was travelling.' He ran his hand through his hair. 'Why do you keep coming back to that?'

'Because that's my remit. The only reason I'm here at all.'

He scooped in a long breath and sat back, looking drained.

She watched him and wondered. What was going on inside that twisted little brain of his?

She carried on, noting that this was still an area he didn't want her to explore. 'Wouldn't you like it to be known that you'd hoodwinked the police for all these years?'

He was smiling now, back on track, sure enough of his ground to mock her. 'You're trying to appeal to my vanity. Oh, Claire. You'll have to be more subtle than that.'

'Acknowledged.' She flapped her hand. 'Look, Kobi, I have more than enough work to do. If you can't help me find out what happened to this poor girl then I'm wasting my time again, aren't I?'

His eyebrows rose. 'I did ask you here for a reason.'

She waited.

He leaned forward, speaking earnestly. 'I know these girls, Dr Roget.' He'd reverted to rolling his 'r's' and rubbing in her French connection. He must have noted how it made her wince and was using it as a barb. She swallowed while he continued, speaking earnestly. 'I understand the way their mind works. The tricks they play. The lies they tell, the way they give you the come on just before the fuck off.'

'So you did know Marvel?'

He shook his head. 'You're not going to catch me like that, Madame Roget. But think of it this way.' There was an urgency in his voice accompanied by a frown and rapid blinking as the words spilled out of him. 'I'm actually sick of all this speculation that I murdered this fucking girl. I never met her so I didn't even know her. But she's not like those other girls. You're looking in the wrong place. And think of it this way. Because *I know* I'm innocent I've got the sense to look elsewhere. That's why I tell you, search in her family. They're hiding something. I know this because I've been a killer myself. I've squeezed the life out of these little hussies. I know how someone feels when they plot and plan and know what they've done, just waiting for the headlines to hit, the panic to spread like a moorland fire.' His eyes were shining, his lips wet. 'Take my advice. Look into Marvel Trustrom's family. If you won't listen to me there's no point your coming here at all. It's all wasted time. You wanted a lead. I'm giving you one. Handing it to you on a plate. I know these things. I am a killer. I know how killers work.'

She was silent, absorbing his words and the passion that lay behind them. How did he know Marvel's family were hiding something? Yet this felt real and genuine. But it was weird, as though she and Kobi were working on the same side.

She waited but there was no more. He had said all he was going to say. She picked up her bag and gave him a last opportunity, doubts creeping through her mind like a virus, as she watched his shoulders tense. At least she could interpret this one. He didn't want her to go. Not yet. She was providing him with sport, entertainment. Drinking up the barren hours.

He waited until her hand was on the door handle. 'There is something else,' he said quietly. 'Something I can prove. Something tangible.'

She turned, the challenge in her eyes. 'Look at any of the articles about Marvel,' he urged. 'Then read between the lines. That family,' he said, 'was dysfunctional. I know they're hiding something.'

'Where did you get this from?'

'I read,' he said, 'between the lines. Look at the parents, the brother, the sisters.' And then, disconcertingly, he giggled. 'You have to admit it,' he said, 'you're intrigued. I have you on a string.'

She turned and faced him. 'Can you give me any hard evidence that you had nothing to do with Marvel's disappearance?'

'Such as?'

'Well, like where you were that rainy November day when Marvel went missing?'

'I just told you. I can't actually remember. I was probably travelling. It's a long time ago,' He waited. 'The police will have asked me. It'll be in my statement.'

'Stop handing out vague hints. If you have something then tell me. Otherwise . . .'

'OK,' he said, holding his hand up. 'OK. I'm a teacher. I know these girls. I can read them like the veins on the back of my hand. I never met Marvel. I've only read about her but because I knew this would be pinned on me I read everything I could about her. And because I kill girls . . .' He said this as casually as if he had confessed he smoked the odd cigarette or drank a glass or two of wine a day. 'Because I kill girls – of a certain type – I could see into the crime and the person who perpetrated it. It's a family crime.' His eyes were bold. 'It's not me. It's not a crime of hatred. You should know that. I discarded those girls' bodies because I wanted them and their peer group to be afraid.'

Watching his face, Claire felt this was the truth. But if it wasn't him then it was someone else. Kobi could be right it could be someone in the family. She stared at him for a little while, wishing she could divine whether he was lying cleverly or telling the truth, actually trying to help her. But her training had warned her. The character of someone with a severe personality disorder is set for life as is an optimistic nature or pessimism. People do not change. They simply grow older. And in the wake of that their crimes diminish because they grow lazy.

'What have you got to lose,' he urged softly, creeping under her skin with his words, 'by talking to them? With your skills you should be able to suss out lies from the truth and work out what really happened to the poor, little, fat girl.'

Perhaps it was the phrase or possibly it was his tone but something alerted Claire. She looked hard at him but read nothing except a pasted-on, bland, almost innocent expression.

Kobi continued smiling, his head on one side as he watched her. How she wanted to displace that smile. Claw it away from his face. As it was, she used the only weapon she had. 'I thought your wife was rather interesting,' she dropped in casually.

Apart from a miniscule shrinking of his pupils, Kobi did not react.

'I often wonder,' she mused, 'just what it is that persuades a woman to marry a man she has no hope of having any sort of normal relationship with.' She waited for the words to take effect, for the anger to catch fire. For him to defend his virility.

But Kobi simply smiled. 'It's an interesting point to ponder,' he said steadily. 'I daresay you could write a thesis on it.'

How could he possibly know that?

TWENTY-EIGHT

She left the prison with conflicting emotions, questions buzzing around in her head – just as Kobi had wanted. But she had to admit it: Kobi pointing the finger at Marvel's family opened up new possibilities. Ones she hadn't even considered; neither had the police.

He could still be playing with her but the fact that she'd spent some time with Jessica had rattled him. She sighed. Who knew with Kobi? She sat in the car, the prison walls looming in front of her until, frowning, she rang DS Willard, already anticipating his response.

At first, he was evasive when she asked her question. Had they considered any possibility other than Marvel's disappearance being down to Kobi? Had they investigated the family? Fully?

He almost exploded. 'Honestly?' She heard the ring of defence and waited.

'No. We linked it straight away to the other two schoolgirl deaths.'

She hung up on Willard.

The trouble was, apart from Tom, she had no access to the girl's family; Marvel's mother had already displayed her reluctance to get involved.

Cancelling her bike ride, she returned to Greatbach.

Back in her office she opened the file and dragged her finger down the names, reading her own scanty notes.

Mother: Dixie, moving on with her new life, anxious to put it all behind her. Sisters: Sorrel and Clarice, kids when their sister had gone missing. Both in their late teens now. Brother: Shane, married and with a small baby.

Take six years away from them and Shane would have been eighteen, Sorrel twelve, Clarice eleven. A young family who had lost their oldest sister. And that was the correct word. Lost. Marvel was lost.

So where should she start? Try sticking a pin in, she thought sourly, wishing she'd never been dragged into this unholy mess. What had started out as a help to a dying man was somehow turning into a police investigation.

Claire recalled Dixie's words with their hint of something. *Special . . . little . . . girl.* What had she meant by that phrase? That Tom had loved Marvel more than the two younger girls? Strangely enough, recalling the tone of Dixie's voice Claire didn't think so. Resentment? Irony? Claire wasn't sure. Had she sat across from Marvel's mother she could have read her body language, observed each twitch of her facial muscles. But a phone conversation left her with no clues. In that way, she reflected, the phone is a blunt instrument without the accompanying body language and facial expression. The thought was persistent. Was it *only* because Tom was dying that he wanted this 'closure'? Or was it something to do with the exposure of the real truth? So what about Dixie? There had been a hint of bitterness when she had spoken about her daughter's uncertain fate in relation to the other families' tragedies. And . . . was she imagining it . . . was her recall playing tricks? Had Dixie sounded almost apprehensive that her daughter *would* be found? How could that be – unless someone in the family was involved? And not Kobi at all?

The obvious answer was to try her again. Speak to her. See her. Watch her.

She fingered her phone.

Dixie Trustrom listened without comment while Claire explained that her daughter's fate was still uncertain and that Kobi was refusing to cooperate. And then in a tight voice Marvel's mother responded. Calmer this time. Perhaps having been taken by surprise before now she had had time to prepare herself. 'My daughter is dead. I believe Jonah Kobi killed her and the fact that he's never confessed nor told us where her body lies is some sort of malicious, twisted game with him.'

'I realize that, but while we have no proof I am keeping an open mind. I'm hoping,' Claire added, 'that something will give him away. Some small detail, perhaps.' She waited.

Dixie's voice rose. 'I must say I didn't think you'd wring a confession out of him whatever your qualifications. We appealed to him while the court case was going on. We attended court every day. We sent endless messages. We were desperate to find her.'

'I realize—'

Dixie cut her off. 'I'll tell you what I believe. My daughter's dead. I'm not saying this out of a sort of supernatural feeling. I'm saying it because I've rolled the facts around in my mind for years. She's been dead for years now. Ever since I kissed her goodbye on that rainy Saturday. I have . . .' She quickly corrected herself. '*We* have mourned her and come to terms with our loss. I don't want it all dug up again. I don't want the headlines. I don't want the case reopened. Let's just be content with saying that Kobi killed her and for some unknown reason he's refusing to confess.'

'So your husband's wish means nothing to you?'

This provoked a long silence. 'You don't know my family, Doctor. You don't know my husband. You didn't know Marvel. We did. To us she was flesh and blood, a difficult, sometimes unhappy, jealous and resentful teenager. She is still real to us. Not simply another body in that vile man's repertoire.'

'Yes.' Feeble though it was, it was the only response Claire could make.

But Dixie's rant wasn't over. 'Dr Roget, you may be a psychiatrist. But have you any idea what happens when a couple loses a child like that? The poison enters the bloodstream, infects the entire relationship. We blamed each other. We blamed ourselves. We blamed the family dynamics. We blamed the police. We blamed him. The entire family collapsed like a house of cards and we had to rebuild. Card by card.'

'So let me help. Talk to me. Give me something.'

There was a long silence, then Dixie Trustrom said, 'Not over the phone. I don't want to describe my daughter to some faceless person, an anonymous voice.'

'Then come here.'

That drew a laugh as sharp as broken glass. 'To a mental hospital? I don't think so.'

'Then . . .?'

'You come to Birmingham. But I don't want you coming here. I don't want Clarice to know I'm meeting a psychiatrist about her dead sister. Meet me at the coffee bar on the corner of Harrison Street, Acocks Green. Say six o'clock? Tomorrow evening? You can park in the NCP just round the corner.'

'OK.' Claire was intrigued, curious and excited. But at the back of her mind she was mindful of the fact that this was just what Kobi had wanted. He was directing the drama from his prison cell.

TWENTY-NINE

Tuesday 8 October, 4 p.m.

She spent the day reviewing patients' treatment, dealing with discharges and patients who needed to be transferred to other units, changing medication and regimes, reading through the notes made by different disciplines. By four she had finished and felt anxious to get on her way. On impulse, just as she was leaving, she rang her GP friend, Julia Seddon, and arranged to go on a run with her over the weekend. And that would not only take up time but also give her something to look forward to. Since she and Grant had split up the weekends needed filling up with plans. Going for a run would mop up a few of those empty hours.

Plus, as a bonus, if Simon and Marianne were in the house over the weekend, she would be out for at least some of the time. And a run of a few miles would free her spirit and do something for her fitness.

But now it was time to head off and meet up with Marvel's mum.

*   *   *

She didn't know what to expect from the encounter when she parked in the suggested NCP and walked round the corner to a lively, steamy coffee bar which had a feel of the fifties about it. The aroma of coffee hit her as she pushed open the door and a woman, sitting on her own, who had obviously been watching for her, beckoned her over.

She'd pictured Marvel's mum as she must have been six years ago, at the time that her daughter had gone missing.

Time had not been kind to her.

Dixie looked very much like her oldest daughter. As Claire drew nearer the resemblance intensified. She could have been looking at an adult Marvel. Dixie was a large lady with wobbling arms and a succession of chins. Luminous dark eyes and a perma-frown with small, screwed-up eyes. She was dressed in jeans she was spilling out of and a baggy sweater over the top in faded red.

Claire smiled and headed straight for the table where she sat. Dixie's face was pale and, far from having moved away from tragedy, she looked tired, unhealthy and unhappy. She raised her mug to Claire and echoed Kobi's phrase. 'Dr Roget, I presume?'

Claire nodded. 'Would you like another coffee before I sit down?'

'Don't mind if I do.'

'Any particular sort?'

Marvel's mother shrugged and Claire headed for the counter, looking back at the woman who was sitting, staring in front of her, eyes unfocused, her face swamped with that old tragedy. Maybe she was right and it was a mistake to drag it all out again, taking this poor woman back to the time when her life and her family had fractured.

She returned and put the two cups on the table. Dixie picked one up and took a sip before speaking. 'You're wasting your time; you know that, don't you?'

'Possibly,' Claire agreed.

'Kobi's not going to tell you anything,' she said finally, 'because he doesn't know anything.'

Claire felt herself freeze. She hardly dared breathe for fear any air disturbance would blow this confidence away and, like a wisp of a spider's web, or the merest hint of cloud in a blue sky, it would drift away and be gone for ever.

Dixie's eyes looked small, encased in folds of fat. The irises were tawny brown and might, at one time, have been her best asset. In her early fifties now and obese, it was hard to say what she would have looked like six years ago. Now she looked a poor, unhappy specimen. Was it her daughter's disappearance that had done this to her? Or would this have been her fate anyway? Tragedy has its impact on a family. Each member reacts in a different way. So had Dixie turned to food for comfort? Had Marvel?

Dixie seemed to be chewing words over in her mind. Frowning, abstracted. Claire resisted the urge to prompt or question her. She had the feeling that what Marvel's mother was about to say would impact her whole take on the mystery.

After a few deep, steadying breaths she finally spoke. Her first question startled Claire. 'How much of this needs to go further, Doctor?'

It was so far away from the truculent woman who had been on the phone only yesterday that Claire blinked. But she couldn't avoid honesty. 'It depends, Mrs Trustrom, on what you have to tell me.'

Dixie chewed her lip and Claire felt compelled to add, 'I've just been called in as a psychiatrist for a professional opinion. I'm not employed by the police. But surely you want the truth about your daughter to come out?'

Dixie's mouth twisted. 'Depends.'

Claire laid her hands on the table. 'I'm a doctor bound by the Hippocratic oath. Anything you tell me will be kept in strictest confidence unless it impacts on another person's safety, in which case my duty would be to tell the truth and involve the authorities.' She gave an encouraging smile. 'But I'm sure that's not the case now.'

Dixie's eyes dropped but not before Claire had read despair in them.

She waited while Dixie finished her coffee and stared down at the dregs as though they were tea leaves and she could read her fate from them. 'I don't think Kobi had anything to do with my little girl's disappearance,' she said finally. Then she looked up with unhappy eyes. 'I was never convinced. None of the facts fitted. She wasn't like the other girls.'

'But you said when I spoke to you on the phone—'

'I didn't know then what I know now. It's taken me a while to realize things.'

Dixie fumbled in her bag and brought out an envelope. She selected something from it and handed Claire a photograph. It was a different picture of the missing girl than the ones on police files but the essence was the same.

Like mother like daughter. Marvel Trustrom was plump and unappealing. A doughy face stared out of the picture. She had straight, red-gold hair, her one claim to beauty, but the same pallid complexion and small eyes as her mother. Her face was podgy, her stare more of a glare. Claire looked at it for a long time, wondering. She looked again at the picture of Marvel. That cockiness which had so infuriated Jonah Kobi in the other girls was completely absent. Claire laid the photograph on the table, face up, frowning and troubled. Then she looked right into the girl's mother's face and tried to divine what the woman was wanting to tell her.

'We're alike,' Dixie said baldly. 'This is what we look like. This is us.'

Claire sensed something. She reached out and touched Dixie's hand. 'What are you afraid of?'

Dixie closed her eyes as though years of weariness had finally caught up with her. 'Once I knew the facts, I knew something else. If Jonah Kobi had nothing to do with the disappearance of my daughter someone else did. Not for the reasons that he gave but for something completely different. And that person is still out there.'

'Who?'

Dixie put her hands over her face.

'There have been no more schoolgirl killings since Kobi was arrested,' Claire pointed out.

But Dixie kept her hands over her face. Then one hand reached out and slid the photograph back towards her, tucking it back into the envelope. A hen gathering up her chicks. Belatedly.

Claire waited, but nothing more was forthcoming and she sensed the interview was over. Dixie Trustrom was going to say nothing more.

Claire could have prompted her. If not Kobi then who? But Dixie's face was hard, her expression set.

'I have one more thing to ask you.'

Dixie's mouth tightened and her eyes were alert.

'Will you ask your two daughters and your son if they will at least speak to me?'

'Why?'

And Claire couldn't answer – at least not honestly. That perhaps from one of them she would learn the truth.

THIRTY

She drove home in a pensive mood, realizing something else. DS Willard had concerns about this case too. That was the real reason he had asked her for her opinion. Not because he thought she would extract a confession out of Kobi, but because he felt there was another dimension to Marvel Trustrom's disappearance. As soon as she was home to a blissfully quiet house, she rang him. 'You never thought it was Kobi,' she accused.

'That's not true.' But she could hear awkwardness in his voice. DS Zed Willard was not a great liar.

'Really?'

He responded with a gruff laugh. 'Police aren't supposed to have instincts,' he said, 'or feelings. They're supposed to go on hard evidence.' He gave another cynical cough. 'Except in this case there wasn't any.'

'Zed,' she said, irritated, 'you haven't been playing fair with me, have you?'

Silence on the other end.

'It wasn't just the physical differences in the cases, was it?'

'Hrrm.'

'Tell me. When you arrested him and charged him with the murder of Shelley Cantor, did he confess quite readily to the other three girls' murders?'

The only response she got was a heaving sigh as he agreed, 'Yes.' He then continued, sheepishly, 'I probably need to talk to you, Claire. But not at the hospital or the station.'

'You can come here if you like.'

'Sure?'

And she felt irritated. 'I wouldn't have invited you if I didn't mean it. Like you I just want any conversation we have about this to be completely private.'

He cleared his throat – the nearest to an apology he'd ever give her. 'I'll bring the list.' She had to remind herself that the list she was waiting for was the details of Kobi's jobs from 2010 when he had left the Macclesfield school and entered into supply teaching until he had been arrested.

She roused herself to Willard's voice.

'I can be round in . . . twenty minutes or so.'

But it was half an hour before the doorbell rang and he stood there.

She led him into the kitchen and offered him a glass of wine or a beer. He chose the beer and they sat around the table. He handed her sheets of paper stapled together. 'The supply teaching list.'

'So many?'

'I did warn you. He was very busy and very much in demand. Obviously,' he added drily, 'there's a shortage of history teachers. I didn't want to jeopardize or delay the court case, Claire, while we scrabbled around for evidence about Marvel.'

'So Tom's just brought it all back? Evoked all the doubts and misgivings you had years ago?'

'I worried about the family.'

'Go on.'

'They didn't seem right. At first, they were just completely shocked. Then they seemed to freeze over. Then we got Kobi and the focus shifted.' He paused, collecting his words. 'Is it possible,' he asked, 'that you're being hoodwinked by him? That it's all part of the game after all?'

She shook her head. Held up her index finger as a warning. 'It's possible,' she said. 'I keep my mind open to all possibilities. At this moment I still don't know. But I have big misgivings.' She recalled Dixie's words, still baffling, hinting at something so much more personal than the accepted view.

'Zed, I want you to do something for me.'

'What?' His response was guarded.

'I'm doing some research,' she said, 'into women who marry lifers. Will you find out all you can about Jessica Kobi?'

'Jessica?'

'Yes. I've met her and put it like this.' She hid behind legal jargon. 'She's a person of interest.'

He took a long swig of his beer. 'OK,' he said. 'Person of interest? You want to leave it at that?'

'For now. You've met her?'

'Yeah.'

'What did you think?'

'I don't know.'

Zed Willard's face creased into a frown. But if he thought he could will her to explain further it wasn't going to work.

They moved on to other general subjects, but Claire felt uncomfortable with the DS. He was still keeping something back.

THIRTY-ONE

She wandered back into the kitchen and poured herself a nightcap, picked up the sheets of paper Willard had left – and put them down again. They could wait.

And in the silence she made an attempt to answer the questions.

Was Kobi guilty of Marvel's disappearance? She was unconvinced.

What she had learned tonight was how deep Zed Willard's doubt was too.

If Marvel's body was ever found there would be forensic evidence to link victim with killer but, given the ease with which the other girls' bodies had been discovered, she wondered now just how hard the police had searched. Had they expected it to just 'turn up' – like the others? There was something else that Kobi had touched on which she didn't want to acknowledge. But it had the ring of truth.

Because he had been abductor and killer, he had knowledge. So if this was one crime he was *not* guilty of maybe he *could* point her in the right direction. Could Kobi, after all, be useful?

While naturally sceptical of anything he told her, certain words resonated. His words floated back to her as clearly as though he sat in the chair opposite, still talking . . .

Look at her, Claire. Use your common sense. She wasn't the type that riled me. She was rather pathetic. An outsider. A loner.

She frowned. How could he know that unless . . .

She was a lonely, sad girl. Had he deduced that from her picture? Or the articles? She'd skimmed through a few. Marvel had been portrayed as a 'loved big sister, a sweet girl, a lovely, happy daughter'. There had been no hint of family problems. Claire was tempted to smile. You don't speak ill of the dead and the family had come in for sympathy rather than criticism. Sometimes even the press follow the accepted rules. She half closed her eyes and tried to think. Big mistake. Into the room wafted that prison scent – carbolic soap, disinfectant, cheap deodorant and the scent of a community laundry.

My advice to you is look closer to home.

So now she had no option but to speak to him again, try and find out what he was, so far, only hinting at.

Wednesday 9 October, 10 a.m.

She sensed a change in him the moment she entered the interview room. He was fidgety whereas before he had been outwardly still. His upper lip held a bead of sweat. She met his eyes and they looked uncertain, uncomfortable. His mouth was set rigid, lips pressed hard together and his hands on the surface of the table had a fine tremor. She sat down, sensing desperation.

'*You* wanted to see *me*.'

She nodded.

'Claire,' he pleaded. 'Please. Listen to what I've been telling you. Use your common sense. Your instincts, if you like. Look at her, Claire, and just think. Marvel wasn't anything like the kind of girl I would want to shove off the face of the earth. She just didn't light that spark.'

She leaned in, studied his face. Glanced up at the dual cameras, one in each corner. She had insisted they have no sound. This was Kobi's right – to speak, in private, to a psychiatrist, hopefully volunteering information and have no one listen in.

'Tell me about . . . the spark.'

Kobi thought about this for a while. But she could wait. She had time on her side and Claire was used to allowing her patients to choose their own rhythm.

'The spark,' he said finally. 'Have you ever stood in front of a class of pubescent girls awash with hormones they can neither understand nor control?'

She shook her head.

'They taunt you,' he said, 'lead you up a garden path although they have no insight into where it will lead. They flounder and act' – he screwed up his face in disgust – 'in provocative ways and then . . .' His hands flew out before forming a stranglehold in the air. 'It is all an act and when anyone is taken in by it they shout and scream and beg for mercy.' His voice was raised now, his eyes bulging with hatred. This then was the last face the girls had seen before they'd lost consciousness and died.

He brought his hands back down to lie flat on the desk again. There was still that fine tremor that he couldn't quite control. 'Marvel could not have made me angry. She was not the right sort.'

'So how did you feel when you snuffed them out?' She used the cruel language deliberately.

And it surprised him. He regarded her with a frown, and she realized her use of the disparaging word had made him uncomfortable.

She kept her face impassive and waited for his answer.

'How did I feel?' He leaned in, surer of his ground now. 'How do you *think* I felt, Claire?' She'd lost her advantage.

'Probably you felt nothing. Perhaps you felt some anger.' She'd affected disinterest as though she didn't care either way.

'I suppose I didn't feel much. When I watched them giggling and flirting I felt angry. I wanted them to suffer. I did not want them to ever grow up. But when they were dead, I felt nothing.'

'Which is why you just chucked them out of the car.'

'Mmm. I suppose so.'

'Detective Sergeant Willard said that you watched the girls. You drove around, stalked them and selected your quarry before you took them and killed them.'

Kobi laughed out loud. 'In his dreams,' he said. 'I was spoilt for choice. Have you any idea how many of these girls are stalking the streets, playing their silly little games, pretending to be women when they are still . . . just . . . little girls?'

She didn't respond.

'I had a job to do, Claire, to clean up the streets.'

'But you could never have continued doing this.'

Kobi sat back, folded his arms. 'I managed four,' he said.

'Five?'

Kobi wasn't going to be caught out with this. Smiling, he shook his head. 'Listen to me, Claire,' he said. 'Listen very carefully. Because I killed the others, I know things.'

Claire listened.

'When you find Marvel's body, it will be fully clothed and you will not find a single cell of my DNA.'

'Do you know where her body is?'

'Aa-ah.' He shook his head. He gave a little cough. 'You're not listening to me, Claire.'

'I am. And I've read the police notes. You were quite good at keeping the girls forensically clean.'

'I can't bear carelessness. Speak to her family. They know the truth.'

It was his final word. So what had she gained from this interview? Perhaps she was asking the wrong question. Maybe she should ask herself what had *he* gained?

THIRTY-TWO

Thursday 10 October, 9.15 a.m.

The next day she had two problems to deal with. One of the nurses had left a message to say that the Birmingham clinic where Ilsa was now an inpatient had contacted them to say that she was expressing a wish to go home.

Alarm bells jangled loud in Claire's head. She immediately rang the clinic and spoke to the manager. 'Do you feel she's robust enough to go home? How is her mental state?'

The manager sighed. 'We're not trained here, Dr Roget. How can we assess her?'

'Has she been having hallucinations? Is she deluded?'

'Not as far as we can ascertain,' the manager said cautiously.

'I'd better speak to her.'

'I'll bring her to the phone.'

There was a pause and then she heard Ilsa's voice. 'Hello.'

'I understand you want to go home. Is that so?'

Ilsa's voice was flat. 'It's where I belong.'

'Have you spoken to John?'

'I was just going to ring him.'

'Well, see what he says. I guess if it's OK with him . . . But I thought you were anxious about being home. You've claimed that his behaviour towards you has been a major contributory cause of your anxiety and depression. That you feel threatened and manipulated by him. Something which he denies.'

'It's something I need to face up to,' Ilsa said bravely and then, quite smartly, she turned the tables. 'Isn't that what *you* advised?'

Claire felt uneasy. 'Why not wait a week or so?'

'I want to see my son. He's only eight. He'll be missing me.' Her voice was steady.

Claire had to remind herself. This was Ilsa who on admission had been so anxious she could not cross a street or leave the house, who now appeared perfectly in control of her emotions. This was a welcome turnaround but it felt unnatural. There was no drug which could have wrought such a dramatic change even in the weeks Ilsa Robinson had been an inpatient and on medication. Claire felt unconvinced and troubled.

Ilsa tried to persuade her, almost wheedling. 'I want to be with my son. I won't get better here, Claire. I'll get better much quicker at home. I feel ready.'

'You're there as a voluntary patient, Ilsa. If you want to go home no one can stop you. But be certain that's what you want and you really feel ready. And,' she felt bound to add, 'if things don't work out you must get back in touch with us.'

Ilsa responded calmly. 'Thank you.' Her voice lightened. 'I promise to take my medication and I promise to attend the day centre regularly.' She trotted the words out like a catechism. 'And,' she added, 'I need to spend time with my son, my husband and my friend. Goodbye, Claire,' she finished.

Claire could only hope it was goodbye and not an *au revoir*.

Afterwards Claire knew at that point she should have responded differently. But she had had no grounds for restraining Ilsa. She had not been sectioned and was a voluntary patient. She tried to ring John Robinson but he wasn't answering either landline or mobile. She left messages on both phones saying only that she was concerned his wife was discharging herself and would soon be on her way home. She had a bit of a head start. There would inevitably be a slight delay while the pharmacist gathered her take-home drugs.

One solution that did cross her mind, of course, was to ring Grant. He was working at the house and maybe he knew where John Robinson was, but she was reluctant to drag him into her work life. Besides, it would break every rule of patient confidentiality.

Afterwards she would regret all the decisions she had made.

Feeling even more uneasy, she left a second message on the Robinsons' home phone.

THIRTY-THREE

S he left instructions with the ward asking them to keep trying John Robinson's phone and let him know that his wife was on the way home. When she put the phone down, instead of feeling relief, her concern compounded. She didn't believe in miracles, particularly in psychiatry. Anxiety and depression were frequently embedded in a person's character. One could use methods – cognitive behavioural therapy, psychotherapy, pharmacology – but cures tended to be slow. There was no 'quick fix'. This apparent miracle was more an indication of instability than a cure. As the atmosphere can feel heavy just before a storm breaks while the insects bite and sting, Claire could feel the same pressure building up.

And the day wore on.

Coincidentally Grant did ring later. 'I have a favour to ask.'

'Are you at the house?'

'Just heading back,' he said. 'Been to pick up some wallpaper sample books. He now wants a sixties pattern. Honestly.'

'Is Mr Robinson at home?'

'I'm meeting him there later. Why do you want him?'

'I can't say, but if you do see him can you ask him to please ring me? Urgently,' she added.

'Sounds intriguing.' Grant paused but she was not leaking private facts.

After a moment's silence he spoke, sounding slightly sulky at being excluded. 'When or if I see him, I'll pass the message on.'

'So what was it you wanted to ask me?'

'Have dinner with us? Mum moves back down to Cornwall next weekend. I'm giving her a hand with the move. Just spend some time with us before she goes.'

Recalling the hostile stare and the obvious resentment towards her that had emanated from Laura Steadman, even at her daughter's funeral, Claire was silent. So was Grant. He knew better than to try and persuade her. So not even a please passed his lips.

If she and Grant were ever going to resume their relationship, Laura Steadman, his mother, would be part of their lives. She had lost her only daughter. Grant was all she had left. 'OK,' Claire said quietly, feeling cornered and already apprehensive. 'How about Sunday lunch?'

'Great,' he said, sounding pleased. 'I'll go ahead and arrange it.'

Claire was already feeling sick at the thought.

And she was, frankly, worried about Ilsa Robinson's homecoming.

Suddenly Kobi's case seemed the least complicated. At least she knew or thought she knew what she was dealing with. She was prepared for his swerves and lies. They did not ambush her like Ilsa. She knew his diagnosis. Ilsa's true mental state was anybody's guess.

The knock on her office door broke in as loud as a thunderclap. DS Willard stuck his head round the door. 'Just passing,' he said, grinning at her, friendlier than of late.

'You'll give me a bad name. My colleagues will be wondering exactly what I've done to warrant a visit from a policeman.'

'I'm sure you've done something naughty,' he said, still smiling. She waited.

'Tom Trustrom's not got long to go,' he said. 'We're running out of time. I wondered if anything in the notes might help hurry things along?'

'I haven't looked at them yet, but I did have a few more questions.'

'I'll answer them if I can.'

'Why was he able to murder Teresa and Shelley?' She deliberately left out Marvel. 'Why hadn't you caught him?'

Zed Willard looked embarrassed. 'We had someone else in our sights,' he confessed. 'We were short on DNA analysis and our suspicions centred around another guy who had committed similar crimes back in the eighties and was out of prison.' He shook his head gravely. 'We ballsed up and two more girls paid the price.'

'Or three,' she reminded him.

'Yeah,' he said abruptly, 'or three.'

'Talk me through it. Make me see it from your point of view.'

Zed Willard practically squirmed. 'Kobi wasn't in our sights. Prior to Petra Gordano's murder he'd never been convicted of anything. He was just a teacher who got on with his job.'

'Wait a minute,' she said. 'That's not strictly true, is it? He'd had that allegation made against him by a teenage girl. Didn't that flag him up?'

He shook his head, frowning. 'That was an internal enquiry. We had nothing to do with it. The school were sorting it out. It hadn't come to the notice of the police so he was still under our radar.'

She made no comment and he couldn't resist adding, 'He was found not guilty and allowed to carry on teaching in the same school.'

When she didn't respond, he tried again. 'Claire,' he said earnestly, 'those are the ones who give us trouble, the "perps" who have been clean right up until their first crime. I mean it's shit, I know, but that's what happens. They get away with it because they're not on any list.'

'So he was hanging around Newcastle-under-Lyme bus station and picked Petra up. No one saw her get into the car?'

'According to her friends she'd twisted her ankle in hockey practice so was limping along and caught an earlier bus home but still later than the general school bus. It was an unusual time. She was sitting down looking fed up. Loads of people saw her. But she wandered off when the bus was a bit late and that's when we believe Kobi picked her up. Within half an hour, Claire, that girl was dead. Her body was found less than two hours after she'd gone missing.'

'And there was no sexual assault?'

'No.'

'No DNA evidence?'

'No. All we had were some fibres from a car seat. And it was a material used by six manufacturers. We're talking Fords, VWs, Nissans. All the cheaper, common models. It didn't exactly narrow the field.'

'And Jodie?'

'Congleton is Cheshire,' he said defensively, fingers drumming on the desk. 'We had resources right through schools, bus stops, bus stations. We were warning girls not to accept lifts from people they didn't know. But we focused our warnings on Staffordshire or more specifically Stoke-on-Trent. Jodie was last seen standing at a bus stop. The weather was very hot that day and she looked exhausted, according to eyewitnesses. One woman approaching the bus stop saw her speak to a man in a blue Ford Focus, window down.' He groaned. 'One of the most common cars on the road. She saw him offering her a bottle of water. Jodie got in. The woman simply assumed the driver was someone Jodie knew. Her description was pathetic. She thought it was a man but it might have been a woman with short hair. She thought he – or she – had brown hair. She got the car number plate all mixed up, as it turned out, but she did get the make and colour of car right.' He looked gloomy. 'Her brother-in-law had one just like it.' He looked even gloomier. 'Sometimes we can be so unlucky,' he said. 'Robbie August, known paedophile, whose taste was for teenage girls. "Budding women", he called them.' The disgust in Willard's voice made him almost spit the words out. 'Once we have a likely suspect all our attention is focused on finding evidence to support that theory.'

She swallowed her retort.

'Robbie August lived in Biddulph halfway between the two crimes. He fitted the profile and . . .' Willard groaned. 'As luck would have it he drove a blue Ford Focus and the fibres from Petra's clothes looked like a match. There was no DNA evidence to link either him or anyone else for that matter to the two crimes. We questioned him under caution. He was very vague about his movements on both days. We put a watch on him.'

'And then Marvel went missing.'

Zed Willard sank back into his seat and seemed to shrink. 'Because we had been keeping a close eye on August we knew he hadn't had anything to do with Marvel's disappearance. We'd been watching him.' He looked shamefaced. 'To be honest at first we wondered if she'd just gone AWOL.'

Willard shrugged and his voice rose. 'I managed to convince myself, fall in with the general view that it was Kobi.'

'There's no need to shout, Zed.' She could feel her own anger rising. 'You should have told me about Marvel's family.'

'I couldn't see that it was anything to do with it,' he said sulkily. 'Well, to put it in a nutshell her mother and father were on the verge of a divorce. They couldn't agree on anything. Her mother was a cow, quite frankly.' He glanced apologetically at Claire. 'She called her daughter the Ugly Duckling.' He paused, frowning. 'I wasn't sure it was used as an affectionate title. In fact . . .' he continued after a short pause, '. . . poor girl. I think everyone in the Force felt sorry for the kid when it started coming out. As it had nothing to do with the case we kept it out of the papers.'

'Her dad?'

'Tom? He was . . .' Willard was frowning. 'He was an odd sort of guy. Quite retiring and shy while his wife harangued him. And then every now and then he would burst. I've never seen anything like it. He would shout and scream as though he was in agony. And a lot of his anger appeared to be directed towards his wife.'

'Not anymore.'

'Well they're divorced and he's so ill. Back then he was a different man. I think if we hadn't been there he got so furious I could have imagined him beating his wife to a pulp. She was frightened of him.'

'So did you look into the rest of her family? Her siblings? Teenage brother, two kid sisters?'

'None of them was much help. I mean, the girls were young. And they were upset. Shane put a brave face on it but of course we had to have appropriate adults when we spoke to the girls and I think that might have inhibited them. They painted a picture of a strange sort of home life where there was this odd one out. But the truth was our investigation into the family was pretty cursory. We never thought it was one of them.'

'Tell me about the teenage brother.'

Zed Willard shrugged. 'What can I say? When he got his ear buds out and stopped playing games on his phone he hardly said anything. Typical teenage lad, I suppose. Didn't want to engage with the police.' He chuckled. 'In fact, like many teenage lads he didn't really want to engage with anyone, I suspect, not even his peer group. Certainly not his parents or sisters.'

'Did he say anything significant about his sister's disappearance?'

'Not that was recorded.'

'So you knew by then it wasn't Robbie August. And Marvel's body didn't turn up. So you were casting around for a new suspect. At the time did you think it was the same killer?'

Zed Willard nodded. 'When her body didn't turn up we just thought he'd changed his MO. And then Teresa Palmer went. And we knew even more certainly that it wasn't Robbie. He was, in fact, in custody for flashing at a girl in Tunstall Park.' His mouth was grim and he was frowning.

'We knew then it was our schoolgirl killer again. Same MO as the first two. Girl picked up near a school, still in uniform, body found within hours. We drafted in more men.'

And Claire sensed unease. 'Shelley,' she said softly.

Zed Willard drew in a deep sigh. 'Kobi being clever again. She vanished from Newport.'

'Shropshire.'

Willard nodded. 'Body found weighted down in Westport Lake this time.'

'So he drove her all that way to dump her in the Potteries. And then . . .'

'A bit of luck,' he said, 'that the Staffordshire Wildlife Trust took such an interest in wading birds and egrets.' He cleared his throat. 'Someone remembered . . . took down the same number. That led us straight back to Kobi. He was arrested two days later.'

Willard's phone broke in, strident and insistent. He frowned at the number. 'Excuse me,' he said. 'I need to take this.' He moved outside the door and she heard his responses.

'OK. OK. I'm on my way. Just text me the address and postcode. Anyone there already? Good.'

He put his head round the door. 'Sorry,' he said, 'I'm going to have to go. It looks like there's been an incident.' He tried to smile. 'Looks nasty,' he said. Then repeated, 'Sorry. I have to go.'

She managed a smile better than he had.

THIRTY-FOUR

When he'd gone, scuttling out of the room, as though the 'incident' depended on him getting there in seconds, she was left with the phrase Marvel's mother had used to the police when describing her daughter. The Ugly Duckling. A familiar moniker. Used affectionately? Willard had spoken to Marvel's mother and had wondered. So what had the sisters thought of her? Clarice and Sorrel had been eleven and twelve when their sister had gone missing and although DS Willard had claimed they had been upset at her disappearance, they too had described their sister as the odd one out. Dysfunctional was the word Willard had used when describing Marvel's family. But he had kept this back from her. Why? If Kobi had murdered the girl what relevance could her family dynamics possibly have on her disappearance? Absorbed in the subject, she cleared her desk and put Marvel's picture back, at its side the list of family members.

Her mother, Dixie, getting on with her life, trying to erase the fact that once she had had three daughters. Not just two.

Marvel's father, Tom, the only one apparently anxious for the truth to come out. Presumably Yvonne, his new partner, wasn't particularly interested in his former life except where it impacted on their current happiness.

Shane, her brother, eighteen at the time of his sister's presumed murder. Not distracted by the marital disharmony he would possibly have had more insight into his sister than her parents. Teenagers who plug their ears with music are often blocking out something else, usually something unpleasant. She needed to speak to him to claw at the truth. But it was the same old problem. She had no powers to force him to attend an interview and she anticipated he would be reluctant. But she had to try. He might be able to help.

And then she thought about Kobi. The more she learned about Marvel Trustrom the less convinced she was that he had had anything to do with her disappearance. Maybe that was why Tom was so insistent on learning the truth. Maybe he wanted to exonerate his own family.

So whom did *he* suspect? His wife? His son? Surely not his daughters?

Feeling chilled, Claire shook her head. Surely not?

Sorrel and Clarice might hold some information, but the probability was that they were simply younger sisters, wrapped up in their own lives. They were nearer each other in age, Marvel the odd one out. But they might have seen something, heard something. Claire put her chin in her hand, half closed her eyes and thought. Kobi was too intelligent to fall into any trap. If he had murdered Marvel, he would only tell her if he had some reason for wanting to. Something to gain. And her gut feeling? DS Willard had painted a vivid picture of family life back then. It was an ugly picture, but it had thrown up another possibility. Maybe Marvel hadn't been murdered by either Jonah Kobi or anyone else. Maybe she'd simply run away from an unhappy family.

A phone ringing somewhere down the corridor reminded her. She had a job to do, wards full of patients, fully booked clinics and urgent referrals arriving daily. She left her office and headed for the wards. The next three hours were spent reviewing treatments, interviewing patients and checking drugs charts.

It was nearly six when she returned to her office.

She'd left her bag in the locked bottom drawer of her locked office. As she drew it out she saw her mobile phone was flashing. Six missed calls – all from Grant. Worried and with a feeling of misgiving, she connected. 'Grant? What is it?'

'Mayhem,' he said. 'When I got back to Robinson's place there was a scene like something out of a horror movie. Blood everywhere. Police. The wife came home, burst into the house and attacked her husband and friend Maggie with a knife.' He still sounded shocked.

Not as shocked as she. It was as though all her fears had suddenly found a form.

'Are they seriously hurt?'

'I suspect Maggie more than John. They were taken away under a blue light. There's blood everywhere. And the police, of course. Including your friend, the DS.'

So that had been the urgent call he had taken.

'Where's Ilsa?'

'They took her away. Shit, Claire, she was in a right state. Like a mad thing.' He remembered whom he was talking to and said, 'Sorry. They said she was a patient of yours?'

'Do you know which station they've taken her to?'

'No. And now I don't know what to do. Truth is,' he said, and she could hear the wobble in his voice, 'I feel a bit shaky. Will they blame you? How the hell do you deal with stuff like this all the time?'

'It's a rare occurrence. And yes. They will blame me.'

'I feel awful.'

And she sensed the subtext. 'Is this a request to come home?' Too late she realized she'd just used the "h" word.

'You just read my mind.'

'I'll see you later. But I don't know when.'

So was this how their relationship was to be resolved? Nothing more dramatic than a casual invitation and, almost imperceptibly, Grant would sidle back into her life?

Even now she could not be sure. Should she just allow their relationship to drift back into the groove?

Reluctantly she tried Zed Willard's phone and got him on the fourth try. Understandably he sounded stressed when she finally connected. And thankfully he didn't ask how she seemed to know about the drama at the Robinson's house.

'Ilsa Robinson is one of my patients,' she said. 'Or at least she was until a week ago when I discharged her.' This provoked a long silence before he let rip.

'And you didn't realize she was a danger to her husband?' He was snappy with her. Patently angry.

She saw where this was coming from. He'd seen the crime scene. 'She was transferred from here to a private clinic in Birmingham.' She was aware how weak this would sound. 'I judged her not a danger to anyone.'

Zed Willard's response leaked anger. 'Well, she's just stabbed her husband and a woman who was in the house at the time so it kind of depends on your definition of *a danger*. Her husband has minor injuries, but Maggie Levand was in a bad way by the time she got into the ambulance.'

Claire could only repeat lamely, 'She wasn't considered a danger.'

'It's fucking obvious she was.' Any friendship between them was fast melting away.

'Where is she now?'

'Hanley,' he said.

'Prison is not the right place for her. I want to admit her back here as soon as possible. On the locked ward,' she added as a sop.

'I guess that's your prerogative.' And he ended the call.

But however logical the process of readmitting Ilsa to Greatbach it would take some time. Two doctors had to sign the form to place Ilsa under a section of the Mental Health Act. Then she could be transferred back to Greatbach. And then what? Ilsa's future was even more uncertain now.

She picked up her car keys and let Rita know she was heading for Hanley police station. It would be hours before she was home. She only hoped Grant would hit it off with Simon Bracknell and his wife if they'd returned from their travels.

Her problems were compounding. And she was still no nearer learning anything about Marvel's disappearance. It was still all guesswork.

THIRTY-FIVE

I t was after nine that evening when she arrived back at Waterloo
Road. She had spent some time waiting at the station for the
second psychiatrist who had quickly agreed with her that Ilsa
should be readmitted to Greatbach Secure Unit. When she and the
other psychiatrist had spoken to her in the cell, she had initially
appeared shocked and almost unaware of what she had done. But
this could be a front. A way of wriggling out of a conviction for
GBH and a prison sentence. A desperate plea for 'while the balance
of her mind was disturbed'. Within minutes of Claire's arrival
Ilsa's manner had changed. She appeared composed. And Claire
decided she knew exactly what she'd done. In fact, as she watched
Ilsa's facial expressions, she wondered whether Ilsa had planned
this all along. Her assumed innocence and now bland manner
seemed to almost deny that the incident had even happened. There
was no need to sedate her. Ilsa was perfectly calm. And so she
would be interviewed in the morning. In the meantime, she would
be transferred to a locked, single room, staff advised to watch over
her carefully. And in the morning Claire would begin her assessment. As she left Greatbach Claire wondered. Was this an acute
paranoiac episode or the result of an orchestrated setup? As she
reached her car she stopped and wondered. In her way, was Ilsa
as much of a psychopath as Jonah Kobi? Perhaps even more
devious?

She recalled the words and tone Ilsa had used. '*I didn't mean
to hurt them. I was just upset and . . .*'

By the time she'd reached home Claire was mentally exhausted
with exploring the seemingly endless possibilities. She finally
unlocked her own front door and heard voices in the sitting room.

Bemused, she stood in the doorway. The three of them were
sitting there like old pals. Grant spotted her first and grinned. 'Just
getting to know your colleague,' he said, 'and Marianne.' They
all looked as though they'd had a fine time of it. A half empty
bottle of wine stood on the coffee table and Grant had kicked his

shoes off and was just rising from a prone position on the sofa. He met her eyes and perhaps read her warning.

This is my house.

And right now all she wanted was a shower, to put a dressing gown on and flop in front of whatever shit was on the TV.

She turned and left the room and heard the silence behind her. She'd broken up the party.

She did feel better after a shower and lay on her bed in the towelling dressing gown. She didn't want to go downstairs and make small talk.

She'd almost dropped off to sleep, still lying on top of her bed when she sensed Grant standing over her. 'Hi,' he said. 'Sorry about that. Sometimes I forget how hard your job is.'

She looked up at him. 'Well, you've had a shit day as well.'

'Yeah . . .' He dropped down beside her. 'It was a shock. And I was glad to have some company. But at least I can't be held responsible.' He caught her look and added hastily, 'Not that you are, of course.' Doubt crept into his voice when he added, 'Not really.'

'Thanks for the vote of no confidence.' But it was hard to stay cross with Grant, particularly when he nestled beside her, his stubble scratching her face. Grant always looked a rogue. She called him her pirate. But now he looked more like a recalcitrant Just William Brown. Ruffled dark hair, gleaming eyes, a swarthy complexion, almost Mediterranean and a muscular build which she felt as he put his arms around her and pulled her on to his chest, kissing her hair and murmuring something. If not sweet nothings something very similar and just as effective. She closed her eyes, beginning to block out the day's dramas and smiled as she pictured him with an eye patch and bandana waving a cutlass.

Unfortunately Grant hadn't quite finished with the subject. 'When you rang and said you wanted John to ring you, I sort of sensed something was wrong. But . . .' He drew his fingers through her hair. 'I didn't imagine anything like that.'

'That's the trouble,' she said softly. 'Neither did I.'

'Hey. It isn't your fault, Claire. It can't be.'

'Whatever,' she responded, 'I will be blamed.'

She closed her eyes. If anyone could wipe away the dramas of the day and the fear of what tomorrow could bring, Grant Steadman could. And his body next to hers through the night would make her feel safe, secure and loved. His arms tightened around her and then he moved away to look at her.

'You do,' he said, grinning, 'look absolutely knackered.'

It was the last thing she remembered hearing before falling asleep.

Friday 11 October, 8.45 a.m.

The morning brought reality.

The assessment of Ilsa's mental condition would not be just down to her. It would be a multi-disciplinary decision made by herself and another psychiatrist less involved than she had been, as well as Edward, the clinical psychologist, the nursing staff and other professionals who had had contact with Ilsa Robinson. Claire could already anticipate the result. Balance of mind unsound. Temporary insanity. Ilsa would get her way.

She spent more than an hour with her patient but at the end of it could not have put her hand on her heart and been certain that Ilsa was not deliberately vengeful but suffering from an extended delusion that her husband and her best friend were having an affair. Either was perfectly possible. But even if it was true and Ilsa had been perceptive rather than deluded, it still wouldn't justify the knife attack. None of the clues were there: the knife had been to hand, in the kitchen. And either cleverly or otherwise Ilsa had seen the changes her husband was making to her home as another effort to exclude her. Claire left the room with the same feeling of dissatisfaction that she had felt on leaving Stafford Prison.

One decision was made. For the time being Ilsa could stay at Greatbach while the CPS, police, the courts and herself decided what to do with her.

Now back to the Marvel situation. Claire was anxious to find out whether there was any truth behind Kobi's hints that the family was involved in Marvel's fate. So reluctantly she contacted Tom again. He sounded weak and exhausted, his voice thin and reedy. And she felt guilty for breaking her lack of news. 'I'm sorry, Tom,' she said, 'Mr Kobi still denies having any knowledge of your daughter's disappearance.'

'Murder,' he corrected. 'My daughter was murdered – I believe,' he added. 'I just want the truth to come out. I want her body found.' His voice was soft and weak and he paused between words as though the very effort of speaking was tiring. He sounded breathless, gasping for air like a goldfish. She could hear Yvonne murmur something in the background.

His words combined with the desperation in his voice alerted her to something. Exactly what was he asking for? His request wasn't that she find Kobi guilty of his daughter's murder. He was asking her to find her body.

Tucking that fact away, she spoke calmly. 'Well, Mr Kobi isn't playing ball, at the moment,' she said. 'He isn't telling me anything, so far.' She paused, knowing she could use his plea to her advantage. 'I wonder if you might persuade other family members to speak to me about the day your daughter went missing.'

'Why?'

She had her answer ready. 'I'm trying to surprise Kobi with facts that weren't published. If we can find something to show that he had insider knowledge it might persuade him into a confession.'

'But we spent hours with the police then.' His voice had changed. He now sounded panicky.

'Yes,' she soothed, 'and I've studied the police records in detail. But there might be some minor detail that one of you remembers. I need to present Kobi with something that wasn't in the public domain. I need to catch him out, Tom, knock him off balance if I'm to get anywhere.'

There was a long pause. 'Have you explained to him that I am dying? Have you told him I don't have long to live?' Now he was sounding appealing, beseeching her to . . . Do what? Reason with Kobi? Appeal to his better self? Squeeze out a confession? She frowned and tried to reason with him.

'I've explained all that, Tom. There isn't much point appealing to his better nature. He doesn't have one. He's only going to confess to your daughter's murder if he has something to gain by it.' She didn't add: *And if he actually killed her in the first place.*

'Has he given you *any* detail about my daughter's abduction?'

'I'm afraid not, Mr Trustrom.'

'So what do you suggest?' He'd run out of energy, all fight drained away like sand in an hourglass.

'I want to speak to your son and daughters.'

He didn't like that. 'Sorrel and Clarice were just kids. They probably hardly remember Marvel.'

'They weren't that young. I think it's worth a try.'

His voice became peevish, squeaky and high-pitched. 'And Shane? You want to speak to Shane?'

'Of course.' She kept her voice calm. 'He was that bit older, wasn't he? A teenager.'

'This is wasting time. Time I don't have.' His voice was squeaky now.

'I'm doing all I can, Tom, and will continue to do my best.'

Something in her had changed. She couldn't put her finger on it but even she could hear something dubious in her voice, something she didn't quite understand. She was on a cake-walk, doubts tilting her perspective.

She battled her way through the afternoon clinic before heading back to her office. She had an hour spare. She'd rung the ward and there were no issues. Ilsa was settled on the new drug regime. Edward Reakin was with her now. She would receive his report after the weekend. Salena Urbi was currently interviewing relatives of another patient and Simon Bracknell was in Hanley on a domiciliary visit to a patient with deteriorating schizophrenia.

Shane Trustrom was positively hostile when she spoke to him. 'I heard you'd been harassing our family,' he said. 'Just because my dad has a weird death wish. My sister's dead. She probably died within an hour of being abducted by that psycho. I don't want anything to do with this mad, pointless investigation. You'll get nothing from it.' And he slammed the phone down. She stared at it for a moment or two. She hadn't exactly expected willing cooperation, but in his voice she had heard something more like fright. A squeaky panic.

She rang Tom again to see if he held any influence over his son.

'What was his response?'

'Not very helpful, I'm afraid.'

He sounded unsurprised.

'Would you have a word with him?'

'I . . . can.' He sounded reluctant, as though it was being dragged out of him. 'I don't think it'll help though. He always was difficult.'

'I'd like to speak to her sisters.'

'They were just kids.'

'I'd still like to . . .'

'Well, Clarice lives with her mum. You'll have to get past Dixie to speak to her. And good luck with that one. She's as overprotective as a mother hen.'

'Sorrel?'

'I do have a number for Sorrel.'

She made a note of it.

While she had him on the phone, she homed in on something that was missing from the police report. 'Did Marvel have a boyfriend?'

'Oh.' It was a sigh of distress. 'She would have loved to have had a boyfriend but I'm afraid Marvel wasn't the most attractive of young women. They weren't exactly queuing up.'

'What about her school friends?'

'Marvel was a bit of a loner.' He sounded sad but something alerted her.

'But that day she went shopping with friends?'

'I don't know who those friends were . . .' Tom paused. The silence stretched so long Claire wondered if he was still there.

'She said she was going shopping with friends.' Claire remembered something from the original statements. 'Karen and Lara?'

'They weren't her friends. And they weren't with her that day. They just wanted to be part of the drama.' Another pause. 'I'm afraid Marvel didn't always stick to the truth. She didn't really have any friends.' He paused before confessing, 'I wasn't always the best of fathers, Dr Roget.'

She could have added to this. *Who is? Certainly not my bloody father who abandoned me and my mother and left for France when I was just a baby. Leaving my mother to vent her spite on me.* Claire could still hear the poisonous words. *Monsieur Roget* and the *French Frog*.

'I want the truth,' Marvel's father said. 'I want to know – for sure.'

She assured Tom that she would do her very best to find it and got some assurance from him that he would speak to his son and try and persuade Shane to speak to her again. Claire was silent. Families are strange and this one certainly took the biscuit. DS Willard had used the word dysfunctional and maybe he wasn't far wrong.

However, somehow the sands had shifted. The more she dug into this strange family the more she wondered. What was the truth behind this dying man's request? What were they all afraid of?

THIRTY-SIX

Saturday passed as planned with an exhausting run with Julia followed by a shower at the house Julia shared with her partner, Gina Aldi. While Julia was a GP and an old friend from medical school, Gina was an artist who painted and sculpted bizarre creations, hybrids of more than one animal, often using mythological creatures. Gina and Julia were always good company, full of laughs and interesting conversation. Claire avoided any talk of work. The day flashed by and Claire gave no thought to Ilsa Robinson, Marvel Trustrom or any of the people who had filled her working week.

At ten p.m. she rose to leave, kissed them both and set off for home. Tomorrow would be a very different day.

Sunday 13 October, 1 p.m.

Grant had texted her that he'd booked Sunday lunch at The Swan with Two Necks, a gastropub recently refurbished, at Blackbrook, just outside Newcastle-under-Lyme, on the Nantwich Road.

Grant's van was already outside when she pulled up and through the window she could see Laura Steadman's stiff back, Grant talking rapidly, hands waving, as though he was pleading with her.

She pushed open the door.

He rose to meet her while his mother still sat, back ramrod stiff. She managed a smile as Claire approached and the two women's eyes met.

'Mrs Steadman,' Claire managed.

Grant's mother held out a thin hand. 'Laura,' she said. 'Nice to see you, Claire.'

There were plenty of subjects they could explore without abandoning polite conversation: the house Laura Steadman had just bought, the job she was returning to and so on. But there were many more that they had to avoid: Maisie's illness and death, the bloodbath Grant had witnessed just days before.

Luckily Laura Steadman was on her best behaviour.

She was full of ideas for the house she'd just bought. 'Isn't it funny,' she said, managing a tight smile. 'You buy your perfect house and the first thing you do is start knocking it about.' She eyed her son. 'It needs another bathroom, Grant.' And Claire could see exactly where this was heading. She knew who would be installing that bathroom. And then there would be other projects. Laura Steadman gave her a comfortable smile.

Mothers, Claire thought viciously.

Monday 14 October, 9 a.m.

Monday swung round all too soon and Claire was on call the following weekend so she'd had the last of her carefree days – for a while.

Ilsa was subdued according to the ward staff when she rang. John Robinson had been discharged from hospital, but Maggie had taken a turn for the worse, Zed Willard informed her, managing to keep any criticism, real or implied, out of his voice. She tried Shane's number again and left a message but without much faith that he would ring back. Dixie said bluntly that she was 'not keen' for her to speak to Clarice and Sorrel didn't answer her phone. Claire left another message, leaving her number and asking her to make contact.

Reluctantly she returned to HMP Stafford.

Kobi looked a bit flat, disappointed when she confronted him this time. It was as though the game was losing its appeal even to him. When she looked at him, he regarded her steadily back, but his eyes looked tired, his lids drooping. He'd lost that spark.

Looking at him Claire realized how much she wanted an end to these visits.

'Why don't you just confess, Jonah, and be done with it? Let us all move on with our lives. Let Tom die in peace. Just tell me where she's buried and I'll leave you alone.'

Kobi looked up. Even though he looked weary there was still a mocking light in his eyes and he shook his head from side to side. 'How are you getting on with the family?'

Claire could have responded in a number of ways.

Not that well really.

They don't want to speak to me.

They're convinced you're just playing a game . . .

She said none of these and Kobi whined on. 'Because *I* didn't do it, Claire. How many more times? I'm serving time because I murdered four girls. Not five. They could never pin the fifth one on me. You need to look elsewhere for Marvel's killer. I've given you enough hints.'

'What do you actually know, Kobi?'

'I've given you my answer.' He stood up then and immediately Claire saw the face of one of the prison warders peering through the window. She smiled at him and he retreated but it was a reminder of how edgy the atmosphere surrounding Kobi was; even though he sat still as a sphinx she could feel malice emanating from him. How he wanted her to fail. It had become a personal battle. Only one would win.

She pursued her point by trying to belittle him. 'What do you actually know about Marvel's family – apart from what you've read in the papers?' And from the smug expression on Kobi's face she knew he'd just swallowed the bait. He'd come alive and his face was plastered with the look of a psychopath who has just seen one of his little stories believed.

His reply was smooth. 'That's it,' he said. 'Only what I read in the press.' He leaned forward. 'But I told you, Claire, I can read between the lines.'

She felt irritated. 'This isn't a competition, you know. You've actually told me nothing.'

His smirk broadened, a tacit response: *Isn't it?* 'Her mother and "father"' – he scratched the air with speech marks – 'despaired of their Ugly Duckling, didn't they?'

This detail had not been in any of the press reports. He knew the phrase. How?

'Her brother loathed her.' Kobi's smile curved. 'Or did he?'

What was he implying? She kept her face rigid. Kobi waited for a moment before continuing. 'And as for her baby sisters. Have you spoken to them yet? The little ballerinas.'

She was being pulled along by the nose. Kobi was watching to see how far he could take her, with the little breadcrumbs he dropped along the way. She needed to regain control of this interview.

'I think we're diverting a little.'

'I thought you wanted to find the girl's body.'

'That's the object of all these visits,' she said coldly. 'Nothing else. My interest isn't in you.'

It didn't ruffle Kobi. 'Quite,' he said. 'But I'm afraid *I* won't be able to help you find your missing girl. You need to look closer to home.' He put his face near to hers so she could see the flecks in his eyes and his expression changed. 'I won't be able to help you because I didn't fucking well kill her.' And as abruptly as a sudden summer downpour his voice changed to a smooth, chocolatey polite. 'So naturally it follows that I didn't bury her body.'

Claire kept her voice steady. 'This is a waste of time. You're not going to help me.'

'Only because I can't,' he crooned, sounding almost apologetic. But it didn't quite make it. 'However, I can help you in another way. Focus on the charm.'

Did she want to play this by asking, noun or verb?

As though he was playing a game of charades, he dropped in another clue. 'The silver bracelet?'

'What on earth are you talking about?' His pseudo-mysterious tone was annoying her while she recognized the way of a sociopath, to tease and lay out a false trail of breadcrumbs, giggle as they watched when someone stumbled after it. She wasn't going to get caught by this, so she continued in the same cold, bored, disinterested voice. 'The silver bracelet you possibly stole from her?'

Kobi sank back into his chair, looking satisfied. 'I don't do trophies,' he said. 'I don't steal the cheap little trinkets these girls adorn themselves with. It really isn't my scene. And if you'd done your homework, Claire,' he admonished, 'you'd know that.'

'Petra's school bag?'

He looked annoyed. 'No. That must have been someone else. I told you, I don't collect pencils and stuff.'

She badly wanted to rattle him. 'There's always a first time, Kobi.'

He just laughed. A dry, desiccated sound. 'You know what, Claire?'

She didn't rise to the bait.

'I really enjoy our little sparring sessions.'

'I'm not here for your enjoyment, Kobi.'

Kobi laughed again. This time a high-pitched, hysterical giggle while he rocked and held his sides as though to prevent splitting them.

What must he have been like as a teacher, Claire wondered, with those bold eyes and sharp intelligence. He could have been . . . inspirational. Or mocking, belittling, cruel. His pupils would never know which 'sir' they had for the day. But then teenage girls are naturally drawn to danger.

On her way out she chatted to one of the prison warders. 'How often does his wife visit?'

'Often as she can,' he said. 'Most weeks.'

'How do they seem to get on?'

'Plenty to talk about. They sit in a huddle laughing, joking, though what they've got to joke about I ain't quite sure.'

'Me neither.'

As soon as she'd left the prison, she rang Zcd Willard. 'I'm getting nothing out of him,' she said. 'He continues to deny that he had anything to do with Marvel. I'm going to pursue other avenues.' Mentally she added, *If I can.*

There was a brief silence while DS Willard recovered his voice. When he spoke he sounded disappointed. 'That's a pity.'

In spite of herself she couldn't not ask the question: 'Do you know anything about the charm bracelet?'

'Uum. Yes. I think there *was* mention that the reason she'd headed off for Hanley in such shitty weather was to buy a charm for her bracelet. I don't think much importance was attached to it.'

'Silver?'

'I suppose so. In fact, now I remember CCTV showed her buying something from a jeweller's in one of the stalls on the ground floor of the Potteries Shopping Centre.'

She was going to have to drag this out of him. 'And?'

'And nothing,' he said waspishly. 'We left that detail out of the press.'

But again, somehow, Kobi had known. How?

THIRTY-SEVEN

G rant had commented once that she was like a terrier, unable to let go of something that was puzzling her.

This, he would have said, was a perfect illustration.

She tried Shane again, but he was still adamant he would not speak to her and she had no authority to force him, although she felt his resolve weakening. There were pauses between his words and somehow she knew he was frowning. She also knew she would get to him at some point.

Sorrel Trustrom, in contrast, was only too anxious to spill the beans on her sister.

Sorrel worked in a beauty parlour. It was a smart establishment offering everything from Botox to derma fillers plus nail extensions and anything else that might just possibly make a woman look more attractive.

She agreed to speak to Claire between clients, around five o'clock.

At four thirty she set off for 'Sorrel & Yvonne's', heading for Cellarhead crossroads, the point where the city of Stoke-on-Trent concedes defeat to the Staffordshire Moorlands. Once famous for having a pub on each of its four corners, these days it is a betwixt and between sort of place, with odd collections of isolated terraces of tiny cottages, one pub currently an Indian restaurant, another still derelict and Sorrel and Yvonne had turned a third into their beauty parlour. They had made a very clever business choice. The old pub was accessible from Leek, the moorlands and the city, only a few miles from Hanley. But out here they had large premises, probably bought for a song, plenty of parking and business rates would be low, the Moorlands Council intent on preserving the surrounds and encouraging businesses. Like 'Sorrel &

Yvonne's'. And, Claire reflected as she locked her car, old pubs are about as cheap a building as you can find.

Sorrel was a sharp-eyed girl, with enhanced red hair and, unlike her missing sister, a petite figure. She was wearing a white overall and a trowel load of make-up.

As expected, she was perfection itself, stick thin with impossible breasts, a flawless complexion, spray tan, huge eyelashes which almost seemed to glue her eyes together and teeth as white as icebergs. She greeted Claire in the way that a woman who is confident of her beauty greets a lesser being.

'Hello there.' Her voice matched the rest of her, a sort of cutesy, high-pitched sound with only the softest of Potteries accents. 'You don't look like a psychiatrist.'

Claire laughed. It wasn't the first time this had been said to her. 'How should I look, Sorrel? Thick black glasses and tied back hair?'

Give Sorrel Trustrom her due. She giggled, put her hand over her mouth and led the way into a small back room, shelves stacked with products. 'You don't mind coming in here, do you?'

'No.'

They both sat down on fold-up chairs.

Sorrel leaned forward giving a good view of ample cleavage and a waft of strong perfume.

'I don't know why this is all being raked up.' She tossed her head. 'It was years ago.'

Claire let Sorrel ask the question. 'So tell me exactly what your involvement is?'

'You know your dad's ill?'

Sorrel nodded and dabbed at her eye without dislodging the lashes or smearing the mascara. 'Yeah. He's very poorly.'

Which was one way of looking at it, Claire thought. Like most doctors she disliked the use of euphemisms when applied to illness. It muddied the waters.

'And you possibly know that he is anxious to find your sister's body.'

At which point Sorrel Trustrom showed her true character, fluttering her eyelashes as she gave Claire a very challenging and direct look. 'We don't actually know there is a body, do we?'

Claire could have applauded her. She was right.

'Yes,' she agreed. 'But the assumption is—'

Sorrel interrupted her. 'That's what it is, Dr Roget. An assumption.'

Claire changed her words. 'The police have asked me to interview Jonah Kobi who—'

'I know who Kobi is. The teacher turned serial killer. But we don't know he . . .' She then changed the track of her words. 'You didn't know my sister. I did. She was an absolute bitch.'

Claire blinked but did not interrupt.

'She nicked my stuff. Stole my perfume, pinched money out of my money box. Took my jewellery. Nothing was safe. She just took it. And if I said anything she'd simply beat me up. She was a cow. A big, fat, ugly cow.'

Claire took a moment to absorb the words. 'You were how old when she . . .?'

Sorrel anticipated her question. 'Twelve. I was twelve when Marvel disappeared. She bullied me practically every day of my life. She was a horror.'

'You don't think she's dead then?'

Sorrel picked at a fingernail. 'To be honest I don't care whether she's alive or dead. I don't care if her body is unburied. I don't care who killed her. It doesn't matter to me.'

'But it does to your dad.'

Sorrel shrugged her dainty shoulders. 'So he says.'

'Tell me about the last day you saw her. That Saturday when she was last seen.'

Sorrel half closed her black-outlined eyes, the lids a pale beige gold. 'She looked ridiculous,' she said. 'She was wearing a tight, black, leather skirt, very short. Her waist bulged over the top of it. She had on a really low-cut sweater. She looked like a tart. She stank of *my* perfume . . .'

'Which was?'

'Charlie. I used to love the stuff and she'd obviously used it. Smelt like she'd had a bath in it. When I told her she wasn't to use it she slapped me really hard. I went to Mum crying and Mum just took no notice. I think she was fed up with the lot of us. Shane had just been gated from school. He'd been smoking pot. When Marvel came downstairs looking like something the dog's sicked up she just couldn't be bothered to argue with her.

Marvel got away with a lot basically because we couldn't be bothered.'

'Can you remember anything different about that day?'

Sorrel's eyes flickered. She scooped in a long, slow breath. 'Not really . . .' she began before adding, 'I just wondered where she'd got the tenner from.'

'Pocket money?'

Sorrel shook her head. 'It wasn't that,' she said firmly. 'Someone gave it to her.'

Claire stiffened. It was the first hint that something else was different about this case.

'Any idea who?'

Sorrel shook her head. 'No. I did puzzle about that.'

'Did you tell the police?'

'No. I didn't see it had anything to do with it.' She looked preoccupied as she finished. 'And then, of course, it was all put down to Kobi so I just forgot about it.' The look she gave Claire was very straight. 'It was him – wasn't it? Kobi, I mean.'

'We don't know. He hasn't confessed to it.' She decided to put the cat amongst the pigeons. 'In fact, he denies it.'

'Pooh. And if you believe that . . .'

'Is there anything else you can think of that might help us?'

'No.'

Claire left a card and Sorrel promised to contact her if she remembered anything else that might have a bearing on her sister's disappearance. But as Claire drove away she felt sure Sorrel would not be ringing any time soon.

The encounter had left her sad. Not to care whether your sister was alive or dead seemed dreadful to her until she recalled how she had felt about Adam, her half-brother, whom she had resented enough to want to stuff a pillow over his face. Thank God she hadn't. She would have been labelled a child killer. No medical school would have wanted her with such a record. It had happened in her mind and gone no further. At least Sorrel hadn't gone that far or rather she hadn't admitted to going that far.

Little by little, fact by fact, she was learning about the missing girl. Sorrel had painted a vivid picture of her. A misfit, quarrelsome, difficult. And Claire supplied the rest: unhappy, the odd one out. The Ugly Duckling.

So her brother had been gated from school for smoking pot. Was that what Kobi had meant by those dark hints about Shane? As well as the suggestion that Tom was not Marvel's father. But if he wasn't why was he so desperate for her body to be found?

THIRTY-EIGHT

She realized she had no idea what was really in Tom's mind. And Shane? What did he have to do with it? Did the entire family have something to hide? But why hide any of it? They weren't even under suspicion. Or were they? The police investigation had been sloppy. Zed Willard was loyal to the Force but even he was admitting this. And she wasn't convinced that he wasn't wondering, after all these years, whether his theory had been misguided.

So, she thought, she needed to look at motive. Why would all these people do their best to mislead her? Kobi for entertainment, and now to the list did she have to add Tom and Shane?

In the morning, she vowed, the first thing she would do would be to comb through Kobi's work record. Then she needed to cross reference that with details of Marvel's life and schooling. There was something there, she was convinced of it. A little thread that she just needed to pull.

And now there was Shane's relationship with his sister. She put her head in her hands. To make any sort of assessment she needed to talk to Shane to decide for herself. And so far he wasn't playing. And as for Tom, he hadn't even hinted that he wasn't Marvel's father.

She parked her car, unlocked her front door and let herself in.

It was only then that she realized that though she could hear muted music from the top floor there was no Grant in evidence. He must have left. And then she understood. Coming and going would always be what suited him.

And maybe it suited her too.

Tuesday 15 October, 11 a.m.

She found Astrid sitting at the nurses' station, leafing through the drugs charts. She looked up as Claire approached. 'You all right, Dr Roget?'

Claire settled into the chair at the nurse's side. 'Yeah,' she said. 'I'm good. How's Ilsa?'

'Ominously quiet,' the nurse said. 'How are her two victims?'

'I think her husband's home, but the woman is still in hospital as far as I know.' She settled down in a chair. 'I never would have thought Ilsa would turn so quickly from victim to villain. She hid it well.'

Astrid was quiet for a moment, then she said, 'She's manipulative. But you really think she planned it ahead?'

'I think so,' Claire said quietly. 'I think all that business about claiming her husband was controlling and trying to belittle her was part of the act. We have no evidence he was like that. In fact, if you look at it objectively the evidence all points the other way. He was doing up the house, making everything good for when she was discharged. And I don't believe she thought he was having an affair with her friend. We have no evidence that she was psychotic which means we have to keep at the back of our minds another explanation for the assault. My current instinct is that this was a deliberate criminal offence.' She smiled at the nurse. 'Having said that her barrister will move heaven and carth to claim she was suffering from anxiety and depression and I'll be hard pushed to go against that.'

'So . . .?'

'She'll be returned to our care long term. She won't go to prison. It isn't the right decision but it's what'll happen.'

And the nurse nodded.

'I'll go and talk to her and explain the due process.'

But Ilsa was asleep. Looking as innocent as a baby. Claire watched her for a moment, speaking her name softly but it was obvious Ilsa was not going to rouse.

Late morning, without much hope, she tried Marvel's brother again. Surprisingly he responded to her call and didn't hang up when she introduced herself, though, as before, he was hostile. If anything, even more so.

'I wish you would just leave us all alone,' he said. 'This is bordering on harassment.'

'It's nothing of the sort,' she said, speaking calmly. 'I'm a psychiatrist who has been asked to grant your father's wish that your sister's body be recovered, so when he dies, which I am assured, is not far off, they can be buried together, father and daughter.'

Shane snorted. 'Father and daughter,' he derided.

'He wants the truth.'

'And what exactly do you think my contribution might be?' There was something wary in his voice.

'I don't know, Shane. I suppose I'm hoping you might go over your sister's movements on that last Saturday?'

His response was a hostile silence before answering, 'And what good do you think that'll do?'

She decided to show her card. 'I'm not convinced Kobi is responsible for your sister's disappearance.'

There was a long silence followed by a cynical grunt. 'So he's managing to fool you, is he? I thought you were a psychiatrist, someone with insight.'

She kept her cool. 'Psychiatry is a lot more than just insight, Shane.'

And then he caved in. 'You don't get it, do you?'

She kept her voice steady. 'Get what, Shane?'

'Why would he want to be buried with her? Why is he really so insistent that he wants the truth? Dad and Marvel. They couldn't stand each other. If you'd seen them together you'd have realized that within minutes. He hated the way she sometimes looked, the way she behaved, the clothes she wore, the make-up she slapped on with a trowel, the skirts too short, blouses unbuttoned, T-shirts halfway up her chest. He hated everything about her. He hated her. So why this obsession with being buried with her?'

'Guilt for not . . .?' She'd meant to say, 'loving her', but Shane got there first.

'He was glad to have her off the scene. Called her a slut. Mum and Dad. They were embarrassed by her. The rows, the fallings out. She made the house a battle zone. Mum doesn't want Marvel resurrected. Marvel stole from us. She couldn't be trusted. She was just about anybody's. But no one wanted her. Guys gave her a wide berth.' And then his voice stopped abruptly.

'Maybe your father's remorseful and wants to make it up to her.'

That drew another snort. 'Or maybe he just wants to pretend that our family was one big happy set of people. I don't know.' His voice was bitter and angry.

'When did you last see your dad?'

'Last week. I go to see him as a duty. I sit there. Yvonne watches, making her own contribution. I've nothing to say to him. We're OK, Dad and I – as long as we don't spend more than half an hour in each other's company and don't really say anything. Truth is . . .' he couldn't seem to stop this from spilling out, '. . . we don't trust each other.'

Claire heard and was thoughtful. Something deep and dark was opening up right under her feet.

'Did he mention my efforts to have Jonah Kobi confess to your sister's murder?'

'He touched on it.'

'Did you discuss it?' She wished she could have seen his face as he responded.

'No.'

'Does it mean anything to you? Do you feel the same urge to find your sister's body and convict her killer?'

'No. For God's sake. Let sleeping dogs lie.'

There was a long silence while she absorbed this, wondering if she had imagined that note of fright in his voice?

'After all this time I don't think I'm bothered about her skeleton.' There was a real gravelly bitterness in his voice now.

'And do you think Kobi is responsible?'

'Put it like this,' Shane said, 'it would suit us all.'

Which didn't answer her question.

'What about you, Shane. How did *you* get on with her?'

'I didn't hate her. I felt sorry for her. She was so pathetic. So desperate to be loved that . . .' Again, he stopped dead. The silence stretched and then he caved in. 'Maybe it's time the truth came out. I will come to the hospital if you like. I'll let you know when I can speak to you.'

And she had to be content with that.

To try and actually move forward in this frustrating morass of rumination she started to read through Kobi's work record as a supply teacher. She cross-referenced them against Marvel's schooling.

And there it was in black and white. Just two days at a comprehensive school in Biddulph, filling in for a teacher's absence in 2013. Marvel had been a pupil at the very same school.

She was about to pick up the phone when she read the note Willard had attached to the front:

> He didn't teach her. He taught the older pupils and had no contact with year nine. Also, she didn't take history.

Typical, she thought disgustedly. Just when you think you're getting somewhere.

She could almost sense that he was thumbing his nose at her for her 'cleverness'.

It didn't improve her mood that Kobi was asking to speak to her again.

THIRTY-NINE

She would have refused this time but now she had ammunition, something to fire back at Kobi, and he wouldn't be pleased that she was learning facts independent of the ones he wanted to feed her.

Until he looked up Kobi had seemed terminally bored. He also looked tired and depressed, shoulders sagging, facial expression lacking affect. Prison was ageing him.

She watched him through the window and realized. This wasn't a game to him anymore. He was actually worried that she would find the truth. Possibly he had even lost his cue and was unsure how to play this. She entered the room and sat down.

His eyes narrowed. He sensed she knew something.

But he held back, eyes fixed on her as he tried to read her mind. Then he leaned back in his chair, put his hands flat on the table, palms down, and spoke. 'So?'

'You taught at Marvel's school.'

He blinked.

She fed him the lie. 'You taught Marvel.'

He stirred, ran his tongue over his lips. She sensed relief. *So that was it.* And she was wrong. 'I didn't,' he said slowly, 'actually teach her, though I believe I was in the same school for a couple of days, I think. Clap clap,' he said, irony spilling out, 'for your detective work. Well done you. May I ask how you came by this knowledge?'

'It was all there,' she said, 'in the notes.' As she watched him she sensed that there was another small detail he was worried she might learn.

She pressed forward. 'You saw her at school?'

'Not that I remember.' His voice was casual now. Comfortable.

'But you knew details about her family. Perhaps from a schoolfriend?'

'From the newspaper,' he corrected.

Inwardly she acknowledged. That was not it.

They waited, skirting round each other like boxers in the ring. 'Kobi, why did you ask to see me today?'

He leaned back and folded his arms behind his head, casual now and disdainful. 'Curiosity perhaps?'

That was not it either. He wanted to drop another little breadcrumb.

'You mentioned a charm from a silver bracelet.'

He put his finger on his chin and pretended to look puzzled. 'Did I?' It was a hackneyed impression of confusion.

Something erupted in her as the faces of the dead girls flashed across her mind. 'You brutally killed . . .'

He held his hand up in a stop sign. 'I didn't brutally kill them,' he said. 'I simply extinguished their far too bright lights. Their deaths weren't brutal.'

'Their loss was to their families. They would have grown up, perhaps had children of their own. You robbed their mothers, fathers, siblings, friends. Put fear into countless schoolgirls.'

He lifted his eyebrows. 'A lesson. No more.'

'I intend to speak to some of your ex-pupils,' Claire said.

This lit a fire in his eyes and he responded quickly. 'They won't be able to tell you anything.' He pursued the point. 'Why my ex-pupils? There must be hundreds of them. I don't see what you can learn from any of them.'

Claire smiled sweetly. 'One never knows until one tries.'

He was breathing hard as he responded. 'The girls I taught in the private schools are probably all married by now, living in detached houses and driving fast cars.' He even put his hands up as though wrapped round a steering wheel turning a sharp corner. 'And the rest will be following their various boringly similar paths. You want to waste *precious* time interviewing all the girls in all the schools I taught at when they won't take you a single millimetre nearer to learning where this fucking girl's body is.' He slapped the desk with both hands. It was a loud, startling sound. 'I didn't personally know any of the girls I killed. So what's the point of wasting time?' He couldn't resist adding the barb, 'Time Tom Trustrom doesn't really have.'

Claire didn't react which goaded Kobi further. 'If you need to find her rotting corpse before her Daddy dies. And if you don't mind me saying, as Tom Trustrom has been "dying"' – he wiggled his fingers in mock exclamation marks now, chortling as he did so – 'an awfully long time, you need to look wider afield.'

'Where?'

Kobi paused. Then: 'Why not try Miranda Pullen?'

She knew he was diverting her but listened anyway.

'She's as good as anyone at a tissue of lies, probably married to some wealthy guy by now. And while you're at it fish out some of her best buddies. See what *they* thought of me.' He folded his arms, confident and relaxed. 'Truth is they fancied the pants off me, but I wasn't interested in their clumsy, adolescent little tricks. As a psychiatrist you can surely see that these girls wanted my attention. Well, they got it – or some of them did.'

'At least Miranda made good money out of it.' Claire closed her notebook and yawned, not bothering to suppress it. 'Actually,' she said, returning the notebook to her bag, 'I've already had a chat with your old friend Miranda Pullen. I'm not sure she has anything more helpful to add than you do.'

He smiled and held out his hands. 'She had lovely hair,' he said. 'Did you notice from the photograph? Very soft.' He stroked the desk. 'Red gold. Quite beautiful. Different from her "siblings". I imagine it smelt' – he gave a noisy sniff – 'of coconut shampoo. It was by far' – he slid his eyes up to meet hers – 'her best feature.' Then he frowned. 'Correction. Her only good feature.'

She knew exactly what he was doing, goading her.

'If you have anything concrete to tell me,' she said, 'let the prison guards know and I will come back, otherwise I shan't be coming again.'

She picked up her notebook and headed for the door. She was almost there when Kobi whispered, 'So I'll be seeing you then, Claire.'

'I doubt it. Goodbye, Kobi,' she said.

He glared at her, eyes hot with hatred as she knocked on the door and was let out.

She could still feel the heat of his hostility as she walked down the corridor behind the prison warder.

She joined the D road and a queue of traffic. The M6 must be diverting the flow between Junctions 15 and 16. Another accident? She tapped her steering wheel in frustration. These prison visits were taking up too much time, diverting her from her work at Greatbach.

At last, after crawling along for forty-five minutes she arrived back and, not for the first time, reflected what an ugly building it was: Victorian, forbidding and it always appeared dark, in the shade, which was perhaps an analogy for the dramas that happened inside. The modern wing, which accommodated mainly outpatients and offices, was at the back of the building so one was presented with the nineteenth-century facade, reached through a grey arch which could seem as though you were entering another world. A grim, cruel, unenlightened world where Victorian attitudes and misunderstandings of mental illness prevailed. But actually it was not so. That was an illusion.

She manoeuvred the car into a tight parking space and sat for a while, trying to puzzle it all out, going over Kobi's words and she knew why they'd chilled her. She could see the photograph of Marvel Trustrom as clearly as if it was in her hand. Not the photo of her in school uniform, hair neatly plaited, face scrubbed, or her Facebook picture. Not even the picture that had been given to the press, but one of the pictures her parents had given the police and had been kept back by them. Long, red, gold hair, soft and straight, gleaming, freshly shampooed and straightened. Marvel Trustrom's one claim to beauty.

Claire released her seat belt, climbed out, locked the car and walked through the arch into her other world, the inside world of a secure psychiatric unit.

As soon as she reached her office she took another look at it. It was just as she – and Kobi – had remembered it. She could almost smell coconut shampoo.

She bounded up the stairs. This coming weekend, Grant was helping his mother to move back down to Cornwall and so, she promised herself, she would go on a long bike ride. Out in the Peak District, somewhere really challenging, with long, steep climbs. She would ride until she was exhausted and then she would drive home and drop into a bathtub filled to the brim with expensive and fragrant skin-softening products, glass of champagne in her hand. The weather forecast was perfect. Cool but dry and not too windy. Nothing to slow her down.

She reached the locked ward and keyed in the code, changed on a monthly basis, and headed straight for Ilsa's room. Any decisions she presented would need to be reinforced by facts and interviews. She peeped through the window. Ilsa was huddled on the floor, knees up, back against the corner, eyes staring at nothing. Claire watched her for a while before she entered her room. Ilsa started and pressed herself harder into the corner. 'What's going to happen to me?'

Claire didn't answer and knew it all depended on 'dangerousness'. To herself or other people.

Ilsa had a son of eight years old. She couldn't send her home and put the child in danger. Was there a cure? An absolutely certain cure?

No. She would always be a risk.

Claire spent almost an hour interviewing her and at the end felt convinced Ilsa had planned the entire assault, relying that Claire's testimony of mental illness would protect her from a criminal charge.

On her way out she spoke to Astrid who was in charge of the locked ward. 'Keep a watch on Ilsa. She's in a strange state.'

Astrid's take on her patients was notoriously hard. 'You think?'

'Yes. Keep a close watch on her.'

Astrid nodded. She was an experienced nurse who had worked for years at Broadmoor. She knew what the words 'close watch' meant.

They spent the next two hours discussing various other patients on the ward, altering medication where necessary and then Claire had to dictate some letters. It was almost seven o'clock when her mobile phone bleeped a message. *I can cook dinner for you if you like. Eight thirty OK? G X*

She typed back. *Brilliant. I'm knackered and rapidly approaching terminal starvation. See you later. C X*

So this was the relationship they were falling back into, easy, comfortable, undemanding. Here today, gone tomorrow. Nothing too heavy and no real commitment. Someone there for her as she was for him. And as she locked her office door behind her she acknowledged this could be what she wanted. She looked forward to arriving home.

FORTY

Wednesday 16 October, 8.15 a.m.

She needed to meet up with Shane Trustrom. He'd promised to get in touch, but she didn't want to wait any longer. She added it to her morning's list.

With all the challenges at work and the added complication now of Ilsa's case, she wondered why her heart was skipping. And then she remembered.

Last night, after a delicious dinner of poached salmon, watercress sauce and fresh vegetables she and Grant had shared a bottle of wine and talked.

Grant had a deep voice, slow, steady and sexy, expressive dark eyes with long lashes and what he said he meant. There was no duplicity in him. His manners were almost blunt. You could trust him. He was an anchor. This was why his sister had relied on him during her years of illness and his mother would continue to do so. He was – in spite of his roguish looks – dependable. With him she could confide her doubts about Ilsa's integrity and her misgivings about Jonah Kobi. 'He tosses me around as though I was a kitten's plaything and I still don't know whether he had anything to do with the disappearance of Marvel Trustrom.'

He'd laughed and his arm had pulled her towards him on the sofa. 'And I always thought as a psychiatrist you'd have an instinct for when people were trying to pull the wool over your eyes.'

She'd shaken her head. 'I wish,' she'd said. Adding, 'Psychiatry is a minefield.' He'd kissed away any more words and she knew Grant Steadman would always turn his back on anything he found unpleasant.

In return he'd confided in her where his plans lay. His mother was heading back down to Cornwall. 'I expect,' he'd said ruefully, 'she'll want me going up and down the M5 because a tap's sprung a leak or something.'

Her response of, 'Well, she is your mum,' had earned her a quick, questioning look. As they'd talked Claire had realized how much she'd missed these quiet evenings when they chatted, polishing off a bottle of wine and spending the night together.

The conversation had turned then to Grant's future plans. The police had closed off the Robinson home as it was a crime scene and there was little chance of it being released any time soon which put paid to the home interior Grant had been designing. It was possible John Robinson would entirely abandon his plans to revamp the family home. Everything was in limbo. The court case would take some time to put together, the outcome uncertain. In the meantime, Ilsa would be confined at Greatbach and Grant was . . . unemployed. And now her heart had stopped skipping because she had the odd feeling that ill luck might just follow her boyfriend around. Some people were like that. Just when it appeared they were riding the crest of a wave a tsunami would come along and sweep them under again.

To add to the downward turn of mood her clinic that afternoon seemed full of alcoholics and drug abusers, each one with their own pet reason for straying from the path of good and true. One thing about these people with addiction problems was that they were inventive with their excuses. They dragged in damaged childhoods, abusive parents, boring upbringings which had resulted in a thirst for excitement, overly religious parents, strict Catholic teachings, parents with addiction problems themselves, broken marriages, sick children, pressures of work. The list could go on and on and on. And by the end of it Claire was mentally exhausted. She wanted to ring Shane but put it off until she had checked on Ilsa.

She found Ilsa alert, watchful and wary, sitting in a chair, staring out of the window as though she was planning an escape. Claire spent some time explaining the court process to her and informing her that she would be detained under a section of the Mental Health Act until it was decided what should be done with her.

Ilsa listened without responding. It made any assessment very hard to read. Ilsa was watching her.

Then her face changed and she lunged forward. 'It's you,' she said. 'Your fault.' Claire felt her nails rake down her cheek, tasted the blood. She struggled to her feet and stumbled out of the room. Not the first time she had been assaulted by a patient and it would not be the last. One can remove all sharp objects or anything that could be used in a suicide attempt. But you can't remove a patient's fingernails.

After speaking to the staff to make sure they knew Ilsa should be locked into her room and attended always by two members of staff as well as having her scratches tended by the nurses with antiseptic, she left Greatbach in reflective mood.

She wanted to go home. Take a bath and think. Read a book, watch TV. She couldn't face chasing Shane Trustrom up.

But the day's challenges were not over yet.

Annoyingly Simon's car was slewed across the drive forcing her to overlap the pavement as Grant's was pulled up tight towards the front door. She let herself into what sounded like a battle zone.

Simon and Marianne were having a noisy quarrel in the kitchen. Marianne was screaming. Simon's voice was low and subdued. This is not working, she thought angrily.

Grant was hunched up on the sofa. He watched her enter without a word but she'd noticed the door had been tight shut and the sound on the television louder than usual. He managed a grin before rolling his eyes heavenwards.

FORTY-ONE

Thursday 17 October, 2.30 p.m.

It was all right saying speak to Shane but what if Shane didn't want to speak to her? He'd promised he would get back to her with a time and date when they could meet but so far there had been no contact.

She left another message urging him to get in touch. And at last, at three o'clock in the afternoon, Shane Trustrom did ring back and this time seemed more willing to talk. Almost friendly. He began with a blunt question. 'Do you know yet what happened to my sister?' There was a note of anxiety in his voice.

'No.'

On the other end of the line there was silence. She could almost hear rusty cogs of thought processes whirring around desperately trying to find their notch. Finally he sighed. 'OK,' he said. 'I can come to your place or you can come here if you like.'

Her relief was great. 'I'll come to you,' she said.

He gave her an address in Stone and she arranged to visit him on the following afternoon. She felt there was no time to waste. Tom was dying and her curiosity was compounding.

Her surprise visit later that afternoon was John Robinson. He had lost weight since she had last seen him and was looking gaunt and unhappy. He began by apologizing for simply dropping in. 'I was upstairs visiting Ilsa,' he said, a broken man. 'She tried to hit me. I don't understand what's happened. What has happened? Why has she changed so much?'

It was hard to explain to a lay person when it didn't really make sense even to her. 'She's going through a psychotic episode,' she said. 'Which means that she has ideas which seem real . . . to her.'

'So when will she be well enough to come home?'

'That's for the courts and myself to decide. Hopefully when she seems safe.'

'But when will that be?'

She simply shook her head. He waited for a while then asked, 'Can I be honest with you?'

'Of course.'

'I'm frightened to have her home. I'm ashamed to say this but if you'd seen her face when she . . . And Augustus. I can't risk him being hurt. She could kill him. And you can't guarantee that she won't do something like that again, can you?'

She shook her head.

'I'm not short of money. I'll be generous towards her. I can pay for her care, for supervision if that's what's necessary. She won't lose out. But I'm frightened of her. I don't feel I'll ever be able to relax in her company. I don't know what to do.'

She felt a flood of sympathy. 'Considering the assault on you and Mrs Levand, I don't think your wife returning to the family home in the near future is currently an option. The courts will decide.'

'But you'll play your part.'

'Yes. And how is Maggie Levand?'

'Struggling. Still in hospital having breathing problems. The knife punctured her lung.'

'I'm sorry.'

His face hardened. 'You're the one who let her loose,' he accused. 'You let her go.'

She didn't want to say this but she had to. 'It is possible that your refusal to have her home contributed in some way to her paranoia and conviction that you and Maggie were having an affair.'

He looked at her steadily without a visible response. She tried to reassure him. 'Until Ilsa's future is decided by the courts she will remain here. But at some point she will be free, Mr Robinson.'

Robinson said nothing but slowly shook his head. As he left, she could feel his wash of dissatisfaction.

And she was aware that she had seen the other side of Ilsa now. The violent, unpredictable side her patient had kept carefully hidden behind her veil of anxiety and depression.

She had failed John Robinson, she had failed Maggie Levand, and now it looked as though she was going to fail Tom Trustrom in his quest to find his daughter's body. And she'd misunderstood Kobi, who was shadow dancing behind her, mocking her, imitating her moves and adapting them to his own devices, dropping little hints that may or may not mean something.

Rita had left a note on her desk telling her that Yvonne, Tom's partner, had left a message asking her to phone back. Wearily she picked up the phone and immediately heard the distress in the woman's voice. 'He's deteriorated, Dr Roget. I don't think he'll last much longer. I wondered if you'd got anywhere in the search for his daughter?'

'Not really,' Claire said. 'I'm afraid Jonah Kobi isn't being very helpful.'

'Oh.' The disappointment in her voice was painful. Yvonne's next words were a whisper. 'What if it isn't him?'

'Sorry?'

'What if it isn't Mr Kobi but . . .?'

The doubt Claire had so far suppressed surfaced and caused a physical thump on the chest. She tried to steady her voice. 'That's something we may have to consider.'

As well as, she added silently, *the possibility that Tom might have had something to do with his daughter's disappearance. Maybe even her murder.* The entire case had turned full circle and hadn't stopped spinning yet.

FORTY-TWO

Friday 18 October, 4 p.m.

Shane Trustrom lived in a pretty Victorian terraced house overlooking the railway in the small town of Stone. It was a town which had clung on to its high street and weekly open-air market as well as a monthly farmers' market. In days gone by it had had a thriving shoe industry and today it boasted not only the Trent and Mersey canal but also its own famous brewery, Joules, friend of a million hangovers.

She parked against the railings and knocked on the door. Shane was tall and thin with a stooped posture and a troubled expression. His breathing was quick and shallow with puffs of exhalation. He was only twenty-four but already balding. He looked more than ten years older, the weight of the world – or possibly his past – resting on his shoulders. Which surprised her. Was it his father's impending death which was causing him so much anxiety, his sister's disappearance, or was there something else? Guilt perhaps? His face was deeply scored and his pale eyes, as he shook her hand, looked evasive. He dropped his gaze quickly. Too late. She'd already read them.

He kept her on the step. 'I really didn't want to do this,' he said. 'Dig it all up again.'

'It's your father's request which has resurrected your sister's disappearance. Not the police nor some prurient interest of my own.'

His head flicked up. 'Disappearance,' he queried. 'Are you telling me you don't even think she's dead?'

'There's no evidence,' she reminded him.

'And if she is dead you have doubts that Jonah Kobi murdered her?' He sounded incredulous – or worried.

She managed a watery smile. 'Mr Trustrom,' she said, 'I take nothing for granted.' She tried to make light of it. 'In my work I've learned to doubt everything.'

'Doubt everything.' It was a soft, uncertain echo.

'OK.' He held up his hand, fending her off. Looked up and down the street. 'You'd better come in,' he said, holding the door open wide.

She followed him into a kitchen/living room which encompassed almost the entire ground floor of the property. At some point in the past walls had been knocked through and this large open space created. In a Victorian terrace it was a surprise, as though one had stepped out of one era and into another. The kitchen end was modern with cream units and dark granite tops. At the far end bifold doors overlooked the garden which was an unimaginative rectangle of grass edged with a high wooden fence.

Marvel's brother indicated a chair by the table. 'You want a coffee?'

'Yeah. That'd be nice.'

So they sat around the table and set their mugs on tiny drinks

mats. The house was pristine, so clean and tidy it bordered on
sterile. There was no sign of the baby; no bottles, sterilizer or
infant paraphernalia. Neither were there family photographs.

Shane saw her looking around. 'My wife, Kristal,' he said with
pride, 'she likes the place tidy.'

Claire nodded, hoping to him it signified approval but really
she was reflecting how little warmth the house had as though it
held itself together tightly, worried that secrets might leak out.
She felt a sudden lust for Grant's shoes scattered around the place,
the scent of woodsmoke and aftershave, deodorant and meals
cooked and eaten, the clutter that went with two people personal-
izing their house so it felt like a home. This place felt sucked in
as though it was not even breathing.

Shane was watching her enquiringly, perhaps still waiting for
her approval.

'I don't know what you think I can . . .' He stopped.

'You need to tell me things,' she said. 'Anything that links to
the time when you last saw your sister. Think back to that day.'

'I don't have to think very hard,' he said, looking stricken. 'I
can remember every single minute of that damned day.'

'You were a teenager when your sister vanished.'

'Eighteen.' He hesitated before speaking. 'Let me get this
straight, Dr Roget,' he said. 'Your role is to get Jonah Kobi,
convicted killer of four women. Schoolgirls,' he corrected, 'to
admit to a fifth, the murder of my sister?' He held his breath while
he waited for her response. 'It would sit nicely on his shoulders,
wouldn't it?'

'Not if he didn't do it.'

'But it would hardly make any difference to his sentence.' He
sounded eager. 'He's not getting out any time soon, is he?'

Was he looking for reassurance? 'No. Whatever comes to light
Jonah Kobi is staying inside for life.'

Shane was silent and, in spite of her assurances, he still looked
unhappy.

'I simply want to help your father, give him peace of mind.'

Shane shook his head slowly from side to side, not as
though he was doubting her words but as though her task was
impossible.

'If you don't believe Kobi is guilty, what then?'

'I'll simply hand the cold case back to the police. My involvement will end.'

'So your job is really only to assess Jonah Kobi.'

'That's right.'

His voice had remained quiet, but in his eyes there was a sudden light of panic. He was skittish and nervy. The hands cradling the coffee mug had a slight tremor. He was uncertain about something and this knowledge was nibbling him from the inside out. She waited while he took a sip of coffee before setting his mug down with a carefully controlled action which hardly made a sound.

'Has Kobi actually confessed?'

She shook her head. 'That isn't the way he plays this. As long as I keep going to the prison and asking questions he'll string me along. So far I've had nothing useful out of him.'

Except hints, she thought.

Shane Trustrom stared down at the pale wood grain before looking up. 'What do you think?'

'I have an open mind. Shane. Now tell me what you remember of that day.'

He half closed his eyes. 'It was a Saturday,' he said, 'a day like so many other Saturdays. Lots of quarrelling and shouting. Everyone screaming and yelling at everyone else. We'd run out of milk so Mum was grumpy but didn't want to go out in the rain to fetch some more.' His pale eyes were seeing that past day as though it was laid out in front of him. 'Sorrel and Clarice were both crying, goodness knows why. That house . . .' He looked at her before turning his gaze around the kitchen. 'It was like a zoo. It was chaotic.' He looked around him. 'The opposite of here.'

He shrugged. 'I made a couple of slices of toast and took them upstairs to my bedroom, ate them there while I played on my computer, headphones on to block out the din.'

'When did you actually see Marvel last?'

'Round about lunchtime. I was hungry again. The house was a bit quieter. Sorrel and Clarice had gone out somewhere – to friends' houses, I think. Mum wasn't there but Marvel and Dad were. They were arguing in the kitchen. Dad had her by the arm.'

He gave Claire a quick glance. 'Maybe that's why he feels so guilty,' he said. 'Because they argued the last time he saw her.' And then he looked downwards again as though having proffered a false explanation he had to conceal the truth.

Claire absorbed the image of Marvel's noisy, conflicted family life.

'Later that day?'

'I don't know . . .' His shoulders drooped even further. 'I suppose everyone came back.'

'Except Marvel.'

'Yes. Of course. Except Marvel. The house got noisy and quarrelsome again. Everything, everyone erupting.'

'So when did anyone realize your sister was missing?'

'I don't know,' he said. 'I stopped in my bedroom. It was the only place I could get any peace. Someone . . . I think it was Mum . . . knocked on my door and asked if I'd seen her.'

'What time was this?'

He shrugged. 'I don't know,' he said. 'Six-ish? It was dark. It seemed late.'

She wanted to goad him, prick his conscience. He knew something. She waited. But he wasn't saying anything more. He finished his coffee and sat, waiting for her to speak, his fingers interlocked. Then he looked up and she felt he had come to a decision. He let out his breath with a strange, relieved sigh. One hand stole up and rubbed his forehead as though erasing some memory. He pushed his chair back, stood up and left the room.

FORTY-THREE

She heard him climb the stairs and a minute later descend lumpily as though he was reluctant to do this, each step a heavy, uneven thump on the tread.

He came back into the room and threw something metallic on to the table. A pair of silver intertwined *pointe* ballet shoes tiny enough to form a charm on a silver bracelet.

She looked at it for a moment and waited for him to explain.

He was looking at the tiny shoe as though it was poisonous.

Then across at her, as though he was waiting for her to put two and two together.

When she didn't, he elaborated. 'I found this in Dad's car,' he said. 'That's why she went to Hanley that horrible afternoon. Sorrel and Clarice had one and she was stomping around because she didn't. Sorrel and Clarice were' – he smiled – 'dainty little things, whereas Marvel was the proverbial baby elephant.' He reflected for a moment. 'Just built differently, I guess. Sorrel and Clarice did ballet classes. Marvel was desperate to go but as she was so big Mum wouldn't let her.' He frowned. 'Maybe she thought Marvel would be teased. I don't know. Anyway, Sorrel and Clarice had passed a ballet exam and Mum bought them a little charm each, just like this, as a reward. Marvel was livid. She screamed and shouted and cried.' His face sagged. 'We weren't fair to her, you know. She was different and we didn't understand why then.'

Claire held the tiny object on her palm. To Marvel, this must have seemed like the final insult.

'Next thing she said she was meeting a friend.' Again, he wiped his forehead. 'She was full of shit. She didn't have any friends. Anyway, she was off to Hanley to buy her own little pair of dancing shoes. Marvel being Marvel she couldn't see how pathetic it was. She could have the charm but she was never going to pass the ballet exam. Sad, really.'

'This could be one of your sisters' charms,' she said, 'not necessarily the one that Marvel went to buy that day.'

Shane shook his head. 'They would have created holy hell if they'd lost it.'

Claire sat back and thought. In which direction was this tiny object sending her? 'When exactly did you find this?'

'Later,' he said. 'Much later. Maybe a month or so after Marvel had gone missing. I was cleaning the car for a bit of extra pocket money. I was studying and really hard up. I'd do little jobs around the house for some cash.'

'But you didn't mention this? To anyone? You didn't challenge your father over this?'

'How could I?' He looked appalled. 'Incriminate my own father when everyone – everyone, the police too – were all saying it was the Schoolgirl Killer. No one made a big thing about the differences in the crimes. Why not let Kobi carry the can? It wouldn't make any difference to him. Marvel was a pain.'

'You can't believe your father killed her?'

'Why not?' he countered. 'He bloody well hated her. They were always rowing. And he'd gone out to look for her. He was gone ages. Hours. Plenty of time to . . .'

'But if that's true why . . .' she ruminated slowly, '. . . would your dad now be making a big thing about her body being found?'

'I've thought about that,' Shane said, without rancour, even with some affection. 'He's a lapsed Catholic. He'll want to go to his Maker with a clear conscience.'

'So why not just confess and tell us where she is?'

Shane shrugged.

'I can't believe it of him,' she said. 'It doesn't make sense.'

'You're just seeing a dying, weakened, old man. You didn't know him then. He was full of fire and hatred.'

'Do you believe he killed your sister?'

Shane shrugged. 'What else am I to believe?'

Both were silent for a minute or two, then Claire moved on to the practicalities. 'And her body?'

'There's places.'

She was silent, her thoughts struggling with the fact that Marvel's brother had preserved this tiny piece of evidence for all these years. He'd kept it but why?

'You've *never* mentioned this to your dad? Never even hinted at it?'

He shook his head.

'Why not?'

He didn't answer but twisted his mouth.

'But you've shown it to me.'

'Don't you understand,' he hissed. 'Someone knows.'

Kobi knew. Or at least he knew something. How? He wasn't a psychic or a medium, able to talk to the dead.

She tossed her thoughts around until she realized that Shane was still watching her.

She recalled his words about limiting his visits to half an hour at a time. 'How do you get on with your dad?'

'OK,' he said, guarded now. And she realized this was all hinging on Marvel's brother's testimony. She picked up the charm. 'Do you mind if I keep this?'

He put his hand out as though to stop her. 'What are you going to do with it?'

'I don't know – yet. Maybe talk to your dad again.'

He spread his hands and drew them back towards his body. 'OK,' he said, 'I guess. It'll all come out but he won't be there to face the music. He'll be out of it.' He couldn't resist adding a jibe. 'Hopefully not in purgatory.'

'Is there anything else you want to add?'

Shane shook his head and at the same time Claire heard the front door open and close and the sound of a baby crying. He jumped up and as she watched he wheeled a small pushchair into the room followed closely by a blonde-haired woman Claire took to be his wife. The baby was in her arms.

'This is Dr Roget,' he said, and with a hard stare at her, added, 'she was just leaving.'

Trustrom's wife gave an unconvincing smile. 'Nice to meet you,' she said. 'Goodbye.'

Claire pocketed the charm and left, questions burning in her mind.

Did the answer to Marvel's disappearance lie outside prison walls?

Sitting in her car, she connected with DS Zed Willard who simply sounded irritated that she hadn't yet squeezed a confession out of Kobi. His irritation compounded when she asked him about the silver charm Marvel had gone to buy.

'What about it?'

'Was it the same as the one her sisters had?'

'I don't know.' Now he simply sounded offended.

'Didn't you check with the jeweller?'

'We didn't make a big thing of it. We knew where to focus our investigation.'

At last he displayed some curiosity. 'What's all this about charms anyway?'

'Marvel's brother found one in his father's car.'

This was greeted with silence before Willard responded gruffly. 'Could have been one of the sisters.'

'He says not. What were Tom Trustrom's movements that day?'

'What do *you* think? He went out looking for his daughter.'

Willard's voice was raised an octave. He was sounding defensive and again she sensed that the murders had been too quickly linked. Like charms on a bracelet, events tell a story. It was possible that Willard and his colleagues had been reading the wrong story. 'And by the way,' Willard continued, fighting back now, 'if Marvel's brother found a silver charm why didn't he give it back to one of his sisters? If it wasn't one of theirs why didn't he ask his father whose it was? Or else hand it in to us if he thought it was evidence?'

The question she didn't want to answer.

'It's even possible,' DS Willard added, 'that he bought it as a sort of memento.'

Unlikely, she thought as she ended the call.

The logical step now would be to tackle Tom and simply ask him, but before she half accused a dying man of his daughter's murder she wanted to make sure. She picked up the phone and connected with Sorrel's salon. She could hear a plaintive female voice in the background and the distant ripple of what sounded like rainforest music.

Sorrel's pickup line was trotted out, a pert, 'Hello, Sorrel and Yvonne's Beauty Salon. Sorrel speaking. How may I help you?'

'Hi. It's Claire here, Dr Roget.'

'Yes?' The response was guarded.

Claire got straight to the point. 'The silver charm that your sister went to buy the day she went missing. Can you describe it?'

'It was a pair of intertwined *pointe* ballet shoes. Tiny. I've still got mine.'

That answered two questions.

'And Clarice still has hers?'

'Yeah. Marvel was sooooo jealous.' There was still a hint of malice in her voice.

'Are you sure that's what she went to buy the day she went missing?'

'Yeah.' There was a pause before she added, 'When you find her,' Marvel's sister said, still with the same note of satisfaction, 'she'll probably still be wearing it.'

'Are you wearing it now?'

'I am, as a matter of fact.' Her voice was still pert.

'Thank you.'

'Is that it?' She sounded disappointed.

'Yes.' Claire put the phone down reflecting on something that had seemed insignificant at the time. Marvel had told Shane she was meeting a friend. She recalled his words. *She didn't have any friends*.

She spent the rest of the afternoon preparing for Ilsa's court case with recommendations mainly restricting access to her family and further psychiatric evaluation.

What troubled Claire now was that she wondered how much Ilsa had planned from the first. The hospital admission provided documented instability of her mental state, then there was her self-discharge from the clinic. Writing her report, she was compelled to point out that it was possible her patient was highly manipulative. If Ilsa was lucky and the courts swallowed the version so carefully planted she wouldn't face a charge of GBH or attempted murder but would slide under the radar with a 'while the balance of mind was disturbed' plea. She wrote her report. It would be up to the courts to decide.

FORTY-FOUR

Monday 21 October, 8.45 a.m.

She had spent the weekend pondering both cases – and failed to come up with a neat solution. Grant had been busy moving his mother back down to Cornwall and she had been on call. She'd popped in to Greatbach on the Saturday morning and been called out in the early hours of Sunday to see a patient who had had an epileptic fit. Otherwise all had been calm. But going in to Greatbach on the Monday morning seemed like a tiresome extension to last week's work.

The obvious person to ask about the charm was Tom and ask him outright how it had turned up in his car. But even she could provide an alternative explanation – one which did not mean that he had picked her up in Hanley on that rainy November evening. He could have bought a similar one out of sentiment – or guilt

– particularly if he'd felt he had not treated his daughter as well as he might.

What did Shane believe when he had suggested his father wanted to die with a clear conscience?

But the fact that Tom was dying held her back from questioning him. She would try any other means to find out the truth. So she decided she should speak to Dixie and perhaps Clarice and hope they might give her some titbit. She looked down at her hand. Such a tiny object to open so many questions.

Without much hope she tried Dixie's phone again. And at least she answered the call but her voice was spiky. 'I have no idea why all this is being raked up again. The man who murdered my daughter is in prison.'

Claire stayed quiet while Dixie ranted and finally she spoke. 'We have new evidence.'

'What new—' Claire heard fear in her voice as she gave her address and suggested she drive down after the rush hour. 'Leave it until seven o'clock.'

The day dragged but finally Claire was driving the stuttering stop/start journey that was the M6 into Birmingham. She drove through the city centre and turned towards the south east.

Marvel's mother lived in a neat inter-war semi halfway along a row of similar houses. It was a few minutes before seven when Claire knocked on the door which was opened almost straight away. Dixie rejected Claire's proffered hand and stomped towards a kitchen where she grudgingly offered Claire a cup of tea.

The kitchen was space age with grey plastic units and a dark granite top. The walls were stark white. At the far end of the room was a grey sofa and a very large television.

Dixie worried away at the subject. 'What good any of this will do I really don't know. My daughter is dead and I believe that Jonah Kobi killed her.'

'Do you?'

The words were enough to stop Dixie Trustrom in her tracks. 'What have you found?'

Claire opened her hand and Dixie stared. 'Where did you get this?'

'Shane found it in your husband's car.'

Dixie said nothing but closed her eyes wearily, her face sunken. 'I wondered,' she said. 'Tom paid attention to young girls.' She licked her lips. 'He . . .'

She began again. 'He . . . I saw him looking at them. Sometimes. I wondered if Marvel knew something. If one of her friends had said something. And . . .' She couldn't go on.

Claire felt bound to pursue her. 'Do you mean you wondered whether your husband had molested young girls?'

'God help me,' was Dixie's response.

Claire spoke softly. 'Why was Marvel such an ugly duckling?'

Dixie's head jerked up. 'Sorry?'

'Why was she always the odd one out, Mrs Trustrom?'

The question seemed to freeze Marvel's mother. She began with an unconvincing, 'I don't know what . . .' but the words faded before they'd even left her mouth.

After some moments Dixie met her eyes. 'You already know, don't you?'

'I don't *know* but I have an idea.'

At which point Dixie's face sagged. 'You can easily know who is the mother of a child,' she said. 'Not so simple to find out who is the father.'

'So who is the father?'

Dixie didn't respond so Claire spoke. 'Not Tom.'

Dixie shook her head. 'It has nothing to do with Marvel's disappearance. He was just a man I met at work. He moved to Australia just before the millennium. I don't think I'd even told him I was pregnant. Tom forgave me. We moved on.'

'He knew Marvel wasn't his daughter?'

Dixie nodded.

'Did Marvel know?'

Dixie shook her head vigorously.

'That last Saturday, how long was Tom gone?'

Dixie's face froze. 'Hours.'

Both were silent, contemplating the possibilities.

'I told everything to the police. I didn't hide anything. When the other two girls were taken and Kobi charged we sort of relaxed. But it's dragged on and he's never confessed. We've appealed to him but have had no response. Tom and I separated. The girls grew up. Shane's made a life of his own.' Her face and voice were pained. 'Now it's all being raked up again and . . .' She put her hand out towards Claire. 'I'm sorry. I don't mean to be rude or unhelpful but I don't see how a psychiatrist' – she managed to make the word sound pejorative – 'can help. I think dragging you in will prove just as pointless as all the other enquiries, investigations and cold case reviews.'

Claire was silent, sensing that even now Marvel's mother was frightened for the truth to come out.

So she nodded her agreement and moved on.

'Do you think I can have a quick word with Clarice?'

'Go ahead. May as well get it over and done with. She'll be in her bedroom, probably listening in. She's a sneaky one. But I don't think she'll be able to help you. She was just a kid.'

Clarice was a complete contrast to her oldest sister. Small, dark-haired with soft brown eyes, she was tiny, delicate and dainty and, unlike Sorrel, was wearing no make-up at all. Her hair was tied back and she had an endearingly earnest look.

'Dr Roget,' she said holding out her hand and smiling, perfectly composed.

Her bedroom was lined with bookshelves and posters; a small desk in the corner was smothered with papers. She sat on the bed while Claire perched on the chair.

'I know why you're here,' Clarice said.

'Tell me about your sister.'

'There was always lots of shouting around her. She seemed to cause trouble. Conflict.'

'I gathered that.'

'You've met Sorrel?'

'Yeah.'

'She's something, isn't she?' There was a note of admiration in her voice.

'You're fond of your sister?'

Clarice laughed. 'Yes,' she said, sounding surprised at her own admission. 'Yes. I am. She and Marvel were always shouting at each other, always quarrelling but Sorrel and I were thick as thieves – most of the time,' she put in with honesty. 'I used to hide in the bedroom under my bed. The house was very . . .' She knitted her eyebrows together. 'Turbulent.'

'And Shane, how did he get on with his sister?'

'I think they got on OK – sometimes.'

'Oh?' Clarice's voice had held a frisson of embarrassment.

'They would go in a huddle together and start whispering. There was something . . . secretive about them.' She licked her lips. 'She'd go in his room and I'd hear noises.'

Claire could have asked what sort of noises but Clarice's face was flushed. 'The rest of the time,' she continued, 'they'd look as though they hated each other.'

Claire was silent for a moment. Sibling relationships are notoriously unpredictable. Was this something more?

'He gave her money,' Clarice finished.

Claire tucked the facts away. 'You've confided this to your mother?'

Another miserable nod.

'Do you have much to do with your father?'

That provoked a deep, guilty sigh. 'I see him a couple of times a month. More of a duty call really. I can't say we're close. And I'm not that fond of Yvonne. She hardly lets Dad get a word in edgeways.'

Tom Trustrom hardly had the breath to speak but Claire let it ride.

'And your mother?'

That provoked a firm head shake. 'She can't wait for me to leave home. She's not that maternal. Look,' she said in a burst of confidence, 'I'm not being funny but we don't want all this dragged up again. It was bloody awful at the time and I was only eleven. Marvel's dead. We've accepted that. She died a long time ago. No one's mourning her now. We don't want it all raked up again.'

'So you don't care who killed your sister or that she's buried with your dad?'

'No. I don't think it's important. I don't believe in God and Heaven and all that stuff. What difference does it make whether she's in a shallow grave or in the local crematorium with a headstone?'

'You don't care if her killer goes free?'

Clarice shrugged. 'What does it matter now? Kobi's in prison. He can't hurt anyone again. Why is it so important that my sister's killer is convicted for her murder when he's already serving life? I can't see the point. We just want to forget about it, Dr Roget. Forget.'

'Can you add anything to the investigation, something that would prove or refute the police theory that Kobi murdered your sister?'

She didn't even think about it. 'No.'

And that was that.

FORTY-FIVE

And now she wondered about Shane. What had the relationship been between brother and half-sister? *'There was something . . . secretive about them. She'd go in his room and I'd hear noises.'* What did Clarice's words mean?

And Tom? How had he really felt about the cuckoo in the nest? Was his interest powered by guilt? Had his emotions erupted and he had killed her? And hidden the body in those missing hours? Was he now seeking not only a body but absolution?

Tuesday 22 October, 11 a.m.

Yvonne picked up the phone, still acting as gatekeeper. 'He's not well enough to speak to you again.' Her voice was uncompromising in response to Claire's request.

'I'm afraid it's necessary.'

'Why?'

'I need to speak to him.'

'Well then, you'd better come soon.'

As before, Tom was lying on the sofa, a blanket over him, his head resting on cushions. The whites of his eyes had turned yellow and even through the blanket Claire could see that his weight had further dropped and his abdomen was distended. He barely had enough strength to lift his eyelids. The last grains of sand were running through the hourglass.

She sat down and watched him for a brief time. His eyes were open, his face strained, cheeks hollowed out.

She waited for him to speak.

He wafted Yvonne away, telling her to leave them.

Claire was a medic. A trained general doctor before she had selected psychiatry, although sometimes she believed that psychiatry had selected her. In her role as a medic she'd seen people die more times than she cared to remember. Each one different and yet all strangely similar when life finally left them. This was a man desperate to cling on to that life until this one last mission was completed.

She leaned in and spoke quietly. 'What do you know, Tom? What have you kept hidden?'

Even now he didn't want to say the words. But he did. Extruding them as though they were painful. 'Where did she get that money from?'

It was not what she had expected.

'She . . . she didn't have a bean to her name but she got money from somewhere. Shane cleaned the car for a bit of extra pocket money. What did he need money for?'

In that moment she understood. Tom too, like his younger daughter, had wondered about the relationship between brother and half-sister.

'Where do you think?'

'He gave it to her.'

'Who?'

'Shane did,' he managed, his eyes forced wide open in appeal.

Claire went ice cold. 'Why?' She'd asked the question while dreading the answer.

Tom needed to stutter out these words. He turned his head so his eyes looked straight into hers. The movement hardly rippled the air around him.

'I think,' he said, 'that she was offering herself to him and Shane took it.' Tom Trustrom was pale now. 'He took it. She didn't even like him. They fought and argued all the time. He gave her money.'

Did he realize what he was accusing his son of?

Tom's lips were cracked and dry. 'The truth,' he managed, his voice hoarse and weak. 'The truth has to come out.'

Claire thought about Shane, his wife, the baby, the life he'd built up around him. 'How do you know this?'

'I wanted it to be Kobi but now I know the truth.'

He closed his eyes before he spoke again. 'He had a scooter, you know, did Shane. He went to look for her too.'

She fingered the tiny object in her bag. Beginning to understand something.

But Tom hadn't finished. He managed to lift his head from the cushion, turn and stare at her. 'I should have protected her but I didn't. In some ways it is my fault. I have to say sorry, Claire. You have to get him to tell you where she is and I will say sorry to her. I will apologize for not having protected her.' He was running out of breath. 'Find her for me. Get him to tell you where she is. Tell him to confess. Find forgiveness. Find her for me. Please.'

Exhausted now he closed his eyes. Claire waited but he didn't rouse and finally she left the room and found Yvonne. 'I think you need to come,' she said, 'and sit with him.' It earned her a hostile look which was only too easy to read. *You've worn him out. You should have left him alone.*

Claire was not going to point out that all this had happened through Tom's request.

As she let herself out, she could hear Yvonne fussing around him, muttering.

Sitting in her car, Claire frowned and put her thoughts in order. Tom had kept quiet all these years. Only now when he was dying did he feel the need to confide the truth. He believed his son had murdered his stepdaughter. Shane was convinced his father had killed Marvel. Dixie feared one of them had killed her daughter. And they all wanted Kobi to be found guilty – including DS Zed Willard.

And Kobi?

As she turned the car back towards Greatbach, Claire recalled some of the conversations she'd had with son and father and started asking herself questions.

Hauling a body on to the back of a scooter is impossible. But Marvel would willingly have climbed on to the back.

So what about Tom's car? Behind these 'tricks' she sensed Loki, the god of mischief. Not a brother who was rebuilding his life after a troubled adolescence nor a father who wanted to clear his troubled conscience. It had Kobi's thumbprint all over it. But how could he have manipulated this situation? What was the missing link?

It was interesting that she had never really been convinced that this was Kobi's crime. Quite apart from the anomaly of the MO, it had never fitted. Leopards don't change their spots. Kobi liked applause. Recognition. He wanted the families' grief, the horror, the graphic newspaper headlines. He revelled in accolade.

Kobi did not hide his light under a bushel.

So was it possible that this was not Kobi's crime but father or son's? And if so, why did she still sense Kobi's mischief behind all this? Hear Kobi's laugh, feel Kobi's pleasure at pulling heart-strings even from inside prison?

She'd arrived back at Greatbach and pulled into a parking space, but Claire didn't move.

FORTY-SIX

Wednesday 23 October, midday

Kobi was curious and a tiny bit apprehensive as to why she was there. He was trying to hide it but a little click in his throat told her enough. 'Claire,' he said as she sat down. 'This is a nice surprise. I didn't think you were coming again.' He giggled. 'A bit like curtain calls. They go on and on and you just wish the people would stop clapping and bloody well go home.'

His mouth leaked anxiety. He couldn't work out why she was there.

She sat down. 'I wasn't going to, Kobi,' she said, 'but I wondered something.' She'd reluctantly made the decision, sitting in her car in the Greatbach car park the previous day, that she needed to see Kobi again and to ask him a specific question.

Now he was watchful. 'And how are the family bearing up?'

'Oh, they're all right. A little confused.'

'Oh. Shame that.' He examined his fingernails. 'Not exactly a happy band, are they? Mother buggered off, father dying. Two sisters who couldn't stand Marvel.' He paused, eyes watchful before rolling out his next comment. 'And then there's the brother.'

Claire stayed silent, simply watching him.

That little click in his throat again.

'I wondered something.'

'What?' When she didn't answer he spoke quickly. 'I expect the entire family are anxious to know the fate of the poor child.'

'I expect they are.'

He wasn't winning. He knew that and tried to regain ground. 'The brother. He's a strange character, isn't he?'

She didn't even blink. She was waiting for him to realize that he wasn't rattling her at all. After the briefest of pauses and a narrowing of his eyes, he continued, 'And as for the father – or should I say . . .' He let the sentence hang, suspended in the air.

'Say what you like.'

He drew in breath to parry again. 'I wonder how the mother is these days. Speak to her mother, Dr Roget,' he said. 'Ask her about her son, her husband, her daughters.' He tapped the side of his nose. 'A mother knows all.'

'So they say.'

He leaned in, intense now. 'Why did you come?'

'I wanted to watch your face when I asked you something.'

His throat clicked again.

'I wondered why you married.'

He blinked.

'When did Jessica first contact you?'

'Soon after I was charged.' His eyes narrowed. 'What is this? Why are you interested in my wife? This isn't about her at all.'

'Isn't it?'

He sat back in his chair, folded his arms and watched her. 'You're just fishing around, aren't you? Still hoping to catch something. Or get a confession' – she shook her head, but he continued anyway – 'that I killed that poor unhappy girl.'

She didn't react except to smile.

Kobi scowled but in his face there was an alertness and a sudden vulnerability she'd not seen before. He was almost quivering with tension and she knew she'd hit home. She was nearly there.

It was hard to leave the prison and Kobi with his secrets. But she was near her quarry. And it wasn't the only step forward she was to make that day.

FORTY-SEVEN

Wednesday 23 October, 4 p.m.

John Robinson was sitting outside her office, waiting to speak to her. He looked different – less self-assured. He was dressed differently too, in casual chinos and a tweed jacket. Somehow the business suit had looked better on him. But maybe today was a day off.

He stood up and immediately started to apologize. 'I'm sorry to just turn up like this again but your secretary said you were coming back after your outside visit.'

Claire wasn't cross. She was more puzzled. What was he doing here?

She led him into her office and he sat down heavily with a loud sigh. 'I think I need to come clean with you, Dr Roget.'

'I'm listening.'

He drew in a deep breath, eyes cast down, voice subdued. 'It wasn't the first time.'

She sat up and stared at him. 'You mean she's assaulted you before?'

For answer he pulled up his shirt. The scar was unmistakably a healed knife wound. 'I would have said but no one else was involved. Only me,' he added hastily.

'You should have told me.'

'I know.' It burst out of him then. 'Why do you think I can't leave her alone with our son? Why do you think I keep my own children – her stepchildren – away? Ilsa flies into a rage. And then she lashes out. She gets an idea in her head and you can't reason with her. You can't shift it. She's accused me of having an affair with Maggie, but I'm not. We both just want the best for her. I hoped if I made some effort with the house that she would change.' He paused, looked around him, licked dry lips. 'I don't want to tell you your job. But is it possible Ilsa needs anger management or something?'

Claire didn't respond. Ilsa needed more than anger management.

'She used a glass ornament once.' John Robinson pushed his hair back to reveal a bald patch and a scar on his scalp. 'Maggie's witnessed these rages.'

'But Ilsa has never assaulted her before?'

'Once.' He looked shamefaced. 'Ilsa smacked her in the face. Broke a tooth.'

'But she didn't involve the police?'

'I begged her not to.'

Claire felt sorry for him. Not only had he been covering for a wife he must at times have felt frightened of, but now he was having to confess all and take some responsibility.

'And the anxiety attacks?'

He looked even more shamefaced. 'I thought that was the cause.'

'Mr Robinson, it's possible your wife has a personality disorder. We can try various therapies when the courts have finished with her but the outlook isn't good.'

He passed a hand across his sweating forehead. 'Believe it or not,' he said, 'I just wanted to protect her.'

'And now?'

'Maggie's not doing well,' he said. 'Her lung's collapsed and she has some sort of infection that doesn't appear to be responding to antibiotics. She might . . .' He tried again. 'If she dies will that make a difference as to what happens to Ilsa?'

'Of course.' She felt she should be at least trying to reassure him. 'But the chances are Maggie will pull through.'

'I hope so. I feel so responsible.'

For once she held her tongue. 'It's probable that Ilsa will be found to have acted while the balance of her mind was disturbed and detained for a period under the Mental Health Act.'

She felt she should add something more forceful. 'But given what you've just told me it will be impossible to guarantee that she won't become violent again.'

He nodded and she managed a smile. The first she had ever given him. Now, it seemed, they were on the same side.

*   *   *

Once he'd left she did her ward round with Salena and Simon and when they'd finished they had a coffee and some cake Rita had brought in (her daughter's birthday). It was chocolate, sickly sweet, just what they needed. A sugar boost.

Back at her desk and with the clinic day over, she was able to focus on an idea boring a hole in her mind. She picked up the phone and connected with DS Zed Willard, diving straight into the subject.

'What do you know about Jessica Kobi?'

'Wha-at?' He was patently thrown by the question, protesting, 'What's she got to do with it? She only came on the scene three – four – years ago.'

She repeated her question. 'What do you know about her?'

'She heard about Kobi through the press and got in touch with him. I think they met six months later and that was that. She can't have anything to do with Marvel, Claire. Why are you asking?' He stopped for a moment, then added, 'You think he might have confided in her?'

'I don't know, Zed. He might. But I would still like everything you know about her emailed over to me including her school record.'

'OK,' he said testily. 'I can do that.'

She hid her motive behind the research she intended. 'I'm interested in people who marry lifers.'

It worked. His response was warmer and less guarded. 'Then consider it done. Anything else?'

'Yes. I want Jonah Kobi put on suicide watch.'

At which point DS Willard chortled with humour. 'You're kidding. There's no one less likely to hang himself than Jonah Kobi. He's hardly human.'

'Have him watched,' Claire repeated.

Willard gave a long, laboured sigh. 'All right. If you think it's necessary.' And then out came that well-worn phrase: 'You're the psychiatrist.'

'Thank you.'

6 p.m.

She had a sheaf of papers to review and comment on, parole hearings, new cases, referrals and the ever-present inpatients. Sometimes she felt she was drowning in her workload. Suffocating under the sheer volume of it.

There was a soft knock on the door and Simon Bracknell peered round. He looked awkward. 'Come in,' she invited. 'Come in. How does Marianne like the UK?'

'She doesn't,' he said, running his hands through his hair, ruffling it so, with his ginger hair, he looked like a bespectacled version of Just William. 'To be honest, Claire, it isn't working out. We were on a rocky road before I came and my being away hasn't helped. Or maybe it has and we're just not compatible.'

'Don't you think you should have stayed in Oz and sorted it out rather than' – she couldn't avoid the word – 'running away?'

He looked shamefaced, nibbled at the nail on his index finger. 'I'm a bit of a coward when it comes to facing up to stuff.'

'Like most men.'

She thought she'd spoken under her breath but he looked up. 'Like your guy? Grant?'

She gave a non-committal shrug. 'So what's the plan?'

'Marianne's going back to Oz. We've decided to split. I was going to talk to HR and see if there is any chance they can extend my contract. Maybe a year?'

She drew in a breath, ready to speak, but he forestalled her. 'I don't mean stay at your place all that time. I know your guy is sort of lurking in the background and I guess at some point he might want to move back in?'

Lurking in the background?

'So if or when that happens and you want me to leave I'll be OK with that. I'll easily find somewhere else.' He smirked. 'Somewhere better than I had before. I just want some breathing space.' She hesitated but finally nodded. He waited for her to say something and when she didn't, he grinned. 'Thanks, Claire. I owe you one.' Then his face changed. 'I still have a place over in Adelaide. If you and Grant fancy somewhere to stay – maybe for your honeymoon . . .'

'I think that's jumping ahead just a bit.'

'No worries,' he responded jauntily. 'Whatever. Do you want me to pop back to the wards, spend some time with Ilsa?'

'Yeah. That'd be good.' She gave him a potted version of John

Robinson's revelations and he responded much as she had. 'Oh. That's a game-changer.'

When he'd gone she sat for a moment. She didn't want to go home to an empty house.

She phoned her best friend.

FORTY-EIGHT

I t was wonderful to escape the troubles and concerns of the day and drive that evening to The Villas. Julia and Gina had bought a house there a few years ago and were slowly transforming it. The Villas was an estate of twenty-four Victorian houses built in the Italianate style with turrets and impressive porches, reminiscent of Osbourne House on the Isle of Wight. Inside was an Aladdin's cave of Minton tiles and large fireplaces, moulded cornices and ceiling roses.

They hugged her and passed her a small glass of wine, urging her to stay the night so she wouldn't have to drive home. She refused. 'I have work tomorrow.'

As usual the conversation descended into work talk while Gina grilled some steaks. Julia was a GP in Hanley with a large list of immigrant patients, many of whom had a poor grasp of English. While the meal was being set out she confessed the difficulty of trying to find a diagnosis through interpreters. 'Quite a challenge,' she said drily. 'Everything takes twice as long. But . . .' She grinned. 'I'm not as badly off as the male doctors. The Muslim women who come in have a husband or male relative with them. And try examining women through the thick material of a burka. Very difficult.'

'Ta-da.' Tea was ready. Claire felt herself relax as she regarded her two very best friends in the world. Julia was comfortably plump with short, thick legs, while Gina was the exact opposite, petite with thick, gypsy hair which she dyed a variety of colours. Their relationship was so happy, with each respecting the other's values. What Claire most noticed was the way they fitted around one another with neither appearing dominant nor submissive. They ate in comfortable silence, their conversation desultory as they focused on their food. They didn't ask about Grant and Claire didn't volunteer. And when she mentioned the two patients whose fates were obsessing her at the moment, they listened without offering judgement.

It was only after the meal, when Claire was sitting on their sofa drinking a cup of herbal tea, that they did offer advice.

Julia speaking first. 'I take it you haven't made up your mind what part Kobi played in Marvel's case?'

'I'm not there yet. At times I think psychiatry is even harder than examining a woman through a burka.' They all laughed at that.

When Claire left she felt she'd been given a tonic. She hugged them both, knowing the evening had been a necessary relaxant and she was ready to face whatever came next.

Monday 28 October, 8.45 a.m.

Thankfully the last few days of the week had been fairly uneventful and she'd had a relaxing weekend, catching up on her running on the Saturday and spending most of the dreary-looking, damp Sunday reading the papers and relaxing.

The first thing Claire noticed in her emails on Monday morning was an attachment from DS Zed Willard pinned on to a jaunty message.

> Don't know how this will help, Claire. If you ask me, she's nothing to do with it and won't advance your case one inch. But whatever – here you are. See you soon, Zed.

And there it was.

Jessica Wilson. Born 1997 to Arthur and Miriam Wilson in Wolverhampton. The family had moved around quite a bit, usually staying no more than two or three years in one place. In 2002 they had moved to Telford. Then in 2005 to Congleton, followed by Chester, back to Wolverhampton, then Macclesfield, and for an even briefer period, in 2008, the family had moved back to Telford. In 2014 the family had moved to Shrewsbury.

Claire sat back, disappointed as she read through Jessica's subsequent story.

Birmingham University. 2015–2018. BA in History. Coincidentally – or not – the same degree as Kobi. Brief teacher's course B.Ed and then to a small secondary school in Stoke. Married Jonah Kobi 2016 when she must have still been a student.

Claire studied the list, searching for a connection between Kobi and Jessica prior to his being charged, but she could find no evidence to support this. It looked as though her idea was just that. An idea. Still she couldn't shake it off. The years between 2008 and 2014 interested her. It was quite a gap for a family who seemed to have moved around fairly frequently. Something was missing.

She spent the morning on the wards. By midday she had finished.

Except Ilsa.

Whom she found sitting on her bed, staring into space, looking blank but untroubled. Claire greeted her warily before sitting down. 'How are you, Ilsa?'

The blue eyes bored into hers looking deceitfully bland and innocent as she countered the question. 'How do you think?'

Claire didn't respond.

Ilsa gave a wry smile. 'I'll go to prison?'

'Not necessarily.'

That produced an ice-blue sheen in her eyes but Claire could see behind this she was thoughtful.

'We have a statement claiming previous assaults against your husband.'

Ilsa gave a cunning smile. 'He's my husband,' she said very quietly. 'I think you'll find there is such a thing as spousal privilege. You can't force him to give evidence against me. He kept the previous assaults a secret, didn't he?' She gave a calm, controlling smile. 'In fact he might even say that I felt threatened. And only picked up the knife in self-defence.'

For a few seconds Claire watched her patient, who seemed to be demonizing in front of her eyes. And then . . .

Something clicked into place. The answer to a question.

FORTY-NINE

The rest of the day passed in frustration. There was no more word from John Robinson or DS Willard. Or Grant for that matter. Claire was thoughtful all the way home. As she let herself into the mercifully quiet house she was piecing together fragments of information.

Tom and Shane had been in Hanley on the afternoon that Marvel had vanished.

Tom thought his son had had an incestuous relationship with his half-sister.

Shane thought his father had killed her and hidden her body.

Dixie believed either her son or her husband had killed the girl. She didn't know which so had distanced herself from them both.

And Sorrel and Clarice possibly shared their mother's doubts.

All had wanted Kobi to be guilty.

But she knew now that he wasn't.

And that was why the crime and the timing and the MO and everything else was different about Marvel's disappearance. Because it was different.

The house was eerily quiet that evening. The phone did not ring; there was no key in the door. It was a house of ghosts.

She had trouble sleeping. She heard whispering in her ear, taunts and threats, promises and delusion. She tossed and turned, thumping her pillows into different shapes and in the end gave up.

How could she prove it?

Then she thought of the school register.

Tuesday 29 October, 9 a.m.

The first thing she did in the morning was to ring DS Willard and make her request. He listened without comment and she could sense his confusion.

'I don't get it, Claire,' he said. 'I just don't get it. And it depends on a guess.'

'Chase it up,' she said. 'Please.' She felt compelled to add, 'If I'm wrong, I'll—'

'If you're about to say you'll eat your hat may I point out that you don't wear one.'

'I'm about to buy one,' she countered. 'For my half-brother's wedding.'

'Right.' And then he entered into the spirit of things. 'I hope you're not thinking of wearing a half-chewed hat to it.'

'No.' And at last she felt she could laugh because she understood.

About the wedding, about Ilsa, about Marvel's killer.

Her mind focused on various phrases, one in particular. Marvel had no friends, according to Shane. But that day Marvel had been meeting a friend.

She added to her list of questions. What had Kobi's movements been on that November day? She searched through the notes Zed Willard had left but couldn't find that one particular detail. In the initial investigation had no one asked him that simple question? And he hadn't volunteered the information except when she had brought the subject up and he'd claimed to have been alone in his flat, watching television. She could pick holes in the original investigation. It had been sloppy. They had skated over Kobi's precise work record, failed to ask even the most basic of questions. No wonder the CPS had not included Marvel's disappearance in Kobi's conviction. A smart defence would have thrown doubt into that conviction.

And, as Kobi had been convicted and sentenced before Jessica had come on the scene they hadn't looked too hard into her antecedents either.

It was no wonder that when Tom Trustrom had made his appeal, Zed Willard had roped her in, hoping for some eureka moment with the help of psychiatry. And a timely confession from Kobi.

She caught Shane on his mobile. His reluctance to speak to her again made his voice sullen and unfriendly. 'I thought you were done with me.'

'Almost,' she said brightly. 'I'm nearly there.'

That was greeted with a silence which even over the phone

sounded frosty but eventually he agreed this time to attend the hospital on the following morning.

She needed to read his face when she passed on the allegation.

Wednesday 30 October, 9.30 a.m.

Shane arrived on time, looking awkward in a navy suit and silky red tie. He stood in the doorway, fidgeting with both hands and feet, the fingers weaving into one another, the feet tapping an impatient, nervous beat.

He began with truculence. 'I don't know why you want to speak to me.' She let the comment pass and he continued. 'I don't know anything about my sister's disappearance.' His eyes were anxious, his brows beetling together in a scowl. He glanced at the door and she read there a longing to escape.

'You were in Hanley in the early evening the night your sister disappeared.'

His mouth dropped open. 'Who . . .? How . . .?'

'It doesn't matter who or how. Shane, I know you were only eighteen.'

Shane Trustrom went white and then red to the tips of his ears.

'Did you find her?'

He shook his head.

'Did you *see* her?'

He shook his head, the movement jerky. 'I'd have said if I did.'

She needed to handle this next subject delicately.

'There is an allegation that you and your sister . . .'

He quickly corrected her. 'Half-sister.'

'You and your half-sister were in some sort of . . . relationship?'

Shane went chalk pale and tugged at his tie as though to give himself air to breathe. 'No,' he said. 'Who made that allegation?'

'I can't say.'

'It's not true.'

'Did you have intercourse with her?'

'No. No. I never did. I didn't.'

She waited but he couldn't speak.

'Or were you smoking pot together?'

He let out his breath in a sharp exhalation which gave her her answer. 'Do you remember a girl called Jessica in school with your sister?'

'Jessica? What's she got to do with this unholy mess?'

'Do you remember her?'

He frowned. 'There was a girl called Jessica but she was only at school for about a term.'

'Can you remember her surname?'

'No. She was a couple of years younger than me.'

It fitted.

'Jessica Wilson.' She produced a photograph and he studied it.

'Could be her.' He looked up, a fresh-faced young man with his life ahead of him, she hoped. He grinned. 'Hard to tell. I didn't really know her.'

'OK. Is there anything more you can tell me?'

He shook his head. The door opened and he bolted. She heard his footsteps hurry along the corridor, shoes tapping on the floor, softer and softer until they were gone.

FIFTY

N ext, she had to tackle Tom. But gently.

And she began by telling him what she knew.

'I know Marvel was not your daughter.'

He bowed his head, closed his eyes and didn't bother to try and deny it.

'There's something else,' she said, to warn him. 'A month or so after Marvel went missing Shane found this' – she held out her hand – 'in your car.'

Tom opened his eyes with great effort. He took the trinket in his own hand, held it near his face.

'Poor, silly little girl.' His voice caught. 'Never would have made a ballerina.' She watched Tom who was still smiling as he looked at the charm. 'She weren't a bad kid. It's just everything was stacked against her.'

Claire watched for any sign of guilt or recognition but all she met was puzzlement.

'I wonder how it got into my car.' He looked up. 'Have you asked Sorrel or Clarice if they've mislaid theirs?'

'They haven't.'

She waited for Tom to put two and two together and then he did. 'Did Shane think I had something to do with it?' He managed to raise himself to a sitting position. 'Did he?'

'Yes.'

'Try and put the blame on me when—' He stopped abruptly.

'When what, Tom?'

Tom was struggling to breathe. Yvonne reached for the oxygen cylinder propped up against the sofa. She turned it on and put the mask over his face, her own expression forbidding. And Claire didn't miss the slight head shake.

She waited while his breathing calmed down.

'You believed Shane and Marvel had some sort of . . . relationship?'

He nodded and tugged at the mask. 'Where did she get that money from?' he demanded. 'And then there was the way he was with her. They'd go in a huddle. In his room. Those two had secrets.'

'Shane's told me they smoked pot.'

He was shocked. 'You've asked him?'

She nodded. 'At the time did you think Shane had something to do with Marvel's disappearance?'

'I've always wondered. I hoped not. But now I just want the truth to come out whatever it is. We owe her that. A Christian burial.'

'Even if your son was responsible?'

He opened his eyes wide, the whites a dirty yellow. Miserably, he nodded. 'For years I've hoped it was Kobi. I hoped he'd confess and put my mind at rest. But when he didn't, I wondered. And then her body's never been found. And now I'm near to meeting my Maker I want the truth to come out.'

Claire was silent for a while digesting all that Tom had said, as well as observing Yvonne's upright posture and disapproving face. She reached across to Tom's hand. 'For what it's worth I don't think Shane killed Marvel; neither do I believe that you had anything to do with it.'

'Well, who then? Was it him after all?'

'I don't know for certain – yet.'

Yvonne stood up. She was about to say, *You're tiring him out* or *You're upsetting him.*

Time to leave.

Claire drove back to Greatbach feeling despondent. When would this morass be cleaned up?

The answer was less than a minute later. An email pinged through from the Biddulph comprehensive. And there it was. One girl's name.

Jessica Wilson, a pupil there for one term in the autumn of 2013.

FIFTY-ONE

I t still didn't prove anything. Kobi had only worked there for two days in July. There was every likelihood that he hadn't even taught Jessica. There was nothing linking Jessica to Marvel who would have been two years younger. But if Jessica had studied a degree in history she would have taken it at school.

Claire had no jurisdiction over Jessica Kobi. She could not force the girl to speak to her. She had no choice but to go through DS Zed Willard.

He listened to what she had to say without making any comment but even over the phone she could sense his disbelief. But as she spoke, gradually, his scepticism melted. She didn't need to help him join up the dots; neither did she now need to convince him to focus properly on the case of Marvel Trustrom. As they should have done six years before.

'I take it,' he said testily, 'that you want us to bring Mrs Kobi in and question her?'

'She will be resistant,' she warned. 'You need to direct your questions to the fact that she has "got away with it" for all these years. Appeal to her ego. Get her to talk.'

That drew a grunt from DS Willard.

'Particularly get her to talk about the relationship between her and Kobi and eventually she will trip up. She's conceited. She's got away scot-free for years and, even cleverer, her husband has taken the blame. After all – what difference does it make to him? He's in jail anyway. He picked *her* out of scores of schoolgirls. Something must have attracted him to her rather than repelled him. Work on that aspect, Zed. Feed her ego.'

'Is there any chance you can be in on it?' He was already doubting his capabilities.

'I'll try and attend. Let me know when you're bringing her in.'

'I will. And, Claire – thanks.'

'For nothing, so far.'

She should have commented that this was simply a theory at the moment, that she had neither proof nor a confession. And, staring at her phone, she realized she had not reinforced the need to keep Kobi on suicide watch.

It was seven p.m. when her mobile pinged with a withheld number and she knew it would be Zed. She'd just arrived home.

'We're going to start questioning her,' he said. 'Can you get here in about half an hour?'

'Yeah. Where did you pick her up?'

'At her home.'

'Has she had a chance to tell Kobi she's being questioned?'

'What?'

'Did she make a phone call?'

'She could have done. She went upstairs to get changed. She had her phone with her. She could have rung him, Claire.' He paused before adding, anxiety in his voice, 'Does it matter?'

'I hope not. But you still have Kobi under suicide watch?'

'Yeah.' She picked up on the hesitancy in his voice and was instantly worried.

'Zed,' she said. 'This is important. The one thing a narcissist can't tolerate is being bettered. He needs watching.'

'OK. I'll call the prison again.'

8 p.m.

She watched through the window as Jessica Kobi was led in and cautioned.

Jessica had lost none of her self-confidence. If anything, she seemed to have grown in self-assurance. She gave a mocking glance towards the window and Claire studied her demeanour. She displayed no concern that her dark past had been rumbled.

Claire had already primed Zed Willard which questions to focus on.

He too seemed to have grown in confidence. She knew he was glad to be doing this and to show – years too late – his determination to find the truth this time around.

Zed Willard gave Jessica a confident, apparently friendly smile. 'Thanks for coming.'

Her response was stroppy. 'You didn't give me much choice.' And yet she had waived her right to have a solicitor present.

'Ah, no. Sorry for that.' His tone was still warm and friendly, the 'I am on your side' fallacy.

'So . . .' He slid a piece of paper across the table. Claire had suggested he do this, present her with a fact. She had been a pupil at the Biddulph comprehensive between September and December 2013. Jessica's eyes slid over the sheet of paper. Then she licked her lips. 'So?'

DS Willard presented her with fact number two. 'You met Jonah Kobi, your history teacher, there.'

Jessica's response was a hard stare and another: 'So?'

'Something clicked between you.'

She gave him a look of scorn.

But Willard held his ground. 'You recognized something in each other.'

Jessica's demeanour changed. She gave a little toss of her head as though to shake something off. A fly on her shoulder or a stray hair; more likely a memory.

Willard pressed on. 'Marvel Trustrom was also a pupil at the same school.'

'Two years behind,' Jessica said before she could stop herself.

'Yes.' Willard picked up. 'That's right. Two years behind. But you knew her, didn't you?'

'I knew her,' Jessica said, 'as in when she went missing I remembered her.'

'Exactly. You know that we're still looking for her body?'

That drew a scornful look. 'Like you've been looking for it for years?'

'Luckily, thanks to your husband, we have a lead.'

It's an old game. Split the team up. They are no longer a team but a pair of liabilities because each knows the truth about the other. Kobi and Mrs Kobi are deprived of communication which makes them suspicious. Feel vulnerable.

For the first time Jessica looked concerned.

'A lead – really?' There was a mocking tone in her voice, and she raised her eyebrows but it didn't quite convince and Zed Willard had picked up on this.

He leaned in further, almost spitting the words out. 'What was it, Jess, that told you that you and Kobi had a shared passion?'

'I don't know what you mean?'

'Did he pick up that Marvel was annoying you?'

'That little—' She stopped abruptly.

'I don't have enough to charge you, Jess,' Zed said. 'But we're working on it.'

'So . . .?'

'You're free to go,' he said. 'But I think it might be worth you considering. If we do pick up that you and your husband collaborated in Marvel's murder we won't be looking at any sort of defence, that you were coerced into it, that there was undue influence, or that you married Kobi so he would use spousal privilege. That was your payoff, wasn't it? Your reward. He would refuse to testify against you. You stay free. He stays inside – for as long as he lives.'

Willard shuffled around in his seat as though preparing to go. 'Is there anything else you want to tell me at this point, Mrs Kobi?'

Jessica didn't respond. Claire could read the signs. She'd lost her way.

Willard's next sentence was spoken quietly, as though he was speaking to himself. 'Of course, when we find the body we're bound to pick up on something that tells us how Marvel died and who killed her. Unless you were very careful, Mrs Kobi. And I suspect that you were actually in a bit of a hurry. And not careful at all. Or not careful enough.'

'Am I under arrest?'

'Not at the moment. Not until we find her body.'

Jessica hadn't quite run out of bravado. 'After six years,' she said scornfully. 'What makes you think you'll find her this time round?'

Willard faced her square on. 'Oh – we'll find her. And by the way, whose idea was it to set family members against one another? Oh, of course. Has to be Jonah, doesn't it? He has to have his little bit of fun.'

FIFTY-TWO

Zed Willard rejoined Claire in one of the side rooms. 'How did I do?'

'Good,' she said. 'Really good.'

'Thanks.'

There was a knock on the door. A uniformed officer stood there. And then all hell broke loose.

'Fuck,' Willard exploded. 'Fuck.'

The look he gave Claire was desperate and she knew.

'Kobi,' she guessed.

Willard nodded, his colour as green as someone who is about to be sick.

'They've taken him to hospital.'

'He's still alive?'

'Just about.'

While Claire felt anxiety, she also felt elation. She had anticipated this. And at the same time, it might just be the lever they needed to persuade Jessica to break.

Thursday 31 October, 8.30 a.m.

Driving into Greatbach the following morning, she reflected on Jonah Kobi's plan. With the delicate touch, rumours and one small silver trinket, he had placed suspicion at the heart of the family, turned mother against son and husband, father against son, son against father. They had lived with this edgy suspicion for years, distancing themselves from each other, at the same time trying to maintain some sort of family relationship. But hostility had been at its heart. The son had tried to protect his father and Tom had tried to protect his son. Until he was dying. When he had needed the truth.

The real tragedy? They were all wrong.

It was wicked. It was worse than wicked. But up until now Jessica was right. They had no body and the police would never prove a case on a psychiatrist's say so. Kobi wouldn't have testified against his wife and no one could force him to now they were married. And Jessica? She was never going to confess.

So how?

And that is the greatest difficulty. Knowing someone is guilty is only part of the solution. Proving it beyond reasonable doubt in a court of law is quite another challenge.

She rang Zed Willard. 'Can you find out where Jessica and her family lived while they were in the Potteries?'

She was banking on the fact that Jessica had only lived in the Potteries for a number of months and was unlikely to know its geography well.

A phone call later, Claire knew the answer. A place with a dark history already. Another unsolved murder.

Many places in England have a dark past, still tangible years later, even to the casual visitor. There is one such place six miles north of Stoke-on-Trent. Mow Cop Castle was a folly of a ruin built in 1754 at the summit of a hill, outlined against a more often than not grey sky. It was accompanied by a sixty-five-foot-high rock feature affectionately called the Old Man O'Mow. Believed to be the site of an ancient burial ground, the area is peppered with numerous quarried areas and caves which have their own history. The village which is a hotch-potch of cottages, terraced houses and a few detached dwellings, winds its way towards the summit. Today the area is under the management of the National Trust, but its dark and unhappy past clings to it and the air around it, reminding visitors of a crime which was all too easy to solve and an ugly mystery which has never been resolved.

On Friday 8 February 1963, the body of Mrs Mary Elizabeth Walton was discovered in a red Mini Traveller parked in the high street. It wasn't a difficult crime to solve. Gwen Massey, a Sunday schoolteacher and choir soloist from nearby Rudyard, had been having an affair with Mr Walton, which had ended in October of 1962, when his wife had found out.

During the subsequent court case, the court heard how Miss

Massey had tricked Mrs Walton to a meeting at the Plough Hotel
in Endon where Miss Massey had attacked her victim with a brick
hammer. Miss Massey had then put the still alive but unconscious
body of Mrs Walton in the back of the Mini Traveller and driven
to Mow Cop where she'd abandoned it. Miss Massey had then
walked the eleven miles home. The case against Miss Massey was
backed up with bloodstain forensic evidence and several witnesses
had seen Miss Massey walk home on that cold February night.

On Wednesday 29 May 1963, the jury returned a verdict of
guilty. Miss Massey was sentenced to life imprisonment.

But Mow Cop has another murder, more recent, which has
never been solved. Taxi driver. Steven Johnson, twenty-five, whose
throat was slashed with a knife by his killer in the early hours of
22 December 1990. Mr Johnson's body was found later that day
by dog walkers, twenty yards from his vehicle, in a snow-covered
farm track off Castle Road.

Despite a high-profile manhunt and repeated appeals for information, the six-foot-four-inch Stoke taxi driver's killer has never
been found. The motive for his murder has never been established
and the deceased's fifty-pound takings for the night were still in
his cab.

So one murder solved and another unsolved. And coincidentally
Mow Cop was where the Wilson family had set up home for their
brief stay in the Staffordshire Potteries.

And now another one was due to join Mow Cop's history.

Suspicion falls like a cloud of dust, blown hither and thither by
the wind, landing indiscriminately on any surface where it will
stay until it is wiped away. Kobi had used both location and this
fact to entertain himself and his wife. In this case the obscuring
dust was about to be cleaned.

Claire picked up the phone and spoke again to DS Zed Willard.

'This is my theory,' she said, 'given the facts.' He listened and
even in his silence she could hear incredulity. Finally he spoke. 'You
are kidding,' he said. 'I just don't believe it. It's impossible.'

'Find Marvel's body,' she said, 'and you'll have confirmation.'

'Find her body? When we've been looking for it for six years?'

'I think I know where it is,' she said.

FIFTY-THREE

Back at Hanley police station Claire met Jessica again face to face. She gave Claire a tight smile and followed her into the interview room. As they entered Jessica gave the red eye in the corner a mocking glance and sat down – almost primly. She was dressed in her usual jeans and hoodie.

Claire sat opposite her. 'I'm sorry to hear about your husband,' she began.

Jessica met her with hard eyes. 'Are you?'

Claire drew in a breath ready to drop her bombshell.

'We have a lead.'

Jessica's face became wary, guarded as an animal under threat, and Claire continued smoothly.

'So, now we have some idea of time, place, perpetrator, we can start on the right track.'

Jessica didn't even blink but regarded her steadily.

Claire had to hand it to her. She had nerve. She decided to circumvent her attack. 'I've made a study of marriages to lifers. Some are motivated by a sort of do-gooding pity, a feeling they can reform a bad character. There are others who are drawn to that dark character.'

Jessica simply looked bored. 'Per-lease,' she said. 'Spare me the mumbo jumbo.'

'But I don't think that's the case here, is it, Jessica. I think you quickly recognized that you and Jonah were the same. And your focus was this unfortunate girl. I daresay she clung to you. Was an irritant. Two outsiders. You were new, she had no friends. Maybe Jonah came across some sort of altercation between you and boy did he see something he admired. You lured her, didn't you? She was going to meet *you* in Hanley that day. That's why she dressed up the way she did and why she insisted on going in spite of the filthy weather.'

Jessica's stare was still outwardly bold but Claire sensed that inside she was shaken. But her stare didn't waver.

'And as for your husband. That was a puzzle. Initially I couldn't work out why you and he married. You're not the vulnerable type. Neither are you impressionable. So that left one explanation. You and he were the same. He'd never shown any real interest in women. His first marriage barely lasted two years. The only thing he had was disdain for schoolgirls. And then I realized. You were partners in crime. You weren't different. He had something over you. And so you were married and he gained a channel to the outside. You could set up this little game where you taunted the police with a missing body, set doubts and suspicion between the family members. So easy to do. A little whisper to someone in school, that Shane was abusing his sister. And a tiny ornament planted in Tom's car. Your entertainment was in observing the family suffer and wonder. I suppose it was Jonah who suggested you marry and then no one could force either of you to testify against the other. It was a devil's pact. How you both enjoyed your game. Put the cat among the pigeons and watched the fur and feathers fly. Tom, Shane, DS Willard and then me. Even I was part of the fun, wasn't I? We were all dragged into your slipstream. Especially Tom who might have died before his daughter's remains were found.'

She waited while Jessica thought for a long time.

'By the way,' Claire said casually. 'You might want to know that your husband is not, in fact, dead, but in hospital. The chances of him making a full recovery from his suicide attempt are, so I'm told, slim. He is almost certainly brain damaged from the prolonged hypoxia. Probably, Jessica, it would have been better if he had died, wouldn't it? Then you could have produced a belated and false "confession" from him, couldn't you?'

Jessica lowered her eyelids so Claire couldn't read her expression, but her hands linked together as though she was praying. Jessica praying? To whom? And for what?

Claire glanced at her watch. 'The police are heading up to Mow Cop.'

Had she not been looking for it she might have missed the tiny start Jessica Kobi gave. But she was waiting for it.

Jessica licked her lips and withdrew, deep in thought. Then she gave a little huff of a laugh. 'I wonder what they'll find there.'

'We'll soon find out.'

*   *   *

Willard was waiting for her outside with a request.

'I don't suppose,' Willard said, 'that you'd consider speaking to Tom and Shane?' He hesitated. 'Try to explain.'

'I don't mind talking to them. In fact, I think it's best. They might hear something through the media.'

She glanced back at the door of the interview room. 'And you're going to need an extension.'

'Agreed.'

'How is Kobi?'

'At the moment he's on a ventilator and they're not sure if he'll be able to breathe on his own.' He looked at her curiously. 'How did you know?'

'He's narcissistic. The one thing a narcissist can't bear is not being top dog. The minute he realized he was about to be rumbled his life was in danger. From himself. He wasn't quite willing to take the blame for Marvel's murder. And, I think we'll find that in no way does Marvel's fate resemble any of the other murders. This one, I believe, will prove to be Jessica's.'

'We have a team up at the Cop. Any clue as to where?'

'Yes, I do. I've been thinking about this. The cairn,' she said. 'The Old Man O'Mow. I think he's hiding her. I would start looking there. And Zed,' she added.

'Aye?'

'Don't speak to Jessica until you have hard evidence. You're going to need an extension to question her. Don't underestimate her. She's a clever girl.'

'Thanks for the advice,' he responded gruffly.

FIFTY-FOUR

While the police were working with sniffer dogs and taping off the area surrounding Mow Cop Castle, Claire was making her way to Tom Trustrom's house. Shane's car was already in the drive.

As she pressed on the doorbell, she could only think that it was better that she broke the news sensitively rather than they find out through a leak on social media.

But it was going to be difficult.

Tom was, as before, spread across the sofa, a blanket over him, his breath coming in short, rasping gasps, while Yvonne watched from a dining-room chair at the far end of the room. Shane was perched on the edge of the armchair. At first the hostility and suspicion between father and son was as tangible as a nuclear cloud. Both father and son were apprehensive about what was going to come next. And, with some surprise, she also realized Kobi's ruse was still active. They hadn't quite shed their suspicion of each other.

She began on neutral ground. 'You may or may not have heard the police are searching the area around Mow Cop for Marvel's body.'

Neither responded to this but still avoided looking at one another. Shane said gruffly, 'What makes them think they'll find it there?'

'They've unearthed new evidence.'

'What new evidence?'

'I'm not at liberty to say.'

'So why are you here?' Shane's voice was truculent.

'I wanted to prepare you.'

Tom spoke for the first time. 'Has this got anything to do with Kobi trying to hang himself?'

Claire was cautious. 'Possibly.'

Both started at this. But for the first time father and son looked at each other and on Shane's face was the hint of a thin smile.

'We don't know much more at the moment,' she said. 'The police investigations, as you can appreciate, take some time, but I wanted you to be aware that your request, Tom, might just bring you an answer.'

Tom closed his eyes and she saw his lips move. He was, she remembered, a lapsed Catholic.

When he opened his eyes he looked straight at his son and something fell from both their faces. That hardness, hostility, suspicion was replaced by light and hope. The thaw was as tangible as the melt on the first day of spring and the cold atmosphere that had existed only seconds before was washed away.

Shane moved first. 'Dad,' he said, reaching out a hand.

'None of this is evidence yet,' she warned. 'But if the case is proven and sticks . . .' She squeezed out a smile as pure white as toothpaste. 'Put it like this,' she said. 'The truth will be good for both of you.'

Tom's breathing became laboured as he closed his eyes. His struggle was almost over. For a moment she almost wondered whether he had died right then. Had this not been about being buried with his stepdaughter but more that he wanted their names to be cleared of the suspicion that had poisoned the relationship between them? Shane watched him before glancing across at Yvonne. Claire reflected on the twisted knots that exist within families. One word and a thousand different scenarios. Yvonne took the hint, crossed the room and knelt by her husband's side.

It was time for her to leave.

Zed Willard had always considered himself relatively fit. But the stiff climb up to the Cop was making him very out of breath. He was on the south side of the ruin, its stone crags sinister against a grey sky. In front of him was a team of forensic investigators ably helped by two cadaver dogs. And it wasn't long before he heard them barking and saw the team move towards the cairn as though drawn by a magnet. He quickened his step. The dogs were now held back. Watched over by the ruined castle he imagined he heard, in the wind, the hymn singing of the Primitive Methodists.

The police worked, marking out a grid around the cairn, pulling away stones that had been laid centuries ago and might have stayed so had it not been for this one lost girl. It was tiring work as, watched over by the representative from the National Trust, they numbered the stones. They would all have to be put back in order.

After three hours' work they found her.

Death sucks out character, changes a living, breathing person into a corpse. Six years takes the process forward, changing a body into a collection of artifacts: hair, teeth, bones, material, cheap gypsy hoop earrings and a silver bracelet, which told its own story via unrelated trinkets – a galloping horse, a paint brush and a miniscule pair of *silver ballet shoes*. And then a sad, cheap, plastic handbag because if we have learnt only one thing in the millennium it is this: that plastic is more indestructible than a person. Predation, time and the elements had done their work. But it always surprised Willard that material, hair, jewellery, a plastic handbag with contents, all these survive when a person's remains are long rotted away.

He watched a woodlouse crawl out of the stones and held up his hand. 'OK,' he said. 'That's enough. We need the team, a tent and a pathologist.' The wind whistled its assent, fluttering a lock of red gold hair while DS Zed Willard made a mental prayer.

Please let us find something that links Kobi and his Lady Macbeth to this poor girl.

And this was where intuition, psychology and psychiatry gave way to science.

Claire's mobile phone rang later that day.

'And there she was,' Willard said. 'Folded up like a piece of lino. We've closed off the scene and will get her to the mortuary as soon as possible. Poor little thing,' he said, 'still wearing her cheap, tarty clothes, plastic handbag. Little else left now of her but bones.'

'They might have trouble finding cause of death.'

Willard nodded. 'Well, we'll have to take that as it comes, Claire. But sure as eggs are eggs she didn't stick her own body underneath that heap of stones.'

'Agreed.'

But it still wasn't enough to convict Jessica Kobi of murder.

Kobi was on the Intensive Care Unit, breathing controlled by a ventilator, tubes running in and out, his only sound the feeble bleeps of machines.

The last sense we lose is hearing. Nurses and doctors are taught this in the very early weeks of their training. *Always assume the patient hears you.*

It is a habit one never loses. Claire bent over him and spoke very softly into his ear. 'We have her, Kobi. The Old Man of Mow was hiding her, wasn't he?'

No response.

'But it wasn't you, was it?'

Still no response.

'It was her, wasn't it?' she whispered. 'But whose idea was it to get married and protect each other? Hers? Yours?'

Still no response.

'We'll get her, you know. If you ever get off this bed and out of here she'll be joining you at HMP Somewhere.'

Was it her imagination, wishful thinking that made her wonder afterwards if one of his fingers, trapped in the pulse oximeter, moved – just a little?

She could never be certain.

Willard rang her later. He sounded cautiously jubilant. 'We've got stuff from the burial site,' he said. 'Including a mobile phone. We're running it through at the moment. I can't believe they overlooked that one.'

'It seems unlikely that they did,' she said. 'I wouldn't start getting excited. Not yet. You're not there yet, Zed.'

'Well, we've plenty of stuff to run through the labs. I'm hopeful, Claire.'

She felt a sudden rush of affection for the detective. He'd been so involved from the first. In the end he had searched for the truth. And for that Claire respected him.

It was now down to the lab. Evidence was provided by Caroline Morton, Home Office pathologist, who carried out the post-mortem, watched by DS Zed Willard and the team. She rang Claire soon afterwards.

'Well,' she said dryly, 'this murder couldn't have been more different from the killings of the other four girls. I've read up on the PMs of those four. They were all strangled. Not this one though.'

'So . . .?'

'Stabbed. Multiple times.'

'I thought the body was decomposed?'

'It was.' Dr Morton couldn't keep the note of triumph from her voice. 'But there were nicks in some of the ribs. Even two in her skull. She was stabbed a total of eighteen times. It was what the press like to call a frenzied attack. I would very much doubt that this is the work of Jonah Kobi.'

'And you're prepared to testify this in court?'

'It'll just be an opinion.'

'Thanks.'

*   *   *

Zed Willard rang to tell her that the Family Liaison Officer would be working with Marvel's family. But after the triumph Claire heard a note of doubt in his voice. It was often like this. Triumph when you put your hand on a collar. But however Marvel had died, whoever had killed her, they had yet to prove contact between Jonah Kobi and Jessica Wilson back in 2013.

FIFTY-FIVE

J essica was not going to confess and she was too intelligent to fool but the results started rolling in, lining up like swallows in late August. Claire had primed DS Zed Willard and his team and watched as he interviewed her, but it was just going over old ground. The girl was as resistant as Teflon. She didn't have her husband's conceit or a need for accolade and recognition. Her ego was unlikely to trip her up. Her speech was not unguarded but carefully edited. She had kept her secret for six years and was capable of holding on to it for another seventy.

However Willard phrased his questions, Jessica Kobi was a stone wall.

'Take me through that Saturday.'

'I don't even know what Saturday you're referring to.'

'The Saturday Marvel went missing.'

Jessica's response was disdainful. 'Just remind me of the date.'

And when he did her response was predictable. 'I can't remember.'

'How exactly did you and Kobi pull it off?'

The response was a simple shrug.

'I'm not talking about Marvel's murder, Jessica. I'm talking about the playing off of members of Marvel's family. A bit of sport, Jessica? Or self-protectionism?'

Jessica's response was a bland stare. She didn't even bother with the no comment response.

Zed Willard screwed up his face. 'You knew that father and son were in Hanley that afternoon? Searching for her. Maybe you even saw them? Maybe they even saw you with Marvel? Looking round the shops together?'

No response.

'So whose idea was it to bait the Trustroms? Yours?'

Still no response.

'Kobi's?'

The flicker in her eyes told Claire that this guess was more likely to be correct.

'Ye-es!' Willard played it like a eureka moment. 'Of course. It was something he could play at even in prison. But you . . .' He stared right into Jessica's eyes. 'When the focus returned to that one missing girl you worried, didn't you? And Jonah was always going to be a concern, wasn't he?'

Jessica Kobi was staring straight ahead. It was anyone's guess what was going through her mind. 'But you never completely trusted Jonah, did you? Maybe Jonah played with you too? He wasn't going to confess and there was always the risk that he would say where the body was.' A flicker crossed the girl's face. 'You knew you'd been careless there, that there might be evidence to link you with Marvel's body. I suppose,' he said casually, 'that you were in a bit of a hurry.'

And that little dart struck home.

Zed Willard studied his fingernails. 'The trouble with Kobi is that you were never quite sure you weren't part of the sport too. He probably goaded you, didn't he?'

For the first time Claire saw real fury light Jessica's face. She was having trouble holding it in, taking great, scooping breaths in and out.

But Jessica wasn't about to break.

'You can say all this stuff as much as you like,' she said with a toss of her head. 'You have to prove it.' Her eyes locked on to Willard's. 'In a court of law.'

'Don't worry on that score, Jessica,' Willard inserted smoothly, 'the labs are busy working on it.'

In his uncomfortable seat the solicitor shifted his weight.

And that was how it was left, unsatisfactory, everything hanging on, nothing finalized. No certainties. Claire left the station worrying that they would never have the evidence to charge Jessica Kobi with the murder of Marvel Trustrom.

But next day, in the light of the morning, a phone call from Zed Willard was more than welcome.

'Thank God for plastic.'

It wasn't quite what she had expected but she could hear excitement in his voice.

'Spill the beans, Zed.'

'Marvel's bag,' he said. 'Like a little time capsule. Everything preserved. Including a tissue and some lipstick.' And then he spoke the words every prosecutor wants to hear. 'Both have DNA on them. We have a match. We've got enough to charge her.'

'Be careful, Zed,' she warned. 'Be warned. She's clever. And Kobi's out of the picture. He won't be testifying against her. Whatever evidence you have she's quite capable of batting it away. She'll say the DNA comes from a previous encounter. She's admitted that she and Marvel were sort of friends. And even if you can put her at the scene, she'll plead coercion.'

'Whose side are you on?' he grumbled.

But Claire had been pulled into many court cases. She knew how prosecution and defence could both manipulate what was, in truth, an inexact science, a reconstruction of a crime.

But she attended the interview anyway. And straightaway she could see where Jessica was heading.

Jessica wanted to emphasize her schoolgirl role even though she was now in her twenties. She had deliberately dressed for the occasion in a plain black pinafore dress with a white shirt underneath. Reminiscent of school uniform. Flat shoes and the final touch, her hair tied back. Very different from the woman Claire had met on the two previous occasions. What hadn't changed though was her air of self-assurance or that confidant tilt of her head.

Willard made a double take as he greeted her. 'Jessica.' He motioned her to sit down. By his side was a mousey looking PC, uncomfortable in her uniform which did look hot and scratchy.

'You understand this will all be recorded?'

Jessica nodded, looking bored. Willard cautioned her and then sat back. 'Why don't you just tell me what happened, Jessica? In your own words.'

She leaned back. Still very confident.

'He was my teacher.'

'Where?'

'The comprehensive in Biddulph,' she said. 'They were struggling to get a history teacher so I guess they didn't look too hard into his antecedents.'

'So when did you learn about them?'

She lowered her eyelids. Had Claire not been a psychiatrist she might have thought it was through modesty or embarrassment, but she could see Jessica Kobi was actually enjoying herself. The hand passing across her mouth was to hide a smirk.

'He seemed to like me,' she said with a tiny toss of her streaked hair. 'And I had a bit of trouble with some of my homework.' A flicker of her eyelashes and a sideways flick of her eyes warned Claire that her next statement was likely to be a lie. 'I was anxious to pass my exams so I was grateful to my teacher taking special trouble with me.' Another flutter of the eyelashes.

'When was this?' From his tone Claire knew Willard wasn't taken in by the act.

'Work it out,' she said carelessly. 'I was sixteen years old.'

'So we're talking about 2013.'

It threw Jessica's rhythm in storytelling. She paused as though uncertain which line to choose next. She took a swift look at Willard and must have realized she wasn't cutting any ice with him. 'It sort of grew from there. I realized there was something – different – about him.'

Claire leaned forward, watching Kobi's wife intently. Searching for signs. As a psychiatrist she would love to have questioned her about this 'difference', but in the role she was playing now – part doctor, part fact finder, part helper of the police, behind plate glass – she wasn't going to head down that road. Neither, it appeared, was Willard.

'And Marvel,' he prompted. 'Tell me about Marvel.'

'I knew Marvel,' Jessica admitted. 'I was a bit of an outsider, joining the school for a brief time. I lived just down from Mow Cop and she lived in Gillow Heath. We walked to school every day. I'd seen some guys being horrible to her and told them to bugger off. After that she clung to me. I couldn't get rid of her. She was like ivy growing up a wall, finding every crack and crevice to climb into. She was really annoying. Every time I went out of my front door she seemed to be there. It got oppressive.' She chewed at her lip before saying, 'I asked her to leave me alone but she just got all pathetic and started crying.' She licked her lips. 'It's possible I mentioned this . . . problem to Jonah. Maybe that's why . . .' She sniffed and tailed off her story.

Her blue eyes managed to look – not innocent – deceitful and watchful. She was waiting to see whether Willard swallowed the bait. 'That's all I would have wanted him to do.' She frowned and pretended to retrieve a memory. 'I think he said something like he would make sure she stopped bothering me. Something like that, anyway.'

The swift, surreptitious glance she gave Willard might have been missed from anyone's notice, but Claire had been waiting for it.

After a suitable pause, Jessica picked up. 'I didn't expect him to do anything but have a word with her.' This time the wide opening of her blue eyes was accompanied by a 'shy' smile as painted on as any one of her previous expressions.

It wasn't fooling Willard. 'Were you with her the afternoon of November the twenty-second?'

'I can't remember.' Somehow she managed to sound affronted. But Zed continued in his most stolid, monotonic voice, slow and unstoppable as a tank. 'When you heard she'd gone missing did you remember?' He shuffled some papers around. 'There's no mention of you being questioned.'

Jessica shook her head, managing to look regretful.

'What did you think had happened to her?'

'I just thought – I don't know what I thought.'

Zed Willard shifted his line of questioning. 'And you decided to renew your acquaintance with Jonah Kobi.' This time it was he who managed to inject the question with an accusation.

Jessica gave him a sharp look. 'I liked him.'

'Even though . . .'

'I read about him in the newspaper. I was curious.'

Willard played along. 'So did you ask him about your one-time friend?'

'For years he told me she must have run away maybe because she was upset that I didn't want to be her friend.'

DS Willard smiled as though he had a fish on the end of a hook and again shifted the focus of his questions.

'How did the little silver ballet shoe charm get into Tom's car?'

Jessica chewed her lips. 'I really don't know,' she said.

'You know that she was still wearing the charm bracelet complete with ballet shoes—'

'She wasn't. We—'

'You bought another charm, didn't you, to plant in Tom's car. Your husband's idea?'

So now, Claire thought, she would fall back on Plan B.

FIFTY-SIX

Tuesday 19 November, 8.40 a.m.

The day started badly.

It was Yvonne who rang. Which caught Claire out.

'He's gone,' she said without introducing herself or preamble. Claire struggled. Who was gone? Where? Yvonne followed the cryptic remark with, 'Tom.'

'I'm sorry . . .'

But Yvonne needed to talk. 'It was so peaceful in the end – after all that illness – he just went to sleep.'

Claire murmured a response and Yvonne began again. 'Doctor, I think it was knowing they'd found her.'

'Possibly.'

'It meant he could let go so thank you for all you've done.'

For all she'd done? She'd done nothing. But it can be hard to deflect thanks even when you know they are undeserved.

Did Yvonne not realize this was just the start of things?

In Hanley police station the case against Jessica Kobi was building as neatly as a flat pack chest of drawers. Marvel Trustrom's handbag must have been open at the time of the assault. Inside was a tissue. And the tissue held some blood spatter.

Wednesday 18 December, 11 a.m.

Crematoria are not designed for double funerals. They had had to erect a second bier for the second coffin. Though when Claire thought about it she realized an entire coffin was hardly appropriate for the remains of the girl who was inside.

They'd all turned up, Dixie, Yvonne, Shane and his wife, Sorrel and Clarice. Dixie looked pale but shed no tears for her daughter – or her husband. They played a Spice Girls oldie as well as Mozart. Claire, standing at the back with DS Willard, doubted either Tom or Marvel would have approved the choice of music. But then who does choose their own Requiem? The entire ceremony was strangely soulless. The pall engulfed her even after Claire had returned to Greatbach, still reflecting on the ceremony. In the end, was it what Tom had so wanted?

Kobi's life was held in the balance, the irony being that the final choice whether or when the ventilator was switched off would be made by doctors rather than the courts. One of the few times he had no control. Had he recovered there was always the possibility that he would have implicated or even accused his wife of murder. Who knew with Kobi?

With the forensic evidence it was hard for Jessica to deny she had been at the crime scene. Her defence was coercion. The prosecution were optimistic that Jessica would be found guilty of Marvel Trustrom's murder. The defence were just as hopeful they would win the case.

And Ilsa?

Claire gave her evidence and her one-time patient was detained at Her Majesty's Pleasure.

So after the double funeral all she had to face now was her half-brother's wedding.

Which would be a trial. Not seeing her half-brother married to Adele. That was the easy bit. Adam was one of those blunt-mannered, easy-going men who take a happy, passive view of life. And Adele was sweet-natured. Although a solicitor, she could find the good in all.

And it wasn't her outfit either which she'd already chosen. A cherry-red dress with a bolero jacket over, killer heels and a jaunty black fascinator which sat easily on her blonde hair which she'd grown a little longer than usual, to just below her shoulders. And it wasn't going with Grant either. He would turn up in a beautifully fitting navy suit and matching cherry red tie, his hair, freshly washed, thick and curly and his expression jaunty and optimistic enough to carry off the pirate-in-his-Sunday-best look. He would turn heads at the ceremony and make the day easier.

No, it would be none of these. It would be the ordeal of meeting her mother. After years of hostility and alienation it would be unavoidable at this family occasion. She could already anticipate the moment when she would watch her mother file into the church, smiling at everyone until her eyes alighted on her daughter when her lips would tighten, her eyes blaze for a moment and she would cling on to her husband's arm. Mr Perfect David Spencer.

Claire knew exactly how Marvel Trustrom had felt.

An outsider.

She sat alone in her office, squared up a few papers and stared into her computer screen. The words were starting to dance in front of her, teasing her, drawing her in.

> Why do women marry serial killers? By Dr Claire Roget MB ChB BSc FRCPsych.
>
> There are eight recorded cases of women marrying serial killers in the UK. Many more cases exist in the US and in Asia, particularly China, where there are eighteen recorded cases . . .

When all else fails, there was always the distraction of academia and her work. The day was growing dark, and Claire carried on typing.